His Bonnie Highland Temptation

Temptation

The Clan Sinclair Book Two

Celeste Barclay

Celeste Barclay
Visit my website at www.celestebarclayauthor.blogspot.com
Printed in the United States of America
First Printing: August 2018
Kindle Digital Publishing
ISBN-9781718157675

This novel is dedicated to all those readers who are in need of a little escape to a land of braw warriors and damsels in distress.
~Happy Reading~
Celeste

Chapter One

The pounding in Callum's head as he awoke made him wonder if he had been mistaken for the blacksmith's anvil. Slowly, he opened his eyes and looked over at the curvaceous blonde sleeping next to him. The previous night began to drift through his memory. His father, Liam Sinclair the chief of Clan Sinclair, had announced less than a sennight night ago that not only had he arranged a betrothal for Callum, his heir and tainiste, but that the woman would be arriving before the sennight was over. She was expected some time late this day, so last night he had celebrated his upcoming nuptials by drowning his sorrows in more drams of whisky than he could remember and taking his current lover to bed for a night of entertainment and pleasure. He had been very sure to tell Elizabeth that this was his last night of freedom and that their short, albeit passionate, liaison was coming to an end. While Callum Sinclair may have enjoyed more than a few women's attention and considered himself a well experienced lover, he was also a man committed to fidelity to his wife. Whomever she might be. Callum had not intended to fall asleep with Elizabeth in his bed as he knew she would awake and want one more tumble. She was insatiable which had suited him just fine before he knew he was to be betrothed. Even after the announcement, he had been sure to enjoy her talents to the fullest as his freedom was rapidly drawing to an end. After all, the documents were drafted but not yet signed. He knew that he must have passed out after their last round of coupling. He never thought of his time with a woman as love making as he had never actually been in love.

As Callum came more fully awake and realized that he wished he could fall back to sleep alone, he also realized that the pounding was not just in his head but at his door. He could hear his brother, Alexander, calling to him.

"Callum! Get up. Yer bride arrives within the next quarter hour. She and her escorts have been spotted coming over the rise. Ye'd best be getting cleaned up."

Callum was suddenly very awake and feeling very shaken, both by the remnants of his overindulgence and the news that his soon to be bride was sonn to be at the keep. Callum jumped from his bed and began looking for a clean leine, his breacan feile, or great plaid, and broach. As he rounded up his clothes, he glanced again at Elizabeth still asleep in his bed and grimaced. There would be no time to bathe and he knew he smelleed of her and their coupling. He went over to the washstand and lathered the bar of soap against a cloth. He did his best to freshen up and wash the sleep from his eyes.

"Callum, are ye awake? Yer bride will be getting here in just a few minutes." Alexander continued to bang his fist against the door.

Callum stumbled over to the door as he pulled his leine over his head. He pulled the door open and stared at this brother. Alexander pushed his way into his brother's chamber and looked at the woman now awake and sprawled across Callum's bed. He glared at her and then at his brother. Callum Sinclair was one of four brothers and none of the other brothers Sinclair had taken a liking to Callum's current lover. They found her to be pretentious, self-serving, and manipulative and had tried to warn Callum on more than one occasion, but Callum had been enjoying her attention and ministrations too much to give any serious thought to her character, or lack thereof. As he glanced over his shoulder and watched her sexy stretch, he knew that she was trying to tempt him back into bed. She rolled onto her side and shamelessly allowed the sheet to fall loose from her breasts as she ran her hand over his side of the bed as she eyed Alexander. The invitation was clear: come back to bed, or your brother can take your place.

For the first time since meeting Elizabeth a few months ago at court, Callum regretted bringing her back with him. She had been a lady in waiting to a noblewoman. She was a widow and of lesser noble birth. He had explained from the very beginning that he was not looking for a long-term attachment and had no intention of marrying her. That had not deterred Elizabeth from agreeing to come back to Sinclair land and staking a claim. Callum had arranged for her to have her own chamber, and, before this night, she had never shared his bed. He had always gone to her. He had wanted to save the sanctity of his bed for his wife. This day was not starting well.

"Lass, ye best be getting a move on. I am needed below stairs and ye canna stay here." Callum looked back at his brother in time to see his grimace of dislike. Callum walked to the bed and folded his plaid quickly. He wrapped it around him and secured it with this broach. He found his sporran and belted it around his waist before putting on his boots.

"So yer little bride to be arrives shortly. How vera nice for ye. I ken how excited ye are to meet her," Elizabeth purred.

A chill ran down Callum's back as he heard a tinge of malice in Elizabeth's voice.

"Dinna be trouble, Elizabeth. I explained to ye that our time was going to end soon when I found about the betrothal. I told ye last eve that it was over. Let us leave things on a good note."

"Of course, Callum. We both kenned this was only to last as long as it was enjoyable for us both." That statement gave Callum no reassurance as it had been highly enjoyable last night. He was beginning to wonder if Elizabeth was going to let go with grace or dig her claws in.

"Get dressed and go, lass." Callum walked out of the door with his brother in tow.

"What the bluidy hell were ye thinking taking her to yer bed the eve before yer bride arrives? Are ye really that stupid or just that selfish?" Alexander fumed.

If it had been anyone other than his brother, who was next in age to him and his second, he would have smashed his fist into his face. Callum ran his hand through his still disheveled hair. He realized that he had forgotten to comb it. *I must look like a right mess and for a first impression.*

"First of all, she isnae even officially ma betrothed yet. Second of all, I canna undo last eve. Ye ken how I feel about being pressed into marriage with a lass I have never even seen. Ye were there drinking with me. I can only hope to make a decent impression on the lass."

"Aye. I was there, but I also left off long before ye. I tried to warn ye when I saw Elizabeth lurking near the fireplace but ye wanted to do what ye wanted to do. Ye werenae listening to anyone but yer cock. I swear it'll cause ye trouble and right soon, I'd image." Alexander turned to walk down the stairs and Callum followed. He heard the door to his chamber open and close as Elizabeth came into the passageway. He attempted to speed up, but Alexander was just as large as he and blocked his way. He knew it would be obvious to all that Elizabeth had spent the night with him. He just prayed that no one made mention of it in front of his soon to be betrothed.

Chapter Two

Siùsan Mackenzie walked into the Great Hall of the Sinclairs' keep, Castle Dunbeath, and wondered if she would ever feel at home here. Her eyes rounded at the site of the massive double door entrance with the iron studs to reinforce the wood. She wondered just how large the Sinclair men must be to need a door so wide and so tall. She had heard the rumors that the Sinclair brothers and their father were mountains of men. Her eyes swept over the two fireplaces that were wide enough for at least three women to stand shoulder to shoulder and tall enough for even a large man to stand within. Only one of the fires was lit as the spring air was fairly warm today considering she was now nearly in the northern most part of Scotland. The temperature had dropped significantly each day that she and her escort had travelled northwest. She took in the Sinclair coat of armor hanging above the fireplace that was lit. Above the empty fireplace was an assortment of weapons that had clearly seen numerous battles.

Siùsan's gaze shifted back to the coat of arms. The two lions rampant seemed to be staring at her and snarling. The two different ships made her wish to escape. She had been shocked when, just a moon ago, her father, laird of the Mackenzies, had announced that he had arranged her betrothal. She still was not sure if she was more shocked that he had bothered to arrange a marriage for her or to whom he had arranged it. She and her father were not close.

Movement from the stairs caught her attention, and she turned to see two men walking down the stairs. They looked incredibly similar, but the first man seemed to have a wary expression that took in everything and everyone. His gaze swept across the Great Hall and quickly caught sight of her. He smiled but it looked more pained than welcoming. The man behind him shared the same chestnut hair and remarkably broad build as the first man, but there was an air of command to him. And an air of dread. She quickly deduced who her intended was. As they made it to the bottom of the stairs, the second man seemed to finally notice her. His eyes widened, and he smiled broadly. The death knell seemed to have stopped tolling for

4

him. Siùsan was immediately on edge. Siùsan knew that she had inherited her looks from her mother as her father's attitude towards her was a constant reminder. She also knew that she was considered more than passably attractive. Apparently, Callum Sinclair would agree with that assessment. She had not missed how displeased he looked to be coming to meet her and his rapid shift of demeanor made her wonder just how shallow her future husband was. *So red hair and green eyes are enough for him. Arenae I lucky.*

The two men were soon joined by two more. Siùsan had never seen such a wall of manliness before. It was obvious that the four men were brothers as they were almost exactly the same height, had the exact same shade of chestnut hair, and from a distance it seemed that they all had brown eyes. One brother was only slightly taller and broader than the other three and one brother seemed to be more barrel chested and slightly shorter than the others. Siùsan's gaze locked on the man that she figured was her intended and she tried to plaster a pleasant and serene look upon her face. It was the look she used when she had to be in the presence of her stepmother. They were not close either.

As her intended, she remembered his name was Callum, approached, she noticed that his eyes were a dark whisky shade of brown. When Callum stopped in front of her and bent to kiss her hand, she realized that his eyes matched the stench of whisky that was rolling off him. There was also another scent, almost more cloying, that seemed to waft from him. It was a bitter scent of roses, and Siùsan attempted to not wrinkle her nose as he stood up.

"Lady Siùsan, welcome to Castle Dunbeath and welcome to the Clan Sinclair." His voice was deep and rough as it was clear he had not been awake very long. It was also warm and welcoming, and Siùsan began to feel a little more at ease. He seemed pleasant after all. She was just about to respond when a voluptuous, tall blonde positioned herself just slightly behind Callum. Her kirtle was tight across her breasts and hips and the laces were not quite completely tied leaving much of her cleavage exposed. The hostility and possessiveness seemed to radiate off her as she glared at Siùsan. It did not take much for her to immediately realize that this woman was her intended's leman. Her ire rose at the insult and humiliation of being greeted by her soon to be husband and his mistress.

"Sir Callum, thank ye for yer warm welcome. I must say that is an interesting fragrance that ye favor. It seems rather floral for a man of yer stature." She bristled and found an almost perverse pleasure at his stunned expression. His brothers guffawed and elbowed one another none too discreetly.

Callum saw that Siùsan was looking over his shoulder. He moved aside slightly in what he hoped would like he was about to introduce his brothers. He looked behind him and almost groaned out loud when he saw that Elizabeth had not only followed him downstairs but was clearly staking a claim. He would have to find time to speak to her and make arrangements for her to either return to court or to her clan.

"Lady Siùsan--" Callum did not get a chance to make introductions as Siùsan moved towards the dais and dropped into a curtsey worthy of the king. Callum turned to see his father had been watching the entire exchange. The hard set of his mouth foretold the conversation that he would be having with Callum, but his eyes were warm as he looked down upon Siùsan. He stepped down from the dais and walked to her.

"Rise, ma lady. Ye dinna need to curtsy to me. We are to be kin soon." He took her proffered hand and placed a gentle, fatherly kiss on it and then pulled her in for a hug. Shocked by the show of affection, Siùsan was not sure how to respond. The hug was not too tight, but it was genuine. She slowly wrapped her arms around him and allowed herself to enjoy the embrace. It had been years since anyone had hugged her besides her half-brothers when she left her clan. She began to warm to the embrace and rested her cheek against the older man's chest.

"Dinna fret, lass. He isnae at his best, but he is a good mon, I promise ye. I wouldnae promise ye to him if he werenae. I ken yer father and I ken yer mother's kin. I look forward to becoming yer father by marriage," Liam Sinclair whispered in the sprite of a woman's ear.

Father by marriage. I hadna really thought that far ahead. Perhaps he will be kind to me. Perhaps there is hope that he will be right. I wonder what he kens of ma kin. He sounded like he kens quite a bit. Siùsan's sense of reassurance quickly evaporated and was replaced by embarrassment. If Laird Sinclair knew her family, or at least knew of them, he would know of her status within the family.

Laird Sinclair turned Siùsan to face the four men who approached.

"Lady Siùsan, ye have already met ma oldest son and heir, Callum. To his right is Alexander, ma second oldest and Callum's second in command of the guard. To Callum's left is ma third son, Tavish, and beside him is ma youngest, Magnus."

Siùsan dipped into a shallower curtsy but was respectful nonetheless. "Thank ye for the welcome. It is a pleasure to be here."

"Have ye broken yer fast yet? Would ye care to join us as we do?" Callum's deep voice filled her with warmth, but it took only a second to remember her distrust and disgust.

"Nay. I havenae broken ma fast yet. I would appreciate the meal after two sennights of sleeping outdoors and eating bannocks every morn." The group moved to the dais. Callum usually sat directly to Laird Sinclair's right but he showed Siùsan to that seat. He sat to her right.

Siùsan smiled at the older woman who placed a bowl of porridge in front of her. The kind woman smiled back and nodded slightly.

"Lady Siùsan, this is Hagatha, our housekeeper. She has overseen this keep since I was a wean."

"Tis nice to meet ye, Hagatha. Thank ye for the porridge. It smells wonderful and sweet."

"A little honey, ma lady." Hagatha whispered with a wink. Siùsan could not help but grin.

As Hagatha moved on to oversee the serving of the meal, Siùsan heard a tinkle of laughter that attracted her attention. She saw Elizabeth seated at a lower table close to the dais. The woman was leaning forward to offer the entire dais a clear view of her more than ample breasts. Siùsan peeked down at her own chest and, while she was well enough endowed, she felt lacking in her feminine shape. Callum studiously kept his head bowed over his bowl and shoveled the food into his mouth. Siùsan, too, looked down at her bowl, however, she looked out from under her lashes several times to see Callum glance at Elizabeth as he ate. *At least he has the decency to not be obvious, but he's still lusting after his leman right next to me. What has ma fatherr done? I dinna want to marry a man who canna keep his philandering away from me.*

Another peel of laughter floated across the din of the Great Hall. Siùsan looked up in time to see Elizabeth swipe her finger across her breast to scoop up porridge she had dribbled. She licked her finger and then sucked it into her mouth. Siùsan could not stop the gasp that escaped her.

"I need to check on ma horse. It was a long journey, and I think he has a loose shoe. I will check in with the blacksmith." She pushed back her chair and scurried off the dais. While she walked out of the keep, she managed to take long strides and rush out while still maintaining some composure.

Shite! Callum was stunned both by Elizabeth's display and Siùsan's reaction. He pushed back his own chair and rose. He looked down at his father and saw the displeasure written all over his face.

"Fix this. Fix both." Liam Sinclair swung his glare towards Elizabeth. "Or I will send the chit away maself." He nodded towards the door. "Go."

Callum stepped down from the dais and moved towards the door. Elizabeth saw his approach and grinned. She started to rise, but he walked past without even sparing her a look. If he had seen her face when she sat down again, he would have known that a woman scorned was a woman filled with spite.

Chapter Three

S iùsan practically sprinted across the bailey to the stables. She entered the stables and was greeted to the familiar scents of horse and hay. She breathed a sigh of relief to be with her horse and to be away from Elizabeth, Callum, and all the other Sinclairs. She wandered along the stalls until she found her horse, Trofast. She had been there the day that Trofast was born. The foal's mother did not live long after the birth as it had been very complicated. The stable master had to assist the mare. As a foal, Trofast took to Siùsan, who regularly came to visit him. She fed him goat's milk and taught him to follow a lead line. He was always happy to see her and neighed whenever he caught her sent. As a tribute to her mother's Norse heritage, Siùsan named the horse Trofast, or faithful.

When Siùsan got to Trofast's stall, she greeted the now fully grown stallion by blowing into his nostrils and leaning her forehead against his nose. She looked around for a curry brush and entered the stall. Whispering, she voiced aloud the question she had asked herself earlier, *"What has ma father done?"*

"Hopefully found ye a good and happy match."

Already Siùsan recognized Callum's voice and spun around. She had not thought that he would follow her out to the stables, let alone hear her. The look on her face would have been comical to Callum if he did not feel so guilty for how things were going.

"Lass, I owe ye a tremendous apology and perhaps an explanation. I am vera sorry for the greeting and meal ye have just received." Siùsan felt choked up and swallowed. She walked along Trofast's side as she brushed him down. She could not bring herself to look at Callum as he continued to speak. "We kenned ye would arrive today. We didna expect ye quite so early in the day. I admit that I was surprised when ma da announced the, our, betrothal. I didna react as well as I should have. I over indulged last night as I saw it as ma last night of freedom." Callum could have sworn that he heard her snort at his confession. "I ended ma ties to Elizabeth last night. We are to sign the betrothal contract today, and I willna have anyone come between us."

"Us?" Siùsan swung around. "Us? There isnae an us. There is ye and her, and then there is me." Siùsan bristled and turned away before she said something she would regret. He was not bringing out the best in her. When had she become such a shrew?

She walked to Trofast's hind quarters. She lifted her skirts above her ankles as she stepped over the hoof she lifted. Callum was surprised to see a woman scraping a horse's hoof. He was even more surprised when he realized that he rather liked knowing that she could and would take care of her own horse.

"Lass, I ken what it looks like, but she insnae ma leman. I admit that I have been involved with her, but it began before the betrothal was arranged. I have never kept an official mistress. I never will." He paused to see her reaction. She had moved on to check her horse's other hooves. Her back was still turned to him, but she seemed to be listening, so he continued. "I ken we dinna ken each other, and I canna ken what the future holds, but there are some things I ken for sure. I give ye ma word of honor that I will be a faithful husband to ye. I willna ever stray, and ye can be sure of that."

"How? How can I be sure?" Siùsan lowered the hoof she was checking and walked out of the stall. She faced Callum and fought the urge to put her hands on her hips.

"Lass, ma mama and ma da werenae a love match, but they quickly grew to love each other because they put in the effort to get to ken each other and to build a happy life together. They had five bairns, and ma mama lived long enough for all of us to see what a marriage should be. Ma da was always faithful to ma mama. Always. I mean even now. Perhaps he has sought his release over the years, but I canna say for sure as he has never made anything known to us. I dinna think he has. I hope to one day have what ma parents had."

"I dinna ken ye yet. How can I ken that ye speak the truth and arenae just telling me what ye think I want to hear?"

"Ma word is ma bond. I am a Highlander, and ma honor is something I can never get back once it is lost. One day, I will lead this clan and must keep their trust. I will pledge maself to ye today. I will do so before God, ye, ma da, and ma clan. To me, we will be as good as married."

Siùsan took a step back. She was not entirely sure what he meant by his last comment. Did he expect that she would be willing to anticipate the wedding? *I amnae letting him bed me. A betrothal contract may be binding but it isnae a marriage. It isnae even a handfast.*

Her thoughts must have been clear on her face. Callum ran his hand through his hair. "I seem to be mucking this up even more. I dinna want ye to think I will ever pressure ye to be intimate with me. I dinna want to and willna wait until we stand before the kirk to make that pledge to keep maself only unto ye. I meant that ma pledge of fidelity begins today." He gave her a shy half smile. "Even if I didna mean all of this, and I do, ma da would flay me alive if I ever dishonored ye or disgraced maself by not being faithful."

"Ye fear yer father?"

"Aye. Of course, I do." Callum laughed. "Do ye nae recall his size when ye sat next to him?"

"Aye, I do. I ken where ye get yer braw size from."

"Braw, am I?"

"Ye ken it as does every woman under five score."

"There is only one woman that I want to notice me, and I thought mayhap ye hadnae."

"How could I nae? Ye take up an awful lot of space." Callum laughed again and his deep baritone warmed Siùsan again. This time, she felt like she could trust him more. Not entirely, but more. "Please, dinna disappoint me. I willna trust ye again easily if ye betray me."

Callum reached out for her hand. "May I?" he asked before lifting her hand. When she nodded, he brought her hand to his lips. He pressed a soft kis to her hand. After he lowered her hand, he stepped forward and brushed a soft kiss on her cheek. Siùsan's hand tingled where his lips caressed her skin, and her cheeks pinkened. She pressed her fingertips to her cheek where he had kissed her. She was shocked that he had done that and shocked at how much she liked it. It scared her how desperately she wanted to believe that he was telling the truth.

"Siùsan, havenae ye ever been kissed before?" Callum asked softly as he watched her dazed reaction to his small acts of affection.

"Of course, nae. I amnae loose." Now her cheeks turned red with embarrassment and annoyance.

"I didna mean that at all. I just thought that a woman as bonnie as ye would have had more than one man attempt to steal a kiss and at least one would have been lucky. I am sorry. I didna mean to insult ye. I seem to only be able to do that today. I ken I need to try harder."

"I am the laird's daughter. No mon has ever tried to steal a kiss, and I wouldnae have allowed it anyway. It wouldnae have been proper."

Callum stepped closer and reached his hands out. He tucked hair behind each ear. He smiled down at her and realized just how much smaller than him she was. She barely came to the center of his chest, and he must have weighed at least nine stones more than her. He rather liked that. There seemed to be an odd blend of a will of iron and an innocent vulnerability about her. It made him want to get to know her better and at the same time protect her. She was not frail or even that small of frame, but she seemed slight compared to his own towering height and broad build. At almost six and a half feet, he virtually towered over her, but she did not seem intimidated by him. She just seemed unaccustomed to male attention or affection. *Odd as I ken she has a father and two brothers. How can she be so surprised by affection or even male attention?*

Siùsan looked up into his whisky colored eyes and felt like she might drown. His sudden concern and kindness were almost overwhelming for her as she was so unused to such caring. His hand gently cupped her cheek, and she found herself leaning into his touch.

"We willna go faster than ye are ready for. I will never force ye to do aught ye dinna want or arenae ready for. I promise ye that I will only ever sleep alongside ye every night for the rest of our lives together."

Siùsan was a little overwhelmed at what he was saying and implying. She swallowed and found enough courage to ask him what he would expect from her. "Once we are wed, will ye be coming to ma chamber, or will ye send for me when ye would like ma-- company?" She did not think she could look him in the eye now that she had asked such a personal question, but she wanted to know how things would stand before she made any mistakes or formed the wrong expectation.

"Neither, mo neach beag." He smiled at her surprise. He was unable to tell if it was from his answer or his calling her his little one.

"I dinna think I ken what ye mean."

"I mean, mo neach beag, there will be nay yers or mine when it comes to chambers. There will only be our chamber. Where ye sleep is where I sleep, and I rather like the chamber I occupy now."

"Oh." Her mouth formed a perfect circle, and Callum's mind immediately jumped to picturing her in his chamber, in his bed, making the same expression as he pleasured her. He had a momentary pang of regret as he remembered that he had shared his bed for the first time last night, and it had not been with his wife.

"Vera well, if ye wish." Siùsan was feeling in over her head and needed to escape and reflect on their conversation. "I would guess that ye are expected in the lists by now, and I need to find the blacksmith. I will see ye in the Great Hall later." She stepped around Callum, and before she walked away, she turned to look over her shoulder and added, "thank ye."

Callum stood still and simply watched her walk out. His eyes took in the sway of her hips, and his cock twitched. He had to admit that he was intensely attracted to his little bride to be. He had found her beautiful the moment he had seen her. He had been surprised by just how attractive she was. He had not let himself hope for a pretty wife as he did not want to be disappointed. Her spunk had come through more than once already especially when her greeting pointed out that she knew what he had done the night before and would not turn a blind eye. He rather admired it and found it beguiling. The sense of innocence and vulnerability that he had felt made him curious. He was not sure how someone who seemed so confident could seem so unsure at the same time.

Callum moved towards the door as a shadow filled the space. The sun shining in made it difficult for him to see who was there but the scent and words that greeted him made him want to bolt. "There ye are, mo ghràidh. I was beginning to wonder how long ye were going to coo over yer little lost lamb."

Callum ground his teeth to keep from rebuking her for insulting Siùsan. He simply did not want to engage Elizabeth in conversation. He moved towards the door, and she met him half way. She reached out and wrapped her arms around his neck, digging her fingers in like claws to hold on. Callum immediately tugged her arms from his neck. The way Elizabeth had acted since the moment she had awoken had been off putting. Callum was quickly coming to understand what his entire family had been trying to warn him about. Yet again, he was filled with a sense of regret and guilt over his selfishness and impulsiveness. He did not want Siùsan to see him with Elizabeth or hear that he had met with her in the stables after she left.

"Elizabeth, have done. I told ye last night that we were finished. That was the end. Let us part on good terms before I send ye away. I willna have ye alienate or humiliate ma wife."

"She isnae yer wife yet. Mayhap she never will be. Ye arenae even betrothed yet. Ye dinna have to go through with it."

"Of course, I do and more importantly, I want to."

"Have ye been sampling her charms? Mayhap a roll in the hay to test her out before ye pledge ye life away."

"Tread carefully. Ye are trying ma patience vera quickly. Regardless of whether I even liked ma betrothed, which I do quite a lot, I willna have ye trying to come between us. This affair was always destined to end, and I have called it quits. Dinna touch me anymore and dinna follow me, or ye will find yerself outside the wall in a heartbeat."

Callum brushed past her and stomped out of the door. He made his way to the lists. The scowl on his face kept others away. He took out his frustration with Elizabeth and himself on his brothers as he trained for the next several hours.

Chapter Four

*R*etreating to the chamber she was shown after returning from visiting the blacksmith, Siùsan felt the need for some solitude. Elizabeth had been obvious as she made a beeline for the stables as Siùsan left. Siùsan had discreetly moved to the side of the bailey and made it look like she was familiarizing herself with her new home but, in actuality, she lingered to see how long Callum and Elizabeth would remain in the stables alone. It had not been long at all. Not long enough for them to have done much, and by the look on Callum's face as he stormed out, he had not been that excited to see Elizabeth. The sense of relief that Siùsan felt when she saw that nothing had happened had been a shock. She realized she had been holding her breath almost the entire time. *Why should I even care? I ken I dinna want a philandering husband, but I havenae aught choice even if he is. Most men would say it isnae any of ma concern and that I should just accept ma lot in life. I just canna. Not after a lifetime already of being ignored.* She also could not help the wicked sense of glee when she saw how put out Elizabeth looked as she left the stable alone. She looked no more mussed than she had in the Great Hall. She was still half hanging out of her kirtle, but she did not seem any more disheveled.

Siùsan moved about her chamber as she found her belongings had already been put away for her. She saw that there was really nothing left for her to do to set up her chamber since she had brought so few belongings, only what could be packed in one satchel. She sat down on the bed and was relieved to feel how soft the mattress was. It had been two long weeks since she had slept in a bed, and the coziness of the pillows and thick plaid blankets called to her. She kicked off her riding boots and shed her clothes down to her chemise. She pulled back the top blanket and climbed back onto the bed. As she settled into the nest of pillows and blanket, she thought back over the morning. She did not want to think about her interactions with Callum as it caused a strange fluttering sensation in the bottom of her belly. Thinking about Elizabeth just angered her, so instead she thought about the people that she had met in the bailey. The blacksmith, Andrew, had been very kind to her. His sons had stared a little, but she guessed them to be about four and ten and five and ten. She could not blame them for gawking as they were at an age where they were beginning to notice the lasses. They reminded her of her stepbrothers.

Andrew had accompanied her back to the stables where she met Hamish, the stable master. Together, the three of them looked at Trofast and changed all four of his shoes so that the other three would not have to be done in a few weeks. Trofast had worn all four down quite a lot during the journey.

After she finished in the stables, she walked over to the well to wash her hands and to get a drink. She had run into Hagatha who was filling two buckets of water. They greeted one another, and Hagatha asked how her morning was going. Siùsan knew she was really asking how things were going with Callum as everyone had been witness to Elizabeth's display. Siùsan answered honestly but was brief. She did not know Hagatha yet and did not know if she was a gossip. She did offer to carry the water back to the keep. Hagatha had objected to a lady carrying buckets for her, a servant. Siùsan picked up both buckets and began walking to the keep before Hagatha could stop her. They entered the keep through the kitchen.

Everything came to an abrupt halt when the soon to be new lady of the keep walked into the kitchen with two buckets swinging from her hands. Siùsan had a moment of self-doubt as almost a score of eyes swung towards her. Hagatha led her to the fireplace and helped her set the buckets down. She then led Siùsan to the woman who was clearly in charge. Elspeth ran a tight ship as everywhere that Siùsan looked was clean and tidy. All the workspaces were occupied, but clearly the women knew to clean up as they worked. Elspeth looked a great deal like Hagatha, but where Hagatha was shorter and plumper, Elspeth was taller and a little leaner. Elspeth's hair was a little closer to white while Hagatha's dark hair was threaded with gray. Otherwise their faces were the same. They both had twinkling blue eyes with laugh lines around them. These creases ran along their mouths. Clearly, these were women who had known happiness and cheer.

"Aye, we do look a tad alike, ma lady. We are sisters if ye hadna guessed," Elspeth greeted her with a smile. Siùsan spent the next hour in the kitchen getting to know the women who worked there. She was given a tour of the storerooms and began to learn her way around. She felt like she was beginning to make friends or least becoming well acquainted with the women she would eventually spend most of her time with. Once her tour was done, Hagatha offered her a bath. Siùsan said she would be happy to fetch clean clothes and her soap to have a bath in the kitchens but neither Hagatha nor Elspeth would hear of it. They insisted that the tub be taken up to her chamber. Siùsan felt guilty that she was taking men and women from their work simply, so she could have the luxury of a bath.

She shook her head and chewed on her top lip. "Nay. Point me to the loch, and I can bathe there. I believe the men are still in the lists, so I should be alone, right?"

That had brought everything to a screeching halt for a second time. The women all stared at her aghast. She felt her cheeks flame as everyone looked at her.

"Ma lady," Hagatha patiently explained, "nay woman bathes in the loch here. All women can bathe in the privacy of the keep. The laird insists that women in this clan nae be molested or harassed by any mon. He believes everyone is due their privacy. The unmarried lasses share three large chambers below stairs and married women have cottages at the far end of the bailey. Only the unmarried men sleep in the Great Hall. The unmarried guardsmen stay in the barracks. Ye canna be traipsing off to the loch to bathe. Ye shouldnae even be bathing in the kitchen. Noblewomen bathe in their chambers." With that, Hagatha began barking orders to find two men to carry the tub up to her chamber and to have water warmed then brought up. Unused to assistance when she bathed, Siùsan politely declined then firmly refused help from one of the maids. She knew that she would have to accept help in the near future lest rumors begin that she was hiding something, but she was feeling tired and simply wanted to be alone. She soaked and scrubbed which made her feel much better. When she got out, she had to decide which of her three kirtles she would wear. The gown she had worn while travelling needed laundering badly, she had one serviceable gown that she wore while doing chores at her father's keep, and then a more elegant gown that she planned to wear for her wedding. Deciding to keep her fancier kirtle for any celebrations, she donned her serviceable kirtle and put back on her boots. The one pair of slippers she owned were already wearing thin, so she would save those as well. Once dressed, she did not know what to do with herself. She walked to her window and pulled back the window coverings. She was surprised to find glass in the window encasement. Her chamber at the Mackenzie keep only had a fur hanging over it. It was cold and drafty in winter and stiflingly warm in summer. Siùsan was not sure how long she stood gazing out of the window. She could see the loch outside of the bailey walls. The light had not been very strong when she arrived that morning, so she had not realized that there were two walls surrounding the keep. The lists were located between the walls near the loch. She could make out movement from the men but was too far away to determine individuals. Her eyes scanned for a particular head of chestnut hair and the broad shoulders she had wanted to touch in the stable but, from this distance, it was impossible to tell. Eventually, she turned from the window and realized she had nothing to do but wait for the noon meal. She walked to her bed.

Chapter Five

A soft knocking awoke Siùsan. She had not even realized that she was drifting off to sleep. She rubbed her eyes and looked around. The sun had shifted its position within her room, and she knew that the day had progressed quite a bit. She darted from the bed and walked to the door.

"Who is it?" she inquired.

"Tis Callum, ma lady. I have come to check on ye. Ye werenae present at the nooning and the evening meal draws near."

Siùsan was only in her chemise but she did not feel right holding a conversation through the door. She knew it was rude not to answer, and she did not want people telling tales of the tainiste shouting through the door at his bride to be. She opened the door just wide enough to lean her head and part of her shoulder around it.

"Hello, Sir Callum. I apologize if I have kept anyone waiting. I hadnae realized so much time had gone by. I will be ready promptly. Thank ye." With that, she began to close the door, but a hand shot out and pressed gently.

"A maid explained that she checked on ye earlier when ye didna come down for the midday meal. I ken ye fell asleep, Siùsan," he said in barely more than a whisper. "Did ye really sleep outdoors during yer entire journey? Did ye nae stop at an inn from time to time? Ye must be exhausted."

"It was a more direct route, so we didna pass through many villages or towns. I was fine to sleep on the ground, but I do admit that I found the bed very inviting."

Callum could not take his eyes off the woman standing just beyond the door. Her sleep mussed hair was a riot of curls and waves. It was the color of fire in the light, but it was a dark russet in the dimness of her chamber. He could see the creamy soft skin of her neck and shoulder. It was almost a honey color and he wondered how it could have seen the sun. It took every bit of restraint that he possessed not to reach out his hand and test his theory.

"I am glad to ken ye had a chance to rest. I have come to escort ye to the evening meal. I will wait for ye to get ready." Her eyes widened, and her mouth made that perfect circle once again. Callum hardened immediately. His cock twitched as he longed to feel if her lips were as soft and plump as he thought. They were the same shade of pink as the evening sky. His longing to taste her was stronger than he had anticipated. He had only been with Elizabeth last night, but he suddenly felt like a green lad longing for his first kiss. He finally registered her shock and added, "Outside yer door. I will await ye outside yer door."

Siùsan just nodded and softly closed the door. Callum could just barely hear scurrying feet as Siùsan moved about the room to get ready. Callum was surprised at how soon the door swung open. He was also surprised at her appearance. Her face looked like it had been freshly scrubbed and her hair was tied back with a ribbon. She looked refreshed and well rested. It was her gown that surprised him. That surprise must have registered because a hard glint entered her eyes as she waited for him to speak. Callum knew he was being tested. The gown was well made but clearly older. It had seen better days as the green was now faded to an almost fawn shade. He took her all in and saw that the hem was not yet frayed but was getting close. She had her riding boots back on instead of slippers. The gown was not at all what he expected her to wear to the evening meal or their betrothal.

"I am ready. Are ye?" She asked with a note of steel in her voice.

"Aye," was all Callum could answer.

"Is there a feast tonight that I should ken about?"

"Nay. That will be in a couple of nights as we werenae sure until yesterday when ye would arrive."

"Then shall we go to the Great Hall? I admit I am rather hungry as I missed more than one meal today." The slight jab was not missed by Callum. He had the decency to blush a little as she stepped out of the door. He offered her his arm. She hesitated for a split second and then lightly placed her hand his upon his arm.

Callum felt like he had been singed by the heat coming from her hand even though she was barely touching the material of his leine. He felt the heat spread up his arm, and he was acutely aware of her fragrance. It was the soft scent of lilacs. He wanted to feel the weight of her hand more firmly on his arm, so he covered her hand with his as they made their way down the stairs. The gesture seemed courtly and polite to ensure her safety as they descended the steep stairs but Callum simply wanted her touch. She looked up at Callum with her emerald eyes, and he saw a degree of uncertainty there. Again, he was taken aback by how unaccustomed she was to male attention or any signs of care. He was becoming more and more curious about her life before she arrived at his home.

"Callum, I can manage. I willna fall, I promise." Her voice was just barely more than a whisper, and she tried to pull her hand away. Callum simply kept his in place. She realized that getting her hand back would be like trying to pry a tree root from the ground.

"Lass, these stairs are steep, and a few are a bit loose. Until ye are used to them, I would offer ma assistance. I dinna want ye to come to harm." Siùsan simply nodded as no argument was going to make a difference. Her mind flashed back to that morning. She remembered that Callum and Alexander had come down the stairs with Elizabeth following them. No one had assisted her. Her pride stung at that thought.

"I amnae weak or clumsy. I dinna need a nursemaid." Her stern words bit into Callum. "I dinna recall ye escorting any other women. Ye dinna think me capable of walking down stairs." This time when she attempted to pull her hand loose, she also grasped the rope railing on her other side, so she would not fall. Callum released her hand from his arm only to grasp it tightly in his hand.

"If ye are referring to Elizabeth, the thought never crossed ma mind to offer her help because, to be honest, I never bothered to worry about her."

Siùsan paused on the stairs. She would have this out and make it clear that she was not as frail as he seemed to think.

"I dinna need yer worry. I have been walking up and down stairs on ma own since I was a wean. I amnae so incompetent as to need ye to be a mother hen over me."

"I've insulted ye. Again. I seem to better at that than anything else. That wasnae what I meant. I dinna think ye incompetent or unable. Any woman who can travel for two sennights with only a group of guards, sleep on the ground, and only eat bannocks to break her fast isnae weak. Ma time with Elizabeth served one purpose and only one. What happened outside of that never really concerned me. I didna and dinna feel any attachment to her. I ken that sounds callous, and perhaps it is, but I just never gave her much thought outside of what I found useful." Callum looked directly into her eyes. He knew that what he said made him sound like a cad, and he knew he was one. He realized how shallow it made him sound, but the arrangement with Elizabeth had been mutual up until this morning. They had both done their own separate things during the day. They had only sought each other's company at night. "With ye, I want to build a life. We are to be wed, and I want to make ye happy."

"Is ma happiness the means to ye having a peaceful life? Do ye want me quiet and content so I willna be a nag?" Siùsan was astute and to the point. She would have it out with Callum any time she felt it necessary. She would never cower again.

"Nay. I would like ye to be happy here and with me, but I am not seeking yer happiness just to make ma life easier. I dinna think ye're a nag nor do ye seem the type to become one. Ye are direct and I like that. I like kenning where I stand with ye. Ye dinna seem the deceptive or manipulative type either."

"Nay, I amnae either of those. Ye seem to have enough of that already." From the corner of her eye, Siùsan had seen Elizabeth hovering at the bottom of the stairs.

Now she looked directly at the woman and arched one brow. She was officially acknowledging the challenge, but before she would engage any further, she turned back to Callum. "I think ye can figure out what would make me happy."

With that, she began to move down the stairs. Her hand was still tucked into Callum's, so he was forced to either follow her or let go. Wild horses could not have made him let go. As they proceeded down the stairs together, he entwined his fingers with hers and lifted their joined hands. He brought hers to his lips and gave it a small peck. When he looked up, he had not anticipated seeing Elizabeth waiting for him. The look on her face, he knew, was meant to be seductive, but after the freshness and innocence of Siùsan, she looked jaded and conniving to him. He was beginning to wonder what he had ever seen in her. As she turned more fully to him, he could see the dusky pink of the top of her nipples just barely visible over the neckline of her kirtle. He remembered now what had once attracted him. She had more than enough in all the right places to fill his hands, and she had fawned over him when they met. She had practically thrown herself at him and he had figured who was he to deny what she offered. Now, her brazenness turned his stomach over. When they met at court, she seemed to only be interested in having fun with him. He had brought her home with him thinking that she was truly interested in a romp, but he was realizing now that she clearly had other intentions. She had her sights set on more. She thought she would be fit to become the lady of the keep, but her willingness to flaunt herself to him meant that every man in the keep was getting an eyeful too. Callum suddenly felt disgusted at her and disappointed in himself. He looked at Siùsan from the corner of his eye. He knew immediately that she had seen what he had, but she held her head high and walked with a grace that he admired. They reached the bottom of the stairs. He chose not to acknowledge Elizabeth and turned to guide Siùsan to the dais. He should have known that Elizabeth would not tolerate being ignored.

"Good evening, Callum. Tis good to see ye after such a long day. This morn seems so long ago. I had hoped to go for a ride, but ye were distracted with business. Perhaps later," she purred. Callum felt Siùsan go rigid beside him. She had clearly understood the double entendre. It was not just the blatant reminder of his time with her last night and this morning. Her insinuation that his betrothal was just business only added further insult. The use of his given name grated on his nerves. He would have to make immediate arrangements for her to leave Sinclair land.

He barely nodded in acknowledgement of her presence and continued to steer Siùsan to the dais. For her part, Siùsan seem to barely register Elizabeth's presence but Callum could feel the tension radiating from her. Once again, he seated her between him and his father and prayed for a pleasant meal.

Chapter Six

The meal progressed nicely for Callum as he was enjoying Siùsan's company, but it seemed interminable to Siùsan. Callum was attentive to her and chose the best pieces of meat and vegetables to put on her half of their shared trencher. He made sure that their shared goblet was always full and within her reach. She knew that he was trying to make things up to her and improve on their rocky start. She appreciated his efforts, but it was just a reminder that there was a problem to begin with. That problem once again seated herself at a lower table directly in front of the dais. For his part, Callum did not look in Elizabeth's direction even once. He appeared to have forgotten about her, but Siùsan was not entirely convinced. Whether or not he had any emotional attachment did not matter to Siùsan because she understood the strength that physical attachment could have. She had seen it plenty of times while growing up in a large keep. While she might still be a maiden in truth, her eyes were not. She had stumbled upon more than one rutting couple over the years. She understood the mechanics of the act and even understood that both people could find it highly enjoyable. She had even wondered whether she would enjoy it and whether she would be any good at it. However, now she doubted her ability to hold Callum's attention for long when she knew who her competition was. She was not entirely convinced that he would be satisfied with a novice bride when he could have an experienced woman who had clearly pleasured him countless times in just the recent past.

Her discomfort only grew as the meal progressed. Callum's kindness and attempts to flirt made her question whether they were sincere, or she was just his current flight of fancy. She barely knew him and had no way of knowing what he was like with women in general. He engaged her in conversation and told her about various members of the clan. When he attempted to ask her about her childhood and her life with the Mackenzie clan, she steered the conversation back to the Sinclair clan. She would offer a comparison between someone from her clan to one she saw in the Great Hall effectively bringing the conversation back around to what she felt was safer ground.

When the meal ended, the trestle tables were pushed to the side and the musicians began to warm up. Siùsan enjoyed music and liked to dance even though she had not had much experience. Her father had frowned upon her joining in when he was present which seemed to be almost always. Her toes began to tap under the table as the music began in earnest.

"Siùsan, would ye care to dance with me?"

"Aye, Callum. I would enjoy dancing, but I warn ye that I amnae that good."

They walked down to the open space and joined hands to join into a country reel. Callum was impressed with her gracefulness once again. He could not understand how she could possibly think that she was not any good at dancing. She moved with a fluidity that made her seem to float across the floor. When the rhythm picked up and they stomped their feet, she lifted her skirts above her ankles and laughed. The sound made him think of how his mother had described fairy bells when he was just a lad and she would tell him tales at bedtime. He was completely enchanted with her.

For her part, Siùsan enjoyed meeting new members of the clan as she swung through the partner changes during the various dances. She particularly preferred being partnered with the older men of the clan. She felt more comfortable since they did not ogle her as the younger men did. The current song was just coming to an end as she thanked her partner. She looked for Callum to partner with him for the next dance. She saw that he was partnered with Elizabeth. The woman had managed to angle herself to join with Callum at the end of the song. The music began again, and it was a much slower, more intimate dance. While Callum tried to release Elizabeth's hands, he was pressed into dancing with her when the other couples moved into his space. He strained his neck to look above the heads of the other dancers. Siùsan knew that he was looking for her, but a knot formed in her stomach as she watched the two move together. There was a clear familiarity between the two, and they looked well matched with his dark head of hair and her blonde curls tumbling over her shoulders and down her back. She had pressed her breasts against his chest and molded her body to his. They looked like they had been made for one another.

Siùsan just could not watch any more. She turned to leave the Great Hall but ran straight into Tavish.

"Ma lady, where are ye going? Would ye care to dance with me?" Siùsan had already danced with Tavish as they moved through the different rounds of country dances. He was very good and a polite partner, but Siùsan suddenly had no desire to continue dancing.

"Thank ye, but nay. I think I will sit this one out. I need to catch ma breath. Perhaps a later one." She slid past him and moved towards the dais. She looked back over her shoulder as she approached the steps to the dais. Seeing that Tavish was no longer watching her, she doubled back and slipped out of the giant double doors of the keep. The cool night air hit her cheeks and immediately cooled her off. She wished that she had a cloak or her arisaid, but there was no way she could go back in, get her arisaid, and make it back outside without being noticed. She moved down the steps and began to walk towards the well. She sensed someone following her, but when she turned to look, there was no one there. Not even a shadow. She shrugged and continued her walk. She got to the well and peered over the edge into darkness. She jolted when she heard boots crunching on the small rocks that covered the bailey ground. She looked around but saw nothing. Suddenly, a hand reached out and covered her mouth. Another arm wrapped around her waist. She was tugged back against a hard body. She could smell whisky on the man's breath. He stank of it. He was clearly drunk. She struggled against his hold, but he simply laughed.

"I like a lass with some spirit. Ye'll be a wild one for sure."

Siùsan almost gagged when she understood what he intended. She lifted her feet and tried to knock him off balance by pushing her feet against the side of the well. It was like trying to knock over a mountain. She was beginning to panic but knew that would not solve the problem and would only mean that she gave up any control of the situation.

When the unseen man grabbed her, he had failed to pin her arms to her sides. She thrust her head back as hard as she could. She had hoped to hit his nose, but she was too short. She did succeed in cracking him in the windpipe, and he gasped. Then he laughed again. She reached her arms over her head and estimated where his eyes would be. She gouged them, and he hollered in surprise and pain. His grip loosened just enough for her to pull his hand from her mouth barely far enough to bite him. Hard. She tasted the metallic stickiness of his blood. He ripped his hand away from her mouth, and she screamed as loudly as she could.

~ ~ ~

Callum had kept his eyes on Siùsan any time he had not been partnered with her. He had found dancing with her to be a delight. She was an able and sure-footed dancer, and the way her tiny waist in his hands felt was enough to harden his rod for the entire night. He had been disappointed to let her go any time the dance called for them to switch partners. He was beyond relieved each time she came back to him. He found that, even though he barely knew her, he already missed her when they were apart. He could not figure out why he was so drawn to her so quickly, he just was.

He also found that he was furious when Elizabeth cornered him into a dance that kept them together. He had told her as much and left her standing among the other dancers. He scoured the heads of the clansmen and women who were gathered but could not find the shock of deep red hair that he longed to find. He had seen she was not happy when he began to dance with Elizabeth, but a series of turns had caused him to lose sight of the one woman he did desire to dance with.

Instead of finding Siùsan, he did spot Tavish, who he knew had danced with her several times that evening.

"Have ye seen Siùsan?" Callum asked as he approached Tavish.

"Aye. She said she needed a break and was going to sit down." They both turned towards the dais, but she was not there.

"Strange. I am sure she said she was going to sit the next one out."

"I dinna think she would retire for the night without saying so. Perhaps she stepped out for a breath of air."

Both Tavish and Callum turned and moved towards the exit.

"Where are ye both headed?" They were stopped by Alexander and Magnus who were both holding pints of ale.

"Have ye seen Siùsan? Did she walk by?"

"What, big brother? Have ye lost her already? Ye charm isnae what it used to be," teased Magnus.

"Mayhap so, but I still want to find her. Siùsan doesnae ken her way around and the men have been drinking tonight."

"Fine. We'll help ye two look."

The four brothers walked through the door of the keep and began descending the steps. They had only gotten halfway to the bottom when a scream rent the air. Callum looked in the direction from which it came, and his blood ran cold at what greeted his eyes. Siùsan was grappling with a man at least twice her size. She had a dirk in her hand and was crouched and moving in a circle to give herself space away from the well. The man lunged at her, and she thrust her dirk into his side. He howled with anger and swiped his fist across her face. She jerked back from the impact, and his hand only grazed her face. She produced another dirk from where Callum could not see. She slashed his arm and leg as she pivoted away from him.

Callum thought he would be sick. He had a quick flash of memory from not so very long ago when his sister had been captured and held hostage, bound to a bed because of her husband's spurned lover. He had a sinking feeling that history was quickly repeating itself. He suspected this attack was no mere coincidence since his father had steep penalties for harassing women. Only another woman would serve as temptation enough to defy Laird Sinclair.

Callum led the charge across the bailey with his three brothers following on his heels. When they reached the two fighters, he pulled Siùsan behind him and wrapped an arm around her.

"Sean, what do ye think ye're doing assaulting ma bride?"

"She put me up to it?"

"What are ye saying about Lady Siùsan? That she asked for ye to attack her?"

"Nay. The other one." He staggered and stumbled to the ground. Between being seriously inebriated and the blood he was losing from his wounds, he could no longer stand. He fell backwards and passed out.

Callum turned to Siùsan and pulled her into his embrace. She dropped her two dirks and wrapped her arms around his waist. She clung to him and burrowed her head into his chest. This time when she took in his scent, it was fresh, clean, and masculine. It was a combination of pine and his own natural scent. She breathed deeply and began to calm.

Callum ran his hands up and down her back and over her shoulders and arms to check for any injuries. His heart was pounding still. He felt like he could not catch his breath after seeing his tiny betrothed fight off a man who would have been an equal partner to him in the lists. He was stunned. He was proud. He was slightly aroused. And he was relieved that she seemed to be uninjured.

"Mo ghaisgeach beag," he whispered into her hair as he bent over her and kissed her temple. She was a little warrior, and more importantly, she was his. He knew in that moment that he would always defend her and always come after her. He could feel her body begin to calm and the trembling slowly stopped. She relaxed into his hold. They stood like that for what seemed like forever. He was only slightly aware that his brothers had carried Sean away, and they were alone together. He pulled back slightly from her and used his forefinger and thumb to turn her face towards him. There was the beginning of a bruise on her cheek and jaw. The sight of her marred skin was enough to set his blood boiling all over again.

"I am alright. Ye and yer brothers saved me. Naught really happened."

"Naught happened?" he barked. "That mon was about to rape ye or God kens what else."

"I dinna need ye to explain to me what he wanted. I was more than aware as he said as much when he grabbed me. Even if he hadnae, I am nay eejit. I kenned what he was aboot." She drew back from his arms and placed her hands on her hips.

Callum had never seen a more glorious sight. The moon shone on her hair making it look as though it were flames dancing in the dark. Her eyes had become a much deeper shade of green. Her face was still pale, but a little color was rising up her neck. She most definitely was a little warrior if ever he had seen one.

"I didna mean ye were an eejit. I meant that it is a big deal that he, or anyone, attacked ye. We dinna stand for men to harm any woman in this clan. I certainly will nae stand for any mon harming ye. I amnae angry at ye. I am angry that someone planned to hurt ye." He pulled her back into his arms. "I was concerned when I couldnae find ye in the Great Hall. I was positively terrified when I saw ye fighting him."

Siùsan tilted her head back to look at him. She searched his eyes and saw that he was earnest about his feelings. He was not upset at her but had been very worried about her wellbeing.

"I didna ken that a braw mon like yerself would be terrified of anything." She could only whisper. It seemed that speaking any louder would destroy the spell that seemed to be winding itself around them.

"I was terrified. I dinna ever want to see a mon raise his hand to ye again. Ye deserve to be protected. Ye shouldnae ever have to do it yerself." He lowered his mouth to hers and softly brushed his lips against hers a couple of times. When she did not pull back but rather leaned in to his kiss, he pressed his lips more firmly against hers. He felt more than heard her sigh. She wrapped her arms around him again and lifted her chin to him. His tongue traced the seam of her lips. She did not understand what he wanted. When he did it a second time, he pressed his tongue against the crease. She opened her lips only. He used his thumb to gently press her jaw open, then she understood what he wanted. She opened her mouth to his invading tongue. He languidly allowed his tongue to search the inside of her mouth. Tentatively, she used her tongue to touch his. She had no idea what to do or what he would want her to do. When she heard his deep groan, she grew braver, allowing her tongue to trace the inside of his mouth. His grip on her waist tightened. She pulled back her tongue and sucked gently on his.

Siùsan was shocked that she was allowing him to kiss her in such a manner but could not have stopped herself even if she wanted. *Just a few hours ago, I could barely stand the mon. Now I canna get enough of him. What is he doing to me? Why am I so drawn to a mon I'm nae sure I even like let alone trust?*

Callum was in heaven and hell. He had never felt anything more erotic than the feel of Siùsan pulling his tongue into her mouth and holding it there. Her body felt perfect pressed against his. Her breasts were much fuller than he had realized before. The flair of her hips tempted his hands as they skimmed over her sides and then gripped her buttocks. His cock had swollen and was twitching with the need to thrust into her. His ballocks ached with the need for release. Her quiet little pants and moans were driving his control to the brink of destruction. He could barely keep himself from carrying her into the garden and laying her on a bench to ravish her. Only the thought of what she had just endured kept him from pushing things further. Slowly, he pulled his mouth from hers. He drew lines of kisses along her battered cheek and jaw to her neck. He licked and kissed his way down to her shoulder. She titled her head to give him more access. He could feel the shudders of desire pass through her slim body as her hips rocked forward. He knew she was not aware of what she was doing. He desperately wanted to make love to her but knew that if they went any further, she would only regret her impulsivity. He released her bottom and ran his hands up her back. When he reached her shoulders, he pressed her back as he took a step back.

"Lass, I could stay here all night just kissing ye, but I dinna want to overstep. We havenae even signed the betrothal contracts yet. If we stay out here much longer, there will be talk as I am sure more than one person has noticed our absence by now. I dinna want to part, but I ken it is the right thing to do. Will ye go riding with me tomorrow? I would like to show ye the village and the surrounding areas."

Siùsan struggled to catch her breath as she looked up at Callum. She was overwhelmed at her physical and emotional reaction to being in his arms. She, too, knew that they needed to stop before they went too far, and she knew they needed to return to the keep, but she longed to stay with just Callum. She could only nod her head.

"Is that an aye to returning to the keep or to the ride tomorrow?" Callum asked softly. He was desperately praying that she meant the ride.

"Tis an aye to both." She reached up on her tiptoes but was still too short to reach his lips, so she settled for a kiss to his jaw. She rather liked the feel of his bristles on her lips. She reached her fingertips up to rub them along his jaw.

"If ye keep that up, I willna let ye out of ma sight for a month of Sundays."

Siùsan giggled softly. This time it was she who took his hand as they walked back to the keep. They entered the Great Hall together. The Sinclair was there to greet them and look very concerned.

"Lass, ma lads were just telling me what happened. Are ye well? Tell me what happened?" The Sinclair was trying not to riddle her with questions, but he had been shocked to hear that his soon to be daughter by marriage had been attacked in his very own bailey.

"Ma laird--"

"It's Liam for now, lass. Mayhap one day even Da."

Siùsan blushed at this. She could not help feeling happy at this invitation to informality. There was something about Laird Sinclair that made her look to him as the father she had not had. He was an intimidating sight. He had to be at least two and half score, but he was still as brawny as his sons. It was clear that he still trained in the lists regularly. He and Tavish were the most similar in build. They were barrel chested and ever so slightly shorter than the other Sinclair men. His hair was still a deep chestnut making it obvious from whom the sons had inherited their hair. His eyes were a slightly lighter shade of brown than Callum's but still very similar.

"Liam, I needed to catch ma breath from dancing and was overly warm. I remembered that Hagatha said that ye make sure the women of the clan are safe among yer men, so I decided to step outside. I walked over to the well. Then a hand covered ma mouth, and another wrapped around me. I fought then Sir Callum and yer other sons came to ma rescue." She did not want to repeat what the man had said to her or after when Callum questioned him. She had already deduced that Sean had meant Elizabeth. She could not think of any other woman who would put a man up to harm her. *Does Callum realize who did this? Is this going to be enough to have her set aside or is he going to let it go? I dinna quite ken what to make of his kiss. Was it just lust, or does he mean what he said about being faithful and making me happy? I just dinna ken. I amnae saying aught yet.*

"Lass, is there naught more that ye can tell me?"

"Nay. He was drunk and seemed to be looking for company whether I was willing or nae."

"Da, there is more, but I will speak to ye after we sign the contracts. Siùsan, if ye are still willing to wed, I would make our betrothal official and binding. Tonight."

"Are ye sure that ye want to do that tonight? Ye dinna need more time to ken that we suit?" She could not keep herself from looking at Elizabeth who gloated back at her as she looked at her bruised face.

"I havenae ever been so sure of anything, lass. I would make it official and be sure that *everyone* kens that I choose ye and ye are under ma protection."

"For ma protection. Vera well then." She whispered as she stepped forward to take Laird Sinclair's arm. *I suppose that is more than I could have hoped for.*

"Siùsan, ma son may be thoughtless at times, but he is a good mon. He seems vera taken with ye. Just give him time to show ye that he will make ye a good husband. If ye dinna agree between now and the wedding, ye can call it off without any fear. Ye can stay here or I will escort ye personally wherever ye care to go." Liam Sinclair whispered all of this to Siùsan as they walked towards the priest.

She was too shocked at his offer to do more than nod her head. She looked back to see Callum following close behind. His brow was furrowed as he watched her with his father. Clearly, he had not been able to hear what his father whispered, and he seemed concerned about what he did not know. She gave him a small smile that she hoped would reassure him. Perhaps, if she could convince him that everything was well, then perhaps she could convince herself.

The priest stepped forward as they both turned to face one another. A strip of Sinclair plaid was wrapped around their wrists. It was just loose enough for Callum to turn his wrist and entwine Siùsan's fingers with his. He gave her a warm smile and a wink. She was encouraged by his smile and returned it. They turned to face the priest.

Father Paul began the vows by directing his questions to Callum.

"Do you, Callum Liam David Sinclair, take Siùsan Allyson Mary Mackenzie to be yer betrothed wife, to be her constant friend, her partner in life, and her true love? To love her without reservation, honor and respect her, protect her from harm, comfort her in times of distress, and to grow with her in mind and spirit?"

Siùsan was not sure how he would feel about the part where he was asked to pledge his love. She did not know if he would ever consider loving her, but he answered in a confident and strong voice that carried clearly throughout the Great Hall.

"Ye canna possess me for I belong to maself but while we both wish it, I give ye that which is mine to give. Ye canna command me, for I am a free person, but I shall serve ye in those ways ye require, and the honeycomb will taste sweeter coming from ma hand. I pledge to ye that yers will be the *only* name I cry aloud in the night, and the *only* eyes into which I smile in the morning. I pledge to ye the first bite of ma meat and the first drink from ma cup. I pledge to ye ma living and ma dying, each equally in yer care. I shall be a shield for yer back and ye for mine. I shall not slander ye, nor ye me. I shall honor ye above all others, and when we quarrel we shall do so in private and tell no strangers our grievances. This is to be the marriage of equals. To ye, I pledge ma troth."

Siùsan had not anticipated Callum reciting a traditional marriage vow for their betrothal, but she understood what he was telling her. She had not missed his addition of "only" when he promised to be faithful to her. She also knew that was not meant for her alone. That left a slightly bitter taste in her mouth, but she chose to look to the positive that he had done so.

Father Paul turned his attention to her now and posed his questions.

"Do you, Siùsan Allyson Mary Mackenzie, take Callum Liam David Sinclair to be yer betrothed husband, to be his constant friend, his partner in life, and his true love? To love him without reservation, honor and respect him, protect him from harm, comfort him in times of distress, and to grow with him in mind and spirit?"

In a clear voice of her own, Siùsan both pledged her commitment and staked her claim on Callum Sinclair, future laird of the Sinclairs.

"Ye are Blood of ma Blood, and Bone of ma Bone. I give ye ma Body, that we Two might be One. I give ye ma Spirit, 'til our Life shall be Done. I swear by peace and love to stand, heart to heart and hand to hand. Mark, O Spirit, and hear us now, confirming this ma sacred vow. To ye, I pledge ma troth."

Callum beamed at her and was clearly pleased that she had chosen an equally traditional wedding vow for her betrothal pledge. Without waiting for the priest, he pulled her to him and lowered his lips to hers. It was a sweet and gentle kiss but quickly became deeper. The clearing of more than one throat finally tore them apart. Siùsan was too aroused to be embarrassed. She did not understand the feelings that Callum generated low in her belly. Her breasts ached, and she longed for him to touch her. All she could do was stare up at him. He seemed to innately understand her thoughts for he tucked hair behind her ear just as he had done in the stables just that morning. The events of the day suddenly churned through her mind and she felt exhausted. She could not believe all that had happened in the space of one day. She began to feel too warm, and black spots danced around the corner of her vision. She swayed slightly, and Callum wrapped his arm around her.

"Ye have had a mighty full day, leannan. Perhaps a few sips of wine before we sign the contract. Then ye can retire for the night. Would that be alright with ye?"

Her head was swimming and it took a moment for her to understand all that he had said. She could only nod. With their hands still bound together, they walked up the dais stairs to the table where the contracts had been laid out. It was only then that she realized that she would be signing the contracts for herself. Normally, a bride's father was present to witness the signing. No one had made any mention about the fact that he had not accompanied her or that her escorts had left once she had dismounted her horse. They had not even lingered for a morning meal as they had been specifically instructed not to dally. Now Siùsan looked around to see all the Sinclairs standing together as a happy family and she had no one to stand with her on her behalf. She choked back the tears that threatened and swallowed her pride as she leaned over the documents. She had not seen them before this, so she had not had a chance to review them. Her eyes quickly traveled over the terms and agreements. She saw that her father had given her a small plot of land to serve as her dowager land. She knew exactly where the land was located. It was isolated and not farmable because of the rocks and clay. If she was ever relegated to live there, she would quickly starve. There was no mention of any money that she would inherit or of her mother's dowager land. Her father had not set aside anything to provide for any daughters that she might have. She realized now that he had not even settled a dowry on her as there was no mention of a bride price, and she had not seen any coin exchange hands when she arrived. She also saw that the place where father's seal and signature should have been, was blank.

Her head snapped up as she looked first at Callum and then at Laird Sinclair. *How can this be? Why would Laird Sinclair, nay, Liam accept a bride for his son who comes with naught? What is going on? Is this why Callum hadnae wanted me?* Her eyes filled with tears as she looked at Laird Sinclair. His kind smile told her that he knew what she was wondering.

"Aye, nighean. It is a bit unconventional, but I kenned yer mother vera well. She was a dear friend of ma wife's. Ye are her vera image inside and out. She would be so proud of ye. She loved yer da vera much as he loved her. Ye are the result of that union. I would be proud to call ye daughter."

Siùsan turned away from the crowd that watched the betrothal ceremony. Her eyes could no longer contain her tears.

"Did he ken? Did Callum ken that I come with nae dowry?" She turned to him. "Is that why ye didna want to marry me? Ye think me a pauper. Or did ye just nae want to be forced to marry a stranger?" She felt like she could not breathe. The room was starting to spin, and she saw black spots before her eyes again.

"Lass, I have seen this contract already and, aye, I kenned the terms. I wasnae ready to marry before I met ye. I admit I was angry at the thought of marrying a stranger. The terms of the contract never mattered to me. They dinna matter to me now. I have pledged maself to ye before God, ye, ma kin and clan. I meant what I said."

All she could do was nod. Callum handed her a goblet of watered wine, and she gulped it down. She knew it was not ladylike, but it was all she could do to keep from fainting. She watched as Callum signed the contract and passed the quill to her. She looked at him, at the Sinclair, the other Sinclair brothers, and finally the crowd that watched them all. She put the goblet back on the table and bent over to sign. When she was done, the Sinclair warmed the wax and dipped his signet ring in to it and then pressed it onto the parchment. It was done. She was now legally bound to Callum Sinclair. She looked out at the crowd again and saw the malice in Elizabeth's face as she stood at the front of the crowd as a constant reminder of Callum's life from before her. A life that had only changed that morning. *Will he truly keep his vows or is he just a charmer?*

Those were her last thoughts before the cheers of the crowd drowned out the sound of her voice within her head. Callum unbound their hands slowly and kissed it. The crowd cheered even louder. He looked down at Siùsan and could see that she had reached her limits for the day. Even though he very much wanted to be the one that escorted her to her chamber, he knew that would not be appropriate. They were betrothed but not handfasted or wed. Instead he called Hagatha over and quietly asked her to escort Siùsan above stairs. Once the women had left the dais, he keenly felt her absence. He missed the fresh scent of lilacs that drifted around her. He missed her smile and her verdant eyes which where a shade of green that changed with her mood and lighting. He sat for a while with his father and brothers. They shared a few drams of whisky to celebrate his upcoming nuptials. The crowd in the Great Hall began to shrink as people sought their beds about the keep or in their cottages. His father went to his chambers soon after complaining that he was too old to stay up that late. Callum was left with his brothers. In quiet tones, they discussed what had happened in the bailey that night.

"Sean said 'she' had put him up to it. I can only think of one 'she' who would want harm to come to Siùsan." Alexander came straight to the point. He was never one to tarry when he had something to say. His dislike of Elizabeth had been a silent wedge between him and Callum ever since he had brought her home with him.

"I can easily imagine Elizabeth seducing Sean into harming Siùsan. She doesnae seem to like competition." Magnus stated between sips of whisky. As the largest of all the brothers, even though he was the youngest, he could hold more alcohol than Callum had ever seen. His legs seemed to be hollow when it came to food and drink. *Nay matter how much he drinks, he never gets in his cups and never awakens with a sore head. Tis nae fair.* Callum thought to himself as he looked at each of his brothers.

"But I told her clearly from the beginning that we wouldnae be getting wed and that I wasna looking for a wife. I told her again when the betrothal was announced. I told her that the affair would come to an end once ma bride arrived for the betrothal signing. I told her last night that we were done once the sun rose."

"Therein is yer problem. Ye daft bugger, ye took the wee banshee to yer bed the night before yer betrothed arrived. What message do ye think that sent? She clearly doesnae think that yer promise to end things was serious if ye were willing to tup her hours before ye pledge yer troth to another." The disgust in Tavish's voice could not be misunderstood. Callum winced because he knew that disgust was not just directed to Elizabeth. If anything, it was far more directed towards him. He winced as he realized how selfish he had been to his family. They had tried to warn him repeatedly, tolerating her for his sake. He had steadfastly refused to heed anyone's advice. He had been sure that no harm would come of his affair with Elizabeth. He had pushed ahead because it was what he wanted. Now he was filled with guilt for how Siùsan had been treated throughout her first day with the Sinclairs, how he had disregarded his father and brothers, and how his selfishness could affect the clan. If he was to one day be a successful laird, like his father, he would have to stop being so thoughtless and selfish.

"I ken ye all are right. Ye've all been right the entire time. I should have listened to ye, but I didna, and now I am nae the only one who is paying the price. This is inconvenient for me, but I fear for Siùsan's safety. I must have Elizabeth leave as soon as possible. I dinna care where she wants to go as long as it is far from here."

The four brothers fell into silence as they finished their whisky. They each went to their chambers and bid one another good night from their doors.

Chapter Seven

allum opened the door to his chamber and was immediately hit with the scent of roses. He cringed. He had hoped that the chambermaids would have changed his sheets and aired out the room. He did not want the reminder of his indiscretion at that moment. He did not want any reminders of his time with Elizabeth. He only longed for her to be far, far away and soon. He moved across the room and drew the window covering aside. He opened the glass and allowed the cool night air to waft over him. It helped to clear the scent from his nose, but it still seemed to linger. As he looked through his window, he could see the sea just beyond the cliffs. He unpinned his broach and dropped it into his sporran. He unbelted his sporran and let his plaid unwind from his waist. He turned towards his bed and was startled to see the outline of someone in his bed. He immediately knew who it was. There was only one woman who was brazen enough to enter his chambers and his bed only a few brief hours after he had just been betrothed in front of his entire clan. There was only one woman who wore such a cloying scent. He stormed to his door and yanked it open. He marched next door and pounded on Alexander's door. It was his turn to wait impatiently for the door to open. When it did, Alexander was still wrapping his plaid around him.

"Come with me. The wicked bitch is in ma bed."

Callum turned around without waiting for Alexander. There was no way that he was going back into his chamber alone with Elizabeth. He knew he would never voluntarily touch her again, but he did not trust her not to tell tales. He wanted to have at least one witness to his kicking her out into the night. Alexander followed closely.

"Ye canna be serious that she is in yer bed."

"Serious as a Norse beserker."

They arrived at his door in just a few short steps. Callum pushed the door open and stepped aside. He would have Alexander enter first and see exactly what he meant.

"I've been waiting an awfully long time for ye." The two men heard a sultry voice coming from the bed. "What the bluidy hell? Why are ye here? Where is Callum?" The sultry voice was quickly replaced by an irate screech.

"Were ye expecting someone else, lass?" Alexander returned her question with one of his own. He wandered into the room like he was stalking prey. Callum watched from the door. "What are ye doing in ma brother's bed? Did ye nae hear him and see him this evening? I thought his choice was rather clear. Did ye nae understand?"

Alexander walked to the bed and spotted Elizabeth's kirtle at the foot of the bed. He threw it at her rather than to her. It landed just short of her. In a play to even her hand, she allowed the sheet to drop from her breasts as she leaned forward to grab her gown. She rose from the bed and looked to the door where Callum still stood.

"Ah, there ye are. Were ye hoping to watch or would ye care to share?" Elizabeth purred as she walked past Alexander. Alexander reached out and caught her upper arm. Never had he ever considered physically harming a woman but, in this moment, he wanted to shake her and then drag her to the gates by her hair.

"Get dressed, Elizabeth. Neither Alex nor I plan to spend any more time with ye than it takes ye to don yer clothes and be gone." Callum called from the doorway. While he felt badly that his younger brother was fixing his mess, he had no intention of getting anywhere close to Elizabeth. He wanted there to be no ground for any rumors that he had spent any time with her in his chamber.

Alexander released her arms and crossed his over his chest. Callum followed suit as it was a more natural stance for them both than being relaxed. Elizabeth dressed slowly. Raising her arms high above her head to show off her breasts. She let the kirtle slide down her body and then ran her hands over herself as if to smooth wrinkles. Then she walked to Callum and presented her back to him.

"Could ye at least help me?"

"Nay. Ye managed to undress yerself. Ye can redress yeself." If it really would not have set tongues wagging, he would have kicked her out of his chamber even with her dress undone.

She tugged on the laces that were inconveniently, for her, located in the back. She managed to look down upon both men even though they towered over her. She harrumphed as she stormed out of the chamber. She paused halfway down the passageway and called back to them loudly.

"Thank ye, ma lords, for such an entertaining and pleasurable encounter." Callum cringed as he knew his other brothers would hear her and possibly his father. He was just thankful that Siùsan's chamber was one floor above and she had retired quite a long time ago.

"Have done and be gone." Alexander called out before walking into his own chamber. The door slammed. Callum returned to his own chamber, locked the door, and finished undressing. His sheets retained the scent of roses. He could not sleep there. He pulled his plaid over him and laid down before the fire. He had slept on the hard ground outside enough times for a night on the floor not to bother him, at least not too much.

Chapter Eight

The next morning seemed to dawn all too soon for both Siùsan and Callum. Siùsan awoke to a pounding headache. The goblet that she had virtually chugged had gone to her head as she made her way up the stairs. Hagatha had helped her undress and combed out her hair. She had been kind and motherly which only brought back the tears that had already started to fall in the Great Hall. Siùsan had ended up confessing that she was scared that Callum would not come to care for her ever and that he would stray soon. Hagatha had soothed her and repeated what Callum had told her in the stables. She told them how all Sinclair men value faithfulness and never intentionally mistreat their women. It had been enough to calm Siùsan as she climbed into bed. Exhaustion swept over her and her eyes were closed as soon as her head hit her pillow. She was deeply asleep by the time Hagatha finished tidying the chamber and quietly pulled the door closed behind her.

Callum's head pounded not from the many drams of whisky he had shared with his brothers and father. It pounded from the memory of his encounter with Elizabeth and the smell of her perfume that refused to leave his chamber. He had slept with the window open all night. All it had resulted in was his body being extra stiff from a night on the floor. He rose from the floor and groaned. He looked around his chamber. Elizabeth had now been in his bed twice. Somehow it felt as though it was sacrilege that she had ever been there. It felt like a sin to bring Siùsan to this chamber since the sanctity of his bed had been violated, even if it had only been by choice once. *Once we are wed, I will take up residence in Mairghread's room. When she and Tristan visit, they can have this chamber. I canna bring ma new wife to this bed. I just canna.* He knew that his sister would understand whether he ever fully explained or not. She would know that something had happened, and she would not ask questions, at least not too many. He snorted at that idea. *Nae bluidy likely. If she doesnae like ma answer, she will just ask the others until she kens the entire ugly truth.* That seemed far more likely to him.

~ ~ ~

Callum came upon Siùsan as she descended to the Great Hall. He took her hand and placed it upon his arm without any thought. It just felt right to him. Her small smile told him that she felt the same.

"I trust ye slept well, leannan."

"Aye, like a newborn bairn. And ye?"

"Well enough."

"Is something wrong?" Her perceptiveness made Callum worry that she would figure out that something had happened before he was ready to divulge the entire story.

"Nay, lass. I think I was just eager to take ye on that ride. I would like to show ye around yer new home."

Home. That is a nice thought. In all ma years with ma clan, it never quite felt like home. This is a pleasant first.

"I am looking forward to that too. When would ye care to go?"

"Let us break out fast and then I will ask Elspeth for a picnic."

They arrived in the Great Hall and made their way to their chairs upon the dais. A servant brought them each steaming bowls of porridge. As it was placed before them, Callum passed a bowl of honey to Siùsan. He offered to add some to her porridge. He smiled at her look of surprise.

"I remember from yester morn that ye like honey in yer porridge."

"I wouldnae have though that ye would have noticed such a small detail."

"I find I have noticed much about ye in the space of just a day."

Siùsan could feel her cheeks warm, so she looked down at her bowl. She was not sure how to respond, so she put a spoonful in her mouth. Despite the generous amount of honey that Callum had added, the porridge had a slightly sour taste. It was not quite the taste of spoiled milk, but it definitely was not right. She tried stirring the honey in more and another bite, albeit much less on her spoon. She could not get rid of the sour taste. It was actually rather bitter. She just could not eat any more. She slid her bowl to her side and reached for a bannock instead. She had sworn not eat to another one after eating so many on her journey.

"I am eager to get some time with ye to get to ken ye." Callum whispered in her ear. She had not felt him lean towards her and jumped when she felt his warm breath against her cheek. She jerked and knocked the bowl onto the ground.

"Excuse me. I am so sorry." She leaned towards the mess to clean it up. She felt a gentle pull on her elbow, so she sat up.

"Dinna fash. It was an accident. I startled ye. One of the maids will tend to it. Just be careful not to step in it."

"Vera well. But I still feel badly that I made a mess, and now someone else will have to clean it up." She had every intention of cleaning it up herself, but she did not want to argue with Callum when they were getting along.

She reached for another bannock, but Callum slid his bowl over to her. He signaled a maid to bring another bowl. Siùsan was not sure her taste buds were ready for more porridge, but she did not want to reject his offer. She put the spoon to her lips and slid her tongue out to taste it. Surprisingly, it tasted normal. It was just as delicious as yesterday's. *Strange. Perhaps I just got a bad batch, but I dinna see anyone turning up their noses. Why did mine taste so dreadful?*

Siùsan finished her breakfast as she and Callum chatted about what he would show her. When they were ready to leave, Callum agreed to pick up the picnic basket and Siùsan was going to fetch her arisaid from her chamber. She pushed back her chair and looked at the floor. She was going to clean up the mess she had made, but the sight that greeted her made her gasp. She took a step back and knocked over her chair. Callum turned to see what was wrong and saw that Siùsan looked a tinge green. She was staring at something on the ground. He stepped next to her and looked down. The sight that met him drove a spike of fear through him that matched how terrified he had been the night before when he had seen Sean's hands on her. In front of them, in the middle of the puddle of porridge, was a dead rat. There was foam around its mouth.

"Poison. Someone tried to poison me." She croaked out. She grasped her throat and wrapped an arm around her middle. Callum's strong hands pulled her back from the dead animal. He turned her towards him and wrapped his arms around her. He looked out above her head at his clan. His eyes searched for the one person he knew was responsible. Elizabeth was nowhere to be seen. *How vera convenient. She thinks she canna be blamed if she was nae present.*

"*Hagatha! Elspeth!*" Callum bellowed as he wrapped Siùsan tighter in his arms. "Dinna fash, lass. The person responsible for this will be taken care of."

This only made Siùsan pull away from him. She glared at him. The look of fear or upset that he expected was not there. Rather the anger radiated from her. She glared at him but did not say anything for a moment. Just when he thought she would not say anything, she bit out her response between clenched teeth.

"We both ken exactly who did this and why. The only real problem is that she is yer mistress and plans to remain such. Better yet, she intends to be yer wife. She need only get me out of the way." She stormed off the dais and out of the doors of the keep. She bolted across the bailey to the stables. She ran down the stalls to Trofast and threw his stall door open. She grabbed the halter that was over his head and pulled him from the stall. She took him to a nearby bale of hay and mounted bareback. Leaning far over his neck, she left the barn at a trot. She saw a clear path to the gates and nudged Trofast to a canter. From the corner of her eye, she saw

Callum run out of the keep. He called out to her several times and then ran to the stables. She knew she had little time to make her escape. She did not know where she was going, but she needed to ride and have a moment to herself. The guardsmen at the gate tried to wave her down but leapt out of the way as she kicked Trofast into a gallop. She followed the path out of the gates but veered off when she saw the loch.

~ ~ ~

Callum had leapt from the dais and run into the kitchens to find Elspeth and Hagatha. He told them about the rat and then ran back into the Great Hall as his family came down the stairs. He yelled to them that someone had tried to poison Siùsan and that she had run off. He charged through the crowd that was growing around the dais and pushed through the doors of the keep. He came outside and was blinded by the sun for a moment. He caught sight of motion as a horse came out of the stables. He saw Siùsan atop Trofast riding bareback. He called to her over and over. She turned to look at him once and then spurred her horse on. He dashed to the stables and grabbed his own horse, Deamhan, or Devil. He took the horse out of the stables and mounted without assistance. He galloped through the bailey and out of the gates. He saw her ride towards the loch at a breakneck pace. She crossed over the ground that divided the path away from the keep to the road. She joined the path to the loch and rode along the shoreline. Callum was unprepared for how fast her stallion was. He had been able to tell he was good horseflesh when she had been checking his hooves the previous day, but he did not imagine the speed and power he could produce. He continued to nudge Deamhan faster as he followed Siùsan. He watched as Siùsan and Trofast scrambled up a hill on the far side of the loch. His heart began to pound against his ribs as he watched her riding up the hill. Unbeknownst to Siùsan, there was a steep drop off from the cliffs above the lochs. They dropped straight into the North Sea. There would be no way for her to survive such a fall. He reached the bottom of the hill and bellowed to her.

"Siùsan! Nay! Stop! The cliffs drop off!" He yelled over and over, but he was too far away, and the wind was blowing his voice away. He watched as she reined in at the top of the hill. She looked around and then looked back over her shoulder at him. He worried that she would take off again, but instead she slid from Trofast's back and waited for him. He nudged Deamhan up the last part of the hill and joined her at the crest.

Callum jumped from his horse and breathed heavily. He wanted to yell at Siùsan for scaring him, but he knew that she was shaken from the near poisoning and the sheer drop that greeted her only moments ago. He could understand how she just wanted to escape. Instead he walked slowly towards her as though he was approaching an injured wild animal.

"Are ye well?" he asked tentatively. He stood patiently and decided to let her make the next move.

"As well as can be expected considering yer leman wants me raped and dead." She had no intention of hiding her anger. It was ready to boil over, and she needed to direct it somewhere.

"Siùsan, I dinna even ken what to say. Ye are right about it all except she isnae ma leman."

"Oh, really? What do ye call a woman that ye brought back from court with ye for the express reason of bedding her at any time ye like? I think most would call her yer leman. Not only that, but ye kenned I was to arrive and ye have let her stay. Ye only ended things with her the night before I arrived. Ye didna seem to think that it might bother yer bride to have yer mistress living in the same keep. Just how daft are ye?" By the end of her rant, she was screaming. She walked up to Callum and stood toe to toe with him. She looked up at him and pointed her finger at his chest. She poked him as she drew breath to continue. "Ye have quite the set of bollacks to think any woman would want her soon to be husband parading his mistress around right under her nose. Ye have humiliated me over and over again in just the space of one day. Yer bonnie blonde has arranged for one of yer guardsman to attack me and try to rape me. That should tell ye something of her wiles that she was able to seduce a mon supposedly loyal to ye and yer family, which I am to be a member of. When that failed, she managed to find a way to taint ma food and have it served to me. Just how am I supposed to feel about this warm reception that ye have put on for me?" It was only when she paused to catch her breath that she realized just how loudly she had been screaming. She suddenly had a very real and very strong fear of how Callum would react to her outburst. She stepped back but bumped into Trofast. She had nowhere to go if he lashed out at her. She tensed and waited for his response. She expected him to beat her or to at least yell at her, so when he hung his head and shook it, she was not prepared for his response. He finally looked up, shamefaced.

"Ye're right. Ye're right about it all. I suppose I canna reason ma way out of acknowledging that she *was* ma mistress. I admit that I should have ended it as soon as I found out about the betrothal rather than indulging in ma selfishness. I didna give her the privileges that a mistress would expect, but she served that purpose, I admit. I am so vera sorry for that. Regardless of whether we suited when we met, I should have respected the role of ma future wife more. I should have thought of someone other than maself. I should have done many things differently. I am trying now, lass. I really am."

"I ken that, but it doesnae change the fact that she is still here. She is getting more and more brazen. At what point are ye going to choose me over her? Ye pledged yerself to me only last eve. Fogotten already? Will ye send her away to keep me safe and give us a real chance?"

"I will begin making the arrangement for her departure as soon as we get back to the keep."

Siùsan sighed deeply. She looked around at the breathtaking views from the top of the cliffs. She turned back towards the loch and looked down at the sparkling water that shimmered under the morning sun. She looked in yet another direction and saw a slope that led down to the seashore. She could hear the waves breaking against the rocks below. She heaved another sigh before looking at Callum.

"I hope ye dinna rush off too soon. Ye promised me a tour after all."

"Ye still want to spend time with me? Ye dinna want me to send her away right this moment?"

"I do. I wish she would disappear before we even return. I also would like to nae see her again any time soon. I would rather avoid her, and ye have already promised me time together. I think it would serve us well to get to ken one another if ye really want the marriage ye described to me yester morn."

She offered Callum a smile. It felt more like a grimace, but she tried to put some cheer into it. He watched her and tilted his head to the side as he tried to decide what had made her change so quickly from being livid to conciliatory. Whatever her reason, he was willing to go along with it. He wanted to try to salvage their day. He really did want to spend time with her and without the distraction of Elizabeth and her vindictiveness.

"What would ye care to see first? The sea or the loch?"

"I have never seen the sea before. Could I put ma toes in?"

Callum could not help but laugh at the eagerness in her voice and face. "Ye can, but they might freeze and snap off. It'll be a might chilly."

"I dinna mind. I have always wanted to see the sea but never thought I would."

They tethered their horses to a small bush and walked down the slope side by side.

Chapter Nine

They made their way down to the pebbly beach, and Siùsan took in the scenery that greeted her. The windswept beach stretched for at least a mile to the north and less than quarter of a mile to the south. Callum pointed to a cliff to the south and explained that there was a cave there that he and his brothers and sister used to explore. He told her how when the tide was at its lowest, someone could walk straight into the mouth of the cave but as the tide rose, anyone who wanted to enter would have to swim. He warned her that at the highest tide, the cave flooded and was not safe for anyone. He promised her that they would explore the cave another day when the weather was warmer since it was inevitable that they would get wet.

They turned and walked to the north. Siùsan collected shells as they wandered, and Callum held them in his sporran. They paused to look out at the crashing waves. The distant waters of the North Sea were a churning gray as the morning sun sent beams across its shimmering surface. Closer to shore, the white caps crashed along the cliffs that had no beach as a buffer.

"I havenae ever seen the sea before."

"How is that possible, lass? Yers is one of the largest clans in Scotland. Yer lands touch the sea on both sides."

"True. But I havenae travelled beyond ma journey here. We didna go anywhere near the coast on the way here."

"Ye never travelled with yer da to clan gatherings or to meet up with any of the other chieftains?"

"Ma father did not seek ma company for such trips." Siùsan quickly turned and began to hunt for more shells. She had no desire to discuss her childhood or her relationship with her father and stepmother. She handed a few more shells to Callum but a barking noise caught her attention.

They continued to walk north as Siùsan was curious about the sound. The smell struck her before she could see the seals on the rocky island just off of the coast.

The odor was almost overpowering for Siùsan, but Callum did not seem to notice at all. Siùsan realized that growing up along this coast, he was probably used to it. As she became accustomed to the stench, she could not help but laugh at their antics. She pointed to the pups that followed their mothers as they learned to fish. She marveled at the size of the fully grown males.

"Selkies," she whispered with a grin. "Do ye think that there is one amongst them?" She playfully elbowed him.

"When ma brothers and sister, and I were weans, we came down here with Mama and Da one summer day. Mama loved to swim and was a strong swimmer. She was a Sutherland before she married Da and often visited the coast with her family. She also grew up with a large loch much like ours. Magnus saw her swim out towards that rock and a few seals surrounded her. They barked and dove but never threatened her. He became convinced that she was a selkie and that she had shed her sealskin when she met our da. He was only about five at the time. He followed Da around for weeks asking if he had stolen Mama's sealskin to keep her. When Da gave Mama a sealskin lined cloak during Christmastide, Magnus was convinced that she was going to go back to the sea. He cried that entire time and begged that she never leave us." Callum stopped there as he looked out to the rock again. A small smile tugged at his lips as he reminisced about his family. It was only four short years later that their mother passed away from a fever.

"Yer mother must have been a hearty woman to swim in the North Sea. Does it ever truly warm up?"

"Nay. Not really but ye do get used to it after a time. Ye would be better off swimming in the loch. Do ye swim?"

"Aye. I learned as a wean and then taught ma brothers. It is one of ma favorite things to do."

"Then I will have to take ye to the loch sometime soon."

"I canna swim in front of ye! It wouldnae be proper or decent. Nay. If I may swim, then I will take a maid with me." She laughed softly, and Callum was mesmerized with the throatiness of the sound. "Hagatha was appalled when I suggested that I bathe there to avoid anyone having to carry and fill the tub."

"When was that?"

"When I went into the kitchens after visiting the blacksmith yesterday."

"Ye've already been to the kitchens?"

"Aye. I helped Hagatha with some buckets of water and met her sister. I met all the women who work in the kitchens."

"I hadna realized ye'd been so busy yesterday."

"I filled ma time nicely. Hagatha would not even consider allowing me to go to the loch, so I had a wonderful soak in ma chambers."

"Good for Hagatha. The men may use the loch for bathing before coming in from the lists, but there is nay reason for any of the women to need to bath there. If ye choose to swim for pleasure so be it but not because ye couldnae have a bath brought to ye."

"Ye shall spoil me rotten. I am used to bathing in a loch year round." She shrugged and bent to unlace her boots. Callum was seeing a pattern. Any time talk turned to her past with her family, Siùsan turned the conversation away from that topic. She did it casually, but he was certain it was on purpose. He watched as she shucked first her boots and then her stockings. The latter she tucked into the belt of her arisaid. She lifted her skirts to almost her knees and gingerly picked her way across the pebbles until she reached the water's edge. She slowly placed one foot into the water to test just how cold it was. When she seemed to decide it was not as frigid as she imagined, she waded in to calf deep. Callum watched as she daintily lifted on foot and pointed her toes. Siùsan drew circles with her toes in the low surf. She kicked water out and giggled as it sprayed back at her in the light breeze. She lifted her face to the sun and let her auburn curls cascade down her back. Callum was in awe. He had never seen such a breathtaking sight as Siùsan standing in the surf with her skirts held up and her head leaned back. He could see the graceful arc of her throat and the roundness of her firm breasts even through the thicker material of her arisaid. She lowered her head and turned towards the rocky promontory where the beach ended. The wind swept the hair from her face and lifted it, blowing back and forth across her face. She used one hand to brush it away.

"It's beautiful here. I havenae ever seen anything so breathtaking."

"Me neither," Callum whispered but the wind carried it away.

Siùsan turned to look for Callum since she had not heard his response. She was surprised to see that he was not looking at the scenery but at her. He walked purposefully towards her. He reached her in only a few short strides, wading in with his boots on.

"Me neither," he repeated for her. He reached out and brushed hair from her cheeks and then wrapped his large hand around her head. He cradled it gently for such a large man.

"Lass, ye are the bonniest sight I have ever seen. I canna help it, but I want to kiss ye now more than I have ever wanted anything else. May I?"

Siùsan could only nod her head. She had been stunned by his kiss last night after he rescued her from Sean, but she had enjoyed it. She had thought about it many more times than once since it had happened. She had wondered if it would happen again.

Callum slowly lowered his head and brushed his lips against hers. This time, she parted them slightly. As he pressed more firmly, he felt the tip of her tongue brush his. He wrapped his other arm around her waist and pulled her into him. He groaned when his sporran created a barrier between them. He pushed it out of the way and pulled her back to him. His cock was hard and throbbing as it brushed against her mound and the bottom of her belly. She could feel it, and her hips had a mind of their own as they pressed forwards. She wrapped one arm around his waist and one around his upper back. She was too short to reach his neck without him bending over or her going up on her tiptoes. She pressed her breasts into his chest enjoying the feel of his hard muscles against her much softer form.

Their tongues dueled as they took turns exploring each other's mouth. At times, they licked and at others they sucked each other's tongue. The feeling of pressure on his tongue only made Callum imagine what it would be like to have her lips wrapped around his cock. Siùsan could not quite describe the feeling in her belly and lower when Callum's mouth pulled her tongue in. She felt her breasts grow heavy and even fuller. She ached with need and rubbed her mound against his iron rod. She moaned as she tried to relieve the growing pressure.

Callum lifted Siùsan up, and she wrapped her legs around his waist. Her skirts fell back and bared her knees. His cock found its resting place at her entrance even though the material of her kirtle and his plaid served as a shield. He walked them back up the beach until he found a rock to lay her back on. His superior height meant that he was able to lean his entire torso over her and she pulled him down to her. She felt more air on her thighs than before. She opened her eyes to see Callum looking down at her. She could not believe the look in his eyes. She had never seen a man look at her with such desire and longing as Callum did now. His hand trailed whisper soft up the inside of her thigh until her reached the juncture of her legs.

"I willna take what isnae mine to have, but I can bring yer pleasure if ye will let me." Callum breathed next to her ear. Siùsan could not do more than nod. The thought that they had known each other only for a day flashed through her mind before it floated away. Somehow this all seemed so right. *I will marry him soon. At the vera least, we desire one another. Perhaps it can grow from there.*

His fingers brushed against her warm, moist skin. Callum groaned as he felt her slick entrance and slowly pressed one finger in. She was so wet and welcoming that he had to take not one but two deep breaths to keep from tossing up his plaid and plunging into her. He could feel his cock leaking as he pressed a second finger into her. Her sheath seemed to swallow his fingers whole.

"Callum," she breathed out on a sigh. The sound of his name on her lips almost made him spill his seed. He began to move his fingers inside her as the tip of his cock pressed into her through his plaid. She wriggled her hips down the rock to try to get closer. "Callum, please." She sighed again.

"What is ye want, lass. Tell me."

"I dinna ken. Just more. Something more." She arched her back and pressed her breasts into his chest. He used more pressure as he slid his fingers in and out. He loved the feeling of his fingers being coated in her dew. He longed to taste her but did not want to frighten her by moving too quickly. He would save that for another day. His thumb brushed against her pleasure button and she practically bucked off the rock. She moaned loudly.

"What are ye doing to me?"

"Bringing ye pleasure, leannan."

Her hands ran up and down his back and she leaned forward so she could grasp his backside. Her hands gathered his plaid and he suddenly felt a breeze across his buttocks, then small but strong hands began to knead him. He thrust his hips forward, rubbed her nub, and thrust a third finger into her. He was quickly losing control but was careful not to be so rough as to breach her maidenhood.

Suddenly, he felt one of her legs fall away and a hand was pulling up his plaid in the front. Before he could fully understand what she was about, Callum felt one of Siùsan's hands circle his cock. She held him firmly but gently in her grip.

"I dinna ken what to do. Tell me. Tell me how to please ye as ye are me." Her desperate plea made Callum leak more as he felt the tip of his cock rub against the inside of her thigh. It would be so easy to enter her and spend himself there. The temptation was so very real. She was his betrothed after all. They were all but married in the eyes of the law and his clan, but he just was not able to bring himself to do it. He wanted their first joining to be after they had said their vows and when she was entering into it with forethought not in the heat of the moment. He knew she would regret it otherwise. He pulled his hips back slightly.

"Stroke me. Move yer hand up and down as ye hold me." She followed his directions and quickly found a rhythm that had his hips moving on their own. He still made sure that he was not near her entrance. One feel of her wetness against his tip and he would be lost.

He focused on rubbing her nub in small circles as his fingers rubbed against the inside wall of her sheath. He could feel her muscles tightening and her breathing sped up. She moaned and panted. Suddenly, her entire body went rigid as the most intense and pleasurable feeling she had ever had shot through her in waves. She was not sure what was happening. One hand clung to Callum's shoulder and the other seemed to have a mind of its own as it sped up as she stroked him.

Callum could not hold on any longer. The feel of Siùsan shattering around his fingers and in his arms along with her tight hand fisting him was more than he could take. He pulled back in time to keep his seed from being too near her entrance. He spilled into his plaid and onto her thigh. She released him, and he pulled his fingers from her. He fell forward over her but was sure to brace his weight on his elbows. The consequence of their quick movements was that his cock fell to her entrance. He felt the wetness of her and she reacted in the same moment by lifting her hips to meet him. She moaned, and he jerked back as though he was on fire. He saw the surprise and hurt on her face as she thought he was rejecting her. She tried to pull her skirts down quickly. He reached out and stopped her. He gently rearranged her skirts and then scooped her up. He cradled her in his arms as he turned and slid down the rock. When he was seated, he nuzzled her neck.

"I moved away because I didna trust maself not to take ye even though I just spent maself. Ye are the greatest temptation I have ever faced." He murmured against her neck as he tried to catch his breath. He ran his hands over her back as he breathed in her lilac scent. Siùsan was not sure how to respond.

One moment, she was feeling the most unexpected pleasure and the next she felt like someone had dumped a bucket of cold water onto her. The rapid switch between emotions and their depth frightened her. *How can I feel so much for someone I just met? Someone I amnae even sure I like and can trust?* The feeling of vulnerability was one that she was all too familiar with, and the feeling of staggering loss when her trust was broken was a feeling she knew all too well.

They sat together for a while, but as her body calmed, she began to feel chilled even though the breeze was fairly warm. She shivered once, and Callum unpinned his plaid and wrapped the extra material around her effectively making a cocoon against his chest and shoulder. Siùsan allowed herself to relax and settled in.

"Ye are fortunate to have grown up in such a beautiful and serene place." She ventured to start up a conversation, but she really did not know what one said after such intimacies.

"True but the winds and storms that blow up from this coast can be fierce and dangerous. This place is both breathtaking and dangerous. Dinna ever come along the cliffs alone. The force of the wind can take ye by surprise and blow ye to the edge." He kissed her temple. "I wouldnae forgive maself if ye came to harm here. I havenae ever brought anyone here but ma brothers and sister. This has always been our special family spot."

"Why did ye let me come down here if this is a place reserved for yer kin?"

"Because ye will soon be ma kin, and I wanted to share it with ye and only ye."

She looked into his whisky brown eyes and saw an emotion that she could not quite distinguish. It was not the desire and passion from just a short while ago. It was not laughter or humor or even the anger she had seen the night before in the bailey. Instead it was a seriousness she had not yet seen. She nodded and kissed his cheek.

They settled in and spent the rest of the morning talking. Their conversation varied in topics moving from Callum's memories of his childhood growing up at Castle Dunbeath to history, which included Siùsan's mother's Viking heritage, faith and even current politics. Callum was surprised at Siùsan's wealth of knowledge. He learned that she could both read and write which was unusual even for a laird's daughter. She had taught herself French to teach her younger brothers and admitted that her accent was probably atrocious since she had never actually heard anyone speak the language. He learned that she loved music and enjoyed singing but confessed that she could not carry a tune. In turn, Siùsan learned that Callum had been to court a number of times both with his father and as his father's representative. She learned about his younger sister, Mairghread, and her recent marriage to the Mackay and birth of her son, wee Liam.

"Aye. There is naught wee about that bairn. He came out looking like he was ready for the lists. I can tell he already takes after his father and his Uncle Magnus. He will be a giant soon. We only call him wee to distinguish between him and ma own father."

They fell quiet as they both reflected on the idea of bairns and family. Siùsan was not sure how she felt since it was obvious that once they wed, they would try to make their own bairns. They had very nearly begun practicing just a short while ago. However, the idea of her life being permanently linked to Callum's because of parenthood still seemed very strange. Furthermore, the realization that people would expect them to have a bairn soon was also disconcerting. Despite their conversation this morning, which had helped her gain many insights into her future husband, she still felt like she barely knew him. The idea of sharing a bed and making babies seemed surreal even if pleasurable. Callum's mind swung in the opposite direction. He had never before had any desire to have a bairn. He had felt entirely the opposite and had always been very careful never to sire any children. However, now that he knew Siùsan and he held her in his arms, he could not think of any other woman he had ever met that he would prefer to marry or make a child with. He knew that he still had much to learn about her, but his intuition told him that his father had chosen exceptionally well for him. He wondered just how much his father knew about Siùsan and how much that had influenced his decision to arrange the marriage.

The sun soon moved overhead, and a flock of seagulls came to fish near where they were seated. The squawks of the birds soon drove the couple from their spot beside the rock. Callum repinned his plaid as Siùsan donned her stockings and boots. They climbed the slope back to the top of the cliffs and found their horses where they had left them, grazing on the tall, windswept grass.

"Ye didna eat much for yer morning meal. Ye must be starving by now." Callum grasped Siùsan about the waist and hoisted her onto Trofast's back. Siùsan was accustomed to mounting by herself, so she squeaked at the unexpected motion. Callum gave her a crooked grin. "Any excuse is a good one, ma bonnie temptation." He quickly mounted his own horse, and they rode back towards the keep.

As they approached the loch, Siùsan looked out over the water. Away from the wind of the sea and under the bright noon sun, it was quite warm. She had begun to sweat in the short time they had been riding. She looked over at Callum and when she caught his attention, she grinned and winked. She whirled Trofast in the direction of the loch and issued a silent challenge for Callum to catch her. She leaned low over Trofast's withers and used the extra length of her reins to spur him on.

She reached the shores of the loch only slightly ahead of Callum. He bounded down from his horse and pulled her into his arms. He kissed her soundly, devouring her mouth as his hands ran over her body. His large hand came to rest on her full breast and he gently squeezed it. He kissed her cheek, along her jaw, and down her neck to where it met her shoulder. She gripped his shoulders and simply held on as he bent her backwards to kiss the exposed skin of her chest. Finally, he raised his head to look into her sparkling emerald eyes.

"Must ye always ride yer horse like the hounds of hell are on yer heels? Ye give me such a fright each time. Ye dinna ken the lay of the land here yet. If yer horse misses his footing, ye would go sailing over his head and possibly break yer back or crack open yer head." He was not speaking loudly but there was a force behind it that made Siùsan feel immediately regretful.

"Ye're right. I am sorry. I didna mean to frighten ye. I should be more responsible especially with Trofast's safety. I have had him since the day he was born. I couldnae live with maself if I was the cause of his injury. I wanted to continue having fun with ye, but I was irresponsible and childish. I really am sorry, Callum." She could not bring herself to meet his gaze. It was that type of playfulness that her father had considered foolishness. Now clearly Callum did too. She felt slightly ill at the idea that she had disappointed him so soon after she had arrived and after spending such a wonderful morning with him.

He tucked his finger under her chin and lifted it, but she still would not look at him. He could see the contrition clearly on her face but there was something more. She was internalizing something. Now it was his turn to feel guilty. He had wanted her to take him seriously, but he did not want her to feel badly about herself.

"Little one, I ken ye didna mean any harm. I like this playful side of ye. I simply want ye to be safe. All is forgiven. Will ye let me show ye the loch?" He leaned forward and gave her a soft peck on the lips. When she looked up and saw that he was not truly angry, she gave a small nod of her head. It was enough for Callum, and he wrapped his arm around her waist and guided her towards the loch. He looked back over his shoulder at the horses that he had not secured. They did not seem interested in going very far. If anything, he thought they might wander down for a drink.

"Ye said that ye enjoy swimming. Would ye care to go for a dip now?" He winked at her remembering her earlier objection. He was completely caught off guard by her answer.

"Turn away until I tell ye I am completely in the water." With that she grasped his shoulders and attempted to turn him around. It was like trying to move Ben Nevis. She laughed and simply moved around the far side of a thick bush. She knew he could not see her through it. She quickly shucked off her kirtle, stockings, and boots. She kept her chemise on even though she knew it would do little to hide her once she was wet. It just seemed like the least she could do to try to maintain some modesty.

"Is it deep over here by the rocks? Can I jump in or should I wade?" She called to Callum. She heard a rustling near the bush and realized he was most likely undressing too.

"It is deep enough to jump in there but be careful not to go too deep. There are some rocks that stick out about six feet down. Jump out rather than down." Callum felt a strange sense of protectiveness wash over him at the thought of her jumping in. She said she was a strong swimmer and it was a placid loch, but he suddenly worried that he was not there to catch her. He pried the bushes aside just in time to see her hike up her chemise as she scrambled up the rocks. She had the grace of a mountain lion as she moved higher and closer to the edge. She climbed far higher than he expected and was about to call out to here when she took three running steps and dove over the edge. She did one summersault and yelled, "wee," just before she hit the water. She emerged just moments later but much further out than he would have expected.

Callum had already stripped down and was naked. He jogged over to the shoreline and began to wade in. At the sound of his approach, Siùsan turned in his direction. She caught sight of him in his full glory. She could not turn her eyes away. The sun shone on his chestnut hair and made it look like it was aflame. The muscles in his chest rippled as he swung his arms. His abdomen contracted as he entered the chilly water up to his knees. His powerful thigh muscles allowed him to use a wide stride to enter the water faster. But what fully captured her attention was what hung between his legs. She had never seen a man's private parts before even though she had stroked him to completion only that morning. She had not thought to look down during their interlude. Now she could not believe what she saw. It seemed so large even from a distance and at rest. She thought back to how it had felt in her hand. It had been almost too wide for her to close her fingers around. Now it seemed inordinately long as she thought back on their love making.

Lovemaking? Where did that notion come from? It wasnae love. It was lust. I am sure he isnae going to think of it in such a flighty manner. Ye best not start fooling yerself into thinking he cares more for ye than he does. Ye will only disappoint yerself. Those thoughts brought Siùsan's mind crashing back to reality. She yelped and ducked under the water. She knew he had seen her examining him. She swam quickly away as she needed more distance between them.

"Siùsan! Siùsan!" Callum had waited for what felt like an eternity, but he knew had to have been barely a minute since she ducked under the surface, before he began calling out to her. He could not see any ripples or bubbles on the surface. He had no idea if she had sunk straight to the bottom or swum away. He quickly swam, kicking as hard as he could, to the spot he had last seen her. He prayed that his pride in showing off as he entered the water was not going to harm her. Just as he was about to dive down to search for her, he heard her spring from the water. She was nearly across the loch from him. He could not believe how far she had swum in such a short time. "Dinna move. Just dinna move!"

Callum swum his fastest towards her. She treaded water until he came closer. She felt like she was a tiny fish that was about to be swallowed by a much larger one. She began to push herself backwards. As he got even closer, she flipped onto her stomach and began to swim in earnest. She had only taken a few strokes before she felt his hand grasp her ankle. Not only was her forward momentum ended, she was yanked back into his embrace.

"I told ye nae to move." His hands moved to her thighs and wrapped them around his hips. He could just barely touch the bottom as they were nearer the far shore. He took a few more steps until he could stand easily on the sandy bottom. He grasped her bottom and squeezed, hard. She yelped more in surprise than in pain. She could feel his cock once again grazing the seam of her sheath. It was only the bunched up material of her chemise that kept him from having skin to skin contact. She could feel that she was instantly aroused. If she were honest with herself, she had to admit that watching him enter the water had aroused her. Now she ached for the feeling of him touching her like he had only hours earlier.

"Ye're a cheeky one. I think ye are the one who is part selkie. I canna believe how fast and far ye can swim. Ye will seriously be the death of me today. That is three times ye've made ma heart race. I told ye nae to move." Once again, his fear for her safety transformed into a hunger to hold her and taste her. His mouth crashed down onto hers but this time she was ready and parted her lips. Her tongue darted out and entered his mouth. She wrapped her arms around his neck and tightened her legs to hoist herself higher, so she could more easily reach his mouth. She gave as good as she got. She rocked her hips against him and moaned loudly. The sound of her arousal made his cock throb for release. Release inside of her. He longed for it. He craved it. He walked them out of the water and onto the sandy shore. He lowered them to the ground and rested his weight against her. He thrust his hips forwards as she pressed her mound into him. Callum tried to catch his breath and slow down. This young woman made him want to throw caution to the wind. He wanted her more than he had ever wanted any other woman, but he also wanted to protect her more than he had any woman but his sister. He forced himself to take several slow, deep breaths. As his heart rate slowed down, his common sense began to return. He could not take her before the wedding, and he certainly would not have her first time be on a sandy beach. He could, however, introduce her to yet another pleasure of the flesh. *I suppose I amnae going to wait for another afterall.*

He reached back and unhooked her legs. She stilled and looked up at him perplexed. He gave her a soft kiss on her lips and then eased himself back. Her chemise was still bunched up around her legs, but it was almost to her hips. He ran his fingers over her mound and then brushed them along the seam of her nether lips. She was wet, and he knew it had nothing to do with the loch. She desired him as much as he desired her. He was sure of it. He plunged two fingers into her, and she moaned as her hips arched off the ground. He quickly pushed her chemise out of the way and grasped her hip with his free hand. He worked his fingers in and out of her as his thumb rubbed her nub. He bent over and inhaled her sweet scent. He could feel his cock pulse as he drew his tongue along her flesh for the first time.

Siùsan was shocked to feel his tongue on her, there of all places. She had heard servants talk about doing such things, but she had never considered that a man might one day do it to her. She attempted to sit up, so she could see, but Callum's hand pressed her back into the sand. She looked down to see his dark head between her legs. She let her knees fall open as she pulled her feet closer to her. The sight of him between her legs was the most erotic thing she could think of. He laved her from top to bottom and back up again. He swirled his tongue along her nether lips and then delved into her depths. He moved his fingers out of the way and began to suck on her nub. Sparks of fire shot through Siùsan. She began to writhe on the sand as the sensations overwhelmed her. She could hear moans. It was several moments before she realized they were coming from her and were quite loud. She bit her lower lip to try to silence herself. Callum's head jerked up when she went quiet. He saw her trying to keep quiet.

"Dinna hold back. I want to hear yer moans. I want to hear ma name on yer lips again. I want to make ye scream it as ye come." He went back to work. His cock throbbed for release. He could not hold back as he listened to Siùsan and tasted her. He reached down and fisted himself. He began to fiercely stroke himself as he felt the shudders and spasms begin within Siùsan.

Siùsan looked down again but could only see one of Callum's arms. She leaned to the side and saw that he was holding his rod in his hand and doing exactly what she had done for him earlier. As she watched him pleasure himself as he pleasured her, she felt two very differing emotions. She was even more aroused by how sinful the entire scene was, but she also felt slightly cheated as she longed to be the one who gave him such pleasure. Only moments later, all thoughts fled as she felt her release wash over her.

"Callum!" Siùsan screamed his name.

Callum began to stroke himself at a furious pace. He was so very close. He had hoped that they could climax together, but he was not quite ready. Before he knew what was happening, he felt two small hands shove hard against his shoulders. As he was supporting his entire weight on one forearm, he lost his balance. Just as he felt he was falling, he was flipped onto his back. Siùsan scrambled to move over him and then slide down the length of his body. She wrapped both of her hands around his length as she contemplated how to proceed. Callum watched in awe as she licked her lips as she stroked him. Then she did the unthinkable. She looked up at him for only a moment and then, grasping her hair in one hand and stroking him with the other, she lowered her mouth onto him.

It took only the feel of her warm mouth on his sensitive skin for him to erupt. He tried to push her away, but she clamped down onto him. She sucked with a fierceness that might have hurt if he was not already so overwhelmed with the need to spend himself. He felt his seed shoot into her mouth in hot squirts, one after another. He fell back onto the sand. He could not believe his little bride to be had pushed him off her and turned him over. He could not believe she had taken him into her mouth. And he absolutely could not believe he had just spent himself so completely into her mouth.

She crawled up his body and laid herself alongside of him. He pulled her tight to him and lifted her leg over his hips. He pulled one of her arms to drape across her chest. He wrapped her in his embrace and never wanted to let go.

"I just couldnae let ye cheat me out of bringing ye the same pleasure that ye brought me." She whispered as she closed her eyes. He looked over at her as her breathing softened and deepened.

What manner of woman have I been blessed with? She truly will be the death of me one of these day. She is most certainly ma bonnie temptation. With that, he closed his eyes too and allowed himself to doze lightly. He could not let himself fall into a deep sleep as he was ever aware of his overwhelming need to protect her. He remained alert just in case.

Chapter Ten

allum awoke from his light sleep when he felt Siùsan shift in her sleep. He looked overhead and saw that the sun had moved further than he realized. It was now midafternoon, and his stomach was growling. He looked over at the woman who slept curled up at his side. He had always tried to avoid falling asleep next to a woman unless he was passed out drunk. He did not like the discomfort of trying to leave with pleasantries and noncommittal goodbyes. He had certainly regretted waking to find Elizabeth in his bed. He realized that was only yesterday. It stunned him to realize that so little time had passed, and yet, it seemed like a lifetime ago. Much had shifted in the space of a day and a half. As Siùsan continued to sleep next to him, Callum reflected upon just how selfish he had been the last few months. He had put his physical desires ahead of his family and their wishes. He wished he could go back in time and heed their warnings. He had brushed them off at the time and made light of them as he enjoyed the pleasure he sought with Elizabeth. He had refused to heed their warnings about her true nature. He had even gone so far as to wonder if his brothers were secretly jealous of his relationship with the stunning and talented blonde. As he reflected on the conversations and thoughts that he had had over the last few months, he realized that he had been a genuine arse to those who cared about him the most. As he looked at Siùsan, he knew the difference was that no one had attempted to harm his brothers because of his relationship, so he had not felt any reason to change.

He was plagued with worry as his mind returned to the events of that morning. He thought about the sight of the dead rat in the puddle of porridge by Siùsan's feet. It was not some mere coincidence that the rat drowned in the porridge. The frothing around the rat's mouth and its rigid body were sure signs that the rat had been poisoned. It was even more obvious that the poison had been meant for Siùsan. As he thought more and more about little things that he had noticed in passing about Elizabeth, they began to take shape in his mind as he realized that the delightfully entertaining woman was really a very calculating and cunning seductress. She was after the title of lady of the keep and was clearly bound and determined to either gain it through marriage or by default as his leman. While he had no proof, therefore, he could not imprison her, Callum knew he could waste no time making arrangements for Elizabeth's departure. He also knew it could be several weeks before he had a response from court as to whether she could return. He knew that she had few friends there. She had claimed that the women were jealous of her and bitter. Now he suspected that they had been wise to her real nature.

Callum decided that Elizabeth would need to be moved out of the keep and away from Siùsan. There was a vacant croft within the bailey walls. He could have her moved there. She would not feel completely shunned as she would if he banished her to the village. *This should be a happy medium. Bah! Who am I kidding? She is going to be furious. Unless she thinks that I am doing this to create a hideaway for us. Damn. I dinna want her thinking that. Perhaps, I should have Alexander make the arrangements and help her settle. Her charms are completely lost upon him. It's as though he has ice in his veins when it comes to her.*

With his mind made up, he leaned over and kissed Siùsan's forehead and gave her a little nudge.

"Siùsan, ye must wake up. We need to make our way back to the keep before ma kin sends out a search party. I dinna think ye want them to find ye in yer shift." Siùsan awoke to his voice and stretched as he talked. His last comment caught her attention. She looked down to see that she really was only in her chemise. It had dried and was no longer transparent, but that did not stop her from remembering that there was very little left to hide from Callum after what they had done earlier. Twice.

She looked over at Callum and saw that he was still naked. She quickly averted her eyes and turned bright red.

"It is a bit late to be timid, little one. Ye have seen me in all ma glory." Callum's deep laugh filled the air.

"That may be, but ye dinna need to flaunt it. People will talk if they find out what we have done. They'll say I'm loose. I'm wanton. What if someone saw us?"

"Nay body has seen us. This part of the loch is very secluded. Ye canna easily access it without coming all the way aroundfrom the other side and from a distance, nay one can make out any details other than seeing two people across the loch. We can either walk back around or swim."

Siùsan looked at the path they would have to take if they walked. It was not terribly far, but it was farther than she could manage with Callum completely naked. She looked at the loch and knew that her chemise would be soaked when she climbed out. She would either have to carry her dripping chemise or put on her dry clothes only to get them wet too. While she did not relish any part of the latter option, she knew it was the only one she could manage.

She stood up and brushed the sand from her back and hair as best she could. She gave Callum only a passing glance before she ran into the loch and dove under the water. She kicked hard as she rubbed her head to try to knock loose and flush out the rest of the sand. When she surfaced, she took long, strong strokes that had her crossing the loch quickly. She could hear Callum following her. When she reached the shore, she did not bother to look behind her. She scrambled up the shore and behind the bush where she had left her clothes earlier. She pulled off her wet chemise and tugged on her kirtle. It was extremely difficult to pull it down over her wet body and to fit her arms into the tight sleeves, but she managed. Once it was on, she realized that it had been far easier to unlace the ties at the back when she was dry than it would be to redo them while she was wet. She listened for Callum and when she no longer heard him moving about, she called out to him and turned away.

"I canna do the laces maself. Will ye please help me?"

"Ma pleasure." The voice beside her made her jumped.

"I didna hear ye approach."

"Ye shouldnae have. I am a warrior. Stealth keeps me alive."

"It also nearly scared the life out of me."

"Hmmm. Now ye ken how I've felt thrice today." He leaned over and nipped her ear playfully as he quickly pulled her laces tight. She tried not to think about how skillfully he served as a lady's maid. She did not want to know how many times he had done this before or with how many women.

As though he sensed her line of thought, he kissed her cheek again and whispered, "I used to help ma sister. When we would all go swimming together, she needed help with her laces too."

Siùsan could only nod her head. She appreciated him trying to distract her and shift her thoughts away from his past, but they both knew it was not going to work. She turned towards him and placed her hands on his shoulders. His hands rested on her trim waist.

"Callum, I clearly ken ye have a past. I canna change that. And if I am to be totally honest, I have already benefited from it twice today alone. But I just hope that it truly is in the past."

"Siùsan, I told ye yesterday, but I ken it bears repeating often. I will always be faithful to ye. The men of ma clan do not dally once they are married. Our betrothal is all but an official marriage. I willna stray. I give ye ma word as a mon, a warrior, and a Sinclair."

Siùsan looked up at him and nodded. She believed him for the most part but a small, niggling voice in the back of her head warned her that this was all too good to be true.

Callum and Siùsan returned to the keep. Hagatha took one look at them as they walked into the keep and immediately called for tubs to be taken to their chambers. They each retired to their respective chambers for a soak in the warm water. Callum made his bath a short one though as he needed to find his brother, Alexander. He had a task for him and knew that he was in for a battle.

~ ~ ~

"Ye canna be serious. I amnae telling yer mistress that ye want her to move into a croft so ye dinna have to deal with her."

"If I tell her and see to the move, she will believe that I am simply trying to arrange a trysting place for us. I dinna want her thinking that it will be some type of love nest for us. I want her away from Siùsan before the evening meal is served. I dinna trust her and want Siùsan safe. Tell Elizabeth that she may take her meals in the keep, otherwise she is to occupy herself elsewhere.

"In the meantime, I must draft a letter to the First Lady of the Bedchamber to see if Elizabeth can be reinstated to her position as a lady in waiting. I ken she didna serve the queen, but I suspect that even if the lady she did serve agreed, there may be some discord if I dinna get permission for her return."

"Ye finally ken what we have all been trying to tell ye for months. Ye didna believe us. Ye had to wait until she almost killed someone." Alexander crossed his arms over his massive chest and looked at his brother.

"Ye can relax, Alex. Ye ken that stance doesnae intimidate me. I do it just as well as ye. I amnae asking ye to take her as yer own leman. I simply need ye to help me. We dinna ken for certain that she is responsible but I, too, suspect she is. If ye willna do it for ma sake, please do it for Siùsan's. I am honestly worried. I want Elizabeth as far from Siùsan as is reasonably possible."

At the mention of Siùsan, Alexander relaxed and nodded his hear. "I am only doing it for the lass. She is innocent in all of this. It isnae her fault that our fathers agreed to marry her to an arse."

With that, Alexander turned and left Callum's chambers. He ran his hand through his freshly washed hair. He looked over at his bed and felt disgusted. He looked around the chamber and felt taint of Elizabeth's presence. She had been in his chamber before, but nothing intimate had ever occurred. It was usually when he changed or was gathering something before descending to the Great Hall. It had never bothered him before. Now he felt stinging regret that she had ever crossed the threshold. He was sure that he could never bring Siùsan to this chamber. He would explain everything to his father and ask that he move to Mairghread's now empty chamber. The sooner the better. With that, he sat down at this desk and pulled out a fresh sheet of parchment. He dipped a quill into his ink pot and began the arduous task of crafting a letter that would carefully request Elizabeth's reinstatement without giving away the details of why she could no longer remain. He focused on his upcoming marriage as his rationale for his request. Once he was finished, he brushed sand over the ink and let it dry. He folded the parchment and warmed a small amount of wax with the candle he lit from his chamber's fireplace. He placed the wax where the seams of the parchment met and then pressed his signet ring into place. He waited for the wax to dry and harden before he left his chamber to find one of his best and fastest messengers to carry this missive with haste to court.

Chapter Eleven

O ver the next three weeks, Callum and Siùsan settled into a routine of sorts. They would meet to break their fast and then go their separate ways. Callum generally went to the lists to train unless there was something with which his father needed assistance. Siùsan became more familiar with the kitchens and the servants. She felt comfortable with them and proved herself more than capable of one day taking on the role of lady of the keep by demonstrating she had plenty of firsthand knowledge of how to serve within a keep so large. She raised more than one eyebrow when she rolled up her sleeves and carried fresh sheets to her own chamber where she stripped the bed and remade it. She then proceeded outside and dumped the linens into the boiling cauldron and began to help the laundresses. She surprised all the women in the kitchen with how quickly she could pluck a fowl and chop vegetables. She made loaves upon loaves of bread while chattering away with the women about their families and their lives. She was always very careful to steer the conversation away from her own family and past. She explained away her experience as a need to understand how a keep is run so that she might one day do so efficiently for her future husband and his family. Not everyone believed that to be the whole truth, but since Siùsan was always kind and willing to help in any way needed, no one ever pressed her.

Callum knew that she found things to do around the keep as she often came to the noon meal with flushed cheeks and a glistening forehead. When he asked what she had been up to, she would tell him she was learning this or that around the keep. He was satisfied with her answers as he was always happy to be in her presence. Their noon meal conversations usually turned quickly to how they would spend their afternoon together. They set aside their afternoons for each other. Twice they went out riding and Callum took her to the village to meet the crofters who lived outside the walls. He bought her a ribbon for her hair as one of the afternoons was market day. He was surprised that her eyes watered. She was speechless for a couple of minutes when he gave her the trinket. He watched her swallow several times before she was able to thank him. He once again wondered just what her life must have been like before coming to the Sinclairs if something as simple as a hair ribbon almost moved her to tears. He had not thought much of it as he admitted to himself that he had given countless women such a trivial gift. He looked about at the different stalls. He wanted to find a gift that would be uniquely hers. She may not have known that she was not the first or not the only woman he had given a hair ribbon to, but he did. He wanted to make her smile more as he had noticed that she was often very serious when they were together in the Great Hall. He knew it was because it was the one place they could not avoid Elizabeth. Since Elizabeth took all her meals in the keep, she was a thunderous weight upon their shoulders. She was still shamelessly flaunting herself at the table in front of the dais but now she had a murderous scowl whenever she looked at Siùsan. At first, Elizabeth had tried to hide her malice from Callum, but when he caught her starring at Siùsan more than once, she gave up all pretenses and was openly hostile.

Callum's gaze landed on a vendor who he knew sold various types of brushes both for people and for animals. While Siùsan was busy talking to a sweatmeats vendor, Callum leaned over to Tavish who had accompanied them.

"Keep any eye on Siùsan. I would like to get her something more special as a surprise. I dinna want her to ken what I am aboot." Since the day that Siùsan was nearly poisoned, Callum insisted that she always have a guard with her if he was not nearby. He gave her free movement within the keep but would not allow her out of the Great Hall doors without someone to protect her. It had caused their first and only real fight to date. It had not lasted long. She yelled that she would not be a prisoner when she was not the one trying to murder anyone. Though she might be moved to do so if he did not relent. He yelled back that he would bind her to his bed and keep her there until their wedding if that was what it would take to keep her safe. He continued to yell that he refused to even consider any harm coming to her and he would run through anyone who tried. She had turned the deepest shade of red he had ever seen on anyone as he realized the implications of his words which had rung through the Great Hall as he bellowed that he cared about her too much to leave her safety to chance. She had simply nodded and turned back to the noon meal they were sharing.

Later that afternoon, when they were alone walking through the meadow near the castle, she had rewarded his concern with her tender ministrations. She had stopped them and tugged on his leine until he bent over far enough for her to kiss him. Then she had dropped to her knees and dipped her head under his plaid. He could not believe that this woman who seemed proper in front of his clan and his family would do something so brazen out in the open. As he felt her tongue run up and down his length and then swirl over the tiny opening in his tip, his mind went completely blank. He could think of nothing but the pure bliss of her lips sliding down his length as she took as much into her novice mouth as she could. It was obvious that she was inexperienced, but what she lacked in knowledge, she made up for in effort. What she could not manage, she used her hand to stroke. His hips had rocked in tandem with her sucking motions. It had only taken a matter of minutes before he felt the telltale tingle at the base of his spine. He tried to press her shoulders back and took a step back, but she would not let him go. Instead she simply sucked harder and faster. There was nothing he could do to stop the resulting release that flowed out of him. When he was finally done, she sat back on her heels and daintily wiped her lips with her fingertips. She looked up at him and gave him the most radiant smile. He all but mauled her as he dropped down on to the grass and pushed her onto her back. He growled as he loosened her laces and pulled down the shoulders of her kirtle. He unfastened the belt that kept her arisaid in place and pushed her skirts up to her waist. He pulled one then the other breast free. He realized that this was the first time he had an unobstructed view of them. They were magnificent. He had felt them and knew that she was more endowed than she appeared in her gowns, but he had not anticipated just how full they were. They sat high and round. They were tipped with dusky nipples that pebbled as he stared. He leaned forward and ran his tongue over one of the pointy darts. He swirled his tongue around her nipple just as she had the tip of his cock. He brushed his fingers along her seam and felt how wet she was. She was eager for him and let her knees fall apart. As he sucked her nipple and as much of her breast as he could fit into his mouth, he thrust three fingers into her sheath.

They managed to find time to slip away more than once each day, even if it was only a storeroom or an alcove. As she became more experienced with the intimate feel of his fingers, she demanded more. She wanted more of his fingers, more speed, and more force. He was always careful never to pierce her maidenhead, but he sought to bring her more pleasure with each encounter.

While in the meadow, he had worked her breasts, alternating between the two suckling and massaging, and he worked her core as he rubbed and stroked her to release. He was growing addicted to the sounds she made during their love play, a name for their activity that no longer seemed to bother him when he thought about it, and the look of bliss on her face when she came.

He thought back to that particular interlude as he picked out a curry brush for Siùsan, or really for Trofast. He would take it to the blacksmith and see if he could add a design to the metal back of the brush. He would have their initials added if possible. He wanted to do something nice for her that would match her practical nature. He had picked flowers with her a few times already, but she politely let him know that while she enjoyed their time together, she did not care for the mess they made when they began to die. He had laughed when she just shrugged and said she knew she was not a typical woman. Instead, they had agreed that searching for shells together was more enjoyable. She had quite a collection that she said she laid on every available surface in her chamber.

When he had made his purchase and safely stashed it away in his sporran, he returned to Tavish and Siùsan. Siùsan was gently fingering a bolt of material that was a dark green velvet. It was almost an exact match for her eyes and would make a bold contrast to her creamy skin and auburn hair. When she saw him approach, she dropped her hand and moved towards him. She smiled and took his arm in an attempt to steer him away. He knew she would never ask for such a thing for herself. She was modest in her tastes, but he had not missed the longing in her eyes. He looked over her head to Tavish and then slightly tilted his head back in the direction of the fabric seller. Tavish nodded and dropped back.

Callum unhooked his arm and wrapped it around her waist. He looked down at her and saw that she wore the same serviceable gown that she alternated with an only slightly better kirtle. He knew that she had one other gown that she had yet to wear as she was saving it for their wedding and holy feast days. He was concerned with how little she seemed to have brought with her from her home. He had learned from Hagatha that she had only arrived with a satchel. The same afternoon he sent off the missive, he had asked the groomsmen if she had arrived with any more luggage that he might not have seen. They said they never saw anything. She never once alluded to wanting more or that she even needed more. He knew she would never ask but he had a remedy in mind. He only hoped that she would accept.

~ ~ ~

"Will ye come above stairs with me?"

Siùsan looked around to be sure that no one could overhear them. "I canna be going into a chamber alone with ye. We already risk enough sneaking into the storerooms."

"Are ye worried ye might compromise me," he snickered. When she did not laugh, he continued. "I willna attempt to compromise ye. In fact, we will keep the chamber door wide open if ye would feel better."

She looked around and saw that no one was watching them. She nodded and tried to discreetly move towards the stairs. She turned back to tell him that she would go first, and he could meet her above stairs, but he was ready to step onto the same stair as she was already on. She looked around again and then darted up the stairs. When they reached the passageway on the second floor, he took her hand and led her to the very end of the hall. A beautifully carved door that featured a scene with a wood nymph hiding from a hunter behind a tree stood in front of them. Siùsan had never seen such craftsmanship in her life let alone on a door. Callum reached around her and opened the door.

"Da had it done as a wedding gift for Mama." He said as he ushered her into the chamber and made sure to leave the door open.

Siùsan looked around the large chamber in awe. It featured the largest bed she had ever seen in her life. She blushed as she realized that one day, that would be her bed that she shared with Callum as his wife. Her eyes took in the rest of the room. There were vases of flowers all over the room. A table with a small stool sat near the window. It still had a woman's brush and perfume bottles on it. Siùsan's forehead wrinkled in confusion. She was certain that Callum had told her the day that she arrived that after his mother's death, Laird Sinclair had not taken a leman. Callum had not even been sure that his father had been with another woman in the time since he became a widower.

"It is exactly as Mama left it. Da canna stand the idea of making any changes. He says that he can feel her presence still here and she visits him often in his dreams. Mama loved having fresh flowers everywhere. She would pick them daily when she could. After she died, Hagatha took up the duty of making sure there are always vases full."

Siùsan felt a bit embarrassed now that she realized how much his mother loved cut flowers and she had turned her nose up at his offer to give her fresh ones daily.

"Leannan, dinna fash. If ye dinna care for flowers that is fine. Ye arenae ma mama. Besides, I prefer walking on the beach with just ye than having to share the gardens with ye and the women who till and tend the vegetables."

Callum took her hand and pulled her further into the room. Two large chests sat side by side at the foot of the bed. Callum reached down and lifted the lid to one of them. Siùsan peaked around him and saw an array of colors in the form of numerous women's gowns.

"I spoke to Da, and we agreed that we would like to offer ye the use of these gowns. I ken they are outdated, but they are in excellent condition and ye are fairly close in size to Mama."

Siùsan looked at the gowns and then kneeled in front of the chest. She reached a hand out to touch one, then snatched it back and folded both in her lap.

"Callum, I canna take yer mother's belongings. I believe Hagatha said that there are some unused bolts of fabric in the attic. I can sew ma own clothes. I will find something appropriate and begin work this evening." She attempted to stand but felt a soft pressure on her shoulder as Callum kneeled beside her.

"Siùsan, I asked ma father and he agreed. We both have noticed that yer wardrobe is limited. We would like to do this for ye." He reached out and took her hand. He was surprised to feel how rough it was that day. He looked down to see blisters on them. He realized that she had artfully avoided holding hands with him and she had only touched him over the material of his clothing. They had not had any time alone before this. "What has happened to yer hands?"

"Naught. I havenae been using them for chores in several weeks between the journey here and then settling in. I have also been using a hand lotion every night.

It has softened them too much. Holding the large wooden stick that the laundresses use to turn the clothes in the cauldron simply gave me blisters today. That along with the lye soap that we use has made ma hands a bit rough." She tried to pull her hands back but Callum held fast. He inspected each fingertip and palm. He gently ran his thumb over her palm, avoiding the blisters, then he brought them both to his lips.

"I canna say that I am pleased to see yer hands so raw and chapped. I am proud, though, that ye are willing to help any and everywhere and that ye work so hard."

"I have to earn ma own keep. I have been here longer than hospitality demands, and I am not yet yer wife. I am but an extra mouth to feed. It is the least that I can do. I should be doing more but, well, there isnae time when I leave for the afternoons." Siùsan's cheeks tinged pinks as she looked at her tiny hands in his large ones. His hands were roughened with callouses just as hers used to be and would be again soon. "Ma hands will heal and callouses will form just as they used to. The work willna bother them as it doesnae bother me now."

"Siùsan, ye are ma betrothed. Ye are neither a guest nor a servant. Ye dinna have to earn anything. I told ye, I am proud that ye are trying so hard, but I dinna want to see yer hands like this again. Please."

"Ye are right. I amnae a guest nor a servant but neither am I family. I canna keep taking without giving something back." She shook her head adamantly, and Callum knew that they would just go around in circles if he continued to press.

"I will speak to Da about giving ye some of the proper responsibilities of the lady of the keep. I ken ye can read and do figures. Mayhap ye can see to the accounts with the steward. It is early summer now, but the plans for the harvest must be made soon. Hagatha will need help organizing the storage of all the crops that are brought in. Would ye be willing to do that instead of working with the laundresses or scrubbing anything else?"

"Aye. I can do all of those things as I was responsible for it at the Mackenzie keep." Callum thought it odd that she referred to her former home by her clan's name rather than as her home. He still had not pressed her to tell him about her family life. He figured that when she was ready, she would share with him. He realized, though, that he had just stumbled upon a way to get her to accept his mother's gowns, at least for the immediate future until she had her own gowns.

"If ye are to take on the responsibilities of the lady of the keep, ye must look the part. Ye canna go around looking like ye could be confused for one of the servants."

Siùsan opened her mouth to object and was insulted by his insinuation that her gowns were more suited for rags than for a lady. But as she moved to point her finger at him, she caught sight of how faded her kirtle was and where the hem of the sleeve was beginning to fray. She dropped her hand and closed her mouth. Instead she simply nodded.

She looked in the chest and gingerly pulled out the gown on top. It was a dark shade of plum. The material was smooth and soft. She held it up and looked at it. It was almost brand new. She carefully draped it over the lid of the chest. Next, she pulled out a yellow gown but immediately shook her head and set it aside. She did not think she could pull off yellow with her red hair, but Callum reached across her and picked it back up. He held it up to her and smiled.

"It suits ye. I believe ye could wear any color and look lovely. Even a turnip sack would look becoming." He kissed her cheek and laid the yellow gown on top of the plum one. For the next five minutes, Siùsan sorted through the gowns in the chest. She ended up with two piles: those she could wear as day gowns while she went about her chores and duties within the keep and those that she could wear outdoors when they went riding or walking. She replaced the gowns that she felt were too formal. She did not think that she needed them as no one seemed to dress for the evening meal. Her knees were beginning to ache as she stood up. She brushed out the skirts that she wore and saw now just how tattered they really looked. She felt embarrassed that she had shown up with only three kirtles to her name and a pair of slippers that she had yet to wear and a pair of sturdy boots.

She looked down to see that Callum was pulling out a hidden drawer from the front of the chest. Tucked away tightly were several pairs of slippers. He pulled out a pair that could be worn with the plum gown and a dark navy blue gown. He held them out to Siùsan. She could see that they were about her size.

"Ye canna go around barefoot." Callum smiled even though he knew most of the women of the clan did just that. His smile and his kindness warmed her from the inside out. She stepped forward and placed her hands over his heart. She knew it was an intimate gesture that he might intepret as more than thanks, but she felt more than just thankful.

"Thank ye, Callum. Ye make me feel welcome here and that one day I might belong." She stretched up on her tiptoes and pressed a kiss to his cheek. She cupped his cheek and added, "ye are a kind mon. I count maself lucky to be marrying ye."

"And I ye." He pressed a feather soft kiss against her lips. The slippers were forgotten as they dropped to the floor and they pressed their bodies tightly against one another. The kiss grew in passion just as their relationship had over the past weeks. They had spent as much time together as they could. It was far more time than Callum had ever spent with any woman before, but he found that he genuinely enjoyed her company. As much time as they spent in an embrace they spent talking as well. They were coming to know each other very well. However, right now, all he could think about was the feel of her in his hands. He pulled back and quickly pushed his sporran out of the way. He grasped her buttocks and pulled her hips flush with his. She stood up on her tiptoes again to try to feel his iron rod against her pleasure button. She ground her mound against him as he squeezed her behind.

Their tongues dueled with one another and he groaned as he longed to feel her bare skin.

The window was open, and a waft of lemongrass hit his nose. It doused his ardor in a heartbeat. It was a scent that he associated only with his mother. He pulled back gently from Siùsan and looked into her passion glazed eyes. He kissed her temple gently and then her cheek. He pulled her arms from around his neck and gently kissed each of her fingertips.

"I forget maself when I am with ye. I forget where I am and who I am." He looked around the chamber, and his eyes settled on the huge bed that he knew his parents had always shared. "One day, God willing far in the future, this will be our chamber, and that will be our bed. I will make love to ye every night until we grow old and are sent to our maker. But until then, this is Da and Mama's chamber. I canna dishonor them or ye by getting carried away."

Callum hoped that Siùsan would understand. He looked into her eyes and saw admiration and perhaps even a little adoration there. He knew that she not only understood but approved of his choice. He felt proud that he had inspired such feelings in her when he so often felt like he had much to make up for. Siùsan stepped back and gathered up all the gowns into her arms, but before she could move, she felt the weight lifted away. Callum had his arms full and nodded to the shoes in the drawer then he turned to the door. He moved into the passageway without a word and made his way to the stairs. They passed by his door, but he purposely looked away. Siùsan knew which room belonged to each brother as she had been in each to make up the beds. She wondered why he looked away from his own room. A thought began to take root in her mind. She wondered if there was something, or more likely someone, in there that he did not want her to know about. She tried to shake the idea loose, but it was taking root. She watched as he neared the stairs leading to the floor with her chamber. She looked back at his door and thought that perhaps there was no one in there now, but there must have been someone who had been there that he did not want to think of or have her know about. *Elizabeth.* The single name came to rest in her mind as a deadweight. They continued up the stairs and through the passageway in silence. When they arrived at her door, she slipped past Callum and pushed the door handle down to open it. Rather than stepping in or aside to let him pass, she reached up for the bundle of gowns.

"Thank ye," she said more briskly than she intended. Callum's eyebrows shot up. He had heard her tone. She wanted to try to smile to soften her response but all she found she could do was lift one eyebrow in challenge. Callum looked positively confused. He had no idea what had made her mood swing so abruptly from passionate and appreciative to cold and dismissive.

"What is amiss, Siùsan?" He sounded genuinely confused.

"Naught, Callum. Perhaps there is something that ye need to attend to in yer chamber." She spun around and kicked the door closed behind her. Callum stood stunned outside her door.

Bluidy hell. She is too observant by half. I tried so hard to not bring attention to the bluidy room that all I did was make it worse.

He turned back towards the stairs and moved down to the floor with his chamber. He took one look down the corridor and decided that his chamber was the last place he wanted to be. He needed another round in the lists and then a cool dunk in the loch. Had he not been so immersed in his own thoughts, once again, he might have seen what lurked in the shadows of a doorway down the passageway from Siùsan's. A chamber that was supposed to be unoccupied as its former resident now had a croft of her own.

Chapter Twelve

*M*orning broke bright and sunny the next day.

Siùsan had come down to dinner the night before in one of the borrowed kirtles. It was a russet color that set off her flame colored locks beautifully. The gown fitted her like a second skin. Callum could not believe that it was the same gown that he could remember his mother wearing. His response to Siùsan was nowhere near maternal fondness. A shark spike of lust shot through him as he watched her walk to the dais. The gown was snug in all the right places and accented her large bust that had, up until this point, been his favorite little secret. Now every man in his clan knew that his betrothed had a body made for sin. He had almost growled when Magnus reached out to help her onto the dais. He was ready to smack Tavish when he moved out of her way, so she could get to her seat. He wanted to punch Alexander when he pulled out the chair for her without giving Callum, who was standing beside it, the chance. Each of his brothers simply crossed their arms and smirked. They knew that he was fuming with possessiveness and jealousy. The brothers had never seen him react in such a way to a woman, but they immediately recognized it for what it as. He was immensely territorial and easily provoked when it came to Siùsan, so they were doing their very best to get a rise out of him. However, the only person getting a rise out of him was Siùsan. His cock was standing at attention the entire meal. He could not sit still as he tried to find a more comfortable position. His sporran kept his secret, but it also weighed heavily against his sensitive skin that felt like it was on fire. He ached to feel her, any part of her, against him. His knee brushed against her several times. When she did not pull away the first time, he did it several more times until finally he simply pressed his leg to hers and dropped his hand to rest on her thigh. She surreptitiously ran her hand under his plaid and up to the middle of his thigh. She was turned away from him as she talked to his father. Her fingers danced along the inside of his thigh. He squeezed her thigh in response. He was close to bursting and making a fool of himself in front of his entire clan.

When she was done talking to his father and turned back to their shared trencher, he hissed in her ear, "*lass.*" She could hear the strain in his voice and divined an odd pleasure from knowing that she could tease him and arouse him in such a way. She had kept an eye on him. She had leaned back far enough in her chair that even as she talked with the Sinclair, she had been able to see in her peripheral vision what Callum was doing. He was either watching her or staring at their trencher or gulping down wine from their shared chalice. She could tell that he was miserable, but truth be told, she was suffering too. The feel of his leg against hers, the weight of his hand resting on her thigh, and the feel of his skin along her fingertips was making heat course through her body. As soon as they could make their excuses, they separately made their way out of the Great Hall. Siùsan claimed that she was ready to retire early and shortly after she left, Callum excused himself to the garderobe. Instead, they met in the passageway that led to the stairs down to the dungeon. As there was no one currently residing in the dungeon, it was one of the least frequented hallways in the entire castle. It had become a favorite meeting place for them. Callum hurried down the passageway until he could make out the faintest shape in the dark shadows. He reached out a hand and felt the soft material of Siùsan's gown. He pulled it towards him and when her body collided with his, he pressed her backwards against the wall and pinned her there with his body. He growled savagely in her ear.

"What are ye trying to do to me?" He cupped her face and ran his thumbs over it to find her lips. Then he leaned in. She grabbed the back of his head and tangled her fingers into his hair and pulled gently. Their kiss was rough and hard. Siùsan moaned into his mouth as she reached down and pushed his sporran out of the way. She was becoming tired of it always keeping her from feeling the full length of his body and his arousal. They continued to kiss and run their hands over each other until they heard two guardsmen making their way towards them. They broke apart and Callum pushed her into the alcove in which she had been waiting. He pressed her back behind the tapestry that hid the entrance. She burrowed her head into his chest and felt his pounding heart. It raced as wildly as hers. He rested his chin upon the top of her head until the voices faded away. He was not ready to give up their privacy on the chance that the guardsmen would return.

"That gown looks far too good on ye." He muttered.

"I beg yer pardon." She ground out.

"Ye are a beautiful woman, and that is plain for any mon with even only one working eye to see, but that gown shows the entire world what had previously been ma secret. Every mon in this clan now kens that yer body is meant to bring a mon to his knees. I dinna much care for sharing that knowledge."

"Yer're jealous?"

"Aye," he growled.

Siùsan could not help it. A laugh that turned into a giggle which turned into a snort erupted from her.

"I dinna see how this is a laughing matter. I dinna like ma bride parading around for every mon in the Great Hall to drool over."

"Ye are too kind. I appreciate being likened to a hamhock that the hounds will fight over."

"Ye ken that isnae even close to what I mean."

"For starters, I am yer betrothed but not yer bride. We havenae set a date nor even talked about it. Till then, I amnae anyone's bride. Secondly, ye are the one who lent me this gown and told me that it would be the right size. Ye were correct. Thirdly, I dinnae have eyes for anyone else, and I was pleased to see that neither did ye."

"Were ye testing me?" He pulled her against him.

"Nay. At least nae intentionally. I wanted to look nice for ye this evening since ye went to the trouble of arranging for me to borrow yer mother's wardrobe. I still think ye were hiding something from me, but in the grand scheme of everything, that doesnae seem so important when I considered how kind ye have been to me. I wanted to make ye proud. I have never worn a kirtle or anything like this. I admit that ma pride was well served to see people notice and appreciate ma appearance, but ye were the only one I was trying to impress."

"Ye succeeded in every way." He gently kissed her cheek. "I am sorry that I was such a bear. I have never felt so incensed from jealousy. It was all consuming."

"I ken. I ken that all too well."

"Ah, mo ionmhas. I wish that I could make this easier for ye. I am so sorry."

"I ken ye are." She brushed her fingers over his cheeks in the dark. She felt the stubble on his jawline and then paused. What he had called her finally registered.

"Do ye really think of me as a treasure?"

"Aye. One that is mine and only mine." He leaned forward and nipped at her neck. She leaned her head away to give him more access. Their conversation ended as they came together for another searing kiss. When voices passed by them again, they pulled apart.

"We are tempting fate. We shall be found out if we stay here any longer."

"Aye. Ye leave first, Siùsan. I would watch to be sure ye are safe." With that and a pat on the backside, Siùsan made her way to the servants' stairs. Callum followed a short distance behind and watched as she climbed to the third floor.

Now that Siùsan felt more comfortable in her borrowed wardrobe, she chose a pale blue day dress and brushed back her hair. She left her chamber and met Callum on the floor with the family's chambers. They joined hands as they made their way below stairs to break their fast. They had just reached the bottom of the stairs when

Siùsan heard her name called out. The voice was keenly familiar. She looked up to see the last person she expected to be at the Sinclair keep.

"Robert?" She broke away from Callum and rushed across the floor. She wanted to know what he was doing there before he said anything that would upset the balance that she and Callum were working hard to develop. Before she could stop him, he pulled her into a tight hug. She felt his hands rest on the top of her hips with his fingers dangerously close to her backside. She felt a wave of terror as she remembered Callum's reaction the night before just to other men looking at her. She could only imagine what he was about to do.

Quickly, she pushed against Robert's chest and took the largest step back that she could, but he refused to completely let go. He held her waist at arm's length.

"How are ye, mo ghràidh?" He boomed. Siùsan could have slapped him.

"I amnae yer darling. I amnae anything to ye." She hissed. For a heartbeat, she had been excited to see someone familiar. She had known Robert her entire life, but bitter memories came crashing down on her as he tried to embarrass her in front of the Sinclairs.

She stepped back again, and he was forced to drop his hold unless he was willing to tug at her like a ragdoll. She spun around in time to see Callum storming towards them. The look of murderous rage matched what she had seen the night she arrived, and Sean attacked her. She stepped forward and tried to stop him. She pressed her hands against his chest.

"Callum," she whispered. "Callum, please. Stop."

He looked down at her briefly, but she was not sure that he even saw her. He was gentle but firm when he pushed her aside.

"Who comes into ma father's keep and calls ma betrothed his darling?" Callum ground out between his teeth.

"Yer betrothed? Nay. That is not so as she was pre-contracted to me," Robert scoffed.

Callum lurched forward, but a small hand on his arm stopped him. He looked down to see that now Siùsan was as angry as him, and he was relieved to see it was not directed at him but at this interloper.

"Ye may have asked me to marry ye, and I may have said aye, but we were never contracted to wed. Ma father refused ye, and ye only asked after he announced ma betrothal to Lord Callum. If ye dinna remember the details, I can surely remind ye. Of it all." She ground out the last of it between clenched teeth. "I am well and truly betrothed to Lord Callum and couldnae be more pleased with ma father's choice. He picked vera well." She stepped back so that she could lean into Callum's broad chest. He wrapped his arms around her and rested his hands over her belly. If everyone did not know better, it might have looked like he was protecting her womb, but instead he was staking his claim for all to see. There was not a doubt left who Siùsan

Mackenzie belonged to. She placed her hands over the top of his and laced her fingers with his.

From the corner of her eye, she saw Elizabeth watching it all. The hatred and anger oozed out of her and radiated. If Siùsan was not already so distracted with Robert's arrival, she might have flinched. She watched as Elizabeth emerged from the shadows and moved herself closer to Robert. It did not take much for Robert to catch sight of her and to allow his eyes to drink her in. His gaze returned to Siùsan and Callum, but it was clear that his attention had shifted.

"Robert, why are ye really here?"

"Yer father wanted me to check on yer wellbeing. He kens how close we are." The innuendo was not lost on anyone certainly least of which was Callum.

"Well, we were raised like brother and sister. I ken it wasnae easy for ye to offer up yer freedom to marry me, but luckily it wasna necessary. Please, come and join us as ye break yer fast." She reached out and gestured towards the tables where people stared agog during this unexpected morning entertainment. Siùsan remained in the safety of Callum's arms until she saw Robert take a seat with his back to them. She spun around in Callum's arms and tugged his sleeve.

"Quickly, I must tell ye all. I dinna trust him for a moment."

Callum stared down at her for a moment as though she had sprouted a second head. He had not anticipated that she would be asking him if she could volunteer an explanation. He nodded, and they quietly moved out of the Great Hall to his father's study. He opened the door and ushered her in, closing the door behind him. Again, Siùsan spun around, but this time she pinned Callum to the door. She rose up on her tiptoes and pulled at his leine. When he leaned forward she tunneled her fingers into his hair and pressed her lips to his. She nipped and bit and suckled his lips. She had caught on quickly to the art of kissing and enjoyed it. Callum picked her up and she wrapped her legs around him. He walked to a chair in front of the fire and sat down. She straddled him as the chair was wide enough for her to sit comfortably.

"Callum, I dinna trust Robert at all. He is lying about why he is here. I ken ma father didna send him to check on me. When ma father announced that he was considering a betrothal for me, I was shocked. He had never mentioned anything about seeing me married. I didna ken that he had even thought about it. I feared that he was going to arrange a marriage to an auld mon or a mon who might mistreat me. I ran to tell Robert. I was telling the truth when I said that we grew up like brother and sister. I have kenned him ma entire life. I told him that ma father planned to marry me off and that I feared who it might be to. He offered to marry me, and I said aye. I didna want to marry him and had never considered it before that moment but it seemed like the safest option. Back then, I trusted him. I thought I was making a good choice. That evening, I saw Robert step out after the evening meal. I followed him because I wanted to learn when he planned to ask ma father for ma hand. I saw him walk to the stables. I followed him and entered the darkened stables just a little behind him. I heard voices and followed them. I was stunned to see him with one of the village lasses. She was completely naked, and he was kneeling behind her. I saw him toss up his plaid and grab her hips. I couldnae bring maself to watch aught more but what he said as I started to slide away made me stop and stay. He told her that he would marry the dumb sow, meaning me, and move her into the keep as his leman the moment I announced I was carrying his bairn. While they waited for me to get with child, they could continue to meet at her parents' croft or there at the stables. I was just about to walk away when he said one more thing that made me turn from disgust to fear. He said so vera clearly, 'I just have to wait until that bastard dies and then I will be laird. If not by title, then by deed as neither of those little brats is old enough to lead. They might never lead.' I could not believe it. This mon that I had kenned forever was horrid. I was shocked and hurt. I tiptoed out of the stable and ran straight to ma room. I didna care who ma father married me off to after that. I just kenned it could never be to Robert. I didna want him to harm ma brothers. The next morning, I told ma father that I would be ready to leave as soon as he had the betrothal secured. Robert was in the Great Hall when I announced it. I havenae spoken to him since then. I avoided him until I left. He asked to be part of the escort, but even ma father didna trust him around me as Robert had tried to convince ma father to let him marry me instead. It was within a week that I left to come here. I dinna ken why he is really here, but I can promise ye it is not at ma father's request."

Callum had sat silently as he listened to Siùsan's story. He ran his hands up and down her arms, and when she finished, he pulled her against his chest. He tucked her head under his chin. She listened to the steady beat of his heart and began to relax. She felt safe and protected. She realized in that moment that she only ever felt truly safe and protected when she was with Callum. She closed her eyes and breathed out slowly. As she inhaled, she caught the scent that she had come to recognize as uniquely Callum. It was a blend of his pine soap and natural musk with a touch of the outdoors. As she slowly began to relax, she felt her body loosen. Callum must have felt it too because one of his hands stroked her head as the other ran up and down her back.

"Dinna fash. I believe ye. I ken ye are telling me the truth. We will solve this together. Hopefully, we can feed him a meal or two and then send him on his way." Callum was not convinced that it would be that simple. He, too, had seen that Robert had taken notice of Elizabeth. With what Siùsan just told him about Robert and what he knew about Elizabeth, Callum was truly worried that Siùsan was at risk.

Chapter Thirteen

obert stayed through the nooning and evening meal. Callum addressed him directly after Siùsan retired that night. He and his brothers made their trademark semicircle around him and backed him up to the giant fireplace in the Great Hall. They stood with their feet planted apart and their arms crossed.

"I ken what happened between ye and Siùsan. Siùsan. I also ken that ye didna have any real desire to marry her, but ye do desire the lairdship." Callum watched Robert's reaction to his revelation. Robert barely reacted but his eyes widened just a sliver, and Callum saw it. He knew that Robert had not suspected that Siùsan knew his real motivation. He might have known that she was aware that he would be unfaithful, but he clearly had not known she was aware of his plans. "Unlike ye, we have a betrothal contract that is signed and have pledged our troth before a priest. She is mine." He leaned forward slightly. He was half a head taller than Robert but almost twice as broad. Even so, it was clear to anyone that Robert was a warrior. Beyond the broadsword he carried, his entire bearing spoke to his training and experience. Callum knew that Robert would put up a worthy fight, but his commitment to protecting and keeping Siùsan was far stronger. There was that and the fact that he had three equally massive brothers to support him.

"I think ye had best leave by sunrise on the morrow. Dinna ye have a message to convey to Laird Mackenzie? I am sure that he is eager to hear about his only daughter. Ye should hurry."

Robert studied each of the Sinclair brothers in turn. He watched as their jaws clenched, their necks strained, and their muscles flexed. He decided this was not the time to make enemies.

"I think ye are right. I will be gone before Siùsan comes down to break her fast. Goodnight, gentlemen." He walked out of the Great Hall and towards the guardsmen's barracks. There was no way that Callum was going to offer him a chamber on the same floor as Siùsan.

The Sinclairbrothers watched as he walked away. They looked at one another and each shook his head.

"I dinna trust him at all." Magnus whispered.

"Me neither. I am going to sleep outside Siùsan's door. I would ask that one of ye keep watch over him in the barracks and another of ye stand watch near Elizabeth's croft. They are two peas in a pod. I would bet ma last dram of whisky that they are already well acquainted."

~ ~ ~

As her guest, of sorts, Siùsan had been forced to entertain him for much of the the day. He had gone out to the lists with Callum and the other men during the morning. He joined her and tried to convince her to sit at a lower table during the noon meal, but she had at first politely declined then firmly refused. She compromised by offering him a seat at the dais. Fortunately, there were enough people present that they were not seated near one another. Callum kept his arm loosely hanging over the back of her chair for much of the meal when they were not eating. When they were, he was even more solicitous than usual. Siùsan worried that he was overdoing it when he fed her the best pieces of meat. He always offered her the best pieces and served her before himself, but he had never actually fed her. As she watched him and looked into his eyes, she quickly forgot about Robert. In fact, she forgot about everyone else. It was as though the rest of the diners fell away, and it was just she and Callum. She grew brave enough to feed him in turn. He licked her fingers as they brushed against his lips. The braver she grew, the more brazen she felt. At one point, she managed to suck on the tip of Callum's fingers. His eyes widened, and his nose flared. She could not help but laugh. The tinkle of her laughter drew attention, so they drew apart, but only moments later, Callum leaned in and whispered, "I can give as good as I get."

"Do ye promise?"

Callum almost choked on the ale he had begun to sip.

"Cheeky. And, aye, I do. The sun has come out, and the fog has blown off the loch. What do ye say to a dip?"

"Sounds good to me."

However, their plans were cut short when the heavens opened, and it began to pour. Not only did it mean that they could not go outdoors, it meant that everyone was confined to the keep. It rained for most of the afternoon. Callum and Laird Sinclair retreated to the laird's study to go over clan business. Siùsan gathered the castle ledgers and met with the steward in his study. The other Sinclair brothers pulled out knucklebones and cards to play in front of the fire. They allowed Robert to join them only so that they did not have to go anywhere wet to keep an eye on him.

By the evening meal, everyone was feeling confined by Robert's presence. Alexander, Tavish, and Magnus met their father and brother as they emerged from the laird's study.

"Ye owe us, brother. Ye owe all of us." Magnus punched Callum in the shoulder jovially. "That arse is pompous and boring. Ye are doing Siùsan a favor by marrying her. She would have needed rescuing from him not some doddering auld coot." Callum had shared the details of Siùsan's story before they all retired the night before.

"Agreed. I will call in yer debt whenever I need to." Tavish laughed.

Alexander simply nodded. Callum knew that it was Alexander who was most likely to call in the debt the soonest.

The sounds of footsteps on the stairs cut their conversation short. They all turned to look. Laird Sinclair stepped forward to meet Siùsan at the bottom of the stairs.

Callum could not hear what his father was saying to Siùsan, and he found he was slightly worried and rather put out to not be involved in anything to do with Siùsan. He crossed his arms over his chest and watched her. She must have sensed his gaze because she looked over the Sinclair's shoulder. She paused midsentence, clearly forgetting whatever she was in the midst of saying. She looked at each of the men and then back to Laird Sinclair. She whispered something and then pointed at them. The Sinclair turned around and looked at his four sons then turned back to Siùsan and nodded. She stepped around the Sinclair and looked at the four towering men. She walked over and looked at them. She exaggerated and tilted her head all the way back as though she had to look up a great distance to make eye contact. She spread her feet and crossed her arms. While the four men looked like a rock wall when they stood shoulder to shoulder with their arms crossed, Siùsan looked like a member of the fae when she attempted to stand like them.

"Are ye solving to problems of the world?" She asked none of them in particular.

"Are ye making fun of us?" Magnus asked with a raised eyebrow, but his gruffness wore off when his lips twitched.

"That I am," Siùsan said with an exaggerated nod. Neither Tavish nor Magnus could keep a straight face. She marched over to Alexander and stood before him in a matching stance. "Ye ken I ken that ye're all bark and vera little bite? Though I dinna plan to cross ye." Alexander looked down at her and lost all sense of seriousness when she winked at him.

Next, she turned to Callum. She walked up to him and tried to pull his arms apart. He would not budge. She tugged again, and he smirked. She pretended to pout and then stuck out her tongue as she turned in a swish of skirts. She had not taken more than two steps when large hands grasped her waist and lifted her off the ground. He tossed her into the air with a twist. She shrieked with laughter as she landed into his hands. He held her up, so their eyes were level. She grasped his cheeks and gave him a quick peck. He returned the kiss and gently set her down. He looked at her clothes and was about to complain about her choice since she was wearing one of her old gowns. When he had seen it that morning, he thought that she chose it because of some task or chore that she planned to do outside. With the uncooperative weather that kept them all indoors, he had assumed that she would change into one of her better kirtles. He opened his mouth to suggest she change when she shook her head and silently tilted it towards the Great Hall. He looked over her and immediately saw Robert was watching them. He looked back at Siùsan and understood her rationale. She did not want to do anything to draw more of Robert's attention to her or do anything that could be construed as provocation to the man who had stood before the entire Sinclair clan and hinted that he knew Siùsan intimately.

Callum realized that Siùsan was far shrewder than he might be. He considered himself more than a fair to middling strategist when it came to planning raids or battles, but Siùsan was able to read people in a way than Callum could not. He took her hand and led her into the Great Hall and to her seat on the dais. All the Sinclairs did their best to ignore their two currently unwanted guests and enjoy their meal.

Chapter Fourteen

*T*he next morning broke with a light rain falling. Siùsan awoke to the sound of it tapping against the glass pane in her window. She stood and stretched. She crossed over and moved the window covering away. She opened the window slightly and felt the damp air rush in. She peeked out and saw a low layer of mist hanging over the bailey. The loch was covered by a dense fog. The day was dreary, and it matched her mood. She did not want to go below stairs and encounter Robert. She waited as long as she could before she knew she would be late and everyone would first notice her absence and then would notice her arrival. She made her way below stairs and looked around as she entered the Great Hall. She spotted Callum on the dais. When he saw her enter, he stood and came to meet her. He placed her hand on his arm as they walked towards the dais. She looked up at him and tried to understand what had caused him to suddenly become more formal with her. She had become very accustomed to his arm around her or holding her hand. She suddenly felt nervous, but he grinned down at her. His smile was infectious.

"The toad has hopped away, ma fair lady" he practically crowed. He paused at the steps up to the dais and bowed before her. His smile made her giggle. She curtseyed in returned.

"Thank ye, kind sir. Ye are ma valiant knight for chasing away the warty toad." She understood now why he was being more formal. He laughed as she joined in is jest.

As they ate their porridge together, Siùsan realized that they were coming to get to know each other as only a couple would. Callum scooped honey into her bowl as she reached to pass him the cream. It had taken over a week before Siùsan had been able to stomach the idea of trying the porridge again. Even smelling it had been enough to send a wave of fear through her. She had gone back to eating bannocks even though she had promised herself on her journey that she would only touch the little baked oatcakes if she was traveling again. It had taken Callum adding copious amounts of honey and sampling her bowl each morning for another week before she believed she was safe. She noticed that he preferred cream in his even though he sweetened and tasted hers with honey. She began to think about other preferences that she had noticed. She had seen that he loved neeps and tatties, or turnips and potatoes, but would not touch the haggis that they were served some evenings. He would eat fish that was baked and flaky but only tasted it out of courtesy if it was cooked any other way. She knew that he preferred roasted lamb to roasted boar even though he had hunted and brought in many boars over the years. She knew that he absolutely refused to eat stewed leeks but liked just about every other vegetable.

She must have been lost in thought because she jumped when he tickled her ribs.

"Ye seem vera far away." He murmured to her.

"Why dinna ye like stewed leeks?"

She managed to catch him off guard. He could not seem to find his tongue as she turned her eyes to him. That morning she was wearing the deep emerald gown that had belonged to his mother. The deep color made her eyes appear even more of a verdant green. They seemed to twinkle in the light cast from the fireplaces and the large candles overhead. It was warm in the Great Hall with so many of the clan present for the morning meal, and her cheeks were a mite pink. He leaned slightly towards her and caught a whiff of her lilac scent. He reached out to twirl a lock of her hair around his finger and could see the various shades of red and gold that ran through her hair.

"Leeks, lass?"

"Aye. Why dinna ye like stewed leeks?"

"Do ye ken that's a rather odd question to ask? I dinna like them because I was sick as a child once, and the healer insisted that ma mama feed them to me to regain ma strength. I couldnae stand the taste of them back then, and I canna even stomach the smell of them now. It reminds me of being stuck in bed while ma brothers were outside. Ma sister, Mairghread, was the only company that I had. She would come sit with me once ma fever broke and Mama was no longer worried that she would catch the sickness."

"I feel much the same about cabbage. Nae because I ate it when I was ill, but because I have just eaten too much of it."

"'Twas a bit of an odd conversation starter, ye ken."

Siùsan blushed slightly and looked away before looking up at him again.

"I had been thinking that we are starting to get to ken each other and each other's preferences. I ken that ye prefer cream to honey in yer porridge. I ken that ye only like fish prepared a certain way. That sort of thing."

"True. I ken that ye like sweetmeats but limit yerself to one. I ken that ye like raspberry tarts more than apple. I ken that ye dinna like too much sauce on yer food." He smiled at her mischievously and leaned over to whisper for her ears only, "And I ken ye taste sweeter than any honey I put in yer porridge."

Siùsan whipped her head around and gasped. That only made Callum laugh as he saw the shocked expression on her face. He gave her a quick peck on her lips and turned back to his porridge.

Two can play at that game.

Suisan reached under the table and ran her fingers up his thigh as high as she could reach. She felt his muscles tense and she smiled. She leaned into him and whispered, "I may like sweetmeats, but I also like salty ones too."

Callum nearly choked on his porridge. He coughed and spluttered as Alexander pounded him on the back, and Siùsan laughed until tears came down her cheeks.

She pushed back her chairs and bid the men a good day. Callum marveled as he watched her walk towards the kitchens. He could have sworn there was an added sway to her hips. He could not believe that his wee innocent bride to be had just referred to how his release tasted to her. He thought he could shock her with his randy comment, but she had given back as good as she had gotten. In spades.

~ ~ ~

The morning drizzle gave way to a bright and sunny afternoon. It was true that if a person waited long enough, they could experience every season in a day when in the Highlands. Callum came to the noon meal hot and sweaty from working in the lists. He went straight to the kitchens and asked Elspeth to put together a picnic basket. He told her that he wanted to surprise Siùsan with a noon meal by the loch. Once a basket was filled, he carried it out to the Great Hall.

He had made a concerted effort to avoid Elizabeth over the last few weeks and generally managed it. He made sure that he would only see her when he was in the company of others. If he was alone and saw her, he turned around or ducked into the nearest room. He detested slinking around his own home, but he did not trust her as far as he could throw her.

However, it seemed his luck had just run out.

"A picnic basket for yer little bride. Ah but she isnae yer bride yet. Ye still havenae set the date. I wonder why that could be. Dinna ye want to marry her as much as ye would have us all think?" Elizabeth's sultry voice had once upon a time aroused him and made him eager for bed sport. Now it made his skin crawl.

"Elizabeth, leave off. I dinna have aught to say to ye." He attempted to step around her, but she sidled over and blocked his way.

"Ye used to have plenty to say when we were together."

"We arenae together now." Callum's patience was nonexistent with Elizabeth. He did not forget that she was the most likely one who put Sean up to attacking Siùsan the first night or that she was the most likely one to have tried to poison Siùsan. He had received a missive only the previous day stating that she was not welcomed back at court. It had not surprised Callum to read the vehemence with which his request had been declined. However, it seriously complicated matters as Callum still needed to find somewhere to send her. He had not wanted to marry Siùsan with his former lover in attendance. He wanted to ensure that day was about Siùsan with no detractors present. He looked now at the woman that he once chased and could not understand what had possessed him not to see her true character. "I may have tossed yer skirts for a few months, but that doesnae mean I ever meant to keep ye."

The flash of anger in her eyes made him regret his words as soon as they left his mouth. He knew that it was Siùsan who would suffer his foolishness. He stepped around Elizabeth and spotted Siùsan watching them. He walked directly to her and presented the basket to her.

"I had Elspeth pack up a meal. I thought ye might enjoy an afternoon at the loch. I ken I wouldnae mind a dip." He offered her a crooked smile but knew she wanted to question him about his conversation with Elizabeth. He decided it would be best to just tell her rather than letting her imagination set to work. "Mo neach beag, she stopped me to ask if we had set a date."

He might not need to tell her the entirety of his conversation with his former lover.

Siùsan nodded her head as her eyes continued to follow Elizabeth as she moved to her preferred spot at the table closest to the dais. Normally, she enjoyed it when Callum called her his little one but somehow it seemed trite in that moment. She tried to shake off her sense of impending doom, but there was something in her intuition that told her there was more to Callum's passing conversation than a pleasant inquiry about their yet to be determined wedding.

Callum offered her his hand and she looked at it for a moment. She reached out and took it. She realized that she felt calmer already simply from the contact. They made their way through the bailey and out of the postern gate. They chatted about the change in the weather from the downpour of the day prior. Siùsan had started to help the village healer as she had considerable knowledge of herbs and medicinals. Callum helped her gather some plants that she found growing along the path. When they reached the loch, Callum spread out a blanket for them and Siùsan unpacked the basket.

They sat down across from each other, but Callum was not content with the distance between them. He felt it keenly and knew it was more than just physical. Siùsan was retreating into herself as she had done the first couple of days after she arrived. Callum felt they had made such tremendous progress, and he cared for her deeply. Seeing her remoteness made his heart ache. He may not have planned to talk to Elizabeth and he certainly would have avoided Siùsan seeing it if he could, but he would not allow the harpy to ruin his time with his beloved.

Beloved? What? She isnae ma beloved. Why did that come to mind? But as he watched Siùsan, he realized that it was true. He was falling in love with his unexpected and initially unwanted bride. *I willna have that retched bitch ruin our afternoon.* Callum reached across the food and grasped Siùsan's waist. He lifted her off the blanket and hoisted her across the food. He settled her in his lap.

Siùsan had been looking down at the wheel of soft cheese when she felt Callum's hands about her waist. She did not have a chance to even look up before she felt herself plucked from the ground. She landed on his lap with a squeak.

"This is where ye belong, mo chridhe." Callum tested out the new term of endearment and found that it felt right. She was his heart and was quickly becoming a part of his very soul. Siùsan looked into Callum's deep brown eyes and saw the sincerity of his words. She had been wary of using any terms of endearment and thought that Callum's were just passing phrases. He had called her little one and sweetheart countless times now and assumed that he was just free with his petnames. This time it seemed to mean much more. He ran the pad of his thumb over her cheekbone and brushed his lips against hers in the softest kiss imaginable. It was one of deep affection not lust. Siùsan lifted her chin and pressed her lips against his and returned the feathery kiss.

"Mo ghràidh," she whispered against his lips. She tested out the term of affection. It was not as uncomfortable to say as she thought it might be, but she was not convinced that ma darling was manly enough for Callum.

Callum responded by cupping the back of her head in his hand and deepening the kiss. He had not realized how badly he longed to hear anything that might hint at her feelings for him. His heart began to beat faster, and he felt his cock harden. He, for once, was pleased that his sporran kept Siùsan from feeling his desire. He did not want to ruin this moment by making her think that it was lust that made him speak. Siùsan opened her mouth wider and stroked his tongue with her own. She pressed her breasts against Callum's chest and he could feel her hard nipples through the fabric of her kirtle. She had not brought her arisaid as the weather was so pleasant. He ran his hand along the smooth skin of her neck and feathered his fingertip across the exposed skin of her throat. He pulled away and kissed a trail down the side of her neck. He nibbled where her neck and shoulder met. He licked his way back up to the shell of her ear. She moaned softly as he took her earlobe into his mouth alternating between tugs with his teeth and suckling.

Callum felt her hands on his chest. After she loosened the strings on his leine, her hands explored his shoulders and neck. She massaged his shoulders and sighed beside his ear. A shiver ran through him when he felt her breath. She turned her head and freed her own ear so that she might return his ministrations in kind. She ran the tip of her tongue over the shell of his ear. She dipped it into the well of his ear and then sucked gently on his lobe.

Their touches were still gentle and loving, but their passion was sparking. Callum shifted them so that he could lay above her. He rested his weight on his elbows as he pulled one of her sleeves from her shoulder. He reached behind her and tugged at her laces. Once her kirtle was loose enough, he freed one of her breasts. He suckled her like a starving babe. His hand found the end of her gown and bunched up the hem. She bent her knee, and he ran his hand from her ankle to her thigh. Callum felt Siùsan tug at his leine. She freed it from his belt and ran her hands up and down his back. She loved the feeling of his muscles flexing under her hands.

Abruptly, Callum stood up and brought Siùsan with him. He lifted her gown over her head and let it fall to the ground. Left in only her chemise, stockings, and slippers, Siùsan reached to unpin his plaid from his shoulder. She dropped the pin into his sporran and then unfasted the belt that held both his sporran and plaid in place. She eased the long length of material to the ground. Callum reached down to untie and kick off his boots and stockings as Siùsan removed her own shoes and stockings. Callum untied the shoulders of her chemise, and it dropped to the ground, pooling at her feet. Siùsan pushed his leine as high as she could reach, but Callum had to pull it over his head. He flung it aside as he looked at Siùsan's bare form for the first time. He had seen much of her through her transparent and clinging chemise when they had swum at the loch more than once. However, this was the first time that he could see everything. He reached out tentatively but was unsure. He did not want to frighten her by moving too fast. This was a new element of intimacy between them. Even though she had seen him bare, she had always had the protection of a thin layer of clothing.

Siùsan ended his hesitation when she grasped his hand and brought it to her breast. Callum groaned, lifted her off the ground, and dipped his head to take her other breast into his mouth. His bare cock rubbed along her bare mound. He ached to thrust inside of her and finally totally claim her. His hand slid to the back of her thigh and lifted it to wrap around his hip. His iron rod pulsated as it slid along her wet seam. She pressed her hips forward to gain more pressure on her pleasure button. She moaned as she ground herself into him. Callum felt his control slipping away. He desperately wanted to wrap her other leg around him and drive himself into her over and over. It was only when he felt himself leak along her moist skin that he forced himself to slow down. She must have sensed it too for she dropped her leg and pulled back her head.

"I think we best go for a dip and cool off." Callum muttered.

"Aye," Siùsan agreed breathlessly.

They walked to the shore and waded in. When the water was shoulder deep for Siùsan and barely mid chest for Callum, he pulled her into the circle of his arms. He could not resist holding her as he watched her breasts float just below the surface. His cock rested against her belly as he gripped her buttocks.

"I dinna ken how much longer I can restrain maself. One of these days, I will give in to ma temptation and not listen to reason. I dinna want to do anything that ye will regret, Siùsan, and I dinna want to dishonor ye by taking yer innocence before we are wed."

"What are ye saying, Callum? Do ye not want to touch me anymore?" Siùsan shivered even though the air was warm, and the water was less cold than it had been just weeks earlier.

"Nay. I am saying that I want to set our wedding date. I want to make ye ma wife in truth."

"Ye want this so that ye can bed me?" Siùsan pushed away from his chest and dove under the water. She felt ashamed that she had thought that he felt more for her than just lust. She had thought that he cared about her and might even be falling in love with her. She knew that she was in love with him. She had not realized it as it gradually creeped up on her, but she found herself drawn to him more and more each day.

She scrambled up the beach and ran to her clothes. She tugged on her kirtle and pulled the laces closed as best she could.

Callum followed her up the shore and grabbed her wrists. He held them pinned against her back. His wet body dripped on her already damp gown.

"That isnae what I meant at all. Ye ken I want to make love to ye, but that isnae why I want to set the wedding date. I think ye want me just as much I do ye. I would wed ye because I dinna want anyone else ever again. I would wed ye to give ye ma name and ma protection for the rest of our lives. I would wed ye so that I can fall asleep with ye in ma arms in a proper bed rather than only on a sandy beach. I would wed ye so that I can wake to ye every morning and have ye be the first and last person I see each day."

Callum waited for Siùsan's response. Her heaving breaths pushed her breasts against him. He ached from his pent up need, and he knew she could feel his cock twitching. She slowly allowed her body to relax. She looked up to see the intense look that he sometimes had when he gazed at her. She saw the determination in his eyes. She knew they would wed one day, and she was tired of sneaking around with him. She felt ready to pledge herself to him.

"I will wed ye as soon as the bans are done being posted. Father Paul has read them once, so we can be wed in two weeks." She smiled up at him. Callum relaxed immediately and released her hands. She wrapped her arms around his neck and he lifted her off the ground and planted a hard kiss. He set her back down gently and stepped back for his leine. His aching cock and bollacks were not pleased to realize there would be no release any time soon. He reached for his breacon feile and began to fold it. Siùsan watched him as he lay on the ground and wrapped the large plaid around himself. Callum looked up and saw that Siùsan's gown was becoming soaked through from her skin and hair. It would soon verge on indecent.

"Lass, ye had better hurry to ye chamber and change into something dry." He nodded his head in the direction of her kirtle. She looked down and immediately understood what he meant. "I will be up in just a moment. Perhaps it would be better if ye returned ahead of me. I dinna want people to talk about us." Callum stood and gave her one last kiss. "We can announce our plans at the evening meal tonight."

Chapter Fifteen

Siùsan had just reached the top of the hill when the last person she wanted to encounter stepped out from behind a tree.

"Ye ken ye are not the only one he brings to the loch for a dip. He has dipped his wick with me here many a time." Elizabeth purposely bumped into Siùsan as she pushed past and trotted down the hill to Callum.

Stunned, Siùsan turned to watch Elizabeth approach Callum. Callum had turned to stare out at the loch and could not have seen Elizabeth approach. Siùsan watched Elizabeth wrap her arms around Callum's waist from behind. She felt ill when she saw Callum reach behind him and pull the evil woman into his embrace. She was only mildly comforted when he stepped back from her embrace when he saw who it was.

Siùsan could not help but watch. She was drawn to the scene like a moth to a flame. She could not hear Callum's voice but saw him shake his head. She watched in horror as Elizabeth's hand ran over the bulge beneath Callum's plaid and cup his rod. Once again, Callum stepped back, but this time Elizabeth followed and thrust her hand under his plaid.

Siùsan thought she would be ill as she watched Callum stand there with his cock in Elizabeth's hand. He grasped her wrist but did not draw away. Siùsan's heart crumbled as she watched Elizabeth pull apart the front of her gown and bare her breasts to Callum. She held one up to him, but he would not look at it. Siùsan could see that he was looking over the top of her head and did not see her drop to her knees until her head ducked under his plaid. He let out a startled noise, but it was Siùsan's whimper of despair that had him swinging his head in her direction. The look of shock and guilt was enough to make Siùsan turn around and bolt for the keep.

Callum thought it was Siùsan who had returned to him when he felt a pair of slim arms wrap around him from behind. He was just pulling the woman around to him when he caught the tell-tale scent of roses and knew immediately that it was Elizabeth and not Siùsan. He stepped back and shook his head. He was not prepared for Elizabeth to reach for his cock and take hold. He caught her wrist as she applied pressure that almost made him groan.

"Ye are hard and ready. Just as ye always are for me." Elizabeth cooed.

"Ye ken it is not from ye and not for ye." Callum growled.

"I dinna care. I am here and she isnae. I can help ease the ache. Ye ken nay one can do what I can with ma mouth. Ye've said as much."

Callum tried to step back again, but her hand was too fast, and he felt her bare skin on his. She stroked him quickly, and he could not stop the small dribble of seed that came from his tip. She grinned as she bared her breasts to him.

"Taste these first, then ye can feast on the rest of me next."

Callum refused to look down at her. He held her wrist as tightly as he dared. He feared that he might snap it if he was not careful. He continued to look over her head, so he was unprepared to feel her sink to her knees and dive under his plaid. He felt her tongue on his bollacks as she lifted them. Then her tongue darted out to lick him from stem to stern.

He could not hold back the groan as his body ached for release. His mind and his heart wanted nothing to do with the woman at his feet, but his aching cock and ballocks seemed to think otherwise. He went still when he heard a whimper from the hill above the loch. He looked up to see Siùsan watching. The look of pure heartbreak on her face was enough to make him cry out. He grabbed his plaid and pushed Elizabeth away. He did not care that she fell backwards as her cackle followed him up the hill.

"Ye are too late. She willna forgive ye for this. Ye could have stopped me but ye didna. Ye ken ye would have let me if she hadnae ruined it."

Callum bolted up the hill with Elizabeth's words ringing in his ears. He knew that he absolutely would not have allowed it. He had tried to diffuse the situation by not giving her the attention she desired. He had grossly underestimated what she was willing to do to have her way. He knew in that moment that Elizabeth had planned all of this. He also knew that there was no way that Siùsan would believe that he was not allowing it from what she had seen.

He watched her dart through the postern gate. He was surprised to see just how fast she could run in her skirts. She had hoisted them to her knees and jumped over several puddles as she stormed into the kitchens.

Callum chased her, calling her name. He followed her into the kitchens, but she was already gone. Elspeth stared at him and then frowned. She shook her head and pointed towards the door that led to the back servants' stairs. Callum weaved through the kitchen and pushed through the door. He saw Siùsan bound up the stairs two at a time. She was just reaching the second floor landing when he began taking the stairs three at a time. She was already making her way up to the third floor when he made it to the landing. She had not slowed and was moving further away from him. He made it to the third floor and sprinted to catch her before she made it to her door. He was so close to catching her when she had to stop to open her door. He reached out to grab anything he could reach when she slipped through and slammed the door shut. He heard the lock turn and the bar drop.

He pounded on the door with his fist and leaned his forehead against it.

"*Siùsan! Siùsan!* Let me in. Let me explain. It isnae what it seemed. I swear to ye. I didna want to antagonize her, but I underestimated her." He continued to hammer on the door, but there was no response. He stopped and listened. He could not hear anything from the other side of the door. It was silence. There was no sound of crying or moving about. There was no sound of angry muttering or things being thrown. The complete void of noise scared Callum far more than any ranting would have.

"Siùsan, please. Let me in. *Please.*" He tried again to no avail. He waited for what seemed like forever but never heard a sound. Finally, he gave up and decided to give her time and space. "I will leave ye now, but I will return for ye before the evening meal. If ye dinna open the door then, I will kick it down." He turned and walked away.

~ ~ ~

Callum made his way down to his father's study and knocked before entering. Once look at his son's face and Liam Sinclair cleared the room of everyone but Callum. He poured his son a healthy dose of *usquebagh,* or water of life. If anyone needed a strong shot of whisky it was the morose man in front of him.

"She saw me with Elizabeth." Callum said as he dropped into a chair by the fire. He did not even look up when his father handed him the whisky.

"Just what did she see?"

"Entirely too much and heard not nearly enough. Siùsan was returning to the keep after we had just agreed to set a wedding date and announce it tonight. She must have passed Elizabeth on the way because she stopped at the top of the hill overlooking the loch. At first, I thought it was Siùsan who had come back down for something. I quickly realized it was Elizabeth and tried to tell her no. She reached out and grabbed ma cock. It was already at full attention from being with Siùsan. I stepped away, but she stuck her hand up ma plaid. She grabbed hold and began to stroke. I grabbed her wrist, but she was tugging her kirtle off her chest. I told her nay, but she dropped to her knees and ducked under ma plaid. Bluidy hell. Siùsan saw all of it. She whimpered like an animal caught in a trap. The look on her face will torment me as much as seeing Mairghread tied to that bed at the McDonnells'."

Callum downed the whisky in just two gulps. The burn as it moved down to his stomach only masked the ache in his heart. He leaned his arms on his thighs and dropped his head.

"I chased after her, but she got to her chamber just before I did. I was almost able to touch her hair, Da. She locked and barred the door. I pounded and begged her to let me explain but there only silence. Da, silence. I couldnae hear her moving about. She wasnae crying, at least not loudly enough for me to hear. She didna stomp about or throw things. It was as if nae one was in there. I decided to leave her be for now but told her I would be back for the evening meal. I probably only made it worse by threatening to kick down the door if she doesnae answer then."

"Ye've made a right cockup of this. Aye, I ken what I said. Ye arenae so big that I canna skelp yer wee behind. Ye have a woman who is falling head over heels in love with ye, who is all things good and honest. It doesnae sound like ye tried to stop the harlot from interfering."

Callum looked up at his father and saw he was angrier with him than he had been in years. Liam Sinclair was known to yell and rave at times, but his family knew best that the calmer he was in times of trouble, the angrier he was.

"What ye say is all too close to what Elizabeth said as I ran after Siùsan. But I didna want her. I tried to tell Siùsan through the door that I didna want to antagonize Elizabeth further but underestimated her deviousness. She must leave immediately. Canna we send her off somewhere like Mairghread's?"

"Ye canna be serious? Are ye truly that daft? Ye sister would murder ye in yer sleep. She's only just had a bairn a few months ago, and ye would send that seductress to her. I thought ye liked Tristan. Why would ye purposely try to ruin his marriage?" Laird Sinclair was practically growling by the time he was done. He loved his children more than his own life, but he was baffled by their selfishness and insensitivity at times. He felt like he had failed them and his wife. The older man ran his hand through his still thick dark hair. "I canna believe ye would suggest that even if it was only in passing or in jest. Are ye really that self-centered?"

"Oh, Da. I ken ye have the right of it, and I wouldnae ever do it. Mairghread and Tristan are simply the closest place to send the bitch." Something that his father said finally permeated his clouded mind. "Do ye really think she might love me?"

"Ah, well. She might have, but I dinna ken now, lad. Ye might be lucky and she forgives ye, but I doubt it. She has too much fire in her." He rested his hand on his son's shoulder and squeezed. He did not envy Callum his position, but he had brought it down upon himself.

"Da, I ken that I love Siùsan. I do. I have to make this right."

Chapter Sixteen

S iùsan heard Callum's pounding on her door, and she heard his explanation. Part of her knew that it was a reasonable one, but she could not erase the sight of another woman touching him in a way that she believed was hers and hers alone. The pain that shot through her chest every time she thought of it was enough to take her breath away.

She made it to her room just before Callum caught her. She slid down the door and silently wept. She felt the overwhelming need to flee. She knew she could not stay and marry a man who would not stand up for her or for their relationship. She could not marry a man who could so easily forget her and allow another woman to tempt him.

So she waited. She waited until she heard Callum walk away. She waited until she was sure that all the chambermaids had made their rounds and that she was unlikely to run into anyone in the passageway. She slowly levered herself back to standing and moved to the wardrobe. She was completely chilled from sitting so long in a wet gown. She shed the gown and looked longingly at the others in the wardrobe.

What a waste. I thought that I had finally found ma chance for a real family. I thought I found a place where I was welcomed and important. But once again, I am so vera easily forgotten. She reached out and touched the velvet plum gown that was her favorite. She looked at her old gowns that she had brought with her. She would leave behind the gowns that had never really been hers. She pulled out the sturdier of the two and put it on with a fresh chemise. She pulled on dry stockings and quickly stuffed the rest of her belongings into her satchel. She slung it across her chest and wrapped her arisaid over it. The billowing plaid material helped to hide the bulkiness of her bag.

Siùsan slowly opened her chamber door and looked both ways into the passageway. When she saw that no one was about, she crept to the servants' stairs. She wound her way down to the ground floor and slid along the wall until she reached a door that she knew led into a storage room that also had a door to the bailey. She felt her way across the room, moving slowly so she would not bump into anything and alert someone to her presence. She found the door to the bailey and once again peeked to see if anyone was around. She considered covering her head to try to hide her hair, but she was the only person wearing a Mackenzie plaid. There was no way to conceal that. She darted across the open space and made for the stables. She ran to the back of the stables and nestled herself among the hay bales. She would have to wait there until the guards were almost ready to close the gates for the evening. She had hours of waiting ahead of her. She forced herself to think about anything other than Callum and Elizabeth. She regretted that she would not be able to thank Laird Sinclair for his graciousness and kindness. She wished that she could say goodbye, but there was no way he would ever let her venture out into the wilds alone.

Siùsan also considered her options. She had absolutely no intention of returning to her father's lands. Instead she planned to make her way to the land on which her mother grew up. She would have a long journey ahead of her. Her mother had been the daughter of a lesser MacLeod chieftain. That sept was on the opposite coast from the Sinclairs. She would have to travel the breadth of Scotland to reach a grandfather that she was not sure was alive still or would welcome her if he was.

When Siùsan considered her options, she knew that remaining with the Sinclairs and marrying Callum or returning to her father in disgrace were untenable choices. She knew that going to her mother's clan was her only option. She pictured the maps of Scotland that she had studied as a lass and when she taught her brothers the geography of Scottish clans. There was no way that she could make it to the MacLeods without crossing through Gunn territory which was her stepmother's clan. The only way to avoid it was to travel much farther north before heading west. She could avoid the Sutherlands by staying in the Mackay territory. The Mackenzies and Sutherlands were on good terms, but she remembered that Callum's mother had been a Sutherland. She worried that if she encountered them, they would return her to Callum and Laird Sinclair. *Then again, Laird Sinclair said that his wife had been a close friend of ma mother. Mayhap they would take me to ma grandfather if he is still alive. But what if he isnae. I dinna ken who the laird is now. If it isnae ma grandfather, then they might nae be willing to help me. I will just have to skirt the border and remain with the Mackays. Though Callum's sister is now a Mackay. Damn! It will be better if I travel at night and sleep during the day. It will be more dangerous for Trofast, but we are less likely to be spotted by a patrol or any lawless men.*

With her mind made up, Siùsan settled in to wait. She knew that she would have to time her departure just right. It dawned on her that if she waited as long as she had initially planned, Callum would have come to bring her down for the evening meal. He would find her door unlocked and her gone. *He will sound the bluidy alarm from here to kingdom come. They'll catch me for sure.*

She listened carefully to everything that she could. She heard a wagon roll to a stop outside of the stables. She crept around the side to see that one of the villagers had brought in more hay. She scrambled to slip into the stables before the wagon was unloaded and her hiding spot found. She made her way to Trofast's stall.

"I think it is now or never, ma friend. I canna wait till it is dark." She hurried to saddle Trofast. She took off her arisaid and folded it. She tucked it into her satchel which she attached to her saddle. She led Trofast out of his stall and looked around. It seemed that all of the groomsmen were helping the farmer move his hay. She looked around and saw that there was another door to the stable. It was not meant for a horse to pass through, but she believed that they could still fit. She opened the door slowly and looked around. The door opened to the back of the blacksmith's shop and then the row of storerooms that ran along one of the bailey walls. The noise of the blacksmith's hammer and anvil disguised the sound of Trofast's hooves. They moved swiftly along the small alley between the buildings and the wall.

Siùsan paused before she moved out of the shadows. She looked to see if there was a guard at the postern gate. She saw that there was one at the inner wall and that the gate in the outer wall was ajar, probably from when Callum chased her back to the keep. She grimaced and forced her mind away from that memory. She looked around and found a rock. She picked it up and threw it behind the guard. It landed against a wooden barrel that was on the opposite side of the guard from her. She watched him to see if he would hear it. He had. He looked in the direction of the sound. As he looked over his shoulder, she threw another rock even harder. The noise was louder. The guard shifted in the direction of the barrel. She threw one more rock, but this time she threw it towards the keep and startled a cluster of chickens. She felt badly and was glad she had not actually hit any of the animals. When the guard went to investigate the disruption, Siùsan led Trofast through the two gates. She led Trofast along the path that she and Callum had used whenever they rode out to the meadow. She knew that much of the path was visible to the men on the battlements, but she prayed that since it was a difficult angle from which to attack, they would not be looking that way often. When she made it a fair distance without an alarm being raised, she mounted Trofast and spurred him into a gallop.

Once she cleared the meadow, she slowed Trofast to a walk and got her bearings. She dismounted and found a large branch from a fir tree. She used it to sweep away her footprints as she looked in each direction. The ground was surprisingly hard considering the abundance of rain that they had only the previous day. She looked up and saw that the tops of the trees were densely packed and not much water would be able to make it to the ground. She said a prayer of thanksgiving since she would not have to worry about her footprints or Trofast's hoof prints sinking too deeply.

She nudged Trofast with her shoulder and he moved forward. She dragged the branch behind them and swept the ground to remove traces of them. After almost an hour of moving almost silently through the woods on foot, she dropped her branch and remounted Trofast. She figured that she had put enough distance between herself and Callum that he would have a hard time finding her trail. She pushed Trofast into a cantor and continued through the woods heading due west.

Chapter Seventeen

allum dreaded the coming confrontation with Siùsan, but he refused to allow any more time to pass before they resolved this matter. After he left his father's study, he actually searched out Elizabeth. He told her that she would need to be gone from the castle's grounds by morning and that if she attempted to enter the bailey wall, she would be forcibly removed. He explained to her that she could find a place in the village or make her way home, but he was done. He was quite clear that if he ever laid eyes on her again it would be too soon. She attempted to seduce him with her breasts, then she tried tears, and finally resorted to yelling. She swore and cursed him, Siùsan, and any children they might have. Callum had to admit to himself that he was truly nervous of what Elizabeth might do next, but for the sake of salvaging his relationship with Siùsan, he had to remove her.

Now Callum made his way up the stairs to Siùsan's chamber. He knocked softly and waited to see if she would answer. When he heard no movement, he knocked louder in case she had fallen asleep. Once again, there was no answer.

"Siùsan, let me in. Or if ye willna let me in, then please come out. We need to talk. At the least, ye need to eat. Ye didna eat earlier, and I ken nothing has come up to ye since ye came back to yer chamber." Callum waited, but once again there was absolutely no sound coming from within the chamber. Callum was starting to get more than just a little apprehensive. He pounded on the door and bellowed her name.

"Siùsan, I swear if ye dinna open this door, I will kick it in." He banged his fist once more. When no response came, he stepped back. "Vera well. Ye better not be near the door."

Callum thrust his weight into his kick and the door flung open so easily that he stumbled forward. He was stunned at how it had only taken one kick. He looked around and did not see Siùsan. Instead, he saw the gown she had worn earlier was draped across the foot of the bed with the skirts fanned out to dry. He saw that the wardrobe doors were still open. He walked over and recognized all his mother's gowns. He counted them and added in the one on the bed. He knew that none were missing. He looked for the gowns that were originally Siùsan's and did not see them. He turned back around and surveyed the room. There was nothing out of place. It looked like the room had not been occupied in ages. As his eyes traveled around the room, he spotted the bar to the door. The wood had splintered on the door jamb, but the bar was propped against the wall. *It wasnae even barred. Bluidy hell! It wasnae even locked because she's run.*

Callum ran out of the room and charged down the stairs. When he reached the Great Hall, he looked for his brothers and father. He saw them standing in front of the fireplace. He barreled his way over to them. They sensed the commotion and turned as one.

"She's run. She's left. I must find her before she comes to any harm. I canna forgive maself for this mess, but I willna let her be hurt. Brothers, will ye come with me?"

Laird Sinclair stepped forward and grasped his son's shoulders. He looked into the face that was a younger version of his own. He saw that his son was finally maturing into the man he was meant to be. His body had made the transition years ago, but his heart was only now catching up.

"Ye can take Tavish and Magnus, but Alexander stays behind. I cannae have ye all run off into the unknown. Alex is yer second and therefore takes yer place as ma tanaiste while ye are away. Ye ken that."

Callum nodded and looked at Alex. He extended his arm for a warrior's shake. They clasped forearms and yanked one another into a hug.

"Ye'll find her. And when ye do, ye had better fall to yer knees and beg her for forgiveness. Ye've made a right shite heap of yer courting." Alex said as they embraced.

"Ye, me, and everyone in sight kens that." Callum looked to his other two brothers. "We ride in the next quarter of an hour. Magnus, see to the provisions with Hagatha and Elspeth. Tavish, have the horses saddled. I will round up half a score of men to accompany us."

The three men fanned out to accomplish their given tasks. Laird Sinclair looked at his second son and grinned. Alexander was quiet by nature, but still waters run deep. Nothing escaped him, and he was a master strategist. All the brothers were very close to one another and close in age, but Callum and Alexander were less than a year apart and often seemed more like twins than anything else. He knew that Alex longed to accompany his brothers but understood his duty.

"Ye are a good lad to stay behind with yer auld da. I dinna get to spend enough time with just ye these days. I look forward to knocking ye on yer arse in the lists tomorrow morn." He clapped Alexander on the back hard enough to make him lurch forward. Alexander looked back at his father and grinned. While Tavish might have been the one who was built most similarly to their father and Callum most resembled him in the face, Alexander was more similar in personality to Laird Sinclair.

"Careful what ye wish for auld mon. I willna take it any easier on ye than ye did any of us when we were but wee laddies."

Liam Sinclair guffawed loudly enough to draw looks from everyone in the Great Hall.

"Ye ken that not a one of ye came out as a wee laddie. Wee beasties the lot of ye were." He slung his arm around his son's shoulder as they walked to the dais together.

Chapter Eighteen

"Will this God forsaken rain never end?" Callum groused as the group of men broke camp for the third morning. It was also the third morning of rain. Callum was in a foul mood. There had been no signs of Siùsan after she entered the woods. They had searched the bailey and to see if they could determine how she had made it out of the walls since no one at the front gate had seen her leave. They found her horse's hoof prints and followed them across the meadow, but they lost her soon after. They continued west even though Magnus and Tavish argued that it would be quicker to turn south if they were going to the Mackenzie's keep. Something niggled in Callum's mind, and he was not convinced that Siùsan would make her way directly there. He had argued with his brothers, but they eventually relented and followed him west.

"Ye ken this is Scotland. We can get all four seasons in an hour." Tavish answered. He knew that Callum was not really looking for a response, but Callum's mood was only growing worse by the day. Tavish and Magnus knew that his irritability was not from the weather, though that did not help. It was because he was afraid for Siùsan.

"We are almost to our border with the Gunns. We will turn south and cross their land and the Sutherlands. We can stop overnight with Uncle Hamish and the Sutherlands. Then make our way to the Mackenzies."

"Have ye thought about what ye will say to Laird Mackenzie when ye show up looking for his daughter? What if she isnae there?"

"I dinna even want to think that far ahead. I will come up with answers to those questions once we are across their borders. Mount up!"

The men spent the remainder of the day trudging through the rain and mud. All of them were miserable but none were as miserable as Callum. He was cold and wet and overcome with frustration and guilt. He did not completely fault Siùsan for running away. He knew he was as much to blame as she was. If he was truly being honest, he knew he was even more to blame, but he was frustrated that he could not find any trace of her. It was as though she disappeared altogether. *Where are ye, little one? Where have ye gone? I dinna think ye ran home to yer da, but I cannae find any hint of ye.*

~ ~ ~

"Callum, we need to make camp soon." Magnus called to him. The rain had finally ceased, and the sun had poked through for the last couple of hours. "There is a clearing up ahead. Do ye remember we stayed there the last time we travelled to the Sutherlands?"

"Aye. We are well into Gunn territory now, but we should be fine to stay there."

The men found the clearing and dismounted. They began to make camp. Some of the men went to hunt and others gathered firewood. There was a stream not far away, so a couple of men went to refill the waterskins. Callum stood with his brothers. He was growing angry at himself because he could not find one small woman, and he was growing even angrier at Siùsan because she clearly did not want to be found.

"Where could one lass get to when she is travelling with only her horse? I ken she is not used to long journeys. Coming to us was the first time she'd left Mackenzie land. How has she managed to give us the slip for four bluidy days?" Callum ran a hand through his hair making it stand on end. He looked up to the heavens and growled. A tiny movement to his right drew his attention. He looked up into the branches and could not believe what he saw.

"*Woman! Get down here now!*" Callum stalked over to the trunk of the tree and glared up at Siùsan. She had the audacity to shake her head. "What do ye mean nay? Come down now or I will fetch ye. If I must do that, I will turn ye over ma knee."

"Ye wouldnae dare, ye beastly mon."

"Would I not? Ye dinna ken me that well yet."

"I dinna need to ever ken ye any better than I do now. I ken all too much."

"Is that what ye think? Ye believe ye ken the whole of it, do ye? If ye werenae so damn stubborn and reckless, we could have resolved this in ma da's dry hall." He hauled himself up onto the lowest hanging branches. He watched Siùsan scramble to move to a higher branch. He was surprised once again at how agile she was. She moved like a squirrel and swung from one branch onto the limb of an adjacent tree. He continued to climb higher. He came even with her and moved out on a branch.

"Ye canna follow me, Callum. Dinna do it!" She was shaking her head vehemently.

"I have come this far for ye. I amnae going to--." He was unable to finish as the branch below him snapped, and he dropped through the branches and twigs to land heavily on his left shoulder and arm.

"*Callum!*" Siùsan swung down and dropped to the ground beside him. She pushed through the circle of men that had quickly converged around him. She kneeled beside him. "Callum, Callum. Please say something." She gently lifted his head enough to run her hands over his head. She felt a goose egg forming where his head had hit the ground. She looked at his arm and saw that it was clearly broken, and the shoulder was dislocated.

Callum was awake and in excruciating pain, but the fall had knocked the wind out of him. He opened his eyes to see Siùsan's breasts straining against the neckline of her kirtle as she leaned over him. Her hair fell around them as a curtain. He could not resist the opportunity to touch her, to taste her. He licked the crevice between her breasts, kissed them softly as she ran her hands over his injured shoulder.

Callum was reassured when she did not jerk away from him. She looked into his eyes, but he could not read her emotions. He wrapped his good arm around her waist and pulled her closer. His mouth found hers, and he kissed her passionately. He was desperate for any contact with her. She opened her mouth and met his greedy kiss with her own desire. Callum was lost in his cloud of pain and lust. He did not really notice that Siùsan shifted her body. He was completely unprepared for the ripping pain that seared through his shoulder as she set it. He groaned and pulled her from him. She flew across him and landed with a thud. He looked over at her and could not believe how he had just manhandled her.

"Siùsan, I am sorry. I dinna mean to hurt ye. Not ever." He watched as she wiped her mouth with the back of her sleeve and stood. She did not look at him but instead spoke to Tavish and Magnus.

"His shoulder is set. That was the worse of the two injuries, but I still need to set his arm. I need two smooth, sturdy sticks to make a splint. Ye will need to hold him down. If he tries to throw me again, I will hit back."

Siùsan was all business. Callum was taken aback with her brusque manner after the passion of their kiss only moments ago.

She kneeled beside him again and saw his confusion. She smiled, but it was cold and did not reach her eyes.

"I needed to distract ye, so I could set yer shoulder. Had ye not tossed me aside, I could have set yer arm too. Or ye could have listened to me when I tried to warn ye that ye shouldnae have followed me. The branches were never going to hold someone as large as ye."

"I didna think ye meant following ye in that moment. I thought ye meant I shouldnae have followed ye at all."

"I meant that too. Prepare yerself. This will smart." Before he could draw another breath, she pulled and pressed on his broken arm at the same time. He howled in pain and his back arched off the ground.

"Ye might have given me a moment to prepare maself as ye so kindly advised."

"Aye, well next time use some sense, and ye willna find yerself needing an arm set."

Siùsan stood up and walked away. She had hidden in the trees very early that morning and had just woken up when she heard the men enter the clearing. She did not dare move because she recognized Callum, Tavish, and Magnus's voices immediately. There was a ravine not far from there, and she had tied Trofast there earlier. She walked towards the ridge now and peered down at her horse. He must have caught her scent because he neighed and nodded his giant head. She smiled and turned towards the stream.

Siùsan had just finished washing her hands and face and was leaning forward to take a drink when she sensed him behind her.

"Ye should be resting by the fire right now. Ye need a sling to keep yer arm and shoulder in place." She said without looking back at him.

"Is that really all ye have to say to me?"

"Nay. It is not even close to all that I have to say but it is the nicest that I can think of."

"Siùsan, I ken ye saw it all, but ye didna hear me, did ye? Ye didna hear me refuse her."

"It doesnae matter what ye may or may not have said. Ye didna force her off ye, and ye didna defend me, defend us. Ye didna try hard enough. I ken what I saw."

"Aye. I will agree that I may not have tried that hard but it doesnae mean that I had any intention of allowing her to finish what she started. I didna want to anger her or antagonize her because I feared, still fear, how she might retaliate against ye. I wanted to be kind and gentle but underestimated her desperation and deviousness."

"I dinna want to hear anymore of yer excuses, Callum. She was yer mistress before I arrived, and she can go back to being yer mistress now that I have left. I already spent one lifetime in a home where I wasna wanted. I dinna need to enter a marriage with a mon who doesnae care for me to feel that way all over again."

Callum did not know what to say to everything that Siùsan just revealed. It was the most she had ever said about her family. He simply stared dumbfounded.

"Ye can shut yer gob. I havenae ever told ye about ma kin because it was too humiliating to admit that ma father could not be rid of me fast enough. That is when he bothered to remember that I was his daughter to begin with. Ye want to ken about ma doting father. Vera well. Ma father was deeply in love with ma mother. They met when he and his father visited their holding. Their part of Clan MacLeod was a smaller sept. Ma father was smitten, and ma mother returned his affections. He asked for her hand in marriage, and ma grandfather agreed, but ma father's father would only agree to a handfast. Ma parents were desperate to marry one another, and so they agreed, believing they would eventually marry. It was nae long after that ma mother discovered she was breeding. They hid her pregnancy for as long as they could, but it became too obvious to ignore. As her time drew near, they decided that they would be wed by a priest before the bairn, me, was born. Laird Mackenzie was not in agreement. He wanted to dissolve the handfast early and was in talks to betroth ma father to the Gunn's daughter. They snuck off to a monastery on Mackenzie land and were married. When they returned to the Mackenzie keep, the laird was enraged that ma father defied him. He called ma mother a whore and told ma father to set her aside because the Gunn lass was on her way.

"They rode out the next morning before anyone was up. They were riding back to her father when they came across a group of riders. The riders galloped towards them and bellowed at them. Ma mother's horse was spooked and threw her. She landed badly and couldnae move. Her labor pains began, and it was not long after that I was born. Travelling with the warriors was a woman. It was the woman ma father was to marry. Elizabeth Gunn was a well-known healer, but she stood over ma mother as she bled to death after giving birth to me. Ma father could not convince her to help.

"Ma father was left with a dead wife and a squalling newborn. He carried his wife in his lap back to his keep. He refused to even look at me from what I have been told. It was one of the Gunn warriors who wrapped me in his plaid and brought me along. Ma father had told them to leave me behind."

She paused for breath and looked down at the stream. She sighed and then started again.

"They returned to the castle and were greeted by the entire village. I can only imagine what a strange sight that must have been: the laird's son with his dead wife in his arms and his new betrothed riding alongside, and a strange warrior carrying the laird's granddaughter.

"I was turned over to a family in the village where a woman had recently given birth and had enough milk to spare. That was Robert's family. I lived with them until I was almost ten summers. I vaguely understood that they were not ma real kinand that the laird, for ma grandfather had passed by then, was ma true father. I was brought to the keep and told that I would be allowed to live there now. I was given a small chamber at the top of the family tower. I learned that I had two young half-brothers who I was expected care for. I quickly came to understand that ma father had agreed to marry Elizabeth Gunn because he didna care what happened to him. He was too grief stricken to consider what he was agreeing to. In turn, he was angry and bitter that he was forced into a marriage to the woman he believed allowed his beloved to die. Elizabeth was no more pleasant that he was. She ignored her sons except for when she wanted to manipulate ma father or me.

"I wasnae allowed in their presence except to receive instructions on what was expected of me. Elizabeth suffered through teaching me to read and write just a wee more than the basics. Once she believed I kenned enough to teach maself more, she abandoned me to a study she refused to heat. It was not until ma brothers were old enough to study there that a fire was finally lit during the winter.

"Ma father so rarely acknowledged me that I was stunned and scared to learn that he planned a marriage for me. I had assumed that I would never marry because I was not worth his time to arrange one. I didna ken to whom he planned to wed me. That is why I sought out Robert. I was scared but ye ken how that turned out. So ye can see, it isnae a pleasant and loving family like yers that I come from. I have a father and stepmother who canna stand one another and who despise me because I apparently look exactly like ma mother. I dinna need a marriage to make me feel unwanted and useless. I never needed to leave ma own clan for that. I willna have a marriage like the Laird and Lady Mackenzie which in now only in name. Laird Mackenzie openly seeks his pleasure any and everywhere but with his wife. I dinna need a new clan to be humiliated in front of."

Callum stood there and stared. He had no idea at all how to respond to all that Siùsan had just explained. She glared at him and turned away. She had not taken more than two steps before she felt a hand on her arm.

"Wait, lass." She heard his whispered voice and stilled. Despite her hurt and anger, she longed for him to comfort her after she shared her most painful secret. He gently turned her to face him again. He cupped her cheek and ran his thumb over her cheekbone. He leaned forward, but instead of kissing her on her lips, as Siùsan suddenly yearned for, he kissed her temple. Then her nose and each of her eyelids. He kissed each of her cheeks, and then finally brushed his lips against hers. He pulled back to look at her. Siùsan stood with her eyes closed, but the tears still leaked out. She reached up to brush them away, but Callum kissed them away instead. As he pressed his lips to hers, she tasted her own salty tears. He gently wrapped his arm around her and pulled her in for a hug. The kiss remained soft and gentle. It was not one of passion and desire but rather love and understanding.

"Siùsan, I should have told ye how I felt about ye long before now. I regret that I told ma da before I am telling ye." He tilted her chin up, but her eyes were still closed. "Look at me, mo chridhe. Ye are ma heart, and I love ye. I would pledge maself to ye here and now for all eternity if ye would have me. I have made a mess of our relationship from before ye even arrived. I have much to atone for, but I would spend every day of the rest of our lives together making up for it and showing ye that I speak only the truth. I want none other than ye. I love only ye."

"I love ye too, mo chridhe," Siùsan whispered. "But I am afraid to trust ye again. I never want to experience that type of pain again, that sense of loss and betrayal. I willna survie it."

"I gave ye ma word of honor that I would never stray and that I would be true unto ye. I ken it seems like I have dishonored maself and ma vow, but I swear to ye,

I truly do, that I was never going to couple with her or allow it to go any further. I was pushing her away when I heard ye."

She searched his eyes and saw her own pain mirrored in his gaze. He was hurting too. Their time apart had not lessened either of their feelings for the other or their pain at their separation. She took a deep breath and took his one good hand in both of hers.

"I believe ye, Callum. I dinna want to be apart from ye anymore."

"Will ye handfast with me now? Here? I would make ye ma wife. I ken ye have already agreed three times, so we are wed by consent, but I would pledge maself to ye. I want there to be nay doubt in yer mind that I want to be with ye as yer husband."

"Three times? We are wed?"

"Aye. The first was when ye agreed to come to me for our betrothal and wedding. The second was when we spoke our betrothal vows. The third was when we agreed to announce our wedding date."

"Ye are right. We are wed by consent," she marveled at the idea, "but I would like to pledge ma troth to ye now in a handfast."

"I will wed ye before a kirk and a priest as soon as we get back to Sinclair land."

Callum unpinned his plaid from his shoulder and pulled the extra material down. Siùsan understood what he meant to do so she helped him wrap their hands with the Sinclair plaid. When their hands were joined with entwined fingers and covered by his plaid, Callum looked into Siùsan's eyes and cleared his throat.

"In the presence of God and before His whole world, I promise to be a loving, faithful, and loyal husband to ye, for as long as we both shall live. With this I pledge ma troth."

"In the presence of God and before His whole world, I promise to be a loving, faithful, and loyal wife to ye, for as long as we both shall live. With this I pledge ma troth."

Callum pulled her in for a kiss. This was one was far from gentle. It was filled with passion and pent up desire. He was wed finally to the only woman he had ever considered marrying, and the woman that he desired above all others.

"I told ye they would make up." The sound of Magnus's booming voice broke the mood for the happy couple.

"I dinna disagree with ye. I kenned it all along. Only a mon in love would traipse through the rain for four days and then climb a bluidy tree only to fall from it. And only a lass as equally addled would jump from that tree to tend him when the eejit mon hurt himself." Travish grinned at them both. "Welcome to the family, lass. It's aboot time ye two sorted things out."

"Aye, well it took a moment, but we are handfasted now." Siùsan laughed along with her new brothers by marriage.

"We are married." Callum was quick to correct. He had no intention of ever having their union dissolved. "There will be no repudiating in a year and a day. Ye are mine for keeps."

"Just as ye are mine too. Aye?" Siùsan looked to Callum, and he vigorously nodded his head.

"Only yers."

Siùsan was about to repeat that promise when she could have sworn she heard something in the distance. She turned in the direction of the sound and noticed that the three Sinclairs were doing the same.

"Riders approach and fast." She murmured.

"Stay close to me, Siùsan. We will all go back to camp. Hopefully, all the men will be aware and gather there. I want ye well surrounded by the men."

The four of them hurried back to the camp and were greeted by the sounds of steel on steel. Tavish and Magnus charged into the fray. Callum understood his weakness and took up a defensive stance to protect Siùsan. The camp flooded with men coming from seemingly all directions. Callum had no choice but to engage. While he could fight with a sword in either hand, he counted himself lucky that it was his left arm and not his right that was injured. He fended off one man after another, but eventually three men began to encroach upon him and Siùsan. He angled himself so that she was sandwiched between him and a tree.

He sensed more than saw that she moved. Then he heard a distinctly male bellow of pain. He could not afford to take his eyes off the men in front of him. One of them lunged forward and engaged Callum. They thrusted and parried as Callum tried to keep Siùsan protected behind him. He locked swords with the man on the left and as he shoved his weight forward, the man to the right surged forward to gut him. A flash of red darted in front of him. He thought he would wet himself as he watched Siùsan plunge a sgain dubh, a tiny but incredibly sharp knife, into the man's throat.

Callum regained his focus and finished off the other man. Once again, he caught motion to the right of him. He turned as he heard the sound of rending material. Siùsan rapidly pulled and threw one knife after another at the attacking men. Callum watched in awe as Siùsan dispatched man after man by sinking her dirks into their necks, throats, eyes, or between their shoulders. She ran forward and launched her last dirk at a man battling Tavish. The dirk sliced into the side of the man's throat and lodged itself there with its tip coming out of the other side.

As their opponents mysteriously began to fall with dirks protruding from them, the Sinclair warriors had each turned to see where the knives were coming from. As a one, they were shocked to see Siùsan throwing them with ease and precision. When the skirmish was over, Callum moved to Siùsan's side.

"I want to yell at ye for once again giving me such a fright, but I am too in awe of how ye handle those dirks. I didna ken ye carried so many." He had watched her go through the ones that were sewn into her arisaid and then pull more from the inside and outside of each of her boots.

"I dinna usually carry so many, but since I was travelling alone, I was sure to have them all on me." She shrugged impassively.

Tavish moved forward and returned a now wiped off blade to her. He paused to look at the blade and then her before handing it over.

"Where did ye learn such skill, ma lady?" One of the warriors called out.

"I amnae particularly close to much of ma kin, but I am vera close to ma brothers. I have taken care of them both for much of their lives. As they have grown older and bigger, they have insisted upon taking care of me too. They taught me how to handle a dirk and how to throw one with the intent to kill. They kenned that I often went into the woods on ma own as I didna have a guard. They didna want me to come across someone or something and not be able to defend maself. I think they worried most that I would encounter a wolf or boar." Siùsan shrugged her shoulders and looked at the men, most of which stood with their mouths hanging open.

"She's just like our Mairghread," Tavish said with a grin.

"Do any of ye need tending? Are ye wounded?" She looked around the group but they all shook their heads.

"Ma lady, ye didna give them the time to do us any real harm. Thank ye." Another one of the warriors said.

Siùsan simply nodded her head. She turned back to find Callum and smacked her face into his chest. She had not known he was quite so close.

He pulled her in and pressed her head to his chest. She could feel his heart was still beating wildly. She ran her hands over his chest and rested them next to her cheek. She turned and kissed the skin that was visible at the opening of his leine.

"I am well. I promise."

"I ken it, but that doesnae mean I dinna worry." He held her there for a long while as the men moved about the camp and straightened up.

Eventually, Siùsan pulled back. She did not want to move from his embrace, but she knew that he needed rest. She guided him back to the tree that had protected their backs. She pressed him to sit down. She then pulled her hair back and wrapped it into a tight roll and knotted it. She took her now clean sgian dubh and cut a large square from her chemise. Callum watched her in confusion until he saw her tie the square over her hair. She had improvised and made a kertch, a traditional head covering for married women. She noticed him watching her and she shrugged.

"I am a married woman now. It isnae proper for me to go around with ma head uncovered. Besides, I havenae a ring to wear yet, so how else will others ken that I am wed."

"They will ken because yer braw husband willna ever be far from yer side." He reached up and tugged her hand causing her to fall into his lap. She tried to break her fall to avoid bumping into his broken arm and shoulder.

"I would say I willane break so easily but apparently I do. I would have ye sit with me for a bit. I just want to feel ye in ma arms to ken it's really true that I have ye back and ye are ma wife." Siùsan was happy to indulge him, but their moment was cut short all too soon.

"Lord Callum, I found this one trying to slink away into the woods while I went to take a pish. Begging yer pardon, ma lady." The warrior shoved a man forward as Tavish and Magnus came to join them.

Siùsan scrambled out of Callum's lap, and he could practically see her hackles rise. He would swear that she hissed.

"James Gunn, what are ye doing here? Was it ye and yer men who attacked?"

"Gunn?" All three of the Sinclair brothers said at once.

"Aye. This mon is James Gunn, the younger brother of both Laird Gunn and ma stepmother."

"Arenae ye going to give yer uncle a hug, ma wee Siùsan?" The syrupy sound of his voice made Siùsan want to vomit and had Callum reaching to encircle the man's throat with his hand.

"Who are ye to be speaking to ma wife in such a way? That doesnae sound like how any uncle of mine would speak to ma sister."

"Ye ken we arenae blood relatives. Nay. Siùsan was meant to be ma bride years ago, werenae ye, ma love?

"Ye may have been angling for that, but the one and only thing ma father has ever done to protect me was to refuse yer request. He believed it would push the bounds of consanguinity. We might not be truly related by blood, but as the brother of ma stepmother, ma father believed the familial relationship was entirely too close to incestuous. I agreed."

"I could have taken ye away from yer disinterested father and bitter stepmother. I could have given ye all that ye wanted years ago. Instead, ye let yer father sell ye to the Sinclairs. Just what was the bride price? Or was ye father finally willing to give ye away simply to be rid of ye?"

James Gunn's words were entirely too close to the truth for Siùsan's comfort. She stepped forward and stopped in front of the man who had tormented her as a young woman. She looked him up and down and sneered. Then she lifted her foot and thrust her knee into his groin.

"Be glad I am forgiving enough not to cut off yer cods because I have dreamt of it for years."

She stormed off towards the steam.

"Tie him up and gag him if ye must. He will be a guest in our dungeons until we can ransom him back to his brother. Dinna hesitate to do what ye must to get him to cooperate." Callum called over his shoulder as he followed Siùsan to the water.

Chapter Nineteen

Siùsan knew that Callum was following her, but she appreciated that he gave her some distance. When she reached the edge of the water, she shucked off her boots and stockings. She tucked the hem of her kirtle into the belt at her waist and waded in. The cool water around her ankles and calves helped to calm her. When she finally felt settled enough after the shock of the battle and then finding out James Gunn was responsible for the attack, she turned to Callum. He was resting his good shoulder against a tree and was watching her.

"Did ye notice that he never did answer why he and his men attacked? We all ken it was him as the attackers did naught to hide their plaids even before he was caught."

The Clan Gunn plaid was unique to them just as the pattern was for any other clan in the area. The pattern of the Sinclair and Sutherland plaids were similar but where the Sutherland had white running through theirs, the Sinclairs had red in the corresponding place. The Mackays were distinctly blue, yellow, and green. There was never any confusing them. The Gunns used both light and dark blue shot through with red and green. It was obvious that the men who attacked them were Gunns but what neither Callum nor Siùsan could understand was why.

"I ken we must be on their land but why attack? I dinna believe I have heard that ye are feuding or even dinna get along. I had tried so hard to skirt their land and stay on yers until I could reach MacKay lands." Siùsan shook her head. The guilt of being the cause of Callum's injury along with endangering so many men who had spent four miserable days searching for her finally caught up to her. Her shoulders sagged, and she bowed her head. Callum watched as Siùsan's shoulders began to shake. He pushed off of the tree and marched into the stream. He stepped around her and bent at the waist. He hoisted her over his shoulder and a carried her onto the grass beside the bank of the stream.

"I ken that isnae the most romantic way to carry ye, but it is the best that I can do for now." He gently set her on her feet and sat down. He patted the grass beside him, and she sat down. He wrapped his arm around her shoulder and pulled her to his chest.

"Cry, mo ghaol. Ye have earned it as I suspect ye have been holding in yer lifetime of pain. Cry and let mine be the shoulder ye lean upon, wife." He kissed the top of her head and felt her arms tentatively wrap around him. She was so careful not to jostle or jar him. He could not help but smile. Even in her own misery, she was still thinking of others. He rocked her ever so slightly and whispered ridiculous endearments into her ear as she sobbed. When her tears finally ran dry, she looked up at the man she had married that day and knew that she had made the right choice. She was still hurt and angry, but it was not as fierce as before and most of it was directed at Elizabeth.

"I canna stand that name," she muttered.

"What name is that? What are ye thinking aboot?"

"I was thinking that I amnae as angry and hurt by ye as I was before. I dinna quite feel right yet, but much of ma anger is directed at Elizabeth. That made me think about the other Elizabeth in ma life, ma stepmother. She is an unkind and harsh woman. She made ma life hell with her attention. I truly dinna ken which was worse, ma father ignoring me and wishing I had died instead of ma mother or Elizabeth's constant attempts to punish ma existence that only served as a reminder that ma father chose Rose MacLeod in both life and death."

"Ye dinna need to have either Elizabeth in yer life from now on. I will see to it. Come now. Ye must be hungry. I am sure the men who went hunting are back by now."

"I am rather hungry, but I ate well enough the last few days. Since I didna make camp at night, I was able to build a fire without worrying about ye or anyone else spotting the smoke. I hunted and cooked each day. I ate berries when I found them and even a few apples."

"Ye dinna make camp at night?"

"Nay. I slept in trees during the day and travelled at night. I didna want anyone to see me, and I figured I was less likely to be spotted by ye or any lawless men."

"Ye seem quite well equipped to take care of yerself. Perhaps ye dinna need me after all." Callum joked, but Siùsan stopped short.

"I do need ye. More than I realized or wanted to admit until I thought I was going to have to make a life for maself without ye in a new place."

"New place? Were ye not going back to Mackenzie land?"

"Nay. I never want to go back there again. I was going to the MacLeods. To ma mother's people." Siùsan began to walk again and Callum followed, but he was taken aback to realize just how far Siùsan was willing to travel alone to get away from both him and her family.

She would have rather travelled the width of Scotland to escape me than stay. She was going to rely on kinship to find a place in an unknown clan. What would have happened to her if they refused her? Where would she have gone to next? How would she have supported herself? Callum's thoughts began to run dark as there were few options available to unprotected women who needed to support themselves. Siùsan might be able to find work as a healer or in a tavern, but a single woman was almost certainly going to be pushed into prostitution at some point. He watched as she greeted his brothers and his men. She moved to the side and spread her arisaid on the ground. She accepted the rabbit that was offered to her. It was still steaming hot. She blew on it and looked around. When her eyes landed on him, her face lit up, and she waved him over. Callum was relieved to see that she was back to being pleased with his company. He moved to her side and sat down. They shared the rabbit together and listened quietly to the talk that surrounded them. They were both lost in their own thoughts.

Will he truly make me his wife tonight? Is he too badly hurt and I should leave him alone?

Will she accept ma attentions tonight and can I even manage it?

Chapter Twenty

*A*s the men began to settle in for the night, Callum looked at Siùsan. He sensed her tension but was not sure if it was excitement or dread.

"Siùsan, would ye like to walk to the stream once more? Ye can see to yer needs."

Siùsan looked down at the plaid they sat upon. Then she looked at Callum and nodded. They stood and moved towards the stream. Callum brushed his fingers against hers. When she did not pull away, Callum took her hand. Siùsan entwined her fingers with Callum's. Reassured, Callum squeezed her hand and felt her calm. Callum, on the other hand, felt nervous even though they had shared intimacies before. As they approached the bank, Callum brought them to a stop. He turned to look at Siùsan and saw the question in her eyes. He smiled down at her and relaxed.

"I would make ye ma wife in truth this vera night, but if ye would rather wait until we return home and to our chamber, I understand."

"Home. I rather like the sound of that. I spent ma entire life on Mackenzie land but never belonged. I do feel at home on Sinclair land."

Callum tried to hide his disappointment. His physical desire to join with Siùsan was ever present, but after learning completely of her past, he longed for an emotional connection. One he had never considered before during the act of coupling. He swallowed and smiled again. He was just about to reassure Siùsan of her choice when she spoke again.

"I ken why Sinclair land feels like home. It's where I met ye. Home is not really the land or the keep. Home is with ye. When I ran away, I felt lost and unsettled even though I kenned where I wanted to go. Being here with ye now, I dinna feel that way. I dinna feel lost anymore. I ken it's because of ye. Because I love ye. I would be yer wife in truth and not just in name." Siùsan chewed on her lower lip for a moment. "I just dinna ken how to do that without hurting ye more."

"Lass, ye ken there is more than one position for people to couple."

A shadow passed over Siùsan's face. Callum knew she was thinking about how he had gained such knowledge.

"Siùsan, look at me."

He tilted her chin up with his finger and thumb, but she would not look him in the eye.

"Siùsan, please. Look at me." She slowly looked up and saw the pleading in his eyes. "I ken ma past has already hurt ye many times, but I canna change it. We both ken there have been others before ye, but I have never told another woman that I love her. That means that I have never made love before. That is something that is for ye only."

"But is there really any difference but a name?"

"There most certainly is. It has only been about physical pleasure in the past. I never had any real feelings tied to the act other than a want of release and entertainment."

Callum tucked the hair behind Siùsan's ear and stroked her cheek with his knuckles.

"With ye, I want to give ye everything. Ma body doesnae seem enough. I want to give ye ma heart. I feel like ye're a part of ma soul. I want to feel as though we are one and not just because our bodies are joined. Ye are as much ma home as I am yers. I would share that with only ye."

Siùsan was moved by Callum's words. Only hours ago, she might have thought he said those words to convince her to return with him for the sake of his pride, but she did not think he could fake the reverence she heard in his voice or saw in his eyes.

She stepped back from him and saw the immediate flash of pain. *He thinks I'm rejecting him. He couldnae be more wrong.*

She undid the belt that held her arisaid. She folded it neatly and then tossed it off to the side.

"I dinna ever need that plaid again as I am nay longer a Mackenzie." She reached up to unpin Callum's broach. She dropped it into his sporran. She undid his belt next. She caught his giant plaid in her hands. She had never really considered just how massive it was, but Callum was unusually tall, so it was at least two yards longer than typical.

"Ye ken yer men will all ken what we've been up to when ye walk back to camp in just yer leine. I claim this one as mine. It smells like ye." She held the material up to her nose and smiled. Callum almost swallowed his tongue. He knew she had no idea just how seductive she looked.

"I would see ye wrapped in just ma plaid," he whispered.

"I would see me wrapped in just ye." Her cheeks turned pink at her own brazen statement. Callum had learned quickly upon getting to know her that Siùsan had an unbridled passion, but she kept it well hidden from everyone but him. He reveled in that secret knowledge.

Callum yanked the plaid from her and laid it on the ground. He reached down and tugged on his boot laces. He hopped from one foot to the other as he tried to toe off his boots as he pulled his leine over his head. Siùsan could not help but giggle.

Once Callum stood naked before her, she unpinned her makeshift kertch and let down her hair. She pulled it to the side and presented her back to Callum. She looked over her shoulder to see if he would accept his invitation. His hand was already reaching for her laces.

Callum's impatience to touch his wife was so great that he almost tore the laces to Siùsan's kirtle. As he pulled them loose, he forced himself to breathe and slow down. Even though they had already done much together, he reminded himself that she was still an innocent. He did not want to scare her as he already worried about hurting her when he took her maidenhead.

Siùsan sensed Callum slowing down and raised an eyebrow in question.

"There isnae aught reason to rush. We have a lifetime together." He learned forward to kiss her shoulder but could not help but laugh when he heard Siùsan growl softly.

She pulled on her sleeves and allowed the gown to pool around her feet.

"Ye might nae be in a hurry but I dinna feel the same. I have spent all evening worrying that ye dinna want to touch me."

"Dinna want to touch ye?" Callum really did laugh now. "When have I ever not wanted to touch ye?" He kissed her shoulder again.

"Ye didna make any move to touch me while we sat by the fire. Then ye made it sound as though ye were only going to have us settle down for the night by the fire. I thought mayhap ye'd changed yer mind about being married to me."

He pulled her back into his embrace and wrapped his good arm around her. She did not lean back all the way to protect his arm in the sling, but her backside rubbed against his cock. He rocked his hips into her.

"Do ye have any doubt now?"

"Nay," she whispered.

He ran his hand up and down her arm as he feathered kisses across her shoulders. He gently turned her to face him. He pulled the ribbons loose that held her chemise in place. It glided to the ground like a feather caught in the wind. Siùsan stepped out of the chemise and gown. She bent to untie her boots but Callum caught her hand and shook his head. He took her hand and kneeled. She followed him onto the plaid. He gently lowered her to the ground. He kissed a warm path from her knee to her ankle as he undid one then the other boot. Siùsan watched the ripples in his back muscles as he moved. She could not help herself and sat up, so she could reach out to run her hands over the hard muscles of his shoulders. She felt him shudder at her touch. He turned to look at her. The hunger in his eyes took her breath away. *Mayhap I willane have to wait so long after all. He wants this as much as I do.*

She almost moaned aloud when he stretched out beside her favoring his injured shoulder and arm. She rolled onto her side to face him. He slid his good arm beneath her and wrapped it around her side. He drew lazy circles on the small of her back and then cupped her backside. He danced his fingers along the divide of her buttocks. He had never attempted to touch her there before. He was curious to see her reaction. As always, he was not disappointed by her own curiosity. She looked up at him as she threw her top leg over his top hip. This gave him more access to everything he wanted. He ran his fingers between the cheeks of her backside and grazed her most sacred of places. She drew in a sharp breath but let it out just as quickly when she felt his tongue on her nipple. She had not even realized that she had closed her eyes. She looked down to see Callum's head bent over her breast as he took as much into his mouth as he could. His fingers slid through the wetness of her seam. He thrust three fingers into her as he suckled hard on her breast.

Siùsan moaned loudly and rocked her hips. She wanted to grab his shoulder for purchase but was careful not to press on his injury. Instead, she fit her hand in the groove of his hip. She had come to learn that this was one of her favorite places on his body.

She waited until Callum lifted his mouth to shift to her other breast. She caught his hair in her hand and gently pulled his head back. She brought their mouths together in a fierce tangle of tongues. She shifted her weight and nudged Callum onto his back. She looked at him as she tried to figure out how to maneuver their positions.

"Straddle me, mo ghaol, just like ye did on the chair in the study." Siùsan immediately remembered their interlude in the laird's study when Robert had come to visit.

She carefully swung one leg over him and as she slowly lowered herself down, she felt the tip of his rod poke at her entrance. She looked up at Callum to see what he wanted her to do.

"Ease yerself onto me. Let yer body get used to the feel of me inside ye." Those were the most erotic words Siùsan had ever heard. She felt her body adjust to the feeling of Callum inside of her. He felt so incredibly large and long that she was not sure that her body could take all of him in. "I will fit, lass. I promise."

Siùsan looked up when Callum seemed to read her thoughts. She felt him press against a barrier inside of her. She knew that was her maidenhead. She took a deep breath, looked into Callum's eyes, and nodded her head. He thrust his hips up as she dropped her weight onto him. The searing pain that shot through her was unlike anything she had every felt before. She could not seem to catch her breath and her eyes watered. *He is too large. He doesnae fit. How can this feel so horrible when everything else feels so good?* She whimpered softly.

Callum sat up and pulled her head into the crook of his neck. He ran his hand up and down her back and damned his injury for taking away the use of one of his hands. He kissed her hair and slid his hand between them. He felt for her pleasure button and began to rub it in gentle but firm circles.

"It will get better, I promise ye. I ken it hurts now, but the pain will ease then I will bring ye pleasure. I am sorry that I hurt ye. It willna ever hurt again." Callum covered her cheeks in kisses as he continued to stroke her. "Rock yer hips, Siùsan. Adjust until ye are comfortable. I willna move until ye're ready." *Even if it kills me.*

Siùsan slowly shifted her weight against him. The pain had already begun to ease and the feel of Callum's finger against her was beginning to make her ache for release. Now, the feel of Callum deep inside of her made her want to explore what more he could do to her. She rocked her hips as he suggested and was rewarded by his deep groan. She cupped his face in her hands and pressed her lips to his softly. She ran her tongue around the outline of his lips and then pressed into his mouth. She used her tongue to draw his into her mouth. When he obliged, she began to softly suck on it. As she played with his tongue, she circled her hips a couple of times. She was beginning to understand what the fuss was all about. She was fully aroused again and wanted to move faster.

"Callum, please move now. I need it."

"What do ye need, Siùsan? Tell me." He wrapped his good arm around her and pressed his hips up into her and he pulled her down onto his cock.

"I dinna ken. I dinna ken. I just need more of this, of ye."

"Ye do ken, mo chridhe. Just let go and tell me how to please ye."

Siùsan tried lifting her hips up slightly and then lowering herself. She felt Callum press so deeply into her that she thought he might touch her heart. She wanted more, and she wanted it faster.

"More, Callum. I want to move faster, and I want ye to move harder. Show me how much ye want to be inside me. Show me that I am the only one ye want."

That was all the invitation that Callum needed. He tightened his hold on Siùsan and flipped them around so that she was on the bottom. He rested his entire weight on one forearm. Siùsan marveled at the strength of Callum as he began to move inside her with fervor.

"Siùsan, I want ye more than anything I have ever desired before. Ye feel better than I could have possibly imagined. Ye're so tight I feel like I am going to explode but I dinna want this to end. I want to make love to ye all night and every night for the rest of ma life. God, lass, I want ye." Callum began to move harder and faster. Siùsan moaned as she pressed her feet into the ground to lift her hips to match each of his thrusts.

"I ken what the fuss is about now. Callum, ye willna break me. Harder, please. Just harder."

Callum could barely breathe when he heard Siùsan repeat her request for him to move harder. His hips pounded into her. He knew she would be incredibly sore in the morning from the rough way he was taking her, but he could not bring himself to stop. He had never, ever wanted to be inside of a woman more than he did with Siùsan. He wanted to find his release and pour his seed into her. He would truly claim her as his when his seed took. He prayed it would be soon. They had bound themselves to each other in word and in deed, but he would have them start their own family as a tie that bound them together forever. *I have never wanted to get a woman with child before. Just the opposite. I have made sure that never happens. Why now? Cause I love her more than ma own life.*

Callum leaned forward to catch Siùsan's lips in a possessive and powerful kiss. He thrust again and again praying that she would find her release soon because he was not sure how much longer he could wait. He felt her inner walls begin to tighten around his throbbing cock. He felt the tingle at the base of his spine. Siùsan arched her back off the plaid and then dropped back as she wrapped her legs around his waist and clung to him.

Siùsan felt her whole body burst into flames as her release took over. It started as a soft clenching in the bottom of her belly and the wave grew until it spread through her. Her nipples tightened, her legs clenched, and she squeezed her sheath as tightly as she could around Callum's cock.

Callum felt Siùsan's release and how she squeezed his rod. He could not stop his seed from shooting forth. The pressure of Siùsan squeezing him was too much. He ground his hips into her as he kept coming. It was the single greatest release he had ever felt. He could not believe how it seemed to go on forever. He did not think he had that much seed in him. He was sure that she had drained every last drop.

He dropped his forehead to rest against hers. Their sweaty bodies did not feel the cool breeze that blew around them. Their hearts pounded as they both tried to catch their breath.

"I havenae ever felt anything like that before. Good God, woman, ye will be the death of me. But what a blessed way to go."

Siùsan smiled as she looked up at her husband. *Ma husband. He really and truly is ma husband, and I am his wife.* She brushed the hair back from his forehead and strained to kiss his cheek.

"Callum, I understand now. I understand what all the women whisper about. I understand why maidens are kept in the dark about the pleasures of the flesh. I understand what it means to make love. That is what we did, isnae it?"

"Aye, Siùsan. That was more than anything I have ever done before. I have never felt so connected with any other soul than I did as I made love to ye. I willna ever let ye go. Ye are ma wife in truth now. I love ye more than anything."

Callum gently rolled them onto their sides. Siùsan was not ready for the connection to end. She threw her leg over his hip once more. Callum stroked her cheek as he looked into her eyes.

"Ye have bewitched me, Siùsan. I didna want a wife only a short while ago, but now I cannae imagine ma life without ye. Ye have made me want to be better for ye, for ma family, and for ma clan. I realize now that I was incredibly selfish before I met ye. It is a good thing ma da is so hale and healthy because I was not ready to lead a clan because I didna really ken how to put anyone else ahead of me. I would do anything to protect ye and to make ye happy. I ken now that loving ye has finally made me into a mon."

"I was so terrified that ye would reject me. Then kenning that ye didna want a wife from the moment I arrived hurt so much. I had been rejected all of ma life and to face it once again nearly broke me. I so desperately wanted to believe ye when ye came to me in the stables, but I was scared to trust ye completely. I didna ken ye yet, but over the past sennights ye have proven to me that ye are the mon I want. I fell in love ye, but I didna think ye could love me when ye had other, better choices. I ran not just out of hurt from what I saw but out of hurt that I believed I wasnae good enough to keep ye. Ye came after me. Ye didna let me go. Ye protected me. Ye wed me by yer choice and made love to me. I want to be yer wife more than anything."

"Siùsan, ye must understand and believe that there isnae any better choice for me than ye. Ye are ma only choice." He kissed her softly and then gave her a crooked grin. "I must be sure to thank Da for once again kenning what was good for me."

They lay in one another's arms for a long time simply looking at one another and running their hands over any part they could reach. As the moon moved higher in the sky, the air began to chill more. When Siùsan shivered slightly, Callum knew he needed to move them back to camp and close to the fire. He did not want Siùsan to get sick.

"Mo neach beag," Callum nudged her gently, and Siùsan smiled as she came fully awake to hearing Callum call her his little one. She realized that she cherished his terms of affection for her. She wanted to use them for him too. She had been nervous and was not sure of his sincerity at first. Now she knew that he truly did use them out of love. She felt more secure in the notion of using a pet name for him.

"I am awake, mo ghaisgeach." She looked up to see Callum's chest puff out, and he stuck his hand out to help her up. He seemed quite proud that she thought of him as her warrior.

"I will strive to never disappoint ye again, Siùsan." He said as he pulled her into his embrace. He realized that besides making love to his wife, holding her in his arms was his favorite thing to do.

"I ken," she whispered as she kissed his bare chest. She looked up at him earnestly. "And I willane ever run from ye again when we have a problem." He kissed the top of her head. They stepped apart and began to redress themselves. Callum bent to pick up his plaid, but Siùsan was faster than he was. She scooped it up, folded it in half, and wrapped it around herself.

"I already told ye it is mine." She grinned as she grabbed her boots and darted towards camp. Callum grabbed his boots and chased after her. His shoulder ached as he ran, but he was not to be outdone. He caught her in a few long strides and dropped his boots as he lifted her off her feet from behind. Siùsan squealed softly, and Callum lowered her feet to the ground. She spun around and kissed him soundly.

"Keep that up, and we willna make it back to camp. I will toss yer skirts up and take ye right here."

"Do ye promise?" Siùsan looked thoughtful as her eyes scanned the area. She spotted a large oak tree nearby that had a smooth trunk. She ran to the tree and turned around to look at Callum. He watched her like a predator. She tugged at her laces enough to pull the neckline of her gown loose. She pulled it and her chemise down enough to bare her breasts to him. She watched Callum and was sure that she saw him lick his lips. She cupped her breasts together in her hands and offered them to him. He scooped up his boots and ran towards her. She nearly had the wind knocked out of her as he crashed into her. He took a breast into his mouth and suckled hard to the point of almost pain. He grabbed the material of her kirtle and began to bunch it up in his hand as he raised it. Siùsan caught the bottom of his leine and lifted it above his waist. She wrapped her hand around his shaft and stroked him. He gave a feral growl as he hooked her leg around his waist.

"I warned ye." He breathed as he thrust into her. This was no soft and gentle melding of two souls. It was primal and base. Siùsan dug her nails in to his good shoulder as she used her other hand to press his head into her breast harder. He bit her nipple and thrust hard. It was all Siùsan could do to keep from banging her head against the trunk as he pressed her harder and harder against it. He lifted his head and looked down at her. The gleam in his eyes matched her. He sensed that she liked this wild side and craved it as much as she did his gentle caresses and soft words. She moaned loudly, and he captured her sounds with his mouth. They were close enough to camp that he worried his men really would hear them. He would not have cared if it had been Elizabeth or a tavern wench. In fact, he would have relished his men hearing him bring a woman pleasure, but this was his wife. He would never dishonor her, and he was not about to share such private pleasure with anyone else.

When they both needed to breathe, he lifted his mouth slightly from hers.

"Yes," she whispered. "More, Callum. Dinna stop. I'm so close. Harder, harder."

"Yer wish is ma command." He thrust over and over. He felt himself lose control as he sank into her warm, wet, tight sheath time and again. Siùsan went rigid and squeezed him as she came. He thrust twice more and exploded. He did not understand how his release could be so strong, almost violent, after having made love only a short while ago. He thought he had drained himself the first time he came inside of her, but he once again poured himself into her.

Siùsan clung to Callum as she was not sure that her legs could support her. She looked up at him in awe. They had made love the first time they joined, but what they had just done was unlike anything that she could have imagine. It was not soft and tender as the first time. They had moved hard against each other as they lay on the ground, but it had been a melding of their souls but this...This had been a primal need to bind themselves to each other.

Callum looked at Siùsan and feared that he had hurt her. He could not believe how nearly violent their coupling had been. *I just fucked ma wife. I fucked her like a whore, and it was only her second time coupling. What have I done?* His remorse for once again being so selfish almost overcame him. He wanted to apologize but did not know how without offending her.

Siùsan smiled to herself as she thought back on what had just happened. *He really does desire me. It is not just me being available to slake his lust. He canna control himself any more than I can.* Siùsan joy was short lived when she looked up and saw the horror and regret on Callum's face. She immediately felt ashamed for teasing him and acting so wanton.

"I am sorry. I willna act so shamefully again." She whispered as she pushed past him. She quickly pulled her gown back into place and pulled the laces tight again. She had dropped the plaid as she righted her kirtle. She opened it wide and wrapped it completely around her. She covered her head as she was not sure where she had left her kertch. She spotted her boots and picked those up too. She looked over her shoulder at Callum and saw him standing there dumbfounded and befuddled. She paused. His expressions were highly confusing to her. One moment he looked disgusted at her and the next he seemed unsure of himself.

Callum realized that Siùsan blamed herself for what had just happened. He spurred himself into motion. He ripped his broken arm from the sling and almost howled in pain as he moved his shoulder, but nothing was going to keep him from properly holding his wife. He watched the shock on Siùsan's face as he reached both arms out to her. He pulled her tightly against him and would not let her go when she tried to ease away from his battered shoulder.

"Nay. I amnae letting ye go until ye understand ma reaction. It wasnae anything ye did. I love yer playfulness and yer desire for me. I am just truly sorry for treating ye so roughly. I didna show ye the respect that is due ma wife."

"I dinna understand. Didna ye like what we just did? I thought ye enjoyed it. Ye seemed to." Siùsan trailed off. She was swallowing back tears. She had just had the two most physically astonishing experiences of her life. She had thought they were closer than ever, but her husband seemed to regret it all.

"Leannan, that is the problem. I liked it far too much. I was much too rough with ye. It was only yer second time. I was not gentle the first time and now this time I-"

He could not bring himself to use such a dirty word as fuck in front of his wife. He wished he knew what to say to reassure her that she had done nothing wrong.

"Callum, I dinna understand at all. One moment ye seemed to be so enjoying what we were doing and now ye regret it. I dinna understand what I did wrong. Why do ye regret making love to me again?"

"Because I didna make love to ye!" He nearly yelled with exasperation. He saw the confusion in Siùsan's eyes. Behind that was a deep hurt, and he realized that she thought he was rejecting her once again. She did not have the experience to understand the different ways that a couple could come together. He knew that he had to be honest. "Siùsan, I love ye, and we shared something strong and passionate, but I wouldnae call what we did making love. I fucked ye. I fucked ma wife." Callum hung his head in shame and shook it. "I treated ye no better than a whore. I took ye against a tree, damn it. I wanted only to stick ma cock in ye until I came. I wanted to make ye come as hard as I could. I wanted to toss yer skirts and tup ye until neither of us could see straight. I fucked ye." He finished on a whisper. He could not bring himself to look at Siùsan.

Needless to say, the sound of her laughter and the shaking of her body came as a shock. His head jerked up as he looked at her.

"That's what upset ye so much? Ye thought ye'd mistreated me. What if I told ye I liked that as much as what we did the first time? What if I told ye I hope ye fuck me again and again just as much as I want to make love to ye for the rest of our lives? What if I told ye that I want to fuck again right now since I enjoyed it so much? I dinna want to be treated like some cold noblewoman whose husband does his duty by her and then seeks his pleasure elsewhere, seeks to fuck someone else."

Callum could not believe his ears. He stared in shock at Siùsan. He was not sure what stunned him more, her repeated use of such a crass word or that she wanted to repeat their coupling over and over. She wanted to do it again right now. He shook his head to clear his mind and looked at her. She stood there grinning like the cat that got into the cream.

"Ye really arenae bothered by how I just took ye?" He found he was rather awestruck by his little wife who barely came to the center of his chest. He thought he should treat her only with delicacy and reverence now that they were wed. Apparently, she did not mind that but wanted it rough just as much.

"I wasnae bothered until ye pulled away. I felt ashamed of being so brazen and taunting ye. I thought ye thought I was acting like a whore."

"And I was afraid ye would think I had treated ye like a whore."

"Ma braw mon, cannae we have it both ways? Making love and tupping?"

"Aye. That we can. We can do it anyway that we want. What we do is between us. As long as ye are enjoying it, we can do it however we desire. If ye dinna like something, ye have only to tell me, and we will stop."

"Vera well, but I havenae disliked anything we have done yet." Siùsan's cheeks turned a dark red, but she forced herself to look up at Callum before she whispered, "Can we do it again like I said? Or is it too soon?"

Callum's cock went from partially aroused to rock hard in the beat of his heart. He could not comprehend how he was ready to go yet again after the last two times. Even in his green youth, when he first discovered his hand and then women, he had not been able to go so many rounds so quickly and so hard. He was ready to thrust into her when he finally came to his senses.

"Leannan, ye are going to be vera sore tomorrow. We have a long ride ahead of us, and I have used ye too roughly tonight. I fear that ye will be in a great deal of pain tomorrow."

"If I am going to be sore anyway, what does it matter if we do it once more?" She cocked one eyebrow.

"I wouldnae make it worse for ye."

"Will ye make time to bring me to the stream to bathe in the morning? I imagine the cool water will do wonders for me."

"Of course. If that would make ye feel better, I will take ye there."

"Then it is settled. We have a solution to ma soreness, so let us not wait any longer." If he had not been aroused again, he might have marveled at her practicality. Siùsan crossed her arms which thrust her breasts up and almost over the neckline of her gown. Callum could not take his eyes off them. He knew how full and round they were from when he balanced them in his hands and his mouth devoured them. "Once when I stumbled upon a maid and guardsman in the passageway near the storerooms, I saw them coupling. I hadnae understood what they were doing at the time as she wasna facing him. Now I think I ken. He was behind her and had her skirts lifted. I could see his plaid was gathered between them. I saw much the same with Robert and the maid." Siùsan paused to take a breath before plunging on. "Is that something we can try? Is that a way that ye like it?" She hated being reminded that Callum had been with other women, but she was curious, and she was committed to keeping him to herself alone.

Callum moved slowly towards her. He nodded his head. Siùsan turned around and pulled her skirts up to present her backside to him. Callum pulled his leine up and fisted his cock. Siùsan looked over her shoulder and swallowed hard as she watched him stroke himself. She reached forward and ran her fingers through her wet seam. Callum nodded his head as he watched her. He moved behind her. He caught her hand and lifted her fingers to his mouth. He licked each finger then sucked them into his mouth.

"The sweetest honey I have ever tasted." He took his cock in his hand and rubbed it between her bottom cheeks. "Lass, do ye ken how some men couple with a woman to avoid bairns and the pox?" She shook her head. "A mon can take a woman here." He pressed the tip of his cock against her tight rosebud. "This is how I avoided siring any bastards. Ye are the only woman I ever spilled inside."

"Did ye enjoy taking women that way? Is that how--" She was not sure that she could bring herself to mention another woman while they were being so intimate, but she had to know. "Is that how ye used to take Elizabeth? Did ye only couple with her this way?"

Callum stiffened and paused. She had asked an honest question, and she deserved an honest answer. He took a deep breath before responding.

"I took her this way most of the time. She accepted that I wouldnae risk having a bastard. I did couple with her in the more traditional way but always pulled out the moment I felt ma release coming." Siùsan looked over her shoulder at Callum, but he could not meet her gaze.

"Do ye want to take me that way? Not because ye fear siring a bastard or to avoid disease but because ye like how it feels?"

Callum could not believe his ears. This night had taught him a great deal about his wife's personality. She had always been far more adventurous in their love play than he could have ever imagined, even from their very first day together on the beach. In general, he realized, she was curious and adventurous, strong willed and stubborn. Her timidity came only when she felt vulnerable to rejection. Now, she seemed to also be very accepting of how men and women could come together. He risked looking up at her and saw that she genuinely wanted to know and seemed eager for his answer.

"Aye, one day." He choked out. He watched her nod her head and then she turned away. She bent forward and pulled her bottom cheeks apart, presenting the dark rosebud to him. When he made no move to enter her, she wiggled her hips from side to side. Callum was still stroking himself, he noticed, and watching her present herself to him made him curse in his head, but he would not take her that way tonight. She most definitely was not ready for that.

"I willna tup ye that way tonight, Siùsan. Ye areane ready for that, and I would use oil to make it easier and less painful the first time." He stepped closer and nudged his tip into her wet folds. "I will take ye this way though." He slid all the way into her and wrapped his good arm around her. The feel of her body sucking him into her hot, smooth depths made him forget about the throbbing in his broken arm. She moaned as he filled her to his hilt. He paused and let her adjust to yet a new position and new sensations. She pushed her hips back against him and wiggled them again. Callum growled and eased almost all the way out of her. He pushed gently into her, aware that she was probably already feeling sore from their last two joinings.

Siùsan was not in the mood to wait. She had waited her entire life to find someone who would care about her and want her for herself. She had waited weeks for Callum to realize her value to him, and he had awoken her passions time and again. She was relieved to finally have a means to fully satisfy them both. She reached behind her and pulled her bottom cheeks apart again. She bent further forward and thrust her hips up. Callum's fingers dug into her hips as he used both hands to hold her in place. He could not even feel the pain in his injured shoulder and arm. All he could feel was his cock plunging deeper and deeper into the woman that he craved.

"Callum, dinna hold back. Show me how ye like it. Show me." She ground out her last words between her teeth as Callum picked up the pace and slammed into her. He leaned over her and whispered to her.

"Ye have the finest arse I have ever seen. Ye feel so good as I stick ma prick in ye. I want to feel ye come around me. I want to spill ma seed in ye and watch it spill out of ye. I can still taste yer honey on ma tongue. I am going to fuck ye until ye scream ma name, lass."

"Callum, oh, Callum." It became a chant, almost a mantra as she pressed her hips back against him over and over. He slammed into her from behind.

"Callum, fuck me. Fuck me harder. I canna stop. I am so close. I can feel it. So close. Harder, Callum. I want to feel yer cock in me. Callum!" She nearly screamed at the end as she felt her release seize her. Its strength almost brought her to her knees. It was only Callum's grip that kept her from sinking to the ground. He thrust harder and faster. He slammed into her over and over again. He panted and growled as he took her. Finally, she felt him jerk harder and press his hips forward while he held her in place. She felt the jets of his seed as they sprayed her insides. She felt another short but strong release surge through her.

They stayed bent over as they tried to catch their breath. Callum slowly eased out of her. Siùsan whimpered.

"Oh, mo ghoal, I kenned I shouldnae have been so rough and that we shouldnae have done it again. I am sorry I hurt ye." Callum knew she should have listened to his common sense, but he had enjoyed each of their couplings more than the last.

"I amnae in pain. Just the opposite. I havenae ever felt better. I just dinna want ye to pull out yet. Feeling ye slide into me is almost as good as the feel of finding ma release. I didna want it to end. I dinna like the feeling of being empty after having ye so deep inside me."

Siùsan's innocent and unassuming words filled Callum's heart. Even when they were not being gentle with one another and it seemed like it was more about the passion than the love, Callum knew that she longed for their emotional connection as much as he did.

"I dinna like pulling out of ye either. I would stay joined to ye, as one, forever if we could."

"So even in our moments of passion, ye still feel that way? It isnae just about rutting then?"

"Nay. I suppose it isnae. Perhaps it isnae just fucking after all. I canna just walk away from ye. I canna separate how I feel for ye in ma heart from how I feel for ye with ma body."

"I dinna mind thinking of us rutting as we seem to have quite a passion for one another. But I also ken that I dinna just think of it as our bodies coming together. Ma feelings for ye are too interwoven with what we do."

"Lass, ye are a wise one. I feel the same. There are times, clearly, when ma desire for ye is overwhelming. I canna hold back how much I want ye, but it is not just because I desire ye physically."

"I suppose that just means we have found more than one way to make love. Sometimes it is urgent and overpowering and others it is more leisurely and affectionate," she said philosophically.

Callum helped Siùsan right her gown once more. She picked up his sling and carefully helped him put his arm back into it. He wrapped his good arm around her and pulled her to his side as they walked quietly back to camp.

Chapter Twenty-One

The first person they encountered was Magnus who had watch. He simply nodded his head and smirked. Callum wanted to smack his brother when he felt Siùsan tense beside him, but when he looked down, she was giving Magnus the most innocent smile he had ever seen on her face. She waved to Magnus and kept moving forward. Callum nodded his head to Magnus and followed Siùsan into camp. Almost all the men had settled in to sleep. Siùsan knew they had been travelling for days just as she had, and she knew they had travelled in the same rain she had. While she had travelled in relative calm once she had put a healthy distance between her and Castle Dunbeath, she knew that Callum must have been a holy terror to travel with if what she had seen from the tree was any indicator. The men were surely relieved to have a night of sleep knowing they would be returning home in the moring.

Home. Is that really where I want to go right now? I want to stay with Callum but before this, I had never realized how much I long to ken ma mother's side of the family. If I go back with Callum now, will I ever have the chance to meet them?

Siùsan's mental wonderings were cut short by the sound of someone snickering. She looked across the fire to see Tavish burying his face in the crook of his elbow as he leaned over his bent knees. His shoulders shook as he finally looked up. He snorted when he saw the two of them together.

"Ye're wed finally? Aboot bluidy time if ye ask me. Enough dithering aboot to last a lifetime, if ye ask me."

"I dinna remember asking ye. I'd thank ye to keep yer neb out of it. I dinna need ye insulting ma wife." Callum relished the sound of calling Siùsan his wife. He wanted to shout it from the treetops to one and all. He looked down at Siùsan and saw that her cheeks were bright red. She did not react to Tavish's comments with quite as much aplomb as she had Mangus's smirks.

She pulled away from Callum and went to spread out his absconded plaid on the ground near her saddle. She rested her head against it and wrapped the plaid around her. There was clearly no room for Callum in her little nest.

Callum looked at his brother and scowled. He walked over to him and grabbed his leine at the shoulder. He pulled him away from the fire and turned him to face Callum.

"Did ye really have to humiliate her?"

"Doesnae she have a thick skin? She willna last long in our family if not."

"Ye ken she does. Look at what she has tolerated so far. Do ye really need to compound how unwelcome she has felt by embarrassing her now that we are wed? If ye need a target for yer barbed comments, then make me the target not ma wife. She doesnae deserve it."

Tavish stood with his hands on his hips and looked up at the twinkling stars.

"Aye. Ye're right. She doesnae. She isnae Mairghread and used to ma sense of humor. I must remember that." Tavish shook his head, properly chastened.

"Dinna be an arse come morning. Ye've done enough damage. Give me yer spare plaid."

"Not warm enough in just yer leine? Good thing it comes to yer knees or yer arse'd be in the wind. She seems to have claimed ye and yer plaid. Why not snuggle up?"

"Ye put a wedge between us already." Callum grumbled and gave Tavish a shove back towards the fire and Tavish's saddle bag. Tavish tossed it over to him and Callum laid it on the ground to pleat it. He then laid on top of it and belted it around his waist. "Thank ye, wee brother."

Callum could not keep himself from taking a jab at Tavish. Not only was Tavish his younger brother, but he was also the shortest of the four brothers. Not by much, a hair's breadth really, but just enough to be a source of teasing. He walked over to Siùsan. He wanted to check on her before he bedded down behind her. She might not be pleased with him, but he would still sleep near her to be sure she was safe. After knowing she had slept in trees for days and after the Gunn attack, he was not going to let her out of arms reach.

He reached down to pull the plaid higher on her shoulders, but her eyes popped open. She smiled at him and opened her arms to welcome him. He just stared.

"Dinna ye want to join me?" He could hear the uncertainty in her voice. She began to lower her arm and pull the plaid back when he practically dove under the cover next to her.

"I thought ye were upset and dinna want me to join ye. Ye rolled up so tightly that it didna look like there was much room for me." He tucked her hair behind her ear and let his hand cup her cheek.

"Ye're ma husband now, and we are newly wed. I wouldnae turn ye away. We may nae have a mattress, but yer bed will always be with me." She grinned as she rubbed her leg against him.

"Ye vixen. What have I unleashed in ye?"

"I dinna ken," she whispered as she ran her hand over his chest. "Wouldnae ye be more comfortable on yer back?"

"I'm most comfortable when I'm inside ye but since I cannae do that right now, I will settle for ye by ma side."

Callum slipped his good arm under Siùsan and pulled her close. She rested her head on his shoulder. He stroked her back and hair. Soon he felt her breath slow and deepen.

I must give her a choice. I cannae keep her from her family, but what if she goes and doesnae want to come back? What if they welcome her better than I did, and she feels more at home there? I dinna think I could leave without her again. Just the four days without her, not kenning where she was, was torture. I dinna think I could bear kenning where she is and kenning she doesnae want me anymore.

Tormented by a possible future he did not want to imagine, Callum finally fell into a restless sleep.

~~~

Callum awoke to a soft warm body next to him. He was disoriented for a moment was filled with dread that he would find Elizabeth or some other woman next to him. As he came more fully awake, he caught the lilac scent that only belonged to one woman he knew. He also realized that his shoulder was screaming with pain. It was stiff and sore from sleeping on the ground. However, the ache seemed to lesson when he looked down to see Siùsan curled around him like a kitten. He gently kissed her forehead and whispered to her.

"Leannan, wake up. It's morning, and we must break camp." He shook her shoulder slightly. He was rewarded when she stretched her entire body pressed against him. She slowly opened her eyes. Her sleepy gaze was the most seductive look he had ever seen.

"Is it really morning? I havenae slept that well in ages. Not a single nightmare." She snapped her mouth shut. She had just shared more than she intended.

Callum shifted to get a better look at her. They were forehead to forehead, nose to nose, and lips to lips. He would have kissed her if he were not so curious.

"Ye have nightmares?" he asked softly.

"On occasion," she answered evasively.

"Siùsan, we will be sharing a bed from now on. If ye have nightmares, I will ken. I amnae a deep sleeper. I would rather ye tell me, so I can be prepared, and I can help ye." He pressed a soft kiss to her nose and then her lips. She attempted to deepen it. Callum pulled back and chuckled at her little growl. "I'd like to think that was because ye cannae resist me, but I believe it was to avoid telling me more."

She had the good graces to look caught in a trap of her own making. She lowered her head. Callum waited. He did not wish to rush her. She took a deep breath before proceeding.

"They always begin the same. The woman who raised me for the first ten summers of ma life told me the tale of ma birth and ma mother's death. It always begins with the scene as it was described to me, but it isnae ma birth that I witness, only ma mother's death. In the dream, I am always ten summers. I watch as ma father runs to her and pulls her lifeless body into his arms. Lady Elizabeth is there laughing at the sight ma parents made. She spots me and comes over. I want to ask her what had happened. She grabs me by ma hair and drags me over. She points and says, 'See what ye have done. Ye did this. Ye ruined everyone's life. If only ye'd die too.' Ma father looks up with such rage. I think he's going to defend me but instead he bellows, 'Ye killed ma wife. Ye murdered her. It'll be by ma hand that ye die.' I always wake up as he lurches towards me."

Callum gently used his forefinger and thumb to lift her chin. Tears streamed down her cheeks

"Ye ken it's only a dream, dinna ye? Ye ken ye were never responsible for yer mother's death."

Siùsan nodded, but it was clearly halfhearted.

"I ken I couldnae really have done it, but ma father's abandonment and obvious hatred makes it hard to overlook the connection."

"Yer father is a bluidy fool. If ever I meet him, I'll be hard pressed to nae break his cowardly neck."

"Cowardly? He hasnae been a coward."

"Aye, he has. A real mon would have stepped up and cared for his bairn. He would have cherished ye and loved ye. He would have appreciated that he still had a small part of yer mama with him. Ma sister, Mairghread, has ma mama's eyes and spirit. Never once has ma da scorned or shunned her. He hasnae ever really recovered from Mama's death, but he doesnae refuse Mairghread because she reminds him on his one great love. Yer father and mother kenned the risk of her riding horseback when she was that far along. The jostling of such a ride probably contributed to her early labor. If yer father cared so damned much, he would have made her ride in a wagon. Instead, he prioritized speed over her safety. He was too cowardly to stand up to his own father. He let himself be bullied over and over. That's how he ended up shackled to Elizabeth. That's why he let her mistreat ye for so many years and let another woman raise ye for almost half yer life. Siùsan, I would never put ye at risk like that, and I would never forsake ye like that by abandoning our child. I may not have been responsible enough to properly care for ye the last few weeks, but I will spend the rest of time atoning for it." He finally stopped for a breadth. He saw Siùsan's awestruck expression. "I love ye."

Callum found himself on his back with his bride half sprawled across him covering his face with kisses. She finally came to his mouth and kissed him fiercely. He had already been hard merely from her proximity now he throbbed. He probably would have taken her right then and there if the sound of coughs and cleared throats had not finally permeated. It must have registered for Siùsan at the same time because she pulled back and looked around her. Her swollen lips would have declared to all that she had just been thoroughly kissed, even if they had not had witnesses. She scrambled to her feet and mumbled something about preparing her horse. She unceremoniously yanked her saddle out from under Callum's head and scurried over to the horses. When she was out of earshot, the jibes and randy comments began. Callum adjusted the plaid he wore and moved his sporran to hide his extremely obvious and prominent arousal. When he believed he was decent enough, he drew back the plaid they had shared. Never had he been so glad for his and his brothers' height and the extra yards of material it necessitated.

"Seems yer wee bonnie bride doesnae dislike ye so much anymore."

"Och, she maynae like him but she seems to love his twig and berries."

"Are ye ballocks blue yet?"

"Do ye think she'll make as much racket tonight as she did last night?"

The last comment made everyone go silent. It was one thing to tease a man about his prowess, but it was entirely another to make reference to a man's wife and what they actually did when they were meant to be alone.

Callum swung around and stepped forward. It was a fairly young guardsman, Gavin, who had made the comment. Callum grabbed him by the collar of his leine and lifted him off his feet.

"That is ma wife and the new lady of our clan that ye speak of. If I hear anything about her and what we do as a wedded couple come out of yer mouth, I will cut off yer tongue and shove it up yer arse." If he had had two good arms, he would have punched him. He felt a tiny hand on his arm. He looked down to see Siùsan there. He calmed immediately.

"Be kind, Callum. He is only jealous. He wishes he had yer prowess with women. The word in the kitchens is that he's all bluster but nae blade." She let her hand hang limp from her wrist. She went up on her tiptoes and whispered loudly, "his twig is a sapling and his berries arenae ripe yet."

The men were utterly stunned. She looked around and worried that she had gone too far. She was just starting to blush when the group burst into stomach clenching laughter. She swore she saw tears falling from some eyes and others held their bellies as they doubled over.

Tavish came up and kissed her on the cheek and then clapped Callum on the back. "And ye were worried that she was easily offended." Tavish looked over at her, "ye give as good as ye get. Welcome to the family, lass."

The men eventually collected themselves and broke down camp. Even Gavin had eventually laughed. He was not particularly put out by Siùsan's comments as they all knew they were not true. He was more afraid of angering Callum again. Callum was well known for his fierceness on the battlefield, but it had been a near murderous rage when he protected his wife.

Chapter Twenty-Two

allum moved over to Siùsan who was about to mount her horse. He saw her grimace as she lifted one foot into the stirrup. He had already taken her to the stream where she had been able to soak her nether region and they had both been able to bathe. Callum had seen her virgin's blood on him. He realized he would have accepted Siùsan even if she had not been a virgin, but he could not tamper down his sense of pride that he had been the first and only one to be with her. He wished he could have offered her the same.

Now, though, he regretted immensely that he had taken her three times the night before, roughly and so close together. He saw her wince as she pulled herself up and began to lift her leg to throw it astride. He wrapped his good arm around her waist and hauled her back. He cursed his useless arm as his attempt at chivalry was not starting very gracefully.

"I cannae bear the idea of ye being apart from me. Ye ride with me, wife," he announced loudly. To Siùsan, he leaned forward and whispered, "I ken ye're sore, and it's ma fault. Ye will ride in front of me so ye dinna have to be astride."

"But how will ye manage with me in the way and only one hand?"

"Ye let me worry about that. Ye cannae ride sidesaddle safely on yers and we have much ground to cover." She nodded her head slowly and Callum realized it was the first actual mention of their journey. They had not discussed their destination before this.

"Will ye come back to Sinclair lands with me for now?"

"For now?" Siùsan's face flooded with several emotions in quick succession, confusion, fear, and hurt. "Are ye going to send me away?" she whispered.

"What? Nay! How could ye think that?"

"Ye said 'for now.' That means it's temporary." She looked at their feet.

"I meant until we can restock our supplies and we can dump Gunn in our dungeon. Then I'll take ye to yer family as ye wanted."

Tears threatened and Callum was truly mystified.

"Did ye just decide this or have ye been planning this since ye learned where I was headed? Why handfast with me? Was it just to bed me?" Siùsan thought she was going to be sick.

"Siùsan, ye arenae making any sense. I thought ye would want to visit yer kin still. I would not have us take such a journey without more supplies."

"Visit?" she squeaked.

"Aye. What did ye--" Callum broke off when it crossed his mind what she must have been thinking. He was not sure if he should be angry or hurt that she would doubt him so soon. They had not even reached her family yet. He once again saw tears threatening.

"I thought ye'd changed yer mind, regretted marrying me. I thought ye were sending me away. I thought ye didna want me anymore." Callum's bad temper faded away when he saw just how frightened she was that he was rejecting her. He paused to think before he reacted. He tried to see what could make Siùsan respond in such a manner, and it dawned on him. He was finally coming to understand the depths of her insecurity and the damage that years of being ignored had done. He cupped her cheek and kissed her ever so gently.

"I willna ever send ye away. Ye promised yerself to me and now ye are stuck with me."

She smiled, and he swallowed. He was going to admit his own fear to try to ease hers. "Mo chridhe, I fear it is ye who willna want me any longer once ye are with yer kin."

"Oh Callum, they may be ma kin and I do want to get to ken them, but I told ye yesterday, ye're ma home. With ye is where I will always be."

"I love ye, little one."

"I love ye, ma braw one."

Callum took Siùsan's hand and kissed it then led her to his Deamhan. He helped her up and then pulled himself up behind her. He helped her find a comfortable position. He almost groaned aloud when she settled the soft side of her bottom against his groin. Since he could not properly hold onto her, she twisted to wrap her arms around him. To avoid his sling, she leaned back slightly. It pressed her breasts together only deepening her ample cleavage. Callum's mouth watered with his desire to feast on the warm, supple flesh.

"Hold on, love." He spurred his horse on and she tightened her hold slightly.

They rode in silence for a little while as they both took in the scenery. It was a bit different from her journey out. This time, they were taking the most direct route. Siùsan watched the ground be eaten up by the horse's galloping hooves. Her mind wandered to what life would be like once they returned to the keep.

Is Elizabeth really going to give up that easily? Will she actually leave with grace? I sincerely doubt it. I dinna think she has any grace to begin with. What should I do if she willna leave be? I want to trust Callum, and he has proven himself these last weeks, but she is such temptation. Am I really enough?

Siùsan's stomach clenched as her mind ran away with itself.

Callum sensed when Siùsan was no longer just watching the trees go by. The tension she was radiating off her petite frame was almost palpable. He tried to think what could cause her mood to shift so suddenly. He had felt her hold on him slacken and then release him. He looked down over her shoulder and saw her holding the edge of the plaid that had been his not so long ago. One hand clutched it almost possessively as though she was worried someone would snatch it away from her. The other hand ran the hem through her fingers. He could tell that she was not giving much thought to her actions. Her mind was too busy ticking over on something that was troubling her.

"What's amiss?" Callum murmured softly.

"What? Oh, naught," she answered distractedly.

"Siùsan, it isnae naught. I can feel the tension in ye, and I can see how tightly yer hand is clenched. What's amiss?"

"I'm just trying to support more of ma own weight so I dinna hurt ye."

"Ma thanks but I dinna believe ye. Ye arenae a liar, so why are ye doing it now? I am yer husband now. Yer troubles are mine. Share them and perhaps I can ease them."

Siùsan looked up at him for so long that Callum was not sure she would answer. He was trying to decide between pressing her and giving up when she finally answered.

"I dinna ken how well ye can withstand temptation. One moment Elizabeth was clearly coming from yer bed and the next ye're pursuing me. What happens when ma novelty wears off? Do ye go back to Elizabeth? Do ye find someone else? If Elizabeth is the type ye choose, then I shall only disappoint ye."

Callum was truly insulted. Had they not had a conversation exactly like this before they mounted up? He felt his temper flair all over again but then remembered that it was seeing true fear of rejection in Siùsan's eyes that had forced him to calm before. Callum now understood that even though she seemed to be a cheerful and happy woman most of the time, deep down she was wounded and vulnerable.

"Ye really believe I'd be that quick to move on from ye? I havenae been in love before. I havenae ever considered wanting to spend ma life with any one woman before--"

"Exactly," Siùsan cut in. "What happens when ye realize ye mistook lust for love or ye realize being with the same woman isnae as exciting as ye thought?"

He frowned and pursed his lips before answering.

"What I was going to say was, since I havenae ever felt this way before, ye must be the right one because ye're the only one to ever inspire those feelings. Ye fell asleep quickly last night," he grinned with male pride, "but I didna. It wasnae ma shoulder paining me. Ma mind wouldnae quiet. Can ye guess what troubled me?"

"Dealing with Sir James and the Gunns."

"Nay. I hadnae even thought of him. Try again."

"Traveling safely with me in tow."

"Nay. Try again."

"Ye shoulder nae healing properly."

"Nay. None of those. I told ye before I worry that once I take ye to meet the MacLeods, ye willna want to return with me. I worry that I willna be enough to make ye leave yer kin. So, do ye see? Our fears arenae all that different."

"We both doubt our own worth and fear that we willna be wanted or needed anymore," Siùsan murmured.

"Aye. Ye have the right of it. I dinna ken what the future holds for us, but I do ken I wouldnae stray from any wife. I willna stray from ye. I have pledged maself to ye before God. I willna break a sacrament."

"Just as ye have pledged yerself to me, I made the same pledge before God. I do wish to meet ma mother's clan, but I already told ye that home is with ye."

"Even if they welcome ye and ask ye to stay?"

"Even if women throw themselves at ye and ye face temptation?"

"Fair enough. I suppose ye are stuck with me for I amnae going anywhere. Ye have me for life."

"I couldnae want aught more."

They kissed softly and Siùsan rested her head against Callum's chest. The steady rhythm of his heart and the horse lulled her to sleep. Callum looked down at his sleeping wife and rested his cheek against her hair.

I willna, nay couldnae, ever find another woman worth giving ye up for.

Chapter Twenty-Three

*T*he group of warriors, Sinclair brothers, and Siùsan arrived in the bailey at dusk on their third day of travel. They were all hot, sweaty, and tired. While Callum and Siùsan were able to slip away for a short time each night, it was nothing as vigorous as the night they handfasted. As a result, Siùsan felt up to riding her own horse by the latter half of the second day. Callum missed the special torture of having his wife's soft bottom nestled against his groin. Just before descending the last hill on their approach to the keep, Callum plucked Siùsan from her saddle and pulled her astride in front of him. He groaned as another surge of desire swept through him with Siùsan seated in a new position. Siùsan had peered over her shoulder and raised an eyebrow.

In response, Callum explained, "not only do I long to touch ye and have missed ye in ma arms, I would have the clan ken ye're ma wife now. And by choice. I offer ye the full protection of ma name and our positions within the clan." Siùsan simply nodded her head and faced forward.

Siùsan was waving and greeting Laird Sinclair when Callum noticed Elizabeth coming down the steps from the keep.

"*Shite.*"

Siùsan's head whipped around to follow Callum's line of sight.

"What's she doing here? I thought ye said ye sent her away. Why is she still here?" Siùsan tried to control the panic in her voice.

Callum dismounted and lifted Siùsan down. He wrapped his arm around her from the back and pulled her against his chest. He was determined to show any and everyone that not only had he claimed and returned with Siùsan but that he was glad for it.

"Lads, ye're back and not looking too worse for wear. Well, all except for Callum. What happened to ye, son?"

Siùsan ducked her head. At first, Callum thought it was from embarrassment, but then he felt her small body shake and realized she was laughing. He gave her a squeeze and that only made her snort. She covered her face with her hand.

"Callum thought himself a tree nymph and tried to prance across the tree tops, but his clod hopping, giant of a body crashed through the branchs." Tavish laughed as he clapped his older brother on his one good shoulder.

"Is that so? Was he chasing a squirrel?"

"More like an elusive dove," Callum looked down at Siùsan.

"Flattery might just get ye everywhere," she murmured over her shoulder. Facing forward, she admitted, "Laid Sinclair, he was chasing me. I hadnae decided yet whether I wanted to be found."

"I take it ye made up yer mind."

"Aye, well, yer son can be persuasive. Though now I'm wondering whether I married him under false pretenses." She jerked her chin in the direction of Elizabeth as she approached.

Elizabeth moved provocatively towards the small group. She swayed her hips and jostled her breasts.

"I truly didna ken she would still be here. I didna lie to ye. I wouldnae lie to ye about aught and certainly nae something like this that could drive us apart." Callum whispered in Siùsan's ear. She just nodded. Callum felt her tense in preparation for a confrontation.

"Did I hear ye say ye were married?"

"Aye, Da. We handfasted four days ago. We are well and truly wed," Callum said proudly.

"Then ye should be calling me Da, lass." He reached out and opened his arms. Siùsan stepped forward without hesitation. Callum released her and immediately felt the loss of contact.

The Sinclair engulfed Siùsan in a massive hug. She felt safe and cocooned by his fatherly embrace for only the second the time in her entire life. She turned her head and rested a cheek on his chest. She wrapped her arms around him.

"Dinna fash at him. He truly didna ken she would be here. He tried to send her away. The storms kept her, and we've had a bit of an emergency where we needed a lady's aid. That's the only reason for her still being here." Laird Sinclair quietly explained.

Burrowing a little further into his embrace, Siùsan nodded.

"Da," she whispered.

"Aye," he squeezed her and then released her. She stepped back and felt Callum's arm immediately come around her. He pulled her to his side.

Elizabeth walked up to the group, but they shut her out. Except for Callum, who with one broken arm and the other gripping Siùsan could not, father and sons assumed their most natural position, arms crossed with their feet planted apart.

Elizabeth tried to squeeze in or look between them but Siùsan was now family and to be protected at all costs.

"Where is Alex? Why isnae he here to greet us?"

"Ah well, we had a bit of our own adventure. Alex is caring for an unexpected guest who showed up during the storms. Our guest is a lady, so that is why we had Elizabeth come in to the keep from time to time. Otherwise, she has been staying in the village." Laird Sinclair stated pointedly.

"Alex playing nursemaid. I dinna believe it." Callum laughed and scratched his head. "I'd like to take Siùsan inside and get her settled."

The small group turned to walk to the keep. Elizabeth seized this opportunity to gain Callum's attention.

"Ma lord, I can have yer bath prepared, so I can wash yer back just as ye like it."

Siùsan gasped quietly but, to Callum's credit, he did not react or take his eyes off Siùsan. Growing desperate, Elizabeth tried again.

"Our chamber is ready, and we can retire now."

This brought Callum to an immediate halt. His tight hold on Siùsan caused her to stop abruptly too. She stumbled into Callum. She felt how rigid he had become.

"Never has it been *our* chamber. One night. One recklessly stupid, regrettable night is what ye spent there. Now yer assistance is nae longer needed. Return to the village. Dinna come back even to the bailey. I will arrange yer escort this vera day. Dinna ever insult ma wife again," he ground out between clenched teeth.

Callum turned to his brothers, "Magnus, Tavish, with me. Da, ye too if ye please."

The brothers shrugged and followed Callum and Siùsan across the bailey. Laird Sinclair walked alongside the couple.

"Aboot time ye took yer bollacks back from that she-devil," Magnus commented.

"Ma bollacks have been just where I needed them." Callum shot him a glare and looked down pointedly at Siùsan. Magus nodded sheepishly.

The small entourage reached the chapel. Callum stopped at the doors of the small kirk.

"Siùsan, we have pledged ourselves to each other when we handfasted and each time our bodies come together, but I would have the blessing of the church so nay person can dispute our marriage. Ye are ma wife, and I would make that permanent as of this moment. What say ye?" Callum held his breath. He believed that Siùsan would agree, but they had already been through much, and a small part of him still worried that she might take the opportunity to end their union after a year and a day, if not sooner.

"Aye."

That one word seemed to lift the weight of the world off Callum's shoulders. They all entered the kirk. Father Paul came out of the sacristy when he heard the party enter the chapel.

"Ma laird, ma lady, lads, what can I do for ye?" Father Paul was one of the few who could still get away with calling the brothers "lad," but he had officiated all their baptisms, and Alexander had even tiddled on him as an infant while receiving the sacrament. He was as much a member of the family as he was the clan's priest.

"Father Paul, Siùsan and I handfasted four days ago, but I would have us say our vows before ye and God right now. I would have our marriage registered."

"Is that so? Ye ken I havenae posted the bans three times yet."

"Father, we are already married in every way in the eyes of God. I would have it made official so nay person can dispute it."

Callum did not need to say more for Father Paul and Laird Sinclair to understand the relationship had been consummated but for good measure, he added, "even if we hadnae handfasted, we are wed by consent. Siùsan has said aloud she wishes to wed with me more than three times."

"I ken yer meaning, ma son. Ye dinna need to convince me." Father Paul moved towards the altar and gestured for them to follow.

Father Micahel kissed his stole and wrapped the vestment around his neck. He cleared his throat and looked at Callum and Siùsan. Callum and Siùsan joined hands and stood looking at one another with Callum's plaid wrapped once more around their wrists by Laird Sinclair.

"Ye will recite yer vows but I dinna think we shall do a full mass. We can save the nuptial mass for when the clan may witness it."

Siùsan looked over at Father Paul with her brow wrinkled. "We will still be really and truly wed even without the full mass?"

"Aye, ma dear. It is the recitation of yer vows and ma blessing that makes ye wed in the eyes of the church. Are ye both ready?"

Looking at one another again, they stated their agreement in unison. Siùsan felt like the ceremony went by in a blur. Having already made her betrothal and then handfasting vows, Siùsan focused more on the man standing across from her. They were both travel weary, and their clothes were stained form the journey. Callum's broken arm was in the splint and sling she had made. Despite all of this, or perhaps because of it all, Siùsan thought he had never looked more ruggedly handsome. So much had transpired in such an incredibly short time. She had spent over a score of years feeling unloved and unwanted. She had arrived at the Sinclairs and had feared more than once that her situation would carry on much the same way only in a new location. However, as she stood before Callum, holding his hand and looking into his smoky brown eyes, she felt his love for her coming off him in waves. She felt it as he squeezed her hand. She felt it in the secret smile as one side of his mouth tilted in a grin. She felt it in the smoldering look in his eyes that promised so much more later. She felt it in the way he leaned forward as if to touch more of her, to be closer to protect her. She knew she truly had found her home, and it was with Callum.

Callum looked down at the woman he had come to love with a stomach clenching, heart squeezing fierceness. She barely came to the center of his chest, but she was filled with enough spirit and bravery to rival any of his men. His mind flashed back to the first time he saw her then to their first time on the beach together. He remembered the relief and anger he had felt when he spotted her among the leaves of the treetops, and he remembered the pride and fierce loyalty he had felt as she defended him and his men with her flying dirks.

I didna want a wife, and I vera nearly ruined it all, but somehow this beautiful woman forgave me over and over and still had enough faith in me to wed me. Twice. I willna fail her again. I will cherish her for the rest of ma days. I just pray we can have the love and happiness ma parents shared. I just hope I have her by ma side longer than Da had Mama. I dinna ken if I could go on without her. I truly love her.

Callum's attention snapped back to the present when he heard the priest say amen. He looked down at the plaid that had been woven around their joined hands. He saw an extra sparkle in Siùsan's emerald eyes. They were like the grass on the rolling hills after a summer rain.

"Wife," he whispered.

"Husband," she said on a sigh.

Much like the night they handfasted by the steam in the forest, Callum pulled his injured arm from his sling. He ignored the sharp shooting pain in his shoulder, so he could wrap both arms around his bride. He pulled her in for a kiss filled with promises of passion and pledges of love. She melted into his embrace as she wrapped her arms around his waist. The laughs and snickers were not enough to separate them. It was only the dire need to come up for air that finally pulled them apart.

"Ye really should be taking better care of that shoulder, or it willna heal properly."

"As ye say, wife." Callum truly enjoyed saying that word now, but he knew it was only because it referred to Siùsan.

The family left the kirk and moved to the Great Hall.

"I wish now that we had summoned Alex. I regret not including him."

"He has barely left our guest's chamber since she showed up. I'm not sure that he would have even come. He seems to have developed some sense of responsibility for her," Laird Sinclair explained.

"I will have to go and see him later. Da, Siùsan and I still plan to visit her MacLeod kin. We just returned long enough to restock our supplies."

"And long enough for ye to rest and heal yer arm."

"I thought ye were in a hurry to reach them."

"They arenae going anywhere. Ye need to heal." Siùsan planted her feet and crossed her arms just as she had already seen the Sinclair men do at least a dozen times. "And at the time, I was running from ye. Now ye're stuck with me." She playfully scowled as she imitated his fierce look.

"Yer wee bride seems to have ye by the bollocks again, brother," Tavish goaded.

"I wouldnae have it any other way." Callum kissed the top of Siùsan's head. "I will remind ye of this when it's yer turn."

"It'll be a day hotter than Hades in Scotland before that happens. I have ye and yer future bairns along with Alex ahead of me for the lairdship. I'm having too much fun to settle down. Besides, I couldnae deprive so many lasses."

"Ye *will* have a wife one day, and I doubt she'll appreciate having yer past in her face, *especially* if ye sire any bastards." Siùsan walked towards the stairs leading to the chambers.

Tavish looked at Callum. "I'm sorry. I seem to put ma foot in shite around her just aboot as muh ye."

"Dinna fash. I ken."

Chapter Twenty-Four

allum took the stairs two at a time to catch up with Siùsan. When they reached the landing, Callum linked his hand with hers. They moved down the passageway. When they came to Callum's door, Siùsan stopped but Callum continued. She looked at him confused. She did not understand why he did not want to enter his chamber.

"Ye havenae been gone so long as to forget where yer chamber is."

"That isnae ma chamber anymore. Ours is down the hall." He tried to continue on, but she would not budge.

"I dinna understand. Why is Mairghread's chamber now ours? It isnae larger. If anything, it's smaller."

Callum ground his teeth and ran his hand through his hair. He really did not want to explain because it would require him to admit something he was ashamed of, but one look at Siùsan's expectant face told him it could not be avoided.

"I cannae bring maself, or ye, to use that chamber. I dinna want the reminder of ma transgressions."

Siùsan swallowed and slowly nodded her head.

"Other than her, no others have shared that bed with ye?"

Callum nodded.

"That woman was there for only one night?"

Callum nodded again.

"It is now ma chamber. She may have had one night, but I will have it for a lifetime. I claim it just as I claim ye."

Siùsan took his hand and tugged him towards the door which she opened. Callum kicked the door closed and swung Siùsan around to press her against the wood. He looked down at her and smiled enigmatically.

"I should have carried ye across the threshold or jumped the broom, but I didna think ye would want to be slung over ma shoulder like a sack of turnips anymore. Tis not very romantic." He lifted his arm in the sling a little.

"Ye wouldnae want me to think ye'd given up on the romance already," she laughed.

Callum dipped his head and captured her mouth. He slid his tongue along the seam of her lips. When she parted them, he pressed his tongue into her mouth. Siùsan sucked on his tongue. Callum's cock became rigid and pulsed. He reached behind Siùsan and locked the door. He pulled at the laces of her kirtle as she unfastened the broach at his shoulder and then unfastened his sporran. They pushed and pulled at each other's clothes and peppered each other's faces with kisses.

Callum bent slightly at the knees and lifted Siùsan over his good shoulder. She squealed as her hair hung down almost to the back of Callum's knees. He walked over to the bed and unceremoniously dropped her on to the bed. He then climbed onto the bed and rolled over onto his back.

"I decided that was easier and faster after all."

"Nae romantic but ever practical." Siùsan ran her hand over the ripples of his abdomen. They flexed and twitched as she caressed his slightly hairy chest. She ran her hand down to where the nest of dark curls began. She teased him by sliding her fingers near his rod but then pulling away. She flicked her fingernail against one and then the other nipple. She leaned forward and sucked one of his nipples into her mouth and bit lightly. She rose up onto her knees and stradled him. She was careful not to rest any of her weight on him but leaned forward to tempt him with her breasts hovering over his mouth. He captured the back of her head and pressed softly until he was able to kiss her swollen lips. He noted that they were extra plump from their kisses. When she pulled back, he grasped one of her breasts and brought it to his mouth. He used his one good hand to knead her other breast as he feasted on the first. When he had his fill of one breast, he moved to the other. He slid his hand down and began to slide his fingers into her moist sheath. She sat back and shook her head. She smiled mischievously as she slowly backed towards his feet. She let her breast trail over his body. As they moved next to his pulsating rod, she squeezed her breasts around his cock. Callum could not take his eyes off his bride who held his cock between her ample breasts. She rocked slowly so that it slid up and down. He could not believe that his bride of four days, who had been an innocent not so long ago, was turning into sin incarnate.

Siùsan watched attentively as Callum's rod slid between her breasts. She used her hands to cup her breasts and to tighten her hold on his cock. She watched, mesmorized, as the tip leaked slightly. She remembered what Callum had done with his tongue several times on their journey home. She remembered what they had done at the loch and in the meadow that seemed so long ago even though it was only just a sennight ago.

Siùsan bent forward and slid her tongue across the top of Callum's shaft. She flicked her tongue over the small slit as it leaked more. Callum groaned and fisted the sheet in his one good hand. The hand of the arm trapped in the sling clenched and unclenched over and over. Siùsan released his cock from her breasts and slid back further to straddle his legs. She leaned down and ran her tongue from the hilt to the tip of his cock. She licked the ridge on the underside of his shaft and marveled when his cock twitched. She swirled her tongue around the tip and then flicked it against the tender spot where his shaft rounded to the tip. Callum growled as his hips surged up towards her. She wrapped her hand around his iron rod and took him into her mouth.

"Siùsan! Ye dinna have to do this." Callum was still always a little surprised when she took him into her mouth. It was something that he never thought his lady wife would do, but that was long before he met Siùsan. More than one woman had serviced Callum with her mouth, but that did not mean that he expected Siùsan to do it routinely. He tried to sit up and push her shoulder up. She batted away his hand and pressed her free hand against his chest.

"Mmm-mmm," she mumbled as she began to suck his cock in earnest. She used her hand to stroke the length of him that she could not take into her mouth. As her mouth slid up, she stroked him with a twisting of her wrist. Callum could not believe how good it was to feel her small hand and warm mouth on his shaft. He watched in amazement as Siùsan worked his cock. He felt himself creeping closer to release and needed to stop her before he lost the opportunity to reciprocate the pleasure.

"Siùsan, I'm close, lass. I dinna want to end this so soon. If ye keep going, it will be over before I have a chance to enjoy the rest of ye."

Siùsan eased off his rod and inched up his body so that the tip of his swollen sword rubbed against the entrance of her sheath. Callum could feel the heat coming from her core, and his cock slid against the dew that met him at her entrance. He rocked his hips up and she slid down into him. Siùsan moaned at the feel of Callum sliding into her. She had concluded several couplings ago that the feeling of joining with Callum, of taking him into her body, was almost as good as the feeling of release that he brought her. She leaned forward and braced her hands by his head. Callum pulled her head down to his mouth. He caught her lip between his teeth. He tugged gently on her bottom lip and she flicked her tongue into his mouth. Their tongues dueled as their bodies rocked together. Each gave as good as they got. They bodies slapped together in a rhythm that had become uniquely theirs and familiar to them both.

Callum grasped Siùsan's hip and dug his fingers in as he guided her into a faster pace. The headboard of the bed slammed rhythmically against the wall. The bed ropes creaked with the force of their motions. Siùsan suddenly arched back and thrust her breast forward as her release washed over her. She clenched her inner muscles and milked Callum until he joined her in his release. Siùsan tried to ease off Callum and move to his side, but he wrapped his arm around her and pulled her down. She angled herself so that they remained joined but she did not put any of her weight on his injury. Her head fit perfectly into the crook on his neck. He ran his hand up and down her back. She hovered her hand over the curls on his chest just barely touching them. Callum was still wondering how his young bride knew how to take him into her mouth in a way that usually only far more experienced women would.

"Ye seem rather distracted," Siùsan observed a while after Callum's hand had stilled on her back.

"Sorry, lass. Just lost in thought."

"Oh?"

"Aye, but naught of importance."

"Ye're wondering how I kenned what I was about. Ye canna deny yer curiosity."

Callum looked down at his wife as she propped helself on an elbow. She shrugged before explaining.

"Ye've never come out and asked. Ye just accepted what I said after the first time. I appreciate that, and it was the truth. I kenned how I enjoyed yer mouth on me and figured ye would enjoy mine. I heard a lot from the ervants and warriors at ma father's keep. Nae one paid much attention to me, so they often spoke freely even when I could hear. I also ken how it drives me to the brink when ye use yer mouth. As I've said before, I thought it might do the same to ye. I havenae done it before ye, if that's what ye thought."

Callum had not thought she had done it before, but he had been disconcerted. However, his curiosity came to an abrupt halt when he was reminded of what Siùsan's childhood had been. He pulled his arm out of the sling and ignored her protests and pain to hold her with both arms.

"Mo ionmhas, ma treasure, ye will never be overlooked again. Ye will never be unappreciated again. Ye will always be loved. Ye will always be wanted."

"I love ye, Callum." Siùsan whispered. They shared a gentle kiss filled with a promise.

Chapter Twenty-Five

or next three sennights, Siùsan and Callum fell into an easy routine. It took them longer to leave than anticipated, but Siùsan refused to travel until she was sure Callum's should was healed. They woke early but did not make it out of their chamber until everyone was almost through breaking their fast. Callum went to the lists to practice. Siùsan had objected and then whittled away Callum's first day back to training. When he returned a bit sore but not battered, she relented. For her part, Siùsan spent time going over the accounts, learning from Elspeth how much food was consumed daily and how much would need to be stored for winter. She collected and hung to dry herbs and medicinals that could be used at the keep on the off chance the village healer could not come right a way. She had her own knowledge and skills that could be useful.

After the nooning, Callum would return to take Siùsan riding on the pretense of showing her even more of the Sinclair lands, but they fooled no one, least of all the guards they took with them.

Seated in front of him, Siùsan would lean into Callum as he held the reins in one hand while the other roved over her body and under her skirts. Siùsan gripped his thighs and clenched the material of his plaid as Callum would use the rocking of the horse's gait to increase Siùsan's pleasure. She bit her lip to keep from screaming out, leaving tell tale teeth marks on her lip.

After Callum finished pleasuring her, Siùsan would swing her leg over the saddle to sit sideways. As Callum kissed away the traces of her ectasy on her lips, Siùsan slid her hand under his breacan feile. Wrapping her hand around his swollen cock, she would stroke him until he groaned, and she felt his release on her fingers.

They would return to the keep only to bathe and take supper in their chamber after which, they would retire for the night. They slept little during those three days.

It was after one such outing that Callum had two surprises awaiting Siùsan in their chamber. The first thing Siùsan saw was the emerald fabric she had admired at the market all those weeks ago, but now, rather than being on a bolt, it was a beautiful kirtle with embroidery on the neckline, cuffs, and hem. Next to it sat a small wrapped package. She had no clue as to what could be in it.

"Go on. I ken ye're curious. Open it."

Siùsan looked over at Callum and slowly stepped towards the bed. Before opening the package, she ran her fingers over the rich texture of the emerald velvet. It was by far the most beautiful and luxurious dress she had ever seen let alone owned. She could not believe that Callum had truly noticed all those weeks ago. Even more, she could not believe that he'd had a gown made. She knew from looking at the stitching which village woman she would need to thank. Christina Sinclair was renowned for her skills with a needle.

"I didna even ken that ye noticed how I was looking at this fabic. How did ye get it?

"I sent Tavish back for it as we left the market. Since ye fit ma mama's gowns so well, I sent one with the material to Christina. I just wish they could have be done sooner and closer to our wedding."

Her eyes travelled to the wrapped package. She could not even begin to tell what it was. It was an odd shape that made it impossible to discern what it could be. She picked it up and could feel what she thought to be bristles on the bottom. She carefully unwrapped it and gasped when she saw the exquisite curry brush. The bristles were sturdy but not overly scratchy. She knew that Trofast would appreciate that. What took her breath away was the intricate etching that had been done in the center. A large S was prominent in the center with a smaller S linked to the top curve and a C was linked to the bottom curve. There was a selkie etched to look like it was swimming along the edge. Around the letters were etched lines to represent waves.

"I canna have a door frame carved for ye, but I thought ye might like this. And Trofast too."

Siùsan had to swallow several times before she could speak.

"I have never been given a gift before. I canna believe how generous ye are to me. This is the most precious belonging I have. Thank ye." The end came out in a choked whisper. She walked over to Callum and wrapped her arms around his middle and held tight as she rested her head against his chest.

"I wanted to give ye something special as a wedding gift. I thought ye would appreciate the practicality of the brush, but that alone did not seem romantic enough. I hope this will remind ye off our first day together. The day I started to fall in love with ye."

Siùsan looked into Callum's eyes and saw the smile that reached all the way to them. She saw love, kindness, devotion, and faithfulness all in one gaze. She crooked her finger, and he bent over.

"I love ye with everything I am." She kissed his cheek and stepped back. She turned and went over to her trunk, one that had been given to her upon her arrival. She opened the lid and moved aside several kirtles and chemises. Towards the bottom she pulled out a bundle of material. She turned to Callum, but he was already beside her. He was peeking over her shoulder the entire time.

"Ye're worse than a wean during Christmastide."

"I ken." He grinned.

She handed him the fabric, and he quickly realized that it was wrapping for something soft inside. He pulled off the top layer and found himself holding a magnificently stiched new leine. The material was soft but sturdy. He opened it up and held it out to examine it. He noticed something small on the cuff of the sleeve. He held it up and saw that much like the monogram on the currey brush, the two S's and a C had been stitched intertwined in white thread. They were bracketed by two horses that looked familiar. Deamhan and Trofast. He looked at the other sleeve and found the same monogram, but on this cuff was a selkie and a man swimming. The white thread was discrete and would make it difficult to see by anyone else, but Callum would know it was there.

"I see we have kept Christina quite busy with our little secret surprises."

Siùsan looked a bit sheepish and shook her head.

"Christina didna make that. Not the leine or the stitching."

Callum looked questioningly at her, and then it dawned on him.

"Ye? Ye made this for me?"

"Aye. I had duties around the keep, but not always enough to keep me busy while ye were still in the lists."

"Ah, lass. I love this. Thank ye. I never kenned ye kenned how to sew so well. I do feel like a wean at Christmastide, ye ken."

A cloud passed over Siùsan's face, but it passed so quickly that Callum almost doubted himself. Something that she said just a moment ago registered before. *I have never been given a gift before.*

He gently moved the gown out of the way and took Siùsan's hand. He gently tugged her hand, and she sat down beside him. He wrapped his arm around her waist and took her other hand in his.

"I heard what ye said before. Aboot never having been given a gift. How can that be?"

"It's vera simple. Moira Mackenzie, the woman who raised me in the village, didna have the means to give us gifts. Besides, I wasna her bairn. Not really. Once I moved into the keep—we ye can guess the rest."

"Aon bheag, ye will be showered gifts from now on. If it makes ye smile as ye are now, then I will happily do it."

He kissed her temple. She turned to look up at him and gave him a gentle kiss. Much like most of their kisses, it quickly turned heated. They retired for the rest of the afternoon and evening. They did not even take a tray that night.

~ ~ ~

As they began their fourth sennight at the Sinclair keep, their morning began as the others had. But instead of their afternoon ride, Siùsan looked in on the mystery woman Alexander had been nursing. Alex was summoned to make an appearance in the laird's solar while the men planned the journey to the MacLeods.

"After the Gunns' attack on us, I am loathe to cross their land but we havenae much choice if we dinna want to go far out of our way. Siùsan was trying to stay on Mackay lands to avoid them too. She just didna ken her way well enough." Callum looked over a map of the Highlands. None of them truly needed the map. They had all criss-crossed the Highlands over the course of their lifetimes.

"As long as we hold the Gunn's brother, there is a chance they will retaliate," Tavish observed.

"Aye. I'd like the four of ye to travel with Siùsan and at least half a score of guards. I dinna want to take any chances with another attack."

"All four of us?" Magnus asked with a raised brow and a glance at Alexander. "Dinna ye want one of us here as yer second?"

"I already have a second as ye well ken. I also dinna often send ye all out together if it can be helped, but ye watch out for each other better than anyone else can."

All eyes shifted to Alexander who kept fisting and unfisting his hands. He would never directly or openly defy his father, but he had a very strained leash on his temper.

"Da, ye ken I am the only one here that she really kens. Siùsan leaving, there is nae body else to care for her. I dinna want her frightened if I turn up gone and she feels trapped in an unfamiliar keep with an unfamiliar clan." Alexander gave his father a hard look and held his breath.

"Ye can stay."

"That's it? Ye'll let him stay on some pretty words?" Tavish looked between his father and older brother in utter disbelief. None of the sons could believe he had relented so easily.

"I ken now that he's serious enough about the lass to put up an argument against leaving her somewhere unknown. I ken more from watching him than from his words. Now, Callum choose yer guardsmen and have Siùsan arrange with the kitchens for supplies." With that the conversation ended and the men each scattered to complete their preparations.

~ ~ ~

Callum and Siùsan joined the family for the evening meal that night. If Siùsan were honest with herself, she would admit that she had been jealous of the easy banter and closeness of the Sinclair family that she had experienced before she ran away. It was partly a fear of never fitting in and always being, yet again, on the periphery that had driven her to take her leave. Now she was included in the jokes and stories as though she had always been a Sinclair, not one who had only officially joined the clan a moon ago. As she looked around the Great Hall, she began to wonder if travelling to see her extended family was a wise choice. *What if they dinna want me anymore than ma own clan did? What if this is all for naught and I humiliate maself by just showing up somewhere I was never invited to go?* Doubt began to gnaw at her. Callum looked over and saw Siùsan's far away look. He gently squeezed her hand until she looked at him.

"What troubles ye, lass?"

"Naught really. Just wondering how I will be received showing up uninvited and unannounced."

"Ye're kin to the laird. Ye'll be received warmly. And if for some reason ye are nae, we will return home immediately. I will be with ye the entire time. I promise."

Siùsan smiled up at Callum, but she could not entirely shake a sense that something would go amiss with this journey.

Chapter Twenty-Six

he Sinclairs set off at first light. Siùsan and Callum slept more that night before than they had since they wed, having only made love once before they both fell asleep with Siùsan tucked into the curve of Callum's warm and solid body. She knew that she never would have fallen asleep or stayed asleep if it were not for the cocoon that his body made around her. She had been restless all through the remainder of the evening meal, and she felt unsettled as they rode out of the bailey. Siùsan scanned the horizon over and over somehow anticipating trouble.

As the day progressed, Siùsan began to relax. They had not encountered anyone along their ride, the sun was high in the sky, and it was pleasantly warm with a cool breeze. Trofast was eager to be on the road again and tugged at the bit to be allowed his head. They stopped to water the horses and take care of their personal needs every few hours. While Siùsan was not as accustomed to long hours in the saddle like the other men, she was able to hold her own despite the hard pace they kept. Callum had explained that he and his brothers had planned how far they wanted to travel each day and would know by natural markers when they would stop to camp for the night. He also promised her a few nights at an inn. He remembered that she had not be afforded that luxury when she left her clan. Now he understood why. Callum did not have to explain that they travelled through Gunn territory and that he wanted them to cross as swiftly as possible. It was inevitable that they would have to spend at least one night on Gunn lands.

As the sun began to set, they stopped to make camp along a stream. Siùsan, with her bow that Magnus had taught her to use, joined Tavish and Magnus when they left to hunt. It did not take long for them to return with several rabbits strung up by their hind legs. Callum and a couple of the guards had fished while they were gone.

"We have a vertible feast tonight. There should be enough left over to eat on the trail tomorrow," Magnus rubbed his stomach as he spoke.

"We can always count on ye to be sure that we willna starve. How ye are not thick about the waist is anyone's guess with how much ye eat. If Elspeth didna start storing food away the moment winter ended, we would all starve with ye in the keep." Tavish teased his "little" brother who was half a head taller than him.

One of the men had begun heating a pot of water with onions and turnips that Elspeth had packed while the others set up camp. By the time the hunting party returned, the camp was set up, and they were ready to help skin the rabbits and debone the fish. It did not take long for supper to cook and everyone settled around the fire.

Everyone seemed tired after their first day in the saddle. Siùsan noticed many of the men yawning and stretching against their saddles while Callum arranged for the first watch. Even the guardsmen assigned to stand guard seemed tired. *That's odd. When I traveled with them the last time, no one seemed this tired after a day of riding. Just the opposite. I seemed to be the only one who could barely keep their eyes open. I'd marveled at how they could last so long when I was almost ready to drop off ma saddle.*

Siùsan once again felt uneasy, but Callum and his brothers seemed to have everything sorted out. Magnus and three other guardsmen would stand the first watch. Callum spread a plaid out a little distance from the fire but still close enough to see and be seen by the others. He laid down and held his arms out for Siùsan. She settled in next to him, and he wrapped a second plaid around them. It was like sticking her body into a furnace. Siùsan did not think she would ever get totally accustomed to just how much heat Callum generated. She would never freeze in winter, but she might swelter in summer. She pushed the plaid down from her shoulders and reached up to kiss Callum's chin.

"How do ye fair, lass? Ye did well today."

"I'm a little sore, I confess, but alright."

"If ye need to stop more often just say the word. We dinna have to be there by a certain day, so we can slow if ye need to."

"Nay. I can keep up." Callum watched as Siùsan set her jaw and fire sparked in her eyes. He would leave this topic alone and slow the pace the next day. He knew she was determined to keep up with the men, but he saw no reason to wear her down this early in the journey. He yawned and felt himself drifting off. *I didna realize how tired I am. The lack of sleep since becoming a married man must be finally catching up to me.* Callum smiled to himself and looked down at Siùsan who had rolled over to watch the fire. The last thing Callum remembered was pulling her tight against him and wishing they had more privacy, but he was simply too tired to take her away from the camp.

~~~

Siùsan awoke to a rustling in the trees nearby. She had definitely heard something that sounded larger, much larger, than a rabbit or a squirrel. She looked around the camp and saw that even the men who had been posted guard near the fire had fallen asleep. The combined snores of the men would give away their location even to a deaf man. She nudged Callum to wake him, but he grunted and rolled away from her. Her brow wrinkled as she looked at her husband. She had discovered early on that he was an extremely light sleeper. Their first night in the keep, she had tried to sneak out of bed to find the chamber pot but Callum had pulled her back into bed and snatched his sword from where it was propped against the bed. He had demanded to know what was wrong as he scanned the room for an intruder. Siùsan's cheeks had flamed red as she explained that she had simply wanted to use the chamber pot. She had not been able to go once she knew that he was awake.

Now Callum's snores alarmed her. His sleepiness, along with that of all of his men, was not normal. She was about to shake him when five men broke through the trees. They moved through the camp swiftly and all moved towards her. Siùsan could not believe her eyes as the shadows shifted into distinct people. Both Sir James and Robert were rapidly approaching her. James reached down and ripped her from the plaids that she shared with Callum. Robert attempted to bind her arms and legs. She thrashed as hard as she could and struck Robert in the shins and used her head to slam into his nose.

"Ye dumb bitch. Ye've broken ma nose." Robert slapped her hard across the face.

"*Callum! Callum! Help me, Callum!*" Siùsan watched as her husband barely moved at her screams. "*MAGNUS!*" She screamed at the top of her lungs. *Where is he? He was on watch too.*

"Ye can scream as much and as loud as ye like, but they willna come to yer rescue. The sleeping draught that was added to the stew will have them out for hours. Ye were to be sound asleep too. Did ye nae eat? That was unwise as it will be a long time before ye receive a proper meal." James growled in her ear.

Siùsan continued to fight and scream until James and Robert had her arms and legs tussed up like a sow. They did not bother gagging her as they knew the Sinclair men would be hard to rouse in their drugged state.

"*CALLUM! CALLUM! CALLUM!*" Siùsan kept screaming as she was unceremoniously tossed over James's horse. He slapped her backside and she yelped. She thought she was going to be sick as the horses thundered out of the forest and into the nearby glen.

Callum awoke with a start to the sound of Siùsan's screams. He thought he had been dreaming, but as he came awake and realized that she was no longer next to him, he looked around in a panic. First, he took in the plaids that had been thrown off him. Then, he saw that all the Sinclair men were still asleep around the fire.

Finally, he watched as a group of men with Sir James Gunn and Robert Mackenzie in the lead ride off with his wife tied across a horse.

Callum roared with anger. He lept to his feet. He looked at the men who were still fast asleep and quickly knew that they had all been drugged. There was no other conceivable reason as to how the were all asleep and had slept through Siùsan's cries for help. Just as he went to Tavish to wake him, Magnus stumbled into the camp will a large gash on his temple and an eye that was beginning to swell shut. He was rubbing his other temple and Callum could see a goose egg forming.

"Callum, I'm sorry. Five men jumped me from behind. I couldnae shake how tired I felt and was slow to react."

"I ken. We were drugged. Help me rouse the men. They've taken Siùsan."

Neither Callum nor Magnus waited to tend to Magnus's wounds. They began shaking the men awake. While groggy and disoriented, all the men woke to the bellows and nudges of their larid's engraged sons.

The men began breaking down camp and saddling horses. It had taken almost a half an hour from when Siùsan was taken to when they rode out. It was still the middle of the night and there was no moon to help guide them or to show tracks.

"Do ye ken who took her?" Tavish asked with a yawn.

Callum gave him a scathing look, and Tavish snapped his mouth shut. Callum did not need the reminder that he, that they all, had slept through Siùsan's attack and abduction.

"Aye. I saw Sir James Gunn and Robert Mackenzie riding at the head of the pack." Callum gritted out between clenched teeth.

"Gunn? What was he doing there? He's supposed to be enjoying the hospitality of our dungeon."

"Well he isnae. I ken who I saw."

"Do ye think that they went to the Gunn keep?" Magnus asked.

"I dinnae ken, but it is the closest place they could ride and hide her."

"Do we head there then?" Tavish asked.

"Aye. We can be there by midmorning if we keep this pace."

With that, the men galloped towards the Gunns' castle, a murderous rage growing inside Callum. He would wipe out the entire Gunn clan if that is what it would take to get his wife back. Self recrimination ate at him. *I promised her that I would be with her the entire time. I've failed her, and it was only the first night out. I will kill any and all who have laid a hand on her. I will get ma wife back and it will nae be pretty if any harm has come to her.* Callum ground his teeth and spurred his horse on faster.

Chapter Twenty-Seven

I t was close to midday with they approached the Gunn keep. They had to stop twice to water the horses and give them a chance to rest. The horses were lathered and flagging when they drew near the proticullis. Callum had paced in circles during each break. He could not rid himself of the image of Siùsan flung across Sir James's horse with her arms and legs bound. As the sleeping draught wore off, he realized that it was her screams for him that had awoken him. The sound of her frightened voice echoed in his head. He could not ease the pain he felt for failing to protect her.

As they approached the gate, guardsmen stationed on the wall above called down to them.

"I am Callum Sinclair, son of Laird Liam Sinclair. I wish to speak with yer laird. I would ken what ye have done with ma wife." Callum called up to them. He watched as the men looked at each other with confusion.

"Why would we ken where yer wife is? Who is yer wife?" A bellowing voice called from the wall near the gate.

Callum watched as Laird Tomas Gunn stepped into view.

"Yer brother stole ma wife last night from our camp. Let us in. Now."

"I dinnae ken what ye're talking about. I havenae seen ma brother in over a moon. I received a message two sennights ago from yer father stating that he was a guest in yer dungeon. I dinna see how he could be stealing anyone's wife if he's locked away. I would like to ken more about how he came to be in yer dungeon though." The last part was said with a hard edge as Laird Gunn raised his arm to signal that the porticullis should be raised. He did not offer an explanation as to why he had let his brother languish there with no ransom payment or even a reply.

"Ye and yer brothers only. Leave yer weapons at the gatehouse." Laird Gunn turned away.

"Aye, ma brothers and me. Nay, I willna leave ma weapons anywhere but on me."

When there was no further objection, Callum, Magnus, and Tavish rode through the gate.

Callum looked around as they entered. There did not seem to be anything out of place. When the Sinclair brothers dismounted, Tomas Gunn approached and extended his arm. Callum simply looked down and then looked the Gunn in the eye. He refused to shake the man's hand until he was sure that Siùsan was not tucked away somewhere within the keep.

He thought he had understood rage when his sister, Mairghread, had been kidnapped the previous year but now he truly understood the blinding fury and devastating frustration that his brother by marriage, Tristan, had felt when he did not know where Mairghread was. Now, Callum would manage a civil word, if only for Siùsan's sake.

"What's this aboot a lost wife? Ye couldnae have been married long and ye've already misplaced her."

Magnus's arm shot out to keep Callum from lunging forward. Tavish stepped slightly in front of his brother.

"Ye ken yer brother attacked us since ye already said ye'd received the missive from our father. Ma wife and I, along with these men, were travelling to the MacLeods to see her mother's people."

"And just who is yer wife?"

"Siùsan Mackenzie."

The Gunn flinched when he heard the name. Callum froze. He would have though the Gunn would know the betrothal considering the connection between the Gunns and Mackenzies. Then again, that would hae require acknowledging Siùsan. He was not sure what to make of the Gunn, but he knew he was not going to like what he heard or saw.

"Ye are welcome to look aboot, but I can guarantee ye willna find her here."

Callum nodded. He looked to Magnus, and he moved away to stand near the keep and began scanning the bailey. Callum and Tavish dashed up the steps to the main door. They entered and began searching the ground floor. They made their way through the kitchens, buttery, and storage rooms before tearing through the chambers above stairs. They split up and each looked under beds and in armoires. When they returned to the Great Hall, Callum was nearly out of his head with worry.

"Show us the dungeons," he barked.

Laird Gunn himself led them into the dungeons and opened every cell.

"Ye see. As I already told ye, she isnae here."

The men returned to the Great Hall. Callum's eyes swept the hall once more before emerging into the bailey. He and Tavish walked over to Magnus.

"Have ye seen aught that would make ye believe she's here?" Callum whispered.

"Nay, but I did get a chance to speak with one of the kitchen servants," Magnus smiled wolfishly. All the Sinclair brothers had a way with women, but Magnus seemed to draw them like flies to honey.

"Aye? Well what'd she say?" Tavish asked as he continued to sweep the bailey with his eyes.

"Apparently, Robert Mackenzie came looking for Sir James aboot a one and a half moons ago. That would mean it was after he visited us and just before Sir James attacked us. I dinnae ken if they kenned that Siùsan had run off, but Sir James was definitely looking for her. The maid said that they sat up drinking most of the night. She was the one serving them. Apparently, Sir James is still hot under the collar that Siùsan was married off to ye instead of to him. Robert was equally angry that the claim he'd staked by agreeing to marry Siùsan to keep her from marrying ye was refused outright without consideration. Both men believe that they are entitled to Siùsan's dowry. That is what both really want. Apparently, Sir James was to meet Robert but attacked us instead. I would hazard a guess that he thought it was his lucky day when he found us traveling. Needless to say, he never made their last meeting."

"Didna they ken that she came with almost no dowry at all? That was part of the reason that I couldnae understand why Da agreed to the marriage. In fact, Da had been the one to make the inquiry about the possibility of a marriage."

"Nae. The maid said that was something they spoke of. They had both thought that even though Laird Mackenzie couldnae stand his daughter, he would have been willing to pay almost a fortune to offload her."

Callum growled at the way Magnus described what he had heard.

"I didna say these things. I'm just repeating what I heard." Magnus stood with his arms akimbo.

"I ken. It doesnae mean it doesnae anger me even more to hear what they and her father think of her."

"So, what now?" Tavish asked.

"If ye dinna mind ma two bits, I would tell ye that ma brother has her spirited away somewhere ye wouldnae think to look. He wouldnae go anywhere that ye could easily guess. He's been sneaky like that since he was a bairn. He couldnae stand to share anything with me or Elizabeth."

The Sinclairs turned to look at Laird Gunn who had quietly approached the trio.

"If ye ken yer brother so well, where do ye think he went?"

"I dinna ken because I dinna ken yer bride. Where would she be least likely to go on her own?"

The Sinclairs looked at one another and stated altogether, "Her father."

Callum, Tavish, and Magnus remounted their horses and charged out of the bailey with nary a thank you or good-bye to the Gunn.

When they rejoined their men outside the wall, Callum led the group far enough away from the keep that no one would be able to hear anything that carried on the wind.

When they stopped by the forest treeline, Callum looked at each of the men. They wore looks of varying degrees of guilt and remorse. They knew they had been drugged but they felt horribly that none of them had been able to prevent the attack. Only Magnus had been awake because, despite eating his share, he was large enough that the dose he received from his portion had not been enough to make him more than drowsy.

"We ride for the Mackenzies. I believe Sir James and Robert Mackenzie will have her hidden somewhere. I doubt her family even kens she is there. It's clear to me now that Laird Mackenzie's disdain and outright dislike of Siùsan is not a secret among the Mackenzies or the Gunns. I wouldnae be surprised if other clans ken this too. If she isnae there, then we move on."

"Do ye ken whether or not Sir James is close to anyone in the Sutherland, Munro, or Ross clans? He could have stopped anywhere along the route to the Mackenzies."

"Nae. I dinna think so. I dinna think that any of those clans would harbor them and risk angering us and the Mackays, and dinna forget Mama was a Sutherland. Everyone kens that we are allied through marriage. Besides, we havenae any bad blood with the other clans. At least not right now. God save them if I'm wrong and she's on any of their land. As the Gunn said, he would go where we least expect and that is to her own kin." Callum swallowed the bile that rose in the back of his throat when he thought about James or Robert touching his wife, the fear she must be feeling, and the fact that she was so unwanted by her father that they could hide her there and he would not notice.

Chapter Twenty-Eight

Siùsan had long since given up trying to fight Sir James's hold on her. Everytime she tried to readjust herself to find a position that did not crush her ribs, he gave a hard swat to her backside. The pounding of the hooves and being tipped halfway upside down had given her a roaring headache. She had to close her eyes since watching the horse eat up the miles as they galloped only made her want to cast up her accounts.

They had been riding for hours before they stopped the first time. It was clearly only out of necessity for the horses. They were all lathered and beginning to flag with exhaustion. It was already late afternoon and the sun was moving towards the horizon. They rested only long enough for the horses to drink from the nearby stream and to catch their breath.

Robert took Siùsan behind a bush to relieve herself but insisted on watching her. She fumbled with her skirts since Robert and James had refused to untie her. She was completely humiliated trying to keep her skirts out of the way without falling over while maintaining her modesty. When she finished, she had to call to Robert to carry her back to the horses since she could not walk on her own. She glared at him as he simply laughed.

"Ye can glower at me all that ye like, Siùsan. It willna change anything. Ye come with us willingly or unwillingly. Ye can choose. Willingly means that ye can ride sitting up. Unwillingly means I'll toss ye over ma saddle like a sack of turnips."

Siùsan forced a smile that looked much more like a grimace. Robert laughed and lifted her onto his saddle then climbed up behind her.

"Mmm," he hummed. "I forgotten just how sweet ye smell. Ye fit in ma arms quite nicely." He wrapped one arm around her waist and used his thumb to stroke the underside of her breast.

Siùsan desperately wanted to wiggle away from his reach or elbow him in the gut but she feared his reaction, so she suffered through his hand wandering over her waist, ribs, and when he cupped her breast. She looked around to see if anyone had noticed his groping. There were a few knowing looks from the men some of whom were Mackenzies that she had known almost her entire life. Not a single man, Gunn or Mackzenie, looked as though he would come to her rescue. The only time Robert's hand stopped moving over her was when James rode abreast of them and scowled.

"Dinna think that ye can have what should have been mine years ago." Sir James stated with a hand on the hilt of his sword.

"Dinna fash. I ken our arrangement. That doesnae mean that I canna enjoy her presence a little before we arrive home."

Home? Robert said this. Home must mean the Mackzenies. Why would he take me there? Even ma father wouldnae condone taking me from the Sinclairs. He was only too glad to be done with me to ever welcome me back.

Siùsan tried to understand what she had just learned. With a pounding headache, she just could not seem to think past her own questions.

They rode well into the night until it simply became too dangerous to continue. The horses could no longer see their way. There was too great a risk that one could stumble and go lame. When they set up camp, Siùsan was dumped so near the fire that she had to scoot back to keep from being singed. Her hands were not untied, and she felt like a rabbit nibbling on the two oatcakes and piece of dried meat that she was given. By this time, she was exhausted from being awake for almost an entire day. She could barely keep her eyes open, but she twisted her hands enough to be able to pinch the inside of her wrists everytime she felt herself beginning to drift off. The sting was just enough to keep her alert. She knew she had a dirk tucked into each boot and one in the small pocket sewn into her skirts, but she had not had an opportunity to use any of them. She had not packed as many as when she travelled alone. The firelight shone on her clearly, so she could not try to sever her bindings until the men had all settled in to sleep.

She almost groaned aloud when Sir James tied a long piece of rope to the bindings at her wrists and another one to the bindings at her feet. Robert approached and picked up the rope attached to her feet while Sir James kept the one attached to her arms. They each sat on one side of her. No one had to explain that these ropes were leashes and if she moved at all during the night, either or both would know. She had no chance to escape even if she could get to her dirks. The movement would alert the men to her attempt. She really and truly was stuck.

~ ~ ~

It took the Sinclairs almost four days to pick up on the trail of the party that had stolen Siùsan. It rained lightly the morning before allowing Magnus to spot fain tracks that had been covered. Magnus was an excellent tracker and could see the smallest indentations and disturbances that no one else ever noticed. The Gunns and Mackzenies had tried to cover their tracks. They discovered there were more of them than Callum had originally thought. Callum had initially seen only five men, two of which were Sir James Gunn and Robert Mackenzie. Now they knew that Siùsan travelled with close to a score of men. That was double what Callum had brought. He was not overly concerned by the odds since the Sinclairs were well trained and had more at stake than the Gunns or Mackenzies. Callum only worried about what might happen to Siùsan if she were caught in the middle of a battle.

"Those tracks are at least a day old. We seem to be gaining on them, but we arenae likely to overtake them. I suspect that they are travelling long into the night before making camp. I havenae picked up any sign of a fire since the first night. I dinna think they are even lighting one. I ken we lost some time going to the Gunns but not enough for them to get that far ahead unless they are riding almost twenty hours a day." Magnus explained.

"I ken what ye're saying. I dinna ken how they have done it without any of their horses going lame. I want to push harder and ride longer, but I dinna want to risk injury to any of the horses. I just canna stand the thought of her being with those men. Ma mind willna stop imagining all that could be done to her." Callum looked at the ground and shook his head. He wanted to ride ahead and leave the others to catch up when they could, but he knew that would be the height of foolishness. If he was set upon or was injured because of his impatience, it would only slow them down further. He remembered the results of his last bout of impetutiousness. His arm ached when it rained.

"We canna be more than a day behind them even if they are riding longer than we are. We will catch up to them. If their desire is to get her land, then they willna harm her," Tavish reasoned.

"Nae. I dinna think that's it. They ken her father wouldnae pay a ransom or at least not much of one. They havenae tried to kill me and make her a widow. I think they have done this to punish us which means they will sorely mistreat her given any chance."

"Perhaps they expect a ransom from us or the MacLeods." Tavish responded. "We are still in Sutherland territory. We can make a choice: we continue as we are and cross Ross land or we head west and stop at the MacLeods. Perhaps Siùsan's grandfather would assist us. At the very least, I think he would want to ken we were travelling to see him when she was stolen. Da made it sound as though the MacLeod would want to see his granddaughter."

"I dinna ken for sure that the MacLeod wants to see Siùsan. He hasnae done so yet, and Siùsan is over a score years old. I dinna want to waste any more time than we already have."

"Callum, we arenae going to catch them before they reach the Mackenzie keep. Once they make it there, they will have any number of places to hide her and any number of people to help them. Clearly, some of the Mackenzie men are willing to assist Robert or at the least they will have Gunns there to assist. I think we need to seek the MacLeod's help," Tavish reasoned.

"Tavish is right. We are not enough to take the keep if need be. I canna see how the MacLeod couldnae help. Siùsan never made mention that she thought the MacLeod wouldnae want to see her. Just the opposite. That's the whole point of why we were on the road."

"Vera well. To the MacLeods then the Mackenzies. I just pray ye are right and we havenae just sentenced Siùsan to more abuse."

With that, the Sinclairs adjusted their route and headed to the MacLeod stronghold. It took them another day and a half of hard riding to reach the MacLeods. They were exhausted, dirty, and hungry when they approached the keep. They were met by three men who rode out of the woods just as they crested the last downhill stretch before reaching the keep.

"Sinclairs? Ye're a ways from home. What are ye doing on MacLeod land?" asked one of the patrols.

"We would see yer laird about a family matter." Callum refused to give away any more information until he spoke to Laird MacLeod and he knew how he felt about Siùsan.

"And what family matter would that be?" pressed the MacLeod warrior.

"One that isnae yer business and is for the laird's ears only." Callum was beginning to lose the very last shred of patience that he had.

"I am Michail MacLeod the laird's oldest grandson. I would ken what ye want with ma grandfather before I let ye go."

"If we meant any of ye harm, do ye think we would have ridden out in the open for ye to see? It's about yer cousin, Siùsan Mackenzie."

"What could ye have to talk to him about her. She's been dead for over a score of years. She was a stillborn when her mother died after falling from her horse."

Callum exchanged a look with his brothers. He was sure the shock on their faces was mirrored on his.

"Nae. Yer cousin is vera much alive. She's ma wife."

Michail gave each of the Sinclairs a thorough look over before nodding his head. "Come."

The Sinclairs were escorted by the three men and led into the bailey.

"Grandda! Ye best come out here sharpish!" Michail called as soon as he was able to make his way up the stairs to the entrance of the keep.

"What are ye bellowing about? Why are ye back already?" Laird Thormud MacLeod stopped short when he saw the Sinclair contingent in his bailey. The laird was a large man and had the same hair and eye color as Siùsan. There was no doubt whose granddaughter she was.

"Grandda, the Sinclairs claim to be here about Siùsan Mackenzie. They claim she is alive and married to this one," Michail pointed to Callum.

Callum stepped forward no longer waiting for Michail to conduct introductions or for the laird to ask questions that would not progress their search.

"I am Callum MacLeod, the oldest son of Laird Liam Sinclair. I married yer granddaughter, Siùsan Mackenzie, just over a moon ago. Her father and mine arranged the marriage. At Siùsan's request, we were travelling to visit ye. She wanted to meet her mother's kin. While camped one night, Sir James Gunn and Robert Mackenzie drugged our supper, how we dinna ken, and stole Siùsan while we slept. We have been to the Gunn keep. She isnae there. We have come to ask for yer assistance. We believe she is back at the Mackenzie keep. There are but a baker's dozen of us, not nearly enough if the Mackenzies resist. Will ye help?"

Laird MacLeod's eyes had grown larger and larger with each word that Callum uttered. He shook his head.

"This canna be. Ma granddaughter died at birth when ma own daughter died from falling off a horse. The old Mackzenie laird and his son, ma daughter's husband, assured me that neither had survived."

"Laird MacLeod, I can promise ye that it is yer granddaughter who is ma wife. Besides the fact that she has yer hair color and eyes, she told me that the dirk she carries has a carved rose in it because that was her mother's name. She showed it to me and there is a ruby set in the center. She'd been told by the woman who raised her that if anyone doubted she was her mother's daughter, that would be proof. It's the only thing of her mother's that she has."

"Dear God above. I ken exactly what ye are talking aboot. I had that dirk made and carved the rose maself for when she turned six and ten. If yer wife is in fact ma granddaughter, why didna the Mackenzies tell me she existed and that she has grown into an adult woman?"

"I dinna ken. I believe it's because her father has tried to remove any memory of his late wife. That includes Siùsan. She was raised by a woman in their village until she was ten summers. Then she moved into the keep serving as more of a maid than laird's daughter. She served her stopmother, Lady Elizabeth Gunn, and her two half brothers. Ma da arranged the marriage and told me that Siùsan's mother was a close friend of ma mother."

"Come inside and we shall talk. It is true that the two lasses were extremely close up until Rose died." The men walked into the Great Hall. Laird MacLeod waved an arm in the direction of the dais. He was ghostly white and distracted as he took in all that had been told to him. "She was on her way here to meet me?"

"Aye. Siùsan and I had a bit of a rocky start to our betrothal. She wanted to come here when she didna want to marry me. We reconciled, and I promised her that we would travel to ye together."

"I canna believe I have a granddaughter." Laird MacLeod kept muttering to himself and shaking his head.

A middle-aged couple entered the Great Hall together and paused when they saw guests. As they approached the raised platform that held the laird's family's table, Callum saw that they man strongly resembled the laird.

"Torrian, this is Callum Sinclair and his brothers." The MacLeod looked at Tavish and Magnus who had not yet been introduced. "They have come with news about Rose – and your neice."

Torrian MacLeod's eyebrows shot up to the fringe of his hair. It would have been comical if the situation had not been so serious.

"Father, ye ken that Rose didna have any living children."

"Apparently, that isnae the case. Mackenzie lied to me when he rushed to marry that Gunn woman. I kenned his father did not approve of their marriage and wanted the Gunn woman to be his daughter by marriage. Rose's husband turned out to be spineless in the face of his father's demands. Turns out, Siùsan, that's her name, has married Callum Sinclair, here, and has been abducted by a Gunn and a Mackenzie." The aging laird looked at least five years older than he had when Callum first laid eyes on him only moments ago.

"Merciful Father! Was it James Gunn who ran off with her?" The woman who had been silently observing finally spoke. "He is ma cousin. I am Catriona MacLeod, but I was born a Gunn. I heard several years ago that there was a young Mackenzie woman that James wanted to marry but she was far too young, and the father would not agree to pay a dowry. If it was a Gunn, I would not be surprised if it was James. He held a grudge if he felt he had been wronged, even as a wean."

All eyes had swung to Catriona MacLeod. She stepped back behind her husband who took her hand. She was clearly a shy woman and not used to speaking up.

"Yer other cousin, Lady Elizabeth, married Siùsan's father immediately after Rose's death. Did ye ken that?" Callum asked.

"Aye. It was only three moons after Torrian and I were wed. I feared that I would be sent back to the Gunns because of their part in Rose's death."

At this Laird MacLeod looked up and gave a wistful smile to Catriona.

"Cat, I never kenned that is how ye felt. We would never have sent ye back. Ye have been a blessing to me and to this clan ever since ye arrived and especially when we lost Rose." Catriona smiled shyly and moved closer to Torrian when he wrapped his arm around her. Callum had a pang of jealousy watching the older couple. He wondered if he would ever get Siùsan back, so they could grow older together just as Torrian and Catriona were.

"Callum, and I assume these are yer brothers, ye are welcome to spend the night here. Eat, bathe, sleep, and on the morrow, I will lend ye as many of ma men as ye want. I ride with ye to fetch ma granddaughter."

Chapter Twenty-Nine

*T*he men gathered in the bailey the next morning before the sun rose. Torrian MacLeod had argued that his father should remain at the keep. Laird MacLeod insisted that Torrian, his tanaiste and heir, remain behind. The MacLeod stated decisively that he had a score to settle with the Mackenzies that was apparently very long overdue. Torrian had relented when Michail said he would accompany his grandfather. Just as the first rays began to peak over the horizon, the Sinclairs rode out with Laird and Michail MacLeod and accompanied by two scores of warriors. As a lesser clan, they did not have more men to spare if any were to stay behind and defend the keep.

Laird Thormud MacLeod rode at the head of the group alongside Callum. Callum snook a peak at the aging laird and could clearly see what the man must have been in his prime. It was clear to anyone who looked that the man could still swing a broadsword and would be fierce if pushed into battle. Callum breathed a silent breath of relief that the MacLeods had so easily and readily agreed to ride out with him. He was thankful that he had remembered the dirk that Siùsan had shown him one night when he had felt it in her kirtle as he undressed her. The carving had been unusual and when Callum made mention of it, Siùsan explained that it was the only thing that she had that had been her mother's. She said she never went anywhere without it.

As the day wore on, Callum felt his nerves fraying even more. He had thought he had reached the end of his patience several times during this journey but, somehow, he managed to keep going. He had to for Siùsan's sake. *It will be almost a fortnight by the time we reach the Mackenzies. What the bloody hell will they have done to her by then? I swear if any of those bluidy bastards have defiled her, I will rip their ballocks off and shove them down their throats then rip their cocks off and shove them up their arses. I just want ma wife back, damnit.* Callum tried to slow his breathing as his anger began to boil over yet again.

"Son, ye must remain calm. Ye willna be any help to any of us, especially Siùsan, if ye let yer rage get the better of ye." The MacLeod spoke for Callum's ears only. "I ken that ye must be out of yer mind with worry and anger. I ken how I feel, and she is a granddaughter I havenae even met. I can only imagine how ye feel. Ye must keep yer wits aboot ye if we're to find her."

"I ken it. I will be fine by the time that we get to her. I just canna stop worrying about how she fairs. I promised her that I would be with her the entire way then I failed her in the worst possible way."

"If yer Siùsan is anything like ma Rose, she doesnae blame ye in the least. This wasnae yer fault anymore than it was hers. Do ye blame her for being kidnapped?"

"Of course nae. Why would I?"

"Exactly. She didna ask for this to happen just like ye didna. Neither of ye could have foreseen this, so neither of ye could have prevented it. We will right this wrong and end this for good." The MacLeod had kept his eyes directed forwards during their entire conversation. Now he turned to Callum and offered him a grandfatherly smile.

They rode on in silence. There was not much to say amongst the men during the ten days that it took to reach the Mackenzie land. Two days before they reached the Mackenzie keep Magnus picked up the remnants of their trail. He estimated that they were only two or three days ahead of them.

Sitting around the campfire, the Sinclair brothers had time to strategize with Thormud and Michail MacLeod. Callum's suspicions that the MacLeod had once been a great warrior were proven true when he listened to the advice that the older man offered. They agreed that Callum and Tavish, along with Thormud and a handful of MacLeod warriors, would enter the keep from the front gate just after sunset. Magnus would attempt to enter from the postern gate. If he was able to unlock it, then five of the Sinclair men would follow him and five would remain hidden in the woods with all the horses. The Sinclairs would enter through the kitchens and make a sweep of the kitchens and dungeon. Meanwhile, Michail would follow Magnus through the postern gate and take half of the MacLeods to sweep the bailey and outbuildings. The other half of the MacLeods would ride through the village to search. There was to be no violence if it could be helped. None of the Sinclairs or MacLeods were to initiate a fight and would only use their swords if they had to defend themselves.

When they arrived at the Makenzie keep the sun was nearly setting. They rested and waited just on the other side of the last hill that separated them from the keep. They were out of sight of the guards who lined the wall. Magnus had not seen any indication that there were patrols in the area. They had not seen anything even when they crossed into Mackenzie territory. Tavish had remarked on how lax the Mackenzies seemed with their security. Callum agreed and noted that it was no great surprise then that Robert Mackenzie had been able to ride out with his clansmen.

Callum tried not to pace as he waited, but he was impatient to move out. Tavish and Magnus gave him his space and instead checked their weapons. They sharpened their dirks and swords. All three of the Sinclair brothers wore dirks in each boot, strapped to each thigh and each wrist, and two at their waists and one in their sporran. It was not unusual for them to travel this heavily armed. However, it was not often that they were prepared to use every single one.

The MacLeods brought along five skilled archers who would keep their bows trained on the wall in case Magnus or Michail were spotted and the alarm was raised. These men checked their bow strings and fletches of arrows. They were prepared and were selected because their night vision was better than an owl's.

When the sun set, and darkness began to kreep across the forest and keep, the Sinclairs and MacLeods set off. Callum, Tavish, Thormud, and a handful of the MacLeod warriors rode out into the open, but the others stayed to the shadows. Callum and the men along with him wanted to be noticed. They wanted to draw attention away from the others who snook to the back of the keep.

"Who goes there? Identify yerselves!" came from the top of the wallwalk.

"Sinclairs and MacLeods. We are in need of yer hospitality and a word with yer laird." Callum replied invoking the unwritten law of Highland hospitality. No one would readily deny someone's request for hospitality even though the weather was clear and warm meaning they were not in need of shelter.

"Wait there."

Several minutes later the gate could be heard being unlocked and the porticullis was raised only high enough to allow the men to walk their horses inside.

"Suspicious bunch considering they have no one on their borders," Tavish murmured.

"Aye," Thormud breathed in reply.

A short and stocky man appeared on the steps to the keep. Callum knew instantly that this had to be Siùsan's father. He had the swagger of a man who was used to getting what he wanted. He was also still in good shape and looked like he could be a potential challenge if it came to that. Callum sincerely hoped he would not need to draw his sword on anyone, least of all Laird Mackenzie. He was still Siùsan's father after all. He did not want that death on his conscience.

"Which Sinclairs and which MacLeods? Why have ye come?" There was a sharp edge to Laird Mackenzie's voice even though he tried to keep it light and jovial.

"Yer son by marriage, his brother, and his grandfather by marriage," called out Callum. At the utterance of the last title, the Mackenzie took a stutter step before moving forward to greet his unexpected, and now most definitely unwanted, guests.

"So ye're Callum. I hope married life is treating ye well though I canna imagine why ye would be here so soon after marrying. I dinna see the woman, so I ken ye arenae returning her already." The Mackenzie no longer tried to hide the sneer from his voice when he spoke of Siùsan. "Thormud, what brings ye here with the Sinclairs?"

"The woman." he practically growled. "If I hadnae already learned that ye're a lying sack of shite, I would ken now. The better question is why have ye been keeping ma granddaughter from me for over a score?" The last words came out as a veritable roar. Callum looked over to see the MacLeod standing with his arms akimbo. Callum and Tavish were in their usual stance, feet hip width apart and arms crossed over their chests.

"So ye learned that the lass survived. She isnae ma concern anymore. She isnae a Mackenzie anymore. Since she's a Sinclair now, I think ye should be at their keep getting acquainted." With that Laird Mackenzie turned to walk away. Callum's arm shot out and grasped his shoulder yanking him back around.

"Do ye ken where Robert Mackenzie is? Or yer brother by marriage, James, for that matter?"

"Nae. Why would I? I dinna concern maself with their comings and goings."

"Robert is one of yer men. Ye dinna ken which of yer men are here and which arenae?" Tavish piped in with disgust.

"Yer man and yer brother by marriage have stolen ma wife. Ye may not care for her, but she is still yer daughter, mon. If she is here, ye can count on a war with not only the Sinclairs but the MacLeods, the MacKays, and dinna forget the Sutherlands since they were ma mother's people."

"I dinna ken what ye're going on aboot. She isnae here. She isnae welcome and well she kens it. I was only too glad to be done with her. Now ye can leave as well. I dinna have to extend any hospitality to those who dinna need it. Get out."

The Mackenzie turned and strode up into the keep. Callum, Tavish, and Thormud exchanged looks and then looked over their shoulders at their men. They charged up the steps as a large wave crashing onto the keep. They stormed into the Great Hall.

"Men, block the entrances to the Great Hall. Tavish with me. We search above stairs. MacLeod deal with the Mackenzie." With that Callum raced up the stairs to the second floor. In the distance, Callum heard swords being drawn. He had already pulled his from his sheath before making his way up the stairs.

Callum and Tavish swept through each chamber upending chairs, pulling bedding off, pushing beds aside, and yanking clothes from armoires. There was one room left at the end of the hall. Callum crashed through the door and quickly realized from the screams that he and Tavish had arrived at the women's solar and seated directly in front of him was none other than Lady Elizabeth Mackenzie, Siùsan's stepmother.

Lady Elizabeth barely looked up from her embroidery. She continued stitching as though two massive warriors had not just broken down the door to her private sitting room.

"I could hear ye searching for the chit, but she isnae here. She wouldnae dare come here." Callum saw the Cheshire cat grin that passed across her mouth so quickly that he barely caught it. He knew Elizabeth knew more than she let on.

"Ye ken where yer brother is. Speak, woman. I willna spare ye if ye're awkward."

"I dinna ken where ma brother is. I assume he is overseeing clan business back at his keep. Ye ken being laird is vera busy."

"Dinna act daft. Ye ken I mean James. I have already seen Tomas." At that, Elizabeth paused before making the next stitch. Callum could tell she had not anticipated that. Perhaps she did not know all the details of her brother's plan, but she clearly knew something had happened to Siùsan and James was a part of it.

"Ye have already ransacked ma home looking for her and turned up with nothing. James may have the chit, or he may not. I dinna ken and dinna care. She has been a thorn in ma side since before she was born. As long as I dinna have to see her again, I couldnae care less who has her."

Callum turned to Tavish. It was clear they were not going to get anything more out of Elizabeth without holding a dirk to her throat. He was not prepared to go quite that far yet. He suspected she would gladly go to the grave without sharing what she knew if it meant that Siùsan suffered. He simply could not understand how anyone, let alone her father and stepmother, could hate her so much. She was everything good in the world, yet she was loathed simply because her mother had died and because Ulrich Mackenzie had chosen a MacLeod instead of a Gunn. If anything, the Mackenzie should loathe the Gunns even though he married one. He should be willing to do anything to aide in their downfall if for no other reason than retribution for their role in his late wife's death.

Callum and Tavish retreated out of the room. They moved into the shadows near the stairs. Tavish shrugged and looked back over his shoulder.

"Did ye get the distinct impression that she kens far more than she says?" Tavish whispered.

"Absolutely. She seems happy that we canna find Siùsan. She's glad that Siùsan is in danger."

"I dinna understand this clan one bit. Let's see if the MacLeod has made any progress."

The men moved out of the shadows and were nearly to the stairs when they both noticed a motion from their left. Swords drawn they turned as one.

Chapter Thirty

Siùsan was exhausted, hungry, and filthy. She looked around the tower room that was on the opposite side of the keep from her old tower room. This one was not much more than a storage room. There were pieces of old furniture and tapestries strewn around the room. There was a cot that was barely long enough or wide enough for her to lie on her side at night. She had been given little more than two bannocks a day and a pitcher of water. The chamber stunk as no one had emptied the chamber pot since she arrived.

Robert had untied her wrists when she was tossed into the room upon their arrival three days earlier. She had barely seen or heard anyone except for Elizabeth, Callum's former lover, who was a shock for Siùsan to see. Elizabeth taunted Siùsan at every turn. She threw the bannocks to her when she brought them. She kicked the chamber pot so that it nearly tipped over. She held the water pitcher just out of Siùsan's reach, and she reminded Siùsan of all the times that Callum had bedded her.

Elizabeth was loose lipped and reveled in Siùsan's captivity. Consequently, she had much to say. Siùsan gritted her teeth and played along once she realized that Elizabeth gave away important information when she was bragging. Siùsan came to learn that it was Elizabeth who had released Sir James from the dungeon by once again seducing a guardsman who fell asleep after their romp. She slipped in through the postern gate up against which she had trysted with the man. She had also covered the onions and turnips in a sleeping draught when Elspeth set the bag aside for Siùsan. Last but not least, Siùsan learned that Elizabeth was related distantly to Robert through his mother. Robert had been sent to court earlier that year on business for Siùsan's father. He was there to seek approval for Siùsan to marry Callum. While there, he met Elizabeth and an affair. It was during a late night pillow talk that Robert shared that he was ever so close to gaining the Mackenzie lands and lairdship. He had sensed a kindred spirit in Elizabeth and shared his frustrations when he learned all those months ago that the Mackenzie was interested in betrothing his unwanted daughter to Callum, who in turn had yet to be informed of the marriage negotions that were proceding. Coincidentally, Callum was at court at the same time. Elizabeth and Robert initiated a nefarious plan that involved Elizabeth seducing Callum and ingratiating herself into his good graces enough to garner an invitation back to the Sinclair castle. She was positively gleeful when she recounted how she had fooled all of the Sinclairs and most importantly Callum. The only part where she became bitter was that Callum had not continued their affair after Siùsan's arrival. Elizabeth had planned to replace Siùsan as Lady Sinclair once Siùsan was stolen away.

Her pride will goeth before a fall. And I will be the one to trip the bitch. I canna believe that she and Robert hatched this entire plan that has been in the works for so long. Doesnae she realize that for Robert to get ma father's lands, several people must die first and that includes Callulm. If Callum is alive, then neither Robert nor James can wed me and she canna have Callum. If I amnae alive, which is the only way she could get to Callum, then neither Robert nor James will help her because they willna have the land or title either. The good fortune they had in James agreeing to assist for a cut of the gains is unbelievable. I dinna think that James is playing them fair, but who am I to set anyone straight. Nae. Let me see if I can breed discontent and distrust among them.

And so began Siùsan's slow plan to work against her captors. She did not know, nor did she really care at this point, if her father or Lady Elizabeth knew that she was being confined to the tiny chamber. She was more concerned with finding a way out than worrying about all the people who might have contributed to her confinement.

Blessedly, both Robert and James had separately told her that they had no intention of bedding her until they knew whether she carried the next Sinclair heir. Neither wanted to be cuckholded into claiming another man's child. They warned that they would rid her of any child either before or after it was born. As she thought about this now, she wrapped her arms around her middle. She was not certain if she might be carrying but even the possibility made her overly protective. She was lost in thought about Callum when she heard the key in the lock. Callum was never far from her mind. She missed him intensely and longed for him to come to her rescue. She was confident that he would eventually find her, she just prayed it was before Robert or James assaulted her.

When the door opened, both Robert and Elizabeth stepped into the room. Siùsan was surprised to see them together. Robert had only been to see her once since they arrived. That was only to threaten her with a beating if she caused any problems. To prove his seriousness and his desire to rid her quickly of any possible child, he had slapped her across both cheeks and when she fell, he squarely planted his boot into her gut. Siùsan was wary of him now. She did not recognize this Robert. He was nothing like the boy she had considered a brother for so many years and then her best and only friend afterwards. She understood now that while he might have seen her as a sister when they were very young, his intentions had shifted significantly as they aged.

"How is our fine captive today," Robert sneered. "Are ye getting enough to eat? Sleep well last night?" He walked up to Siùsan and pinched her chin between his thumb and fingers. He turned her head side to side and examined the bruises that he had left days earlier. They matched well with the bruises that she had all over her front from being tossed over the saddle for a full day and from his kicks.

"Yer chivalrous knight has already come and gone. A few questions and he gave up. He didna search vera long or vera hard for ye. Aye. That's the right of it. He was here. In the bailey. In the keep. But now he has gone, and ye must stay." Robert watched to see if she gave any reaction. Siùsan wanted to flinch away from him but knew that was exactly what he wanted. Her expression remained blank. Receiving no reaction, he moved over to Elizabeth.

He stroked her cheek and glided his hand down her neck until his hand cupped her breast. His other hand began to inch up her skirts. All the while, Robert watched Siùsan. He pulled Elizabeth's kirtle down to reveal her breasts. He fondled them as his other hand found what he searched for. Elizabeth threw her head back and moaned. Robert turned slightly so he could take one of Elizabeth's nipples into his mouth while still watching Siùsan.

"Do ye see what ye will have. I can please a woman. I will make yer body sing with pleasure." He licked Elizabeth's other breast as he tweaked her nipple. Elizabeth moaned again.

Siùsan knew that he was trying to arouse her. Nothing about this scene was appealing. What did appeal to Siùsan was sewing the seeds of discord.

"Elizabeth seems to be enjoying yer ministrations, but ye keep looking at me. Are ye thinking about me, wishing it were me? I'm the one ye've always wanted even if it's just for ma land. Ye willna be keeping Elizabeth once ye have me, will ye?"

Elizabeth's head snapped forward to glare at Siùsan. Robert simply chuckled. He pulled Elizabeth's head towards him and kissed her passionately.

"Aye. Elizabeth may get to the men who want me first but they all seem to choose me over her in the end." Siùsan tapped a finger against her lips. "Robert, ye wanted me for ma lands but couldnae get me so ye took up with Elizabeth. Elizabeth, ye wanted Callum for yerself, but he cast ye off once I arrived. Here Robert is using ye to try to arouse me. Ye seem to come in second even when ye finish first." Siùsan was aware of the inuendo that her last comment held. She grinned as Elizabeth glowered at her, but she was not quite through yet.

"Elizabeth, how does it feel to ken that every man we both ken will toss yer skirts until ye grow tiresome then they cast ye off for me? It seems like none of them are tired of me. James, Robert, and certainly Callum all want me for keeps. That must be very frustrating to ken ye'll never be quite enough for anyone."

Elizabeth shoved away from Robert. She glared back and forth between Siùsan and Robert before turning on her heel and marching out of the chamber.

"Ye think ye are so smart. Ye think that ye can get between Elizabeth and me to cause trouble. Ye didna count on the fact that I couldnae give two shites from Sunday about whether that whore wants me or nae. She isnae the only woman willing to spread her legs for me. In fact, ye are here now, and I'm hard as a plank. Ye will do very nicely."

Siùsan backed up against the wall trying to put as much distance between the two of them as she could. She has seriously miscalculated her game.

"Ye said ye wouldnae touch me until ye kenned whether I carried Callum's child. If ye defile me now and I do end up with child, ye'll never ken whether the bairn is yers."

"Come now. I have heard about how Callum tups ye morn, noon, and night. I ken ye ken there is more than one way to fuck." Robert darted forward and grabbed Siùsan's hair. With a handful of it, he yanked her neck back until it felt like it would snap. He licked her neck and squeezed her breast viciously hard until she could not help but yelp. "Perhaps I should have ye suck ma cock first. I can watch yer pretty, little mouth kept busy and quiet. Or mayhap I will do ye in the arse. There's nothing quite like a tight arsehole to make me come hard and fast."

Siùsan was shaking at this point. She may have succeeded in getting Elizabeth angry enough to leave, but she had only antagonized Robert enough for him to rape her. Robert turned her and pushed her onto the bed. She reached out both arms to brace herself. Before she could try to move, she felt her skirts being pulled up and tossed onto her back. Suddenly there was something warm, short, and hard rubbing against the inside of her thigh. She screamed as loudly as she could. Robert yanked on her hair, but she continued to scream as loudly as she could hopin it would rouse the dead or at least draw someone's attention. Robert spanked her hard across her buttocks three times.

"Shut yer gob, or it will be ma cock that shuts it for ye." She sensed more than felt Robert grasping his cock and then she felt the tip nudge against her most sacred spot. She clenched her bottom as hard as she could. Robert only laughed in response as he continued to try to shove his way into her. She swung her elbows and kicked out her feet trying to gain an inch of freedom.

"Nay! Nay! I willna let ye do this. Ye'll be fucking ma dead body before I let ye rape me. Kill me now before I kill ye!" As she flailed her arms and legs, she was able to distract Robert enough to draw one of her dirks from her boots. No one had thought to check her even once during her entire imprisonment. She grabbed the dagger and thrust backwards just as the tip of Robert's prick began to gain entry into her bottom. She looked over her shoulder as she swung her arm back. She managed to graze the side of his cock. He howled and recoiled in pain. It gave Siùsan enough time to straighten her skirts and jump onto the bed. Robert grabbed one of her ankles and tugged her back towards him. He flipped her over and curled his hand into a fist. It landed across her cheekbone sending a searing pain throughout her entire face. He balled up his other fist and struck her in the left eye. He was about to punch her again when she raised both legs and pushed her feet into his stomach. He stepped back with a woosh and then laughed maliciously. He grabbed her feet and pulled them apart.

"Even better. Now I will enjoy yer cunny, and I'll be able to watch yer face every moment of yer submission to me. Yer cunt and yer land will be mine soon enough."

Siùsan screamed again with every ounce that she had. Just as Robert was about to push into her, the door slammed open. An angry James stood in the entrance.

"What the bluidy hell do ye think ye are doing? Elizabeth just told me ye were trying to seduce Siùsan. Then I hear her screaming bloody murder. Now I come in to find ye about to rape ma woman. Step back, Mackenzie before this little partnership comes to an abrupt end." James surged into the room with murder in his eyes. Siùsan screamed once more before making a dash for the open door.

Chapter Thirty-One

allum and Tavish surged forward with their swords and dirks drawn. They barely stopped before impaling two older boys. They skidded to a halt when the boys raised their hands in surrender. Callum looked at the boys closely. Even though the passageway was dimly lit, it was clear that both boys were clean and well dressed. Their leines and plaids were made of fine quality. Their boots were fairly new and had fur lining. Callum knew these had to be the laird's sons which meant Siùsan's younger brothers.

"Yer Siùsan's brothers," Tavish blurted out before Callum had a chance.

"Aye, we are. We ken ye've come for her. We ken where she is. She's here in the keep. Nae one else kens that she's here but us. We saw her being dragged in to the far tower a few nights ago. We were supposed to be abed, but we were returning from night fishing at the loch. We saw Mother's brother, Sir James, and Robert taking her into the tower that is nae used for anything but storage. We havenae been able to get close to her as there is a guard posted at the bottom and we believe the top of the stairs, but we have heard her calling out for help. At least the first day she did," said the one who was clearly the elder.

"She screamed for help much of the first day. She wasnae loud enough for anyone outside the tower to hear. We snook in when the guards were changing posts. We couldnae get any closer because we didna want to alert the guards." The younger one explained.

"Ye didna think to tell yer father or mother?"

The boys exchanged a look before the elder one answered.

"We werenae sure that Mother and Father werenae involved in her capture. If they are, we didna want to let on that we ken. If they arenae responsible, well, we dinna think they would come to her rescue. At best, they might set her outside the wall alone and unprotected."

"What are yer names, lads."

"I'm Seamus and he's Magnus," the older boy puffed out his chest proudly.

At five and ten, he was on the cusp of manhood.

"I am Callum and this is ma younger brother Tavish. We also have a brother named Magnus. Do ye ken who I am?"

"Nae. Just that ye're looking for Siùsan and are angrier than a starving bull."

"That I am. Siùsan is ma wife, and she's been taken from me. That's how she came to be here again. I vera much want ma wife back."

The boys looked at the two giant men standing in front of them in their customary stance. The boys looked at one another and mirrored the men's poses, they crossed their arms and spread their feet.

"How do we ken ye willna mistreat her? Even though she is the best sister in the world, people arenae kind to her because she had the wrong mother," stated Magnus, who Callum reasoned was about three and ten.

Callum swallowed when he heard the last part. *So, they were meant to be turned against her, too.*

"I love yer sister more than anything and vera much want to take her home with me. She is wanted and needed by me and ma clan."

Seamus and Magnus once again looked at each other. Callum wanted to smile as the boys' silent communication reminded him so much of how he was with his own brothers and particularly Alexander who was much like a twin brother.

The young men nodded their heads and gestured for Callum and Tavish to follow them. Instead of walking towards the stairs to the Great Hall, the boys led them to a chamber that they had already searched.

"This is ma father's chamber." Magnus whispered. "We must be vera quiet as Mother is still in her solar." Magnus walked over to a large tapestry that hung next to the laird's bed. He pushed it aside and pressed against two stones that were just above his head.

"There are secret passageways thoughout the keep. There is one that joins this tower with the older one. It will bring us out under the stairs on the second floor. Siùsan is being held on the fourth at the vera top." Seamus explained quietly.

The secret door swung open and the two older brothers followed the two younger brothers into the dark. Fortunately, Tavish thought to grab a torch from a wall sconce outside the laird's chambers before they entered the hidden corridor. He now held it overhead to light their way. Seamus and Magnus moved through the darkened passageway with the ease of ones who were very familiar with their surroundings. Callum and Tavish followed them as the passageway twisted, turned, and branched out. Finally, the boys came to a stop before what appeared to be a solid wall. Seamus reached out his foot and tapped the bottom of the wall. A small latch released, and he slowly pushed against the unmarked door. Magnus stepped forward followed by Seamus. They looked around and then waved Callum and Tavish out.

"There are the stairs that lead—" Magnus was unable to finish as a blood curdling scream wrent the air.

"*Siùsan!*" Callum roared. He saw red.

He was not going to wait any longer. He drew his sword and began taking the stairs three at a time. He heard Tavish tell the boys to wait there. His footsteps could be heard as he followed Callum up the stairs.

As he made it to the next floor, Siùsan's screams only became louder. He could hear two angry male voices and knew them to be Robert's and Sir James's. He pushed himself to climb the remaining stairs even faster. The noise of their climb reached the guardsman who was posted outside of Siùsan's chamber. He barreled down the stairs to stop Callum. It took little effort to sidestep him and push him down the stairs. The guard stumbled and fell forwards as he met Tavish coming up. Tavish threw a punch into the man's stomach and pushed him further down the stairs.

Callum thought the sight that had greeted him and his brothers when they found their sister was the worst thing he could ever see, but what met his eyes as he entered Siùsan's prison was far worse than he could have ever imagined.

He took in everything as though it was happening in slow motion. He saw the cramped space, he smelled the days old chamber pot, he heard the two men yelling, but nothing prepared him for the sight of Siùsan stripped naked with Robert standing before her and James behind. Even while the men bellowed at her, they fondled Siùsan. Both men were holding and stroking their cocks. Just as Tavish arrived at the door, Robert and James rocked forward as they attempted to enter Siùsan from the front and the behind. Siùsan's scream rang through the small chamber and snapped Callum into action.

Callum roared with a white hot furry that gave him tunnel vision. No longer was he aware of anything or anyone other than the two men about to rape his wife. He charged into the room and grabbed Siùsan's arm. He pulled her away from the men and shoved her behind him.

"*Tavish!*"

Callum swung his sword at the two unsuspecting and unprepared men. His sword sliced through the side of one then the other. Both men were mortally wounded, but Callum was not nearly done. As Robert and James stood staring at each other, Callum dropped his sword and yanked out a dirk in each hand. He swiped one across each of their throats. Blood sprang from their wounds coating the walls and Callum's chest. He was prepared to geld both men vaguely thinking that he wished he had done that first. He looked first at James and then Robert as he tried to decide what to cut or stab next. When a small hand pulled at his arm, he swung around prepared to cut down anyone near him. It was only seconds before thrusting his dirk that he realized that it was Siùsan and not another threat who had stopped him. He had been an unleashed beserker.

Callum dropped his daggers and pulled his shaking wife into his arms. He held her as tightly as he dared. He felt shaking. At first, he thought it was her. Soon realized that it was him, and he was crying for the first time since his mother died when he was a child. Tears poured forth from both Siùsan and Callum. She clung to him and pressed against him as though she wanted to share the same space as him.

It was only a very loud clearing of the throat, a sound that was becoming annoyingly familiar to them, that finally made them look around. Tavish stood at the door with his back turned towards them. He held a leine in his hand which he reached out behind him. It took Callum a moment to understand why his brother had taken off his shirt and was holding it out, but Siùsan had immediately snatched it and put it on. Callum looked down at himself and realized that Tavish had been smart to offer his leine. Callum's was covered with blood and was not something that he would want to use to cover his naked wife.

"I'll just take these two out of here and leave ye both alone. I should also check on Seamus and Magnus to be sure they dinna see aught of this." Tavish pulled both men to the door and then shut it behind him.

Callum quickly unfastened the extra length of plaid and pulled his leine off tossing the latter in a corner. He picked Siùsan up and cradled her in his arms as he walked over to the tiny cot. He took one look at it and knew that he would crush it. He walked to the wall next to it and slid down to the ground. He held Siùsan in his lap and she gratefully rested her head against his broad chest. She had never been so relieved to see someone as she had been when Callum crashed through the door. She finally felt safe after two weeks of the unknown.

"Lass?" Callum asked quietly.

"Aye, Callum. I'm alright now. Ye came. Ye got here in time."

"In time to stop that attack, but I didna get to ye in time to protect ye from them." He gently kissed the top of her head and stroked her back.

"Ye rescued me. That is what matters. I didna think that ye would find me soon enough. They made me look out the arrow slit before they stripped me naked. They pointed out the men in the bailey and said that ye had come looking for me but were giving up since ye couldnae find me. They taunted me that ye were so close but would never get to me. I feared they were right."

"I kenned ye were here somewhere. I wouldnae ever leave without finding ye. I would never leave ye here."

Siùsan looked up at Callum and gently pulled him close for a kiss. It started gently and grew in intensity until Siùsan was shifting in Callum's lap to better press herself against him. Callum's hand tangled in her hair as he held her close. It was only the tenderness in Siùsan's scalp that made her pull away.

"What is it, Siùsan?"

"It is naught really. Ma head is just a bit tender from Robert yanking on ma hair." She absentmindedly rubbed her head and turned back towards Callum. She leaned in, but this time it was Callum who pulled away. He gently kissed her battered face. He kissed the bruises around her eyes and along her jaw and cheeks. He ran his hands over her shoulders and across her front and back. Siùsan winced in a few places as Callum lifted the leine to get a better look at her injuries. In his rage and haste, Callum had not been able to take in the bruising that covered much of Siùsan's face and body.

"Which one of them did this to ye?" he grounded out.

"Does it really matter? They're both dead now."

"Aye, it matters to me. I would ken the whole of it. I would ken exactly what they did to ye every moment that we were apart. I failed ye, lass. I would ken what I need to atone for."

"Why punish yeself like that? What is there to gain from me reliving this and ye learning all the details? Callum, ye didna fail me. Ever. Just the opposite. Ye saved me when I needed ye most."

"Siùsan, ye can tell me any and everything. I willna turn ye away because of what ye tell me or what they did. None of this was yer fault. Naught was by yer doing."

Siùsan looked into the eyes of the man she had grown to adore and trust above all others. She saw the pain and recrimination in his eyes. She believed what he said but was afraid to test the strength of that promise. She stroked his cheek and kissed his stubbled chin.

"Ye arrived before they were able to do aught to me. They didna harm me more than some bruises."

"I saw what they were about to do. I just saw the bruises on yer breasts. They clearly did more than ye're telling me. What happened?" Callum was growing impatient. He knew that Siùsan was scared to speak of it, and he did not want to traumatize her more, but his mind would not rest until he knew what happened.

"Vera well. This isnae what I want to be doing right now, but I ken ye willna give me peace until ye're satisfied."

Her words were like a jump into a winter's cold loch. Callum shook his head. He could not believe what an inconsiderate eejit he was being. He was about to make his wife relive the terror that her tormentors put her through just to punish himself with the guilt he felt.

"Shhh. Not now. Not any time if ye dinna want to speak of it. I'm sorry. I shouldnae pushed ye. I'm an arse. Please forgive me."

Siùsan heard the plea in Callum's voice and the fear in his eyes. She knew he was asking for forgiveness for more than just his pushiness. Just as she feared telling him the entire truth, she could see that he feared she would not forgive him.

"Callum, there is naught in ma mind to forgive. If ye truly believe there is, then ken that I do. I dinna hold aught against ye at all." She needed space. She needed room to sort out her thoughts. She pushed against him and stood up. "I dinna ken if ye would feel the same way about me." She looked over her shoulder at him as she walked to the far wall. It was only five paces away, but it was just enough for her to breathe.

"What do ye mean, mo ghaol?"

"Will I still be your love if I tell ye the full truth?"

"Of course. Siùsan, do ye fear that I will put ye aside if ye tell me that either of them violated ye?" Callum saw the truth in her eyes before she looked at the floor. He did not need to see her nod her head to tell that she was deeply frightened of just that. He slowly approached as he would a wounded animal.

"What happened, Siùsan?" he whispered. "Ye're ma wife. I have already killed two men who got between us. I will do the same to anyone else. I canna kill memories though. I can only help ye work through them and reassure ye that naught, nae a bluidy thing, will make me shun ye or turn from ye. Nae after what I have been through to get ye back."

Siùsan slowly nodded her head as large, fat tears began trailing down her cheeks. She took a deep breath before starting to retell the events of that day.

"Robert and James both decided that they didna want to bed me until they kenned if I carried yer bairn. Neither wanted to be cuckholded into raising yer bairn, and neither wanted any confusion as to whose bairn I carried. I dinna think either of them realized until today just how much the other desired control of me or rather what they thought I could gain them. Neither of them touched me until today. They had each pushed me about and slapped me, but they never did aught before today to defile me." Siùsan paused to see if Callum believed her. He nodded his head and gave her a small smile to encourage her to continue.

"Robert and Elizabeth came in here earlier." At Callum's shocked expression, she laughed quietly. "Oh aye, there is much to tell about her part in this."

"Yer stepmother was a part of this? I kenned it when I spoke to the bitch." Callum grimaced in disgust.

"Nay! Well mayhap, but I didna mean Lady Elizabeth. I meant yer Elizabeth." Callum shook his head furiously.

"She isnae mine! I swear to ye, she isnae mine."

"Callum, calm yerself. I ken ye arenae involved with her anymore. I just meant it to not confuse the two women. Anyway, she and Robert came in here. She has been the one to deliver ma meager rations. She used every opportunity to taunt me.

She relished in ma capture. She was conniving enough to think she would get ye back now that I was no longer with ye. I thought I might distract them by creating a rift among them. When Robert came in here today, he did so to try to tempt me by making me watch him pleasure Elizabeth. Instead it gave me the opportunity to taunt her. I reminded her that every mon she has would rather have me. I reminded her that ye, Robert, and James have either already or will put her aside for me. I told her she was never anyone's first choice.

"She left in a huff and I assume went to complain to James. Already aroused and with no outlet once Elizabeth left, Robert turned on me. He slapped me and punched me when I fought back. It angered him even more." Siùsan paused here. She did not want to tell him more. When Callum nodded slightly and squeezed her hand, which she had not even noticed he was holding, she continued.

"He tried to take me from behind," Siùsan raised one eyebrow and gave Callum a pointed look. She just could not bring herself to say aloud how Robert wanted to violate her. "I fought him off and grabbed one of ma dirks. I sliced the side of his prick and only angered him even further. He tossed me onto the bed and was about to rape me when James burst in. He began yelling at Robert who only became angrier. It came out that both kenned ye had come, so they made it a point for me to see yer men in the bailey and that nay person would hear me yell even if I tried. I kept fighting them. They pinned me down and felt around to see if I had any other dirks hidden. They found the one in ma other boot, but they didna find the one in ma skirts. James said the only way to be sure I didna have any other knives on me was to strip me bare. They kept arguing about Robert trying to take me from James and how James wouldnae be in the picture if Robert hadnae arranged for his escape. The angrier they became, the more they touched me and the more aroused they became."

Callum knew this to be similar to battle lust, but he did not interrupt Siùsan.

Siùsan walked over to the arrow slit and peered out. The stars twinkled over head. There was little movement outside the curtain wall, but there was a swarm of men now in the bailey. She tried to see more clearly who was there, but it was far too dark to be able to see plaids. She assumed they were Sinclairs. Callum walked up behind her and gently wrapped his arms around her. She leaned back against him and sighed.

"Ye dinna need to tell me anymore. I think I ken what happened next. I just give thanks to God that I arrived when I did."

Siùsan closed her eyes and breathed in the unique scent that was Callum's alone. The mix of pine, and a little sweat and horses. She felt a sense of calm that she had not had since the moment she had been ripped from Callum's arms. She did not even realize that tears were leaking from her eyes until one landed on Callum's arm and he reached up to wipe them away. He gently turned her to face him.

"What makes ye cry, leannan?"

"There is more than what ye saw. They made me--How can ye still want me when another man has--," Siùsan sobbed.

Callum pulled her close and stroked her head. He did not know what to do next. He had been so relieved to know that she had not been raped, that he had gotten to her in time, that he had not thought about what might have happened before. Now he was not so sure that he had rescued his wife in time after all. He desperately wanted to ask what she had not told him yet, but he did not want to push too hard. So he just waited.

Siùsan slowly calmed again and the tear stopped flowing. She sniffed and leaned against Callum's chest. She ran her hands over his bare chest and then leaned back to give him a gentle kiss. Callum suddenly had a sense that Siùsan was saying good-bye.

"They may nae have raped me, but they did make me touch them." Callum had to strain to hear Siùsan as it came out as barely a whisper. He had to stop himself from breathing a sigh of relief. She would not look at him and tried to step away from him. Callum refused to let go. He did not want her to feel trapped, but he was not about to let her walk away.

"They didna hurt ye in any other way?"

Siùsan shook her head.

"Wasnae that enough?" She looked up at him with eyes that showed the depth of her anguish.

"I didna mean it that way. I ken now what they did to ye. I just want ye to understand that this doesnae change anything between us. Ye didna do it by choice. Ye didna want to do it. What would have happened if ye had refused?" He ran his finger from her temple down to her chin lightly grazing the bruises that covered her face. "They would have only beaten ye more or tried to rape ye sooner."

"Ye arenae upset to hear that I touched another mon? Ye dinna think I'm a whore? Because I do!" This time when she pulled away, Callum let her go. He ran a hand through his hair and scrubbed his face with both hands.

"Siùsan, I dinna think any of that aboot ye. I havenae thought it and would never think that. Ye are ma wife because I love ye and ye love me. Ye wouldnae have married me if ye didna ken I love ye. That isnae going to change because two mad men kidnapped and then violated ye. Damn it, Siùsan! Ye wouldnae be in this position if it hadnae been for ma self centered choices that I made over and over. If I hadnae taken up with Elizabeth, she wouldnae have been around to help them. Their plan never would have taken root. If I hadnae made ye feel like ye had to run from me, we wouldnae been attacked by the James Gunn. If I had protected ye properly, ye never would have been snatched from me while I snored. Dinna ye see? Ye didna do any of this. Ye survived as best ye could. If anyone is to blame, it's me. I did this to ye!"

Siùsan did not know what to say. She saw the same anguish on Callum's face that she felt. She shook her head and walked back to him. She wrapped her arms around his waist and waited until he lifted his arms to hug her back.

"I already told ye that I dinna blame ye for this, and that all is forgiven," Siùsan said.

"And I have told ye the same. Ye arenae to blame. Ye didna do aught that needs forgiving." Callum held his breath waiting for her response.

"I just canna believe that any mon would want a wife who was whored out to other men."

"I dinna see it that way. Ye arenae a whore. Elizabeth, who throws herself at any mon she thinks will help her gain more, is a whore. I dinna care a whit about whether ye stroked two men if it kept ye from being beaten, raped, or killed!" Callum cupped Siùsan's face in his hands and kissed her passionately. He backed her against the wall and pulled Tavish's leine over her head. He pulled his belt from his waist and let his plaid fall to the floor. Siùsan's hands roamed over his body and down his sides. Her hands found the grooves on the sides of his buttocks that she loved so much. She held onto him as he lifted one of her legs to his hip.

"I am going to make love to ma wife now. I want naught but to show ye how much I love ye. I willna ever turn from ye. I willna ever let ye hide from me. We are bound together, and we will go through life as partners."

Callum pressed gently into her. Siùsan moaned as she felt his long, thick sword slide into her sheath. She had been so afraid that he would reject her once he knew what she had been forced to do. She had not completely let go of her guilt, and she knew that Callum had not let go of his, but she could not think of a better man to spend her life with or a better way for them to start to heal. She desperately wanted to show Callum how much she loved him and how grateful she was that he rescued her. However, he stilled. He also feared that he was rushing her.

"Lass, ye arenae doing this because ye think I expect it or that ye have to thank me for coming to ye, are ye?" Callum's heart sank when he thought that she might make love to him out of obligation rather than want.

"I dinna do this because I feel obligated or that I owe it to ye. I want to make love to ye because I love ye and thought I might never see ye again. I want to feel us joined as one again. This is where we belong. With us in each other's arms."

Callum and Siùsan kissed again. Their tongues dueled with one another. She had a moment of doubt that doing this would make him think of what she had been forced to do with Robert and James. As Siùsan gently sucked Calllum's into her mouth, Callum groaned and thrust into her faster. Their passion rose quickly and crested fast. They were left out of breath and panting. Callum once again lowered himself to the ground and settled Siùsan on his lap. He handed her Tavish's leine and he pulled his plaid around them. He smattered small kisses across her forehead as they both tried to catch their breath. They looked into each other's eyes and knew that things would be right between them. They sat quietly, simply enjoying their time alone together, but it did not last nearly long enough.

Chapter Thirty-Two

The shouts warned them that people were on the way and the heavy thudding of boots on the stairs barely gave them enough time to right their scant pieces of clothing. Callum pulled Siùsan up and moved her behind him. He picked up his forgotten sword and positioned himself in front of the door. They had no way of knowing if these were friends or foes. The voices were nearly outside the door before they could clearly make out what was being said.

"Callum! Where the bluidy hell is ma granddaughter?"

"Where's ma daughter? What have ye done to her. I'll kill ye if ye harm her!"

"Callum! Siùsan! Get dressed!" The last coming from Tavish before two almighty roars were heard.

"Trust Tavish to improve the situation," Callum grumbled. He eased his stance but still used his large frame to block Siùsan from the two men who sounded like they wanted his head.

The door swung open on its broken hinges. In the doorway stood two out of breath older men and one gloating younger brother. Everyone stood and stared at one another for a moment before Laird Mackenzie and Laird MacLeod launched into a tirade of questions. Siùsan stepped around Callum who tried to pull her back behind him. She gave him a quelling look and took his hand. She interlaced her fingers with his and gave her father and grandfather a pointed look.

"I'm fine, as ye can see. I didna come to any real harm—"

"Nae harm! This one dragged two dead bodies into ma bailey and two knocked out guardsmen!" Laird Mackenzie bellowed as he jerked a thumb over his shoulder to indicate Tavish.

Siùsan took a slow breath and tried to relax her shoulders. Her father had an unparalleled ability to rile her.

"As I was aboot to say, nae harm because Callum got here in time. I was mostly left alone for the near sennight I was here."

"Sennight? Ye were hidden here for an entire sennight?" The Mackenzie seemed to deflate in front of them all. He seemed to age a decade before their eyes.

His shoulders stooped, and his head dropped. "I didna ken. I didna ken." He kept whispering.

Siùsan gritted her teeth but showed no emotion to her father because she truly felt none. She thought she would feel anger, hurt, or resentment. She even thought she would feel hate. There was just nothing.

"Siùsan, ye have to believe that I wouldnae let them keep ye locked up in here. I wouldnae ever let either of them touch ye if I'd kenned." Laird Mackenzie's words fell flat to Siùsan. She stared at him as though she had never seen him before and certainly not as though he was her father. She felt completely blank when looking at him.

"I believe ye, Father. I believe ye didna ken and ye wouldnae have condoned them taking me. After all, ye would have worried that you'd lost ma meager dowry for naught and the Sinclairs might demand recompense." While there was no bite to her words, Laird Mackenzie jerked back as though she had slapped him.

"Nay! That isnae so. I dinna care about the money. I have been a failure as a father to ye, but I never wished anyone to abuse ye."

At that, Siùsan gave an unladylike snort.

"Ye may nae have wanted any mon to rape me but ye certainly never cared if I was abused. Yer neglect was abuse. Yer wife's treatment of me when I was only ten summers old was abuse. There was nae other child in this keep who was made to regularly scrub the privvies. There was nae other child in this keep who was forced to sleep in a storeroom throughout the year with naught but one thin blanket. Nae even a candle. There was nae other child who was sent away from meals with nae food simply because her parents couldnae stand the sight of her."

Laird Mackenzie's shocked look could not have been faked. He was truly stunned by what Siùsan just shared.

"Those things couldnae have happened to ye."

"Aye. Each one and for years. Perhaps ye should speak to yer lady wife more often. Ye might ken what happens in this keep when ye're off playing laird."

Now there was bite to Siùsan's words. Years of pent up anger and hurt threatened to pour forth. Callum wrapped his arm around Siùsan's shoulders and pulled her closer. Through this all, Laird MacLeod stood silently. His face just kept growing redder.

"Ye hate me," Laird Mackenzie sounded resigned.

"Nae. I dinna hate ye. I dinna feel anything for ye anymore. I dinna consider maself to be a Mackenzie anymore. I dinna wish anyone harm or foul. I just dinna care."

"Ye piece of shite! I care! Ye lied to me about the death of ma only granddaughter who came from ma only daughter. Ye neglected and mistreated her for her entire life. Thank the blessed Jesu that she married a mon who loves her and cares for her. That was the only damn thing ye've done right in her entire life." Before Laird Mackenzie could think about moving, two large hamhocks for fists flew at his face. One landed squarely and broke his nose while the other blackened his eye. "I could and would have taken her. I would have raised her among people who would have wanted and appreciated her. Yer stole from yer daughter and ye stole from me. This willna be easily forgiven."

Laird Mackenzie held his plaid to his nose to try to staunch the bleeding and looked completely at a loss as to what to say or do next. He knew he was a defeated man.

Laird MacLeod stepped forward tentatively and now seemed shy when smiling at Siùsan.

"Ye look just like her. Ye're the spitting image of yer mother, ma daughter, Rose. I canna believe it. It's like looking at her again. I didna ever think I would."

A tear ran down the MacLeod's cheek. He held out a hand and waited to see if Siùsan would take it. She stepped away from Callum and wrapped her arms around Thormud. It took but one heartbeat before he embraced his granddaughter.

"Ah, lass. Ye even smell like yer mother."

"Grandda," Siùsan sighed. Besides Callum and Laird Sinclair, she had never felt so safe as she did in her grandfather's embrace. She nestled her face against his broad chest and smelled his rather grandfatherly scent which included a lingering scent of whisky. "I was trying to visit ye. Ma husband was taking me to ye."

"I ken. I'm so vera happy to ken ye wanted to meet me. So vera happy."

They embraced for several more minutes before pulling apart.

"Grandda, what are ye doing here?"

"Yer husband came to me for help. Needless to say, it came as quite a shock to learn that not only did I have a granddaughter I'd never heard of but that she was married and had been kidnapped, too. Callum and his brothers worked out that ye had been brought here. He needed more men to accompany him. I wasnae ever quite resolved with the death of Rose. While Callum and Tavish came up here to find ye, yer father and I had a little fireside chat." He glowered at Laird Mackenzie. "I canna make up for all the years ye lost being here, but I would gladly have ye with ma clan anytime ye want, lass."

Here was the invitation that Callum had feared. He knew how much Siùsan wanted a family that loved her and wanted her. He just prayed that she realized that she already had that with the Sinclairs. He held his breath as he waited for her reply.

"Grandda, I am so happy to hear that. I hope that we can visit ye and ye can visit us every year. I dinna want too much time to go between our visits either. If it's alright with ye, and with Callum, I would like to travel back to MacLeod lands and meet ma mother's kin. We just canna stay over long. Callum has already been away for over a fortnight. His father will worry, and we have responsibilities at home."

Callum released the breath that he had only just realized he was holding. *She thinks of Sinclair lands as home. She doesnae want to leave me.* Callum's greatest fear was finally and completely laid to rest.

Siùsan turned and walked back to Callum. She looked up at him with the unspoken question in her eyes.

"Of course, we will visit yer kin, and they are always welcome in our home."

"Our home," Siùsan whispered and smiled.

Chapter Thirty-Three

Siùsan and Callum made their way below stairs after one othe maids brought her one of her old kirtles. Callum insisted on carrying her the entire way. He reasoned that she was exhausted and had not been fed enough to sustain her. He did not want to have come so far just to lose her because she tumbled down the stairs. Siùsan easily relented as she was just as Callum described but more honestly, she knew that they both longed to be in constant contact with one another. She did not want to be out of reach from him and he refused to let her go. They were both perfectly content to let Callum carry her while she wrapped her arms around his neck and rested her head on his shoulder. She silently marveled at the breadth of Callum's shoulders and the weight of the responsibility that he already had on them and that he would one day inherit.

When they arrived in the Great Hall, they were met with silence. All eyes were suddenly on them and everyone stopped what they were doing to stare. Siùsan immediately wanted to shrink into Callum from humiliation. She had planned never to return to this keep and she wanted nothing more than to leave as soon as possible. Her father had already made his way down and was seated on the dais with a large mug of what looked to be ale but Siùsan knew was more likely whisky. He looked haggered. Beside him sat Siùsan's stepmother, Lady Elizabeth. While she was not smiling, there was certainly a sense of glee when she saw Siùsan's condition.

"Why daughter, if only we had kenned yer current circumstances. We would have certainly assisted." Callum stiffened as Lady Elizabeth's comment neglected to state who she would have assisted, just as she intended from her gloating expression.

Siùsan was used to Lady Elizabeth's barbed comments and chose to not respond. She did not even look in the woman's direction. Instead she looked around at all those who were gathered in the Great Hall. These were people she had known her entire life and had chosen to ignore her. She tried to come up with something to say. There was just nothing left to give to them, not even antipathy. Instead it was simply apathy.

I always thought that the opposite of love was hate. That if I ever got away from here, I would hate ma father and Lady Elizabeth and all of those who made ma life so difficult. But I realize now that the oppositie of love is indifference.

Seamus and Magnus stepped forward tentatively. They really were no longer boys but young men. Callum had explained to Siùsan on the way downstairs that it had been her brothers who had alerted him and Tavish to where she was being hidden. He told her about how the set of two younger brothers led the set of two older brothers through the winding tunnels.

Siùsan looked from her brothers up to Callum. He put her down only to wrap his arm around her waist.

"Seamus, Magnus, thank ye for helping rescue me. If ye hadnae shown them the way, I might not be standing here right now."

Siùsan paused for a moment to clear her throat. She suddenly felt tears welling up. The only people she had missed while being away from her clan were standing in front of her. They were the only two people that she loved from her former home. She opened her arms and stepped forward. Her brothers rushed forwards. She had not realized until just now that they were both taller than she was. *So much has changed in such a short amount of time. I have a husband and ma brothers are both bigger than me.*

"Siùsan, I am so vera sorry that we couldnae come and rescue ye ourselves. We kenned we couldnae get around the guards, and we *didna* ken if Mother and Father were a part of this." Magnus whispered while they hugged.

"I kenned it all along. I wouldnae have wanted ye to endanger yerselves for me. I am just thankful that ye sought out Callum and helped him."

"We love ye, Siùsan. It isnae the same here without ye. Mother and Father havenae changed but that only makes it worse. Father berates us in the lists for naught and Mother still ignores us. Ye were the only person who loved us." Seasmus whispered.

"Loves. I love ye. Nae in the past, always in the present and always in the future." She kissed both young men on the cheek. "Wait here a moment."

Siùsan turned back to Callum and stood on her tiptoes to whisper in his ear. He still had to lean far over for her to reach.

"I want to bring them with us. Can they foster on Sinclair land? They willna be sent anywhere and they willna receive proper training here. Seamus must learn to lead a clan properly and Magnus must learn to be tainiste."

"Do ye think yer father and Lady Elizabeth would allow it?"

"Mayhap not but can ye still ask? If not with us, then perhaps the MacLeods."

"Aye." Callum straightened up and looked to the dais.

Laird Mackenzie was still staring into his mug while Lady Elizabeth began to eat her evening meal. She was the only person who had been served as the commotion of finding Siùsan had interrupted the meal that had just begun. She blithely ignored everyone while she sat above them.

Callum turned his attention back to Laird Mackenzie. He tried not to show his disgust at the man. The man who had given him the opportunity to a marry a woman who he loved beyond belief but was the same cowardly man who had caused her such deep and lasting pain. He looked back over his shoulder and saw Siùsan's expectant look. She had her hands clasped as though in prayer and was leaning forward. He did not miss the eager look in her eyes. Once more he looked at Laird Mackenzie and took a deep breath before beginning.

"Laird Mackenzie, I greatly appreciate yer agreement in allowing me to marry yer daughter. She has been a tremendous blessing to me and a much needed and wanted addition to Clan Sinclair." Callum just could not resist the urge to make his point abundantly clear. "In return for such a gracious and beneficial arrangement, I would like to offer to foster both of yer sons."

Laird Mackenzie barely looked up. He simply nodded his head. To anyone who did not know Laird Mackenzie well, they might have thought that he suffered self-condimnation, however, those who knew him, knew it was self-pity that had drained him of his vigor. He would return to his normal self when the cause of his self-pity was no longer nearby. Lady Elizabeth, on the other hand, was very attentive to what was being offered.

"Nay! They arenae going with ye or any other Sinclair. They will go to ma kin. They will be trained by the Gunns."

Laird Mackenzie snapped out of his stupor at his wife's declaration.

"Christ's bones on the cross! There is not a bluidy chance that ma sons will go anywhere near the Gunns. They are the cause of all that has gone wrong in ma life." He turned an accusing finger at his wife. "It was yer brother who hooped and hollered loudly and wildly enough to spook ma wife's horse. It was ye who refused to assist her when she needed a healer all because ye believed ye were due the position of lady of the Mackenzies. It was ye who insisted that I abandon ma own bairn to avoid yer brother and his allies from attacking and by fueling ma grief. I ken now that ye mistreated Siùsan when I trusted ye to raise her. It was also yer other brother who kidnapped her, tried to rape her, and would have killed Sir Callum if he hadnae killed him first. Of that I am sure. Nay. Ye'll nae be sending ma sons to the Gunns but I will be sending ye packing back to them. Ye never wanted to be here but to claim yer title. Now ye dinna have to be. Ye served yer usefulness by giving me two sons but ye have sorely worn out yer welcome. I repudiate our marriage and all ties to ye and the Gunns." Laird Mackenzie was yelling by the time he finished.

Siùsan's father had just said more than she had ever heard him say at one time. She was shocked at how ferocious he sounded. But he was not done yet. He turned his attention to Siùsan.

"I already admitted to ye in private that I failed ye, but I will make it kenned to all present." He turned to face all who still watched the scene in front of them. "I failed ma only daughter, the product of ma marriage to the only woman I ever have and ever will love. I ignored her and turned away from her first in ma grief and then in acquiescence to ma current wife's demands. I ken ma time and chances have run out with ma daughter, but I canna and willna make the same mistakes twice. Ma sons will foster with the Sinclairs as of today."

Laird Mackenzie jumped down from the dais with a newfound vigor. He extended his arm to Callum who grasped his forearm in a warrior's handshake. Next, he gazed at Siùsan, who was smiling before her father looked at her.

"Siùsan, I havenae done right by ye. Ever. But I do have the chance to give yer brothers an opportunity to grow into the men needed to run this clan when I am gone. I ken that it was ye who asked if they could foster with the Sinclairs. I ken ye dinna do this for me but because of me. I still thank ye caring so much for yer brothers, and I do this for ye as for them. I ken they are in good hands with the Sinclairs. I am sorry. Ye'll never ken the depth of ma regret and remorse for having treated ye as I did. Treated ye so poorly that any mon, let alone two, thought they could molest ye. This is more ma fault than anyone else's."

Siùsan looked at her father who she had always thought was a cold and hard warrior and then believed was, in fact, a coward after what Callum pointed out. Now she just saw a mon who never recovered from his grief and was turned bitter by circumstances he felt he could not control. She almost felt pity for him, but she was not there yet. She could at least make peace before leaving.

"Father, I ken that ye have missed ma mother every day since she passed. I ken that it was painful for me to be a constant reminder of what ye lost. I also ken I have moved on. I dinna have any real ties that bind me here now that ma brothers will come with me. Perhaps one day I will return for a visit." Siùsan left it with the vague hint that a visit would not occur until after her father was no longer laird.

"Do ye forgive me? Can ye forgive me?"

Siùsan took a deep breath before she could answer. He was asking too much for her after all that she had suffered and what had happened over the past fortnight. Callum came to her rescue. She breathed easy.

"Siùsan has a big heart and a fair mind. I think with time, she will make her peace with ye and her past." Callum placed his hand on the small of her back and turned to her brothers. "Pack what ye need for the journey. Anything ye canna carry in a satchel will be replaced when we get home. We will meet ye in the bailey. We ride out tonight."

Callum led Siùsan into the bailey followed by Tavish and Laird MacLeod, both of whom had witnessed the family dynamics in silence. Siùsan was surprised to see Magnus waiting for them along with a man who resembled her grandfather. There were also close to a score of men in MacLeod plaids waiting too. Siùsan looked up at Callum and then around him at her grandfather who was beaming. Laird MacLeod stepped forward to the young man who was so like him in looks, build, and stance.

"Lass, this is yer cousin, Michail. He is the eldest child of yer Uncle Torrian, ye mama's brother, and his wife, Catriona." He left off the part about Catriona originally being a Gunn. He did not see any reason to add salt to several still gaping wounds. "He is about yer age and will one day be laird of the MacLeods."

"It's vera nice to meet ye, Siùsan. It came as a bit of a surprise that I have a cousin I never kenned about. I ken Grandda is mighty happy to meet ye and ma parents are eager to meet ye too. I dinna quite ken if saying welcome to the family is right, but I canna help but feel it."

Siùsan looked at her grandfather and cousin standing side-by-side. A warmth flooded through her to know that she had blood relatives who wanted her and who were excited to get to know her. She silently reached for Callum's hand and intertwined their fingers. He squeezed her hand gently.

"Michail, I, too, am happy to meet ye. I seem to have found an entire family in one day. I am excited to meet the rest of yer-- I mean-- our clan and to meet yer parents," she said with a soft chuckle as she realized she was as much a MacLeod as she had been a Mackenzie. "I dinna ken how long we will be able to visit. We must be home before the end of fall and the snows come." She looked up expectantly at Callum. He nodded his head.

"Lass, if ye dinna mind, I would ride back to the Sinclairs' with ye instead. There is still much of the summer left for yer visit." The MacLeod said. "I would like to see Laird Sinclair again. It has been far too many years and far too much has passed to go any longer without seeing him."

"I dinna mind if it is alright with Callum." She knew that Callum would not refuse either of them but out of courtesy, she deferred to him.

"Of course. We would be happy to have ye join us, but we camp in the woods tonight. I willna allow Siùsan to remain here another night."

Siùsan was so relieved to know that they would be leaving even if it was to just stop out of sight of the keep. She looked around and spotted Trofast waiting for her. Just as his name meant, he was always faithful and loyal. She ran to him and nuzzled her face into his neck. Callum quietly came up behind her.

"I ken ye've missed him, but I have missed ye too. If ye want to ride him, will ye allow me to ride with ye?"

She turned to smile at Callum. She placed her hands on his chest and could feel the steady rhythm of his heart.

"If Deamhan doesnae mind seeing ye with another horse, I think he will allow it. I would like that too," she grinned

"Ahem, not to once again break up yet another blissful moment between ye two, but I thought ye would want to ken that Elizabeth was found by Michail trying to escape through the postern gate. Michail has offered to make her a guest in the MacLeod's dungeon until she can be sent back to court to await the King's judgment on her role in all of this. Thought ye'd be relieved to hear that," Mangus stepped back and crossed his arms when he finished delivering that piece of news.

Siùsan and Callum simply looked at Magnus and then at each other before nodding. There really was nothing left to be said about any of the people who had plotted and connived against them.

Her brothers made their way to the bailey and everyone mounted up.

"We ride!" Callum called out. The party left the bailey and none of the Mackenzies looked back.

Chapter Thirty-Four

he Sinclair party rode at a steady pace for nearly two weeks before they reached their land. Siùsan slept heavily at night and ate heartily at each meal. However, the last three days of the journey saw her casting up her accounts before every meal and especially when she was near the cook fire and smelled roasting meat. Callum had rushed after her the first time she dashed out of camp to heave. He quickly learned that Siùsan did not like anyone, especially him, to see her when she was ill. She blistered his ears and then burst into tears for doing just that. After that, Callum gave her space but she was never further than he could see. He also noticed that she became increasingly tired by midafternoon. The first afternoon that she dozed off in the saddle, Callum caught her before she fell off Trofast. After that, she agreed to ride with Callum between the midday meal and when they stopped for the night. While they still made time to sneak off together each night, Siùsan was softly snoring as soon as they wrapped their plaids around themselves near the fire.

On the last morning before they reached home, Siùsan knew she had to tell Callum her suspicions as he was becoming increasingly irritable with everyone but her and as anxious as a mother hen around her. When they stopped to water the horses, she pulled him aside.

"Callum, I need to speak with ye, please." They walked out of earshot of the group and stopped in the shade. Siùsan's cheeks had pinkened from riding so many days in the sun and the warmth of the summer day. Callum tucked hair behind her ears which had become an unconscious habit of his from the first day they met.

"Callum, I believe I ken why I've been feeling poorly that last few days. We've been married now for almost two moons. Have ye nae noticed that something hasnae happened? Or something is missing?" She wanted him to figure it out on his own. She wanted to see the surprise as it dawned on him that he would be a father.

Callum thought for a moment, looking into the leaves overhead.

"Nay. I havenae seen anything go missing and I canna think of anything that should have happened. Other than ye feeling a bit off these last few days, everything seems back to normal, or as close as we can come."

"Callum, it's been almost seven sennights since we handfasted. That is a bit of a while, isnae? In over seven sennights, ye havenae wondered why we've been able to make love every day except for those when we were apart. Ye havenae asked if I was indisposed at all during that time."

"Is it too much for ye? Do wish for us to take a break?" Callum could not figure out what Siùsan was hinting at. He worried that he had been too pushy and now he and his ballocks would suffer for it.

Siùsan grunted in frustration. Callum looked down at her. He had never heard her make that sound before.

"Are ye really that dim? Ye had at least one mistress that I ken of and ye were with her for nearly three moons. Werenae there nights when ye couldnae bed her?"

Callum flushed red and looked out over her head. Never again did he ever want to think of being with another woman. He certainly wanted no reminders of Elizabeth. He ran a hand through his hair absentmindedly.

"Aye. I suppose there were a few days each month when she was indisposed."

"Ye havenae noticed that I havenae been indisposed? At least not in the same way? And I can tell ye I wasna indisposed while I was away from ye either."

"Siùsan, what are ye getting at? Do ye nae want to couple as often? Have I been too demanding?" Callum was beginning to get frustrated, so Siùsan took pity on him.

"Mo ghaol, I havenae had ma courses since before we wed. That is why we havenae had to take any breaks in our love making, nor do I plan to do so now, I might add. Callum, I havenae bled in over two moons, I'm ill every time I smell food cooking, I'm exhausted from doing naught, and even ye noticed that ma breasts are more sensitive than normal." She still wanted it to dawn on him without more prompting.

Callum took in the list that Siùsan just rattled off, his eyes growing rounder and his mouth dropping open wider as the penny finally dropped.

"Do ye mean—do ye mean ye're –that we're—Siùsan, are ye having a bairn?" It came out as a whisper by the end.

"I canna ken for sure until I see the midwife, but I have experience with healing and have delivered several bairns maself. I believe I have all the signs that we'll be having a wee one this winter or early next spring."

Callum whooped and pulled Siùsan into his embrace twirling her around. She giggled and when he put her down, it was with a loud smacking kiss on her lips.

"I'm going to be a da! I'm going to be a da!"

"Sshh! I take it ye're pleased," she grinned. She had been a little nervous telling him. She knew he had taken every precaution not to sire any bastards, but she was not entirely sure if he wanted children yet.

"Pleased doesnae even begin to describe how I feel. Ah lass, I couldnae be happier. I love ye, mo neach beag."

"I dinna ken how much longer ye'll be able to call me yer little one. I may end up the size of the side of the stables."

"All the more to hold onto while I make love to ye," he said with a cheeky grin.

She playfully swatted his arm before becoming more serious.

"Callum, I dinna want to tell anyone yet. It's still vera early and things could go wrong. I dinna want to get everyone too excited and then fail to have yer heir. I only told ye because I saw ye were about to worry yerself sick every time I ran off to throw up."

Callum gently pulled in her in for an embrace. He stroked her back and kissed the top of her head.

"I heard what ye just said. Fail to have ma heir. Mo ghaol, God forbid aught happens to this bairn, it willna be a failure on yer part. I want a bairn with ye and have thought about it often since that first day on the beach, but I dinna want one so badly that I risk ye. If it doesnae work out, this time or any time, I will still be a blessed man to be married to ye. Besides, that's what I have Alexander for and he may be on the way to the kirk as we speak," Callum smirked. "I love ye."

Siùsan breathed a quiet sigh of relief. Callum had done much in their time together to help build her confidence. Yet the fear of failure and then rejection still lurked in the back of her mind.

"I love ye, too."

~ ~ ~

They rode into the bailey just as Liam Sinclair came out of the Great Hall. He waved to the group and came down to greet them. He stopped short when he saw Thormud MacLeod amongst the riders dismounting.

"Thor! What are ye doing here? And what are ye all doing back so soon? I thought ye would have stayed for a longer visit."

"Da, there is much to fill ye in on. Much. First, I would get Siùsan inside for a warm bath and something to eat. She's almost asleep in the saddle again."

Liam Sinclair raised an eyebrow at the word 'again'. He took one look at Siùsan and then gave his son a knowing look. He nodded and turned to the MacLeod. The two older warriors greated each other with loud and sturdy claps to the back and a bear hug. They had not seen each other since before Rose MacLeod's death. Liam knew there was a great deal that he needed to explain to Thormud and the rest of his family. He ushered his old friend into the Great Hall, and they sat before the fire while they waited for Callum and Siùsan to rejoin them.

Siùsan and Callum returned after they had shared a bath, only getting distracted long enough for one round of love making, which Siùsan promptly fell asleep after. As they came into the Great Hall, they saw that the Sinclair and the MacLeod were still seated in front of the fireplace. Tavish and Magnus were seated near them playing a game of knucklebones. Callum was surprised to see Alex standing near a window with a young woman he had never seen before. They were not touching, but Alex was clearly positioned protectively, and she did not seem to mind as she leaned slightly towards him as they talked. Now that this young woman was up and about, Callum hoped it meant he would have time to talk to Alex. He missed his brother fiercely and was not used to being this disconnected from him. He understood that it had started months ago when he brough Elizabeth home with him and that he had much to repair, but he longed for the companionship that they shared. He would seek Alex out later.

Callum and Siùsan made their way to the fireplace. Callum pulled over an extra chair to sit next to his father and then pulled Siùsan into his lap. Magus and Tavish looked up and then moved closer. Tavish called to Alex and he, along with the mystery young woman, followed Tavish and Magnus over to the fireplace.

Once everyone was seated, with only Alex standing behind the chair of his companion, Laird Sinclair looked around at his family. He had an immense surge of pride at seeing his sons before him. He missed Mairghread and wished she and Tristan would visit soon. He also keenly missed his wife who had not been given the opportunity to see their children grow into adults. He knew she watched over them all from heaven.

"I've been filling Thormud in on many of the goings on of this clan over the past score of years. I have shared with him a few things that I would now like to tell the rest of you, especially you, Callum, and Siùsan.

"When Rose died, yer Mama and I travelled as quickly as we could to Mackenzie land for the burial. Ma Kyla and Rose had been close friends since they were weans. The Sutherlands and MacLeods have been intertwined for generations in one way or another. We were two days too late and had just missed Thormud leaving. When we arrived, we spent the night at the keep, but it was uncomfortable with the death pall that hung over everyone and the bitterness that radiated off Lady Elizabeth. We chose to leave the next morning, even though we had ridden long and hard to try to get there in time. As we were leaving, we saw a woman in the bailey carrying a vera wee bairn with a thatch of deep, fiery red hair. It was the exact color of Rose's and Thormud's. When we approached the woman, she tried to rush away, but Kyla called out to her. The woman didna dare ignore a noblewoman. As we approached, we saw that she had another bairn tied to her back with a bedsheet that was not much older than the redheaded one. This bairn was a wee lad who was clearly a few months older than the redhead but not old enough that they could be siblings.

"Kyla asked the woman whose child the lass was. The woman wouldnae come out and say it, but it was obvious that the bairn was the laird's and Rose's, and she was caring for her. This woman was Moira Mackenzie." Liam Sinclair nodded to Siùsan. "Aye, the woman who raised ye and was Robert's mother. We couldnae understand why ye were living outside the keep. We pressed Moira for more information. She was extremely nervous but finally admitted that she was to raise ye as her own because yer father and new stepmother didna want ye in the keep. They wouldnae acknowledge ye.

"While ye were living with Moira, Kyla and I sent money and supplies secretly to her. When ye were moved into the keep, I wrote to yer father asking him to foster ye with us since ye and Mairghread are close in age. But ye father wouldnae even answer any of ma missives."

"I found out during ma chat with yer father that he hadnae received any of the missives that Liam sent. I believe Elizabeth was the reason for that, the spiteful bitch." Thormud could not help but add the epithet. He sat back with a hurrumph.

"That is what we came to believe too. Since we couldnae get any response and we didna think coming to visit would help ye any, perhaps only making it worse, I sent a young couple to live and work among ye. Mayhap ye remember Mary and Alec. She worked in the kitchens and he was a guardsman. They would send me missives as regularly as they could to let me ken how ye faired. The news was never good but never dire enough to warrant me intervening. I didna want to make matters worse and lose ma only means of keeping an eye on ye."

"I do remember them. They were kind to me even when they kept their distance just as everyone else did," Siùsan broke in.

"Aye well, it was best for everyone is they were seen and not heard. It was in one of those missives that I learned that Lady Elizabeth was growing impatient with ye still being in the Mackenzie keep or even on Mackenzie land. She had started to needle yer father into allowing James to marry ye. I couldnae wait any longer at that point, so I sent Lewis, ma second, to meet personally with ye father to negotiate a marriage with Callum. It took several moons and several trips back and forth for Lewis before yer father agreed. I was finally able to convince him when I stated that I wouldnae ask for a bride price, I wouldnae require a dowry, but I would take ye with just the clothes on yer back if that would hurry things along.

"I didna explain any of this to Callum because I wanted him to meet ye and form his own opinion of ye. I wanted ye to get to ken each other and hoped that a love would grow between ye just as it did with me and ma Kyla. I admit that Callum gave me several sleepless nights there in the beginning. As I told ye, nighean, I had faith in Callum and needed ye to too, even if he was making a right cockup of it from the start. Blessed Jesu, Mary, and Joseph. I thought ye were going to turn and walk right back out of the keep when ye first met, or rather smelled, him. But I kenned I'd done right when ye put him squarely in his place. Time after time. Ye've yer mother's pluck, ye ken. Not a wilting flower, to be sure."

Siùsan's felt like her head was spinning with all the information that her father by marriage had just shared. She could hardly follow him after he called her his nighean, his daughter. She had to swallow back tears when she realized that she really did think of Laird Liam Sinclair as her father now. All of it was almost too much to take in at once.

"Are ye well, leannan?" Callum whispered to her. She could only nod her head. He gently pressed her head against his shoulder and she relaxed. Callum was also struggling to make sense of all that he had just learned. He never had a clue that his father had spies among the Mackenzies. He never knew the reason why his father had chosen Siùsan or how he could be so sure they would be well suited. He assumed that it was a favor in memory of his mother. He thought back to how bitterly angry he had been to learn that he was to be betrothed. He had railed against his father and sulked then escaped from thinking about it by over indulging in Elizabeth. Thinking of her soured his stomach. He owed his father and brothers a tremendous apology and his father a debt of gratitude.

"Da."

"Aye, lad."

"I am so vera sorry. For it all. I owe ye all such a tremendous apology. I am ashamed of how I behaved from when I returned from court until I wedded Siùsan. I dinna ken how ye put up with me," he laughed ruefully, "but I am ever so grateful that ye did. Alex, I should have listened to ye from the start. I shouldnae been so self-centered to ever believe ye dinna have ma best interests or those of the clan at heart." He stood and placed Siùsan in his chair. He walked over to Alexander and extended his arm. Alex looked down at it and shook his head. Callum was stunned and was about to pull his arm back when Alex grabbed it and pulled him into a hug.

"Ye may be the older brother, but I am the cleverer, stronger, faster and better-looking brother." Alex teased.

"Mayhap ye are." Callum answered for all to hear but between the two of them, he murmured, "prove that ye are and dinna let the lass get away if ye love her like I love Siùsan." He pulled back from Alex and returned to his seat. He lifted Siùsan back into his lap.

"Tavish, Magnus, thank ye for always being at ma side and for coming to ma aide time and again. Thank ye for all ye did for Siùsan. I am blessed with the best of brothers." He nodded to his brothers and kissed Siùsan's temples.

"Da?"

"Aye, lass."

"Thank ye for it all. I dinna even ken how to begin to thank ye for all ye have done apparently ma entire life. Thank ye for picking me." She smiled and looked up at Callum. The double meaning was clear to everyone.

"Excuse me, ma laird. Supper will be served shortly." Hagatha announced.

Elspeth stepped out of the kitchen to monitor the serving of the meal. The Sinclairs and their guests stood and began to make their way to the dais. Siùsan caught a whiff of hagus and bolted out of the Great Hall. Callum dashed after her.

"She's been doing a lot of that of late," Tavish mused.

"Aye. Every time she smells food. Is it wrong of me to say that it leaves more for me to eat?" Magnus joked.

Thormud and Liam just watched knowingly as the couple disappeared down a passageway.

"Uncle Alex."

Alex, Tavish, and Magnus froze. They all turned as a one and looked dazedly at the previously silent young woman. Alex was stunned at her announcement, just as Tavish and Magnus were, but the latter two were doubly surprised to hear her speak. She was a bluidy Sassanach! They looked at Alex, and he shrugged before escorting her to the dais.

"Come, lads. Ye're catching flies with yer gobs hanging open. Ye'll ken it all soon enough."

Epilogue

Six and a half months later

*L*iam Sinclair leaned back in his chair and sipped his dram of whisky. He looked around his Great Hall and chuckled to himself. Not far from him, his sons were making wagers on whether the wee beastie that was causing all the fuss above stairs was going to be a lad or a lass. Alex and Tavish were betting on a lad while Magnus was stilling holding out that it would be a lass. Brighde, the woman who had arrived during a fierce storm and stayed on, becoming close friends with Siùsan during her confinement, was sure that it was both a lass and a lad. The Sinclair was not sure that she truly believed that, but it allowed her to give a noncommittal answer that did not bind her to either side of the bets.

Liam took another sip as a loud scream came from the chambers above. He had been through this five times with his own dearly departed Kyla and once already with Mairghread. He chuckled again as he remembered when Kyla was delivering Callum and years later when Tristan waited for Mairghread to deliver wee Liam. Tristan had proven to be much like he was as an expectant father. Liam had ended up punching the man, his own brother, who stood in his path to his wife and charged into their chamber after pacing for hours. Callum, Tavish, and Magnus had been on the receiving end of Tristan's ire, impatience, and fists.

Callum had taken note more closely than Liam Sinclair thought. The first sign that Siùsan's labor was beginning came that morning when her waters broke on the way to the kitchens. Callum had raced over, knocking several people to the ground in his hurry. He'd scooped her up and yelled for the midwife and the priest. He took the stairs two at a time and would have done three if he had not been so scared for his wife. Siùsan had tried to reassure him that there was plenty of time and that she was perfectly fine to walk up the stairs herself, however, she began the labor pains on the way to their chamber. Her first gasp solidified Callum's intention to remain with her through the entirety of it. No amount of coaxing from anyone could pry Callum away.

It had been five hours since Siùsan's labor began and there was no sign of things progressing any faster. His other sons kept glancing up the stairs each time Siùsan screamed. They looked anxious and out of place, but Liam knew that these things could take time or could be done in a matter of moments. Each babe came when he or she was ready and not a moment before.

"Da, would ye join us over her for a game of knucklebones or nine men's morris?" Magnus called to him.

He was just considering it when a high-pitched wail came from above stairs. Everyone turned to look in the direction of the family chambers. A round of applause broke out among the clan members in the Great Hall.

"I wonder who won," Tavish said to no one and everyone.

Moments later, another but slightly different high-pitched wail sounded.

"Twins! Brighde, how'd ye ken?" Alex asked quietly.

"I didna really. I just said as much to keep me out of yer squabbles with yer brothers. I wonder though, now, if it's a lad and a lass, or two lads, or two lasses."

"Good question," Laird Sinclair said as he finally joined his sons and Brighde.

They were not left in suspense for long. Callum came running along the landing and leaned over the railing.

"It's a lass and a lad. The lass is older by just a hair. Speaking of hair, the lad has ma brown and the lass has her mama's red. She looks to have a fine temper just like her mama! He's a braw one. Bigger than wee Liam was if ye can believe it!"

With that he ran back to Siùsan and his newly expanded family.

Callum walked into his chamber quietly so as not to disturb Siùsan or the babes. He could not stop smiling like a fool. He had been terrified for hours by the pain that that grabbed hold and seemed to never let go. He had felt utterly helpless through it all though Siùsan would not let go of his hand. She claimed that his presence was the only thing keeping her going. He had nearly panicked when he realized that a bairn was almost there and he saw the blood. He was convinced that Siùsan was dying. He'd yelled at the midwife and hugged Siùsan to the point that she had to beat on his shoulder to get him to let her breathe. He'd very nearly passed out when they all realized that a second babe was on the way.

Now he walked over to the bedside where Siùsan was nursing both babes. She was exhausted and sweaty, but he had never seen a more mesmerizing sight than his wife holding their two infant children. The women in the chamber silently bustled about changing Siùsan and the bed linens, careful not to disturb the young family.

"Ye did it, mo ghaisgeach beag. Ye are a warrior. Ye fought through it, and we've both come out the victors. What would ye have us name them?"

"Rose, for ma mama. Her red hair fits too. What would ye name yer heir?"

Callum paused. His nephew was already named for his father. Three Liams would be too confusing for everyone. There were also two Magnuses running around the keep between his brother and Siùsan's. He did not want to hurt the younger Magnus's feelings by naming the bairn after Seamus. He shook his head. He really did not have an answer until he looked up at Siùsan.

"Thormud. Thormud Seamus Magnus Sinclair."

"That's quite a mouthful, but I thank ye for honoring ma kin."

"Ah, well this will also give Mangus mòr something to gloat about to Tavish." The family had taken to calling Magnus Sinclair by mòr, or big, and Magnus Mackenzie went by òg, or young. It was the only way to distinguish the two as they had formed a close bond and were usually found together while the sun was up. Mangus mòr oversaw Siùsan's brothers' training. He claimed it was because everyone else was busy, but it was no great secret that Magnus mòr relished in not being the youngest male in the family anymore.

"Then I would like it be Rose Kyla Sinclair. I ken it might sound better if it was Kyla Rose. I hope ye dinna mind placing ma mama's name first."

"If it hadnae been for yer mother, I wouldnae have ye or our bairns. I love the name and count all of ma blessings to have the three of ye here, hearty and hail."

Callum kicked off his boots and stockings. He unfastened his sporran and the broach on his shoulder. He climbed into bed and wrapped the plaid around his shoulders and Siùsan's. He helped position her so that she comfortably leaned against him. He lifted Rose into his arms and cooed at his daughter. She grabbed his thumb and squeezed.

"Ei! She's got a tight hold on ma thumb."

"Imagine that strength but when she nurses. She will be a challenge, mark ma words."

In comparison, Thormud gurgled and kicked his legs as he laid in his mother's arms.

"I canna believe how big he was considering they were both crammed in ma belly. I wasnae sure I had it in me to get him out. If ye hadnae been beside me, I would have given up." She leaned over to kiss her husband. It was a soft and gentle kiss because they were both exhausted but none of the heat and passion was missing. They had a lifetime ahead of them filled with passion and love.

A soft knock came at the door and Laird Sinclair slowly peeked around the door.

"Come in, Da. Meet Rose and Thormud."

Laird Sinclair beamed as he ran a hand over the tops of each of the babies's heads.

"Ye've both done well for yerselves. Congratulations, and I'm proud of ye both." He kissed Siùsan's cheek and ruffled Callum's hair, just as he had ever since Callum was a lad. He quietly backed out of the room and shut the door behind him. He could hear the soft murmuring of the new parents. He rubbed his hands together gleefully.

Now to move things along and get the next one to stop dragging his heels. Ye're in for a right challenge with that one. She might just be too good even for ye. Dinna make a dog's dinner out of this one like yer brothers nearly did.

Thank You!

Thank you for taking the time to read *His Bonnie Highland Temptation* (The Clan Sinclair, Book 2)!

I appreciate any all reviews, be they detailed or concise, short or long. I read them all and reflect on your suggestions and comments.

I love connecting with readers and hearing your story recommendations. Get my latest news, upcoming releases, and blog at www.celestebarclayauthor.com.

You can also follow me on Twitter, Instagram, Facebook, and Goodreads at:

Twitter: @CelesteMBarclay
Instagram: @CelesteMBarclay
Facebook: /celestembarclay
Goodreads: https://bit.ly/2LhWkcw (or https://www.goodreads.com/author/show/17959368.Celeste_Barclay?from_search=true)

Books by Celeste Barclay

His Highland Lass (The Clan Sinclair, Book 1)

Arranged to marry his stepbrother, Laird Tristan Mackay cannot take his eyes off of Lady Mairghread Sinclair. When things rapidly sour between Tristan's stepbrother, Sir Alan, and Lady Mairghread, will there be a way to end the ongoing feud between the Mackays and Sinclairs? Unassuming and friendly, Mairghread Sinclair is not prepared for the danger that awaits her while visiting the Mackay clan. Who wants Mairghread out of the way? Why would anyone want to harm her?
Laird Tristan Mackay was not looking for a wife, but could Lady Mairghread Sinclair be the one to open his heart and bring peace to their clans or will their passion tear the two clans apart?

Teaser from Celeste Barclay's *His Highland Lass*

"She entered the great hall like a strong spring storm in the northern most Highlands. Tristan Mackay felt like he had been blown hither and yon. As the storm settled, she left him with the sweet scents of heather and lavender wafting towards him as she approached. She was not a classic beauty, tall and willowy like the women at court. Her face and form were not what legends were made of. But she held a unique appeal unlike any he had seen before...
Mairghread Sinclair was intended for his brother—his stepbrother, Alan. She and her father, Liam, and her four brothers approached with a contingency of guardsmen behind them. They had left even more guardsmen in the inner bailey attending to their horses. The Mackays and Sinclairs had not been on good terms of late, and an alliance between Tristan's stepbrother and the Sinclair's daughter was meant to create a truce between the two raiding clans. Within the last three years, numerous crofts and fields had been burnt by both sides and countless heads of cattle and sheep went back and forth between the two. However, when an out and out clash between raiders who met coincidentally one night left fifteen

Sinclairs dead and eighteen Mackays dead or wounded, both chiefs decided that a truce was needed. The strongest way to secure that and to form an alliance was through marriage. As there were no eligible females in the Mackay chief's family to marry off to one of the Sinclair brothers, it fell to Mairghread to marry a Mackay. Tristan did not think he was ready or even inclined to marry at this point. He did feel that his stepbrother, Alan, would benefit from settling down and sowing his seed in only one woman rather than any he could get his meaty hands onto long enough to lift his plaid. He had a quick pang of guilt as the thought that Mairghread was the sacrificial lamb flashed through his mind..."

Meet the members of Clan Sinclair in this first installment of the five book Highland romance series.

96760507R00132

Made in the USA
San Bernardino, CA
20 November 2018